The Abyss line of cutting-edge psychological horror is committed to publishing the best, most innovative works of dark fiction available. Abyss is horror unlike anything you've ever read before. It's not about haunted houses or evil children or ancient Indian burial grounds. We've all read those books, and we all know their plots by heart.

Abyss is for the seeker of truth, no matter how disturbing or twisted it may be. It's about people, and the darkness we all carry within us. Abyss is the new horror from the dark frontier. And in that place, where we come face-to-face with terror, what we find is ourselves.

"Thank you for introducing me to the remarkable line of novels currently being issued under Dell's Abyss imprint. I have given a great many blurbs over the last twelve years or so, but this one marks two firsts: first *unsolicited* blurb (*I called you*) and the first time I have blurbed a whole *line* of books. In terms of quality, production, and plain old storytelling reliability (that's the bottom line, isn't it?), Dell's new line is amazingly satisfying . . . a rare and wonderful bargain for readers. I hope to be looking into the Abyss for a long time to come."

—Stephen King

PLEASE TURN THE PAGE FOR MORE EXTRAORDINARY ACCLAIM . . .

PRAISE FOR ABYSS

"What *The Twilight Zone* was to TV in 1959, what *Night of the Living Dead* was to horror films in 1968, what Stephen King was to dark fiction in the mid-70s—Abyss books will be to horror in the 1990s."
—Mark Hurst, editor, *The Golden Man*

"Gorgeously macabre eye-catching packages . . . I don't think Abyss could have picked a weirder, more accomplished novel [than *The Cipher*] to demonstrate by example what the tone and level of ambition of the new line might be."
—*Locus*

"A splendid debut."
—*Rave Reviews*

"Dell is leading the way."
—*Writer's Digest*

"They are exploring new themes and dimensions in the horror field. My hat's off to Koja, Hodge, Dee and Dillard, as the others forthcoming! And hats off to Dell Abyss!"
—Gary S. Potter, author of *The Point Beyond*

"Consistently excellent, the most likely place to find innovative horror fiction."
—*Science Fiction Chronicle*

"I was amazed at the high level of quality that permeates all aspects of the series. . . . It's such a pleasure to see Dell doing something original with dark fantasy/horror."
—Richard L. Cooke, Literary Editor,
Tekeli-li! Journal of Terror

"The most exciting line of horror novels to hit the field in a very long time. . . . The Abyss line will not only leave its mark on the field but may very well revitalize it."
—*From the Time Tunnel* newsletter

"The new Abyss line of horror fiction has provided some great moments in their first year."
—*Mystery Scene*

"Inaugurating Dell's new Abyss Books series, this powerful first novel [*The Cipher*] is as thought-provoking as it is horrifying."
—*Publishers Weekly*

"Claustrophobic, paranoid . . . compelling, Dell's new horror line is definitely worth keeping an eye on."
—*Science Fiction Eye*

Also by Kelley Wilde

MASTERY

KELLEY WILDE

Illustrations by Laurie McAroy

A DELL BOOK

Published by
Dell Publishing
a division of
Bantam Doubleday Dell Publishing Group, Inc.
1540 Broadway
New York, New York 10036

The trademarks Dell® and Abyss® are registered in the U.S. Patent and Trademark Office.

ISBN: 0-440-20728-2

Printed in the United States of America

Published simultaneously in Canada

May 1993

10 9 8 7 6 5 4 3 2 1

OPM

For pasta lovers everywhere

1

BEGINNINGS I
NOVEMBER, 1989
TOKYO

 I have trouble with the V-word . . . once one of the joys of my life, I am sure. Now the V-word makes me scream.

The V-word and the *what* word—

Oh!

They have played some dreadful trick on me. Some trick that leaves me screaming.

They have erased parts of my mind as cleanly as a cassette is erased.

Where the V-word used to be—hot, steamy, and soulful . . . that much I seem to remember—there is only static now.

I cannot hear the V-word or begin to imagine its sound. I only know it made me warm and womanly all over. I know it made me swing my legs, one thigh caressing the other.

The V-word . . . The V-word . . . What *was* it!

And the *what* word . . . little *what* word . . . Why did they have to take that from me too? Not even static with that one. White noise. Does it begin with a B . . . or a C . . . ?

What they have done is place me into the cruelest of prisons . . . the kind without walls.

What they have done is jail me in a riddle within an enigma. There is nothing, it would seem, that I am not free to think of. There is nowhere I'm not free to go. There is nothing that I cannot say. Nothing that I cannot do.

Except:

anything connected with two words I can never remember . . .

except—

when, from time to time, I hear them . . . and I start to scream.

The V-word . . .

The *what* word . . .

Lost joys of my life!

I have seen many doctors. Their answers were always the same: Therapy cannot begin with words that I cannot remember. Suppose we start at the beginning, the Past?

I have seen several hypnotists. Failure. Utter failure.

But last week I discovered a doctor who may be able to help me.

He is extremely handsome. He looks like Dr. Kildare. And he is very gentle. He has blond hair and deep blue eyes and a voice as soothing as the burbling of a brook.

I think Dr. Coburn likes me.

I know I like him!

Our first two sessions were hopeless, although he was pretty to look at. They took nearly two hours apiece. But, in the end, a breakthrough when—

quite accidentally—

he stumbled on the V-word.

And I began to scream.

Last night Dr. Coburn—I shall call him Dr. C—began to implement his strategy.

The session has given me my first real hope since—

I cannot recall.

But I said—yes, I *said* it—the V-word!

Then instantly forgot it, just as I always do.

I asked him to write it down on a slip of paper. He refused, though, saying that we must begin with my memory itself. And I was filled with despair.

But . . .

This morning it occurred to me:

Perhaps if I remember our sessions . . . If I describe them honestly . . . and hear his soothing, beautiful voice . . . and picture the warm, blue pools of his eyes . . . Then maybe I can write *it* down, as I remember screaming it.

And then it will be *here* for me anytime I wish to see.

I will *know* the V-word.

And if I can remember it, would it be hopeless to dream that the memory will come back—

of what it is I have lost?

I will have one cigarette and prepare myself to begin.

I need my strength and energy.

Because I am going to scream.

There now. Much better now. Breathe deeply and try to remember.

I am lying on the leather sofa in the doctor's office. I know this is old-fashioned, but from my childhood I have been taught: I must be a traditional girl.

The leather sofa is rich and soft and deep, and it is pleasant to lie here, sinking more deeply into its folds, looking up into Dr. C's eyes. I wish that I could

kiss

them.

Dr. C smiles at me warmly. "Are you comfortable?" he asks.

"Oh yes," I answer. "Very! I wish I could always lie down on this couch."

"Well"—he shakes his head, tugs at one ear—"I have a powerful feeling that the day will come real soon when you won't need this couch anymore."

I say nothing. I smile bravely, still wishing I could

kiss

him.

Knowing that he is about to begin.

"Do you remember what happened," he asks me, "last week?"

I squirm a little on the couch, the move raising my skirt up about half a foot. I do not try to straighten it. There is no need for shame here. Dr. C is going to cure me and I like the feel of it, the soft breeze from the fan on my panties.

Dr. C, though, is shy, which delights me. With his little finger, he squinches up his glasses to the bridge of his long, noble nose.

"What happened?" he says softly. He stares, once, at my legs; then fixes his eyes on my face. He is a shy and gentle man. And that, that, that is why I really want to

kiss

him.

"We found the V-word," I tell him. "I know we must have found it. Because I screamed and *screamed* and—"

"Shhh. I believe I've found a way to help you with the V-word. —My dear, why don't you straighten your skirt for us? I don't want you catching cold."

"It's fine," I assure him. "I like the feel of the air through my panties and on my vagina."

Dr. C, amazingly, squirms—oh, almost imperceptibly—for he is good, and very shy, and that, too, to tell the truth, is why I need to

kiss

him.

(Kiss?)

I straighten my skirt to full length, at mid-thigh, clasp my hands on my belly. I am, I must be, a traditional girl.

"I'm sorry, Dr. C," I say. "I've embarrassed you."

"Not at all." He's back in charge. Good for you, Dr. C! "In fact, this is a perfect beginning. You see, what I want to show you, dear, is that for almost everyone there are certain words that trigger powerful emotions. Many Western men and women have trouble with a . . . V-word that you yourself appear to have no trouble with at all."

For an instant I'm so deeply thrilled I nearly jump off the sofa . . . throw my arms around him . . . and begin to

(kiss)

him.

In a flash of understanding, I see where this is going. But I lie back, a traditional girl, and look, with joy, into his beautiful eyes.

"You mean . . ." I pause, discreetly, "that for certain people . . . the V-word is—*vagina*?"

"Yes," he tells me, smiling as if I've just won a gold star. "But you—"

"Oh no! No!" I cry. "I have no trouble with that word. That word is a part of my body. Why should I be afraid of that?"

"Exactly," Dr. C says. "That's exactly what I mean. It's just a word, no less, no more. It can't do us any harm. Your own V-word, for example, is just a collection of sounds. *Ver . . .*" Dr. C coos. "Isn't that a *pretty* sound?"

I say "Yes . . ." and start to squirm, already grinding my teeth.

"Ver-r-r-r . . ." Dr. C says. "Such a pretty, soothing sound. We have no trouble with this sound. It could belong to—*vermilion.*"

"Yes!" I whisper. "*Vermilion.* I have no trouble with that."

I *do* see what he's doing now! I *do* see how he'll cure me! The V-word . . . What is it, but innocent sounds?

"Ver-r-r . . . M-i-i-i . . ." Dr. C goes on.

My eyes are closed. I dare not move.

The V-word is coming!

Help!

"Those sounds might be *vermilion*, that soothing and beautiful color. Or the sounds might be—yes—*vermin*. Cute, furry little vermin."

"Yes . . . I have no trouble with those words."

"Of course you don't. They're only words. Only harmless and soothing arrangements of sounds. And do you know something funny? We could even take the other sounds—I mean, of your V-word—and put them into other words you have *no trouble with*. Shall we try it?"

I cannot describe how much courage it takes. But I nod, for I so want to please him.

Dr. C's blue eyes—have I told you the blue is cerulean? It is, and they are twinkling. "The *chel* sound, for example. Why, that could be *cello*. A soothing and beautiful cello."

"Yes . . . Yes . . . I see that . . . Thanks! I have no trouble with that word."

"Of course you don't. You're very brave."

Dr. C pats my knee on the top, the inside.

"Do you know something?" he asks me.

He raises his hand, strokes his moustache. And I know he is trying to smell me. A whiff of the Obsession I have dabbed behind my knees. Even though I am, as I've been taught, a completely traditional girl.

"Believe me," he says, "when I tell you: All of the sounds of the V-word can be found in other words that you have no trouble with at all. The *eee* sound . . . as in *easy* . . . as in nice and easy does it . . ."

"Yes," I whisper. "Yes, it's true."

"*Eee* . . . as in *electric* . . ."

. . . as in the electric current of my increasing desire to (*KISS!*)

him.

"*Eee*," he continues, "as in *Eden* . . . or *evasion* . . ."

"Oh, Dr. C, it's working!"

I take his hand. I try to place it back on my knee again, where it belongs. He clasps mine, instead, with his strong, gentle left.

"You're doing fine," he assures me.

"Yes, it's true, it really is. I have no trouble with those words."

"Of course you don't. They're only words. The *eee* sound . . . and the *mi* sound—as in *mission* or in *miss* . . . the *chel* sound as in *cello* . . ."

"Yes!"

"The soft, agreeable *ver* sound—as in the color *vermilion* . . ."

"Yes! I feel it, Dr. C. All they are is only sounds."

Dr. C leans over. He is smiling serenely. His eyes are a priest's. "Of course they are. Of course they are. And you are a big, brave, and beautiful girl. That's why the V-word, this time, will be music to your ears. When you hear the V-word, you will think of nothing . . . but how magically, musically lovely it sounds. Are you ready?"

"Sure I am! I'll have *no* trouble with that word."

"Ready?"

"Yes!"

"Set?"

"Sure!"

"Ver-mi-cell-i," my blond doctor purrs.

"Ver!—mi!—cell!—eeee!"

Sound by sound I get it out.

And then begin to scream.

There it is.

The V-word.

I have locked it in a box. There, on a separate page.

I screamed again while writing it. My bra and panties are soaked through with sweat. My hands are trembling as I sit, half-naked, on the floor.

My doors are locked.

The shades are drawn.

But I do not deceive myself: I have just remembered, for the first time by myself, what the V-word is—

and *They* will not be happy.

And if I have already forgotten again, no sooner than I turned the page, that does not matter, really.

The V-word has been captured and put into a box.

I can go back now anytime: to see it . . . to touch it . . . to speak it again . . . to scream again, yes, if I have to.

Until I can say it like anyone else.

Until I can remember why *They* took the V-word from me.

Until I remember who *They* are—and I can begin to fight back.

BEGINNINGS II
DECEMBER, 1988
TOKYO

Three women in shocking red dresses collected their red leather handbags, synchronized their watches, and took off in three cabs in three different directions for three of the seediest bars in the town.

The year's first light snowfall had started. A soft but steady flurry, like that in an upturned glass dome.

Each of the drivers remarked on the cold, alternating glances through the flopping window wipers with furtive looks in the mirror he'd tipped.

Each of the women, who sat in the back, in a red leather mini that stopped at mid-thigh, looked dreamily out of her window and smoked. And stroked the sleek ends of black waterfall hair that framed her pale, childlike face. Pale as the moon, except for the lips, a shocking crimson Cupid's bow, and the heavily mascaraed eyes.

They looked like children, all of them. Wild, wanton children out for a night's wicked play. And each of the drivers was driven with lust as he snaked in and out of the traffic to his woman in red's destination.

Bad girls, they'd remember.

Three bad girls in shocking red leather, with pale Kabuki faces that were at once twisted and cute.

Three bad girls in shocking red leather, no more. And yet, on the cold-stiffened seats in the back, with the flurrying snowflakes around them, each of them, the three bad girls, the three in their shocking red dresses, just sat. Sat, looking dreamily out of their windows, smoking and stroking their waterfall hair. As unaffected by the cold as they were by the men's heated looks.

As each of the cabs with its woman in red approached its destination, its passenger would check her watch. Clap three times excitedly. And murmur, *"Chōdo ii!"* Very good.

The drivers would remember this. They would remember all of this in the days soon to come, when the questions began. The questions, confusion, and rage.

But what they would remember best, as would the doormen in each of the bars, was the triumphant twinkle in each woman's eyes.

The doormen would remember how a woman in shocking red leather, with a handbag to match and black waterfall hair, seemed to float through the flurry of snowflakes . . . stopped at the door . . . slipped a bill in their hand . . . and said, *Dōzo, I'm wanting no trouble.*

The doormen would remember thinking: *Saa, that is my kind of trouble.* They would remember leading the three women in red to their tables in back, every eye in the room on the waterfall hair . . . the crimson bow of Cupid's bow lips . . . breasts rising out of and over the V's of their shockingly shocking red dresses.

Many of the men were rough and unafraid of anything. Many of the men were rich and accustomed to having their way. They would have cut each other's throats for one look from those Kabuki eyes. Not a man of them moved, though. Not one in three bars where the women in shocking red dresses sat nursing their drinks while they studied the time.

The doormen would remember that it felt as if a wall, insubstantial as a mist, inpenetrable though as cold steel, stood be-

tween them, one and all, and the women in shocking red
dresses.

Then they would remember the vague feeling of an—opening. How each man had looked around the room. And known
with, somehow, both despair and relief, that tonight was not the
night for him. Not for him, not tonight, the hypnotic allure of
red leather.

The chosen rose as in a dream, each floating over on fog feet
to his woman in shocking red leather.

The doormen would remember how the scenes were played
in dream-time: how drinks were brought . . . and cigarettes lit
. . . and words exchanged, with laughter. In mere minutes an
hour or two might have passed, so intimately set upon the
shoulders of rich suits were the pale, tiny heads with black
waterfall hair.

Each barman would remember how the woman had looked at
her watch with a smile . . . then led her man off through the
fog of desire . . . his eyes grown huge with wonder . . . and
hers, oh hers, were twinkling.

In the days and weeks that followed, as news of the horror
continued to spread, more witnesses came forward. Not one of
them had a real story to tell—each had just been driving by
. . . or walking by quickly . . . the hour was late. What they
could not account for was why they would have driven by, or
walked by, just as quickly—if the night had been warmer, the
hour less late. All they knew was that, in passing, they'd born
witness to a flash of some truly remarkable thing: a species of
trouble, delirious trouble, such as they'd dreamed of, yet hoped
not to meet.

. . . A woman in shocking red leather, no more, swinging
her hips in the season's first snow—her ruby lips, a Cupid's
bow, arched in a curious smile . . . the man beside her bun-
dling up in his expensive coat . . .

. . . A woman in shocking red leather stopping her man by
the side of his car . . . pinning him against the door . . . and
snaking one hand through the flap of his coat . . .

. . . A woman in shocking red leather, her head over the

car's lowered window, black waterfall hair almost down to the road . . .

Each witness who came forward had a single haunting flash to share.

But no one—there was no one—remembered the ends in three cars that same night, in three parts of the city, at midnight.

And no one would have believed the old wino who'd followed one girl and her man to the wharf.

Not even if he'd lived to tell.

The wino held back at the edge of the lot. He crouched behind a street lamp, waiting until they were halfway across. Thirty yards ahead, parked alone before the rail that blocked a steep drop to the bay, a black Cadillac loomed in the shadows. The woman in red leather squealed and tugged at the hand of the man she was with.

Trouble, the wino thought. Trouble for sure. But his footsteps quickened, too, across the graveled lot.

Halfway across, his heart half stopped . . . when suddenly the man stopped cold . . . disengaged his hand from hers . . . and slowly, very slowly, turned.

The wino crouched beside a lone car centered in the lot. Painful moments passed before he heard the clicks of the Cadillac's doors.

What he heard next broke his heart in three places, and made him wish he could spin on his heels. He heard the man moan fiercely—loud, long, and rhythmic moans:

Aaa-ummmmmm!

Aaa-ummmmmm!

Aaa-UMMMMMM!

Umm-OHHHHHH!

He heard the high-pitched, bell-like tinkling of the woman's laughter. And then the man began to moan still more fiercely and cry out.

AAAAA!

AAAAA!

HUH-

UHHHHHHHHH!

The wino stood. He rocked in place, tormented by the music.

The steam on the windows grew thicker. The car's rockings, more pronounced. Finally, unable to contain his torment, he advanced till he stood by the door on the right.

Gingerly, he circled three fingers on the glass. No sooner had he cleared a patch than it began to fog again. But for one fleeting second, through the vaguely smoked clearing, he saw:

the man, naked on top, with his pants to his shoes, stretched back on the seat . . . the woman, crouched between his legs, her back arched high against the wheel . . . her hands alternately pumping the rampant and swaggering joystick . . . and then, oh then—dear God!—before the glass fogged up completely, the woman's head dropped like an eagle, in a straight savage line, to its prey.

The wino heard a sound not quite like any sound he'd heard. It was nothing in itself, yet everything at once. Bits and pieces of all sounds—as if they'd been swept by a vacuum and spit out into a crazy collage. He heard pain and ecstasy . . . confusion, terror, joy . . .

The sound erupted, finally, in a blissed-out and agonized scream:

"Nani—Nani—Aaa! Nani!"

What is it! What is it! What's happening!

There was a lull. And then a cry of mortal, spine-tingling anguish:

"Iie!" the man wailed. *"Shite! Toranai!"*

No! Do it! For God's sake, don't stop!

Though his body had long been inured to the cold, the wino started shivering. What teeth he still had were beginning to chatter . . . when he saw a swirling circle on the clouded glass.

He could not move.

He could not think.

The woman's tiny hand appeared, that small hand, the size of a bird, with red nails. And, vaguely still, through the half-misted glass, he saw the arched smile of her Cupid's bow lips. And one small finger beckoning.

Come closer, closer to the glass.

The tiny hand made its circle again.

The wino's hand, not quite his own, slowly rose to match it, until—for just a moment that lasted an eternity—he saw with brilliant clarity:

the woman, crouched like a cat on the floor, her right hand raised in a childlike "Shhh" . . .

her wicked and wanton red Cupid's bow lips . . .

from which, to his towering horror, spewed a bowlful of translucent strands, in peristaltic rhythm . . . spilling out and lengthening . . .

As the glass clouded, she turned with a wink, returning to her work. Strands lengthened and glistened and wound 'round and up every inch of the naked man's torso.

The wino teetered backward, reeling, clutching at his heart.

He stumbled hard against the rail, and might have thought to stop there. But then he heard an awesome

CRACK!

as if a mighty oak had just been snapped like a twig in a storm. And when he looked and saw the clouded windows, front and side, run red, he clutched his heart again, for real.

And tumbled back pathetically, over the rail to the rocks and the bay.

Where large schools of fishes
found him quite delicious
and really no trouble at all.

BOOK ONE
FEBRUARY–
APRIL, 1990
ATLANTA

ONE

 Let me tell you the meaning of terror.

There's nothing tricky about it. No rabbits, or goblins, pulled out of a hat. No jack-in-the-box schlock surprises, the sort that I *will* spend six dollars to see.

No, terror, the real thing, is marked by its simplicity, its unrelenting logic. There's no need for theatrics. No need for screeching violins or weirdly wailing cellos.

Terror is the shadow hanging on each step you take.

The sum of all you would not be.

Till one night it overtakes you.

While you're sleeping, your shadow, caught up, passes through.

With a shudder, you awake.

And you are terrified.

I was forty when it hit.

I knew, the minute I opened my eyes: There had been a massive shift of everything within me.

I saw and I couldn't *stop* seeing: *myself* . . . as the absolute absence of light.

Alone again in the closet-sized bedroom . . . the wallpaper wearily racing sun-fried drapes to hell, while plaster from the peeling ceiling dryly curled and flaked.

Alone again, me and the bureau . . . so scratched and so decrepit it made the wallpaper look new.

Alone again, me and the mirror I turned from with a shout.

Oh God, I thought. Oh God, dear God!

I whimpered and was terrified.

I'd never really seen, not once, the very rooms I lived in. Only the place I had plans for.

Till now.

The shadow said, *Welcome Jack. This is Your Life. I've been waiting. What took you so long?*

It was February. And winter in Atlanta is hell's revenge for summer's death.

There is no snow, or next to none. This is no purifying rite. It is the fire emptied, consumed by its own blazing hatred of life. It is the wet dream of the heat to be raging and full of itself once again.

For five years in Atlanta I'd been planning to escape.

But suddenly, this morning, the winter had nothing to do with my plans. The wind rattled the walls of my ground-floor apartment, lashed the windows with a storm of hailstones big as marbles. Lights crackled fiercely in a black and evil-looking sky. And the door, its bolt slipped in the pounding, rattled away on its chain. The curtains hung, half-ripped from rods, and last week's stack of news was strewn in tearsheets all over the room.

I saw the front page plastered to the grate of the gas heater. The paper crackled into flames, which devoured, in seconds, the headline: JAP COPS STILL MUM ON DEAD U.S. DOC! I hadn't read the paper yet. But none of it was news to me: the rug was on fire and this was My Life. A windowpane exploded from a vicious blast of hail. The lights went next. And, in the dark, I watched the lightning streak the sky and heard the flames crackling behind me. Flaming scraps capered around me, now setting off one of the curtains.

It would have been good if I'd checked out in fire. I'd moved south in a summer on the heels of my divorce.

I stood there, watching, paralyzed; my shadow whispered *Yes!*

And then someone was screaming "Jack!" and banging away at the door.

"Jack—fire! C'mon, open the door!"

I heard a roar louder than thunder. Then the door imploded with a brisk snap of the chain. And an awesome gust of wind came blasting through the opening. The force hurled me backward a couple of yards. I went half through a wall and collapsed to the floor.

I still remember seeing him through clouds of breath and smoke: Hank Boone, a strapping six feet two, muscles rippling on storm-slicked arms. His eyes, thickly hooded, widened in disgust.

I guessed he'd just seen his first terrified man.

"Jack, what the fuck y'all *doin'* there? C'mon, get up and help me!"

I sat, my arms around my knees, watching Hank get down to it like someone in a movie:

slam-bracing the inner door open with a table he tossed with a swing of one arm . . .

grabbing two legs of the sofa, in flames, and lugging it out to the drive . . .

beating the flames on the rug with a mat, still screaming at me, "Jack, come on!"

Finally, Hank plopped his lanky bulk down, cross-legged, Indian style.

He gave me a quizzical tilt of his head and drawled in that raw voice of his, "Well, fuck me up the ole wazoo, what the *hell* are y'all on, boy?"

The storm stopped before I could tell him. The hail and the lightning and thunder. And the rain began to fall as it can only fall in Atlanta: dolorous downpours that just break your heart. The ghost of summer weeping.

I told Hank that it had been nothing. It must have been something I ate. I'd felt stunned.

"Sheee-ittt, stunned my ass, boy." Hank gave his ponytail a

flip that sprayed me from across the room. He was my next-door neighbor. He was quite a bit younger than I was. And, from the glimpses I'd caught of his action at night, he was hell on wheels with the ladies.

He was also manager for two dumps the absentee owner, the never-seen Mrs. Palerno, had quartered into hovels. And it was now as handyman that Hank surveyed the damage.

"Naw, I reckon stunned is what ole lady Palerno'll be. Whoo-eee. You'll be just like that Yankee doc got crushed all to shit in Japan. We're talkin' pussywhippin' that'll take your breath away."

I remembered, vaguely, the headline: JAP COPS STILL MUM ON DEAD U.S. DOC! Crushed, I thought. Sad way to go. But lacking in genuine terror.

Hank stroked that granite jaw of his and blended gravel in his throat. "We'll tell her y'all was stoned, not stunned. Hell, I wouldn't mind a little of whatever—hey, whoaa!"

I was slipping my arms through the legs of my pants, thinking that they were a sweater.

"Listen," I blurted, "I'm fine. It's okay. I'll pay for the damage."

"Heyyy." Hank clambered up in a quick, nimble move. "What the hell y'all *talkin'* 'bout, pay the ole bitch."

"I'll pay her somehow. I mean it." *(Just go.)* "If she wants me to leave, that's okay." *(But please go.)*

But he kept looking at me. And I couldn't stand the pity in his heavy-lidded eyes. He started coming at me. "What's goin' on, boy, this throwin' y'all out? Hell—"

I held the pants up like a shield and tripped back. "For God's sake, don't—"

(Don't help me!)

"I ain't gonna hurt y—"

"Stop!"

Hank threw up his palms. He said, "Whoaaaa, boy. Easy now. All I wanna do is help—"

It wasn't me that screamed at him. I was too quiet and frightened for that. It was the shadow screaming at a threat to its existence. "For God's sake, run!" the shadow screamed. "Get out! Oh, God, I'm—TERRIFIED!"

Hank backed away with both palms raised.

"I'll be back later," he growled. "I'll be fetchin' y'all some paint, boy. An' that ole biddy Lady Palerno'll be forkin' up a respectable couch. A man goes to bed an' wakes up in the mornin', his goddamn apartment's on fire? Kiss my ass."

"Please—"

"An' she's gonna pay for the fuckin' drapes too!" He cocked his finger like a gun, the barrel leveled at me. "Oh, an' one more thing, boy. I don't think I can stand no more seein' y'all walk home alone every night, your shoulders half down to your knees. Goddamn right you're terrified. Hell, that'd scare my damn pecker right off. I'll fix y'all up with a real Southern gal who can suck a fuckin' tennis ball through fifty feet o' hose."

"Please—" I cried.

"Damn straight she'll please! Her cunt'll whistle 'Dixie' when she wraps them legs around your waist. Eeeee-hahhhhh!" Hank roared. "The South shall rise again!"

And with that he shut the door.

The rain was so quiet and steady outside, on the roof and on the walls, it sounded like a single sound, a whispered and ominous:

Thisssssss . . .

TWO

For our debut, the shadow wanted someplace showy. So I followed its lead through the late morning drizzle to the station for a downtown train. I agreed with the shadow: Le Peep would be nice.

A half hour later, we were ushered to our table. And not a moment too soon.

The shadow needed energy. But what it hungered for the most was overdue attention. We got that, all right—in spades. Well-heeled tourists gawked over their shoulders and children giggled behind their raised hands.

> *Mommy, look . . .*
> *That man . . .*
> *He's gross . . .*

As we ate, the shadow ate up every look and whisper. My disgrace progressed from just exquisite to sublime, seeing this *thing* as they saw it: My Life.

I thought I'd got the hang of it—when suddenly the room was hushed.

"Excuse me . . . *Sir,*" the waiter said. "A young couple will be joining you?" There wasn't an empty table in the place. They must have thought mine, filled by only a shadow, was the closest to empty.

I caught a swaying flash of red from over the rims of my specs. A shadowy length of something swirling, and surely it was much too long to be hair. Subtle rounds of swelling breasts, arched over and siding the red leather V. And just a flash of red Cupid's bow lips before, in a funk, I looked down at my plate. I started shoveling food, hard, into my mouth.

The woman said something—Good morning, I guess—in a musical, childlike voice. She had a silky accent, as exotic as a kimono. I grunted, not daring to look. And grunted again when her lover sat down.

I couldn't hear a word they spoke. Only the vaguest impression of speech. They'd switched to their own frequency, in their own private language. As I shoveled, with head down, what I caught were small tortuous slivers: her tiny hands, as small as birds, engaged in a light symphony of slicings with her cutlery . . . soft touches of her lover's arm . . .

There is no pain in all the world like the lust for another man's woman. And once your shadow has passed through, all women are other men's women. They belong to the men who are still filled with light.

Time and again, I would set knife and fork down, hoping to ask for more coffee. The waiter couldn't see me, though. Nobody could see me now. The woman in shocking red leather commanded their total attention.

As if they'd never seen before . . . might not live to see again . . . a woman in shocking red leather with red Cupid's bow lips and great childlike eyes and jet hair that fell clear to her hips.

And so I sat, and continued to sit, sipping from an empty cup as I tried not to see.

"Excuse me, prease," I heard her say. "But I must to reflesh myself. And then we maybe going?"

I watched her walk off in slow waves of red leather and swirls of black waterfall hair.

My gaze shifted across to her lover. He looked average in every way. An inch or two taller than I was, perhaps. Or, I should say, had been. Sandy-haired, with an average cut that did nothing at all for his hairline. Eyes a deep but still average blue, and straining hard for focus behind his own Coke-bottle lenses. The face was thin, almost gaunt, with cheekbones high and pronounced. But the effect was averaged out by a nose that did not go the distance, and a mouth just this side of too small. He wore a gold corduroy sportcoat that might have been mine with a little more wear. A man so average-looking you'd have had to look twice just to miss him.

But the woman in shocking red leather was his.

I held my check, but couldn't go.

He smiled at me. Winner's smile.

"Dave Cotter," he told me. He stretched out his hand. I took it, limply, and felt crushed. That hand had touched her everywhere.

"Jack," I managed, barely.

He leaned back and studied me. "I couldn't help but notice— you noticing Michiko."

"She's—" I started. "She's—"

"All mine. But I'll give you the next best thing."

He took out an average wallet, filled with an average number of bills. And withdrew an average-looking, crinkled calling card. He set the card before me just as she called out behind.

"Dave? Darling? We be late."

"Drop them a line," he urged. "Get a brochure."

I stared at him stupidly.

He added, rising, with a wink, "It'll change your life."

I heard a soft rustle of something like leather . . . then felt a gentle folding in of warmth and light on the nape of my neck, a waterfall of silken hair, a light brush of moist lips.

"*Sayonara,*" she said, "and I prease to meet you."

"Come on, honey," Cotter said. "Let's get crackin' on that packin'."

I heard her squeal, "San Flancisco!"

And then they were gone.

I stayed there and stared at the card he had left. White background with a cherry blossom over the badly smudged type:

ANGEL KISS

For men of real refinement—exquisite Asian ladies. Satisfaction guaranteed!

An 800 number was given that I could barely decipher, with an address in Hawaii that I couldn't read at all.

The shadow beamed its approval.

THREE

It was near midnight and my phone was black, a great antique rotary dialer.

I'd been pacing now for several hours, with the same stops on each round: at the gallons of paint in the corner, from Hank . . . at the crinkled white card on the table . . . and at the black rotary phone.

Its simplicity amazed me. And the longer I watched it, the simpler it seemed. Black, and blocklike, primitive. Each call subtotaled the worth of one's life.

I'd gotten six calls in Atlanta: five wrong numbers, one obscene.

It would never ring again.

Still, I could almost feel my right hand pick up the receiver. As if a shadow could be heard.

How simple it all was!

How simple and black.

One A.M. And there we were, the black rotary phone, the white card, and me. I heard a screech from Hank's place, and then a dreadful banging of bodies on the wall.

"Fuck MEEEEEE!" a woman screamed.

I picked the phone up dreamily. Heard the old-time, get-on-with-it buzz. Leaned over to try to decipher the card.

Of course, there was no question of my ever getting through.
The phone would ring and ring—

"Hello, this is Angel Kiss. And we thank you for taking a
chance on your life!"

A recorded message. Good! I knew how the rest of the message would go. Dissolving any second into a shadowy
THISSSSSS . . .

"Hello," the voice repeated. "Is anybody there?"

All right. I could dial, then . . . and people with real voices
could come on at the end of the line . . . but if I tried to
answer—

"Hellohellohello!" the voice cried.

I said, very softly, "Help."

"Just a second, darlin'. Let me crank the volume up here." A
second's pause at her end of the line. "Now, what was it that
you were sayin'?"

I said, "You can hear me?"

She laughed. It was a nice laugh. "I can hear you fine, hon.
You sound like you got it real bad."

I said, "Yeah . . ."

She started talking, soft and low. As if she were here in a red
leather dress and could see me like I used to be, and like I used
to be was fine. She said, "Now, relax there and listen. There's a
lot of men out there lonelier than you are. We get 'em all ages
and sizes. We get 'em rich, we get 'em poor, and what we do is
connect 'em, you see, with that special someone—she may be in
Korea, she may be in Taiwan—"

"Japan?" I croaked.

She chuckled. "Sure! Why, you wouldn't believe the number
of ladies who've had it to here with the men in Japan! The
sweetest things, the cutest things— Why, you look at their pictures and it breaks your heart."

I said, "I saw this girl . . . in a red leather dress . . ."

She said, "Hon, that's between you and her. But red leather
must be a remarkable sight. And if a woman loves her man, all
she wants is to just make him happy."

She asked me what my name was. And I heard a hushed
clatter of keys as she entered my name in the system.

It would be lost. I knew this. Or it would go up in smoke. But it felt good to play the game. I gave her my address. She entered that too and promised to send, the next day, a brochure.

"Jack," she said. "You mark my words. Your life will change forever the day you take a chance on love. Good night, Jack, and have a nice life."

I asked her what her name was.

She said, "Operator Twenty-three. But you just ask for anyone. 'Cause we're all here to help you, twenty-four hours a day. You took the first step, hon. You picked up the phone. Good things are gonna happen soon. True Love is on the way!"

Outside, the rain still fell and fell. I lay back against the wall and fell asleep while listening to its disconsolate

THISSSSSS . . .

FOUR

"One good turn deserves another . . ."

Miss Chisholm and I were alone in her office, but she wasn't looking at me. No surprise. She was half-blind with her glasses; the left eye had a cataract the size of a droplet of milk. A rather striking contrast to her coffee-colored skin. On those rare occasions when I was called to her office, I'd pull my chair to the edge of her desk. Right by the Copy Chief sign. Not today, though. Not today. I sat back, waiting for Miss Chisholm to pull out the ax. A shadow, I knew, had no business setting its foot in The Store.

I tugged at my shirt collar, baring more neck.

Instead, she raised one wrinkled claw to her crinkled throat.

"One good turn deserves another . . . I'll always remember that one, Jack." A lone tear trickled down one cheek from the unclouded eye. "I believe it was your second day when you wrote that ad for us. I must confess that your bein' a Yankee had, at first, *filled* me with doubt. But right away you'd caught it— the Spirit of The Store."

It had been a one-day sale ad for down-filled reversible comforters: flowery prints on one side, solid pastels on the other. And the lead-in had been followed by the usual rigmarole: savings expressed in percentage as well as dollars saved . . . fiber

content . . . blahblahblah . . . But that first line had made
my bones.

I'd had other moments.

But there had only been one note of affectionate praise from
Miss Chisholm. And no other writer ever had gotten more than
two. Which led Miss Chisholm's *people* to treasure the note
they'd received. A sort of formal notice that they had been
touched by the soul of The Store, if only just in passing. And it
drove you onward, see . . . though this was only Retail and
scorned by the Agency hotshots and snoots.

"One good turn . . ." Miss Chisholm said. "So simple, Jack.
And elegant." Miss Chisholm fingered her high-buttoned
blouse, looking dreamily, dreamily through me. "It's somethin'
special, isn't it, when The Store speaks through us."

"Miss Chisholm," I began. My voice sounded as vague as her
cataract looked. I tried again, addressing it, as if the shadow part
of her could hear the heart of me. "Ma'am . . . You don't have
to do this . . . Please."

"Why, Jack," she said, "what on earth do you mean?"

"I mean—Miss Chisholm, listen. You don't have to try to
make me feel—make me *feel*— You see, ma'am, all that, it's
behind—"

"Jack," she said, "dear, what is it?"

"Let me clear out my desk. I'll be gone in an hour."

"Jack!"

"That's all right. I understand." I didn't really stand, I think. I
sort of levitated. "I'll go right now. You can trash all my stuff, I
don't need a job or apartment."

"Why, Jack Pepper!" cried Miss Chisholm. "Sit yourself down
right this second and tell me what is goin' *on*."

It felt like she gave me a nudge with her eye. My body
plumped back on the cushion.

"*Jack?*" Miss Chisholm stretched this out. The word lasted a
couple of seconds.

"Miss Chisholm. Please. I understand. I've been fired and I'd
like to go—"

I'd never heard Miss Chisholm laugh. I guessed that she was
laughing now, a couple of dry puffs that died in a wheeze.

Then she gave me a look with her good eye while I held on for life to the bad.

"Over my dead body," was what Miss Chisholm said. "Oh no, Jack, you-all haven't been fired. I brought you in here to *warn* you. The huns are here, Jack, the *huns* have arrived. It's us against them, for the soul of The Store. And I don't mind admittin', I am positively *terrified!*"

FIVE

The Store pretty much covered two full city blocks. The monolith had grown around the site of the original store—a crude twenty-by-sixty-foot structure thrown together from pine boards after Atlanta was torched.

They'd called it Britch and Co. then, in 1867. And Morris Britch himself had had to carry the ladies across the wood planks, the ground had been so ravaged.

Within a few years it was Britch's. Within ten, it had grown to a block. Ten more, and Britch's had been magically transformed from a mere emporium into the stuff of legend. It had become The Store.

The marble floors were thrilling, yes.

The brass doors and crystal chandeliers . . .

The liveried doormen . . .

The dazzling displays . . .

But these were . . . things—beautiful things . . . sometimes even priceless things—but not to be confused, you see, with the real magic that The Store offered. You came to The Store, and ignored all the rest, because *this* was the soul of Atlanta.

You found the soul in little things the others couldn't bother with:

A smile . . .

A "Good mornin', how are *you* this fine, fine day!" . . .

You found the soul in touches a Yankee never dreamed of:

The Store had been famed from the start for its total refund policy. The customer was always right. Bring it back: anything, anytime, in any condition, with no questions asked. The Store

accepted, with a smile, altered, ancient shirts and suits . . .
dead canaries . . . shoes with worn soles . . . no matter
where they'd been bought.

You found the soul around you, almost wherever you looked.
The Store had risen, phoenixlike, from the ruined city's ashes.
And as it grew and prospered, it repaid Atlanta with interest and
love. You saw The Store in churches . . . in schools . . . and
in hospital wings. You saw The Store in museums and theaters
. . . in rolling acres of emerald parks.

Miss Chisholm had been with The Store forty years.

She floated along and we followed her lead over carpeted
stretches and oak parquet floors.

That is, I followed her up to a point—when I was stopped in
my tracks. For my shadow had been captured as neatly as a
rabbit, by a familiar, low musical rush, a laugh that could not be
mistaken, once heard.

I turned and saw the two of them on an up-going stairway:
Michiko, dressed in a pair of black jeans and a T-shirt as red as
her red leather dress . . . and Cotter a few steps beneath her.

His eyes seemed glued to the tips of his shoes or maybe some
dust on the step. Michiko stood watching him, giggling.

Suddenly, he turned from her, as if he were thinking of coming back down. He took a step, then seemed to freeze.

Happily, I called, "Hello!"

And I don't think I've ever seen anyone gladder to see me.

"Jack," he stammered, *"don't . . . mock . . ."*

Well, that was what it sounded like. I never did get the
chance to ask him to repeat it. Just before their steps rose out of
view, I saw Michiko raise her hand over the top of his head.
Almost as if in a blessing, but without the T of the cross.

The effect was stunning. He stood ramrod-straight and spun
around to Michiko. She was laughing as she came and took his
head in her hands. Then she lowered her own, in a swirl of
black hair, to plant a kiss upon his lips that broke my heart
completely.

I doubted that I'd ever see them again.

I knew I'd never need to.

The shadow had allowed me one final fleeting vision. A
woman in red leather wore it regardless of what she was wear-

ing. You might turn, in a moment of danger, your shadow catching up with you. But she'd reclaim you easily, with no more than a pass of her hand and that laugh. And when you turned—

"Mr. Pepper!"

Miss Chisholm calling to me. It was time to meet the huns. I gave her shadow a nudge with my own. She pivoted smoothly and floated along.

Morris Britch IV, in his late eighties but still going strong, had a grand cigar going when we floated in in single file.

He looked lost in a cloud half as thick as his hair, a shock of cotton-candy white. That massive, single eyebrow hung over both eyes like a thick, heavy plank. No one, I guessed, had seen his mouth since he first grew the family moustache. More hair on his lip than he had in his ears, and that was saying something. Mark Twain's moustache had been all right as far as size and grandeur. But it was no more, in comparison, than a pencil line of hair on the lip.

Morris waved his cigar at Miss Chisholm, then gestured to the empty chairs at the far end of the table.

On either side of Morris Britch were three hard-looking men in expensive blue suits . . . their gold watches gleaming in the early morning light. The huns sipped at coffee from Britch heirloom cups. The huns had a trayful—pure silver, of course—of watercress 'wiches and tidbits. At our end there was nothing. We would not be staying long.

"Boys and girls," old Britch intoned, "the wolf is knocking at the door. And we'll be makin' some changes."

He stuck the cigar like a bit through his teeth and clasped his hands behind his head.

The hun on his right took the move as his cue.

"Ladies," he said. "Gentlemen." He sprang up to his feet. His voice was clear and high-pitched, roughly the same height as he was, six-two. His blond hair was the shortest and slickest of all. And the blue suit he wore was a killer—double-breasted and cinched at the waist so severely he truly looked halved. His gray eyes were as pale and as cold as dry ice.

"My name is Mr. Blue," he said. "And I don't think you're going to like me. But I'd be less than honest if I said I gave a damn. We are a group of consultants brought in by the family Britch because the writing's on the wall. Macy's, Filene's, Bloomingdale's, Wanamaker's—all the independents are selling out to the chains. The Store is about the last holdout. Now Federated's at your door. And our Canadian friend, Mr. Campbeau. The Store's been taking a bath now for years."

Blue's voice had been steadily rising and it was, honestly, thrilling to hear. There was no doubt in my mind that things were changing for the best. And The Store, for a shadow, would be simply swell. I flooded the man with a soft gooey rush of shadowy love and attention.

"Why's The Store taking a bath?" Blue's voice soared. "Because you fucking geniuses have been getting away with pure murder!"

Miss Chisholm made an anguished sound. Then covered her mouth with the back of one hand, as gnarled as a piece of old driftwood.

Blue snapped his fingers at an aide, who smoothly produced a dark folder.

"Now, I like children, I like dogs, and grandmother's cookies bring tears to my eyes." A wink there for Miss Chisholm. "I like quality time with my family. I like barbecued dogs on the Fourth of July. I like walks on the beach. I like candlelit hugs. I like Mantovani and, hey, Rod McKuen. So I guess that you might say I have a taste for—poetry. But what I really like the best . . . I mean, what really turns my crank . . . what gets my joystick jumping—"

"Oh! Oh dear!" Miss Chisholm cried.

Morris Britch stared at the ceiling and puffed, his hands clenching the edge of the table.

"—what sets my blood to *bubbling* . . . is Good Advertising!" Blue dangled the folder before him. Then, slowly and with an elaborate show, he started pulling out ads that he tossed after reading the opening lines.

" 'Pillows made to dream on' . . . Yikes! . . . 'All that glitters is not sold' . . . Piddle! Twaddle! Balderdash!"

He tore through a tidy stack of our collected moments . . . then threw the file to the floor.

In the rear right corner a green blackboard stood propped on a tripod.

Blue marched briskly to it. From the tray he snatched a chalk that he held up dramatically.

"The party's over and you've had your fun. Since you don't know how to do your jobs, we're gonna teach you. Here and now. The way you write a *great* ad is like this. You take a hot poker and brand on your brains four little words. Four magic words. You brand them hot, you brand them deep, until your brains are *screaming*. Don't whisper at the customers. Grab their damn throats and scream right in their ears!"

And Mr. Blue was screaming as he scrawled in huge letters the four magic words:

BUY NOW!
SAVE BIG!

When he was finished, he stood, hands on hips, screaming at us with his eyes, though his voice was as cool as the overhead fan.

"New York has just come to Atlanta. It's war."

SIX

The writers, as writers, had just disappeared.

Back on our desks we found layouts and fact sheets for items that we hadn't seen. From meetings we hadn't attended.

One look at the top layout showed why our presence was hardly required.

The headline was already written, in stone: percentage of savings, no more. The short subhead was—strongly suggested. And there was no room for copy at all, just skin-and-bones listings and prices.

Not long ago I'd slaved for hours over each line of my copy. As if it made any difference.

Who cared?

This was the work I was born for. And I had a real home in The Store.

The others shifted through their stacks, muttering and whispering. I dealt myself, from the top of the deck, that black ace: the jewelry layout.

The headline was perfect, of course, as it stood: 50% OFF! As I copied it, I heard Blue screaming.

The subhead suggested was not all that bad. But—SAVE ON OUR GLEAMING ASSORTMENT?

No, no, my fingers flew. And they were screaming as they flew:

READY . . . SET . . . HALF-TIME! RUN, RUN AND SAVE ON EVERY GOLD-PLATED TIMEX WATCH!!!

And that was it—the ad was done! Only the prices remained to be typed.

I'd finished my first batch by lunchtime.

Then I treated myself to a walk in the rain.

Underground Atlanta was only six blocks from The Store. Overhauled and sanitized, it had just reopened after a decade in limbo. Tourists loved it. Natives loathed it, yearning for the old one with its touch of New Orleans.

I floated in through the street-level doors, wondering how I would like it. And I liked it just fine from the start.

The papers were wrong. And the people were wrong with their whinings about the lost soul. They were as wrong as The Store's writers were, bemoaning the glorious Past.

Underground, the new one, was a place that a man such as I could call home:

low ceilings with the pipes exposed . . .

dim spots casting shadows on bricks underfoot . . .

echoes of Old Underground emerging from the shadows: reconstructed storefronts of gray stone and red brick . . . gas lamps lushly flickering . . . wares set in pushcarts, both sides of the street . . . an old-time country store with barrels for candies and trinkets . . .

I thought the shadow deserved a real treat. A small sign of my growing esteem.

I bought a cappuccino and found a good seat in the food court that stretched for two full city blocks.

I sat alone, dripping and watching the show. I felt right at home in my rain-stinking cords, the cold leaking into my bones. Life was good.

And when the time came to go, I felt happy. There would always be a place here for the shadow to . . . well, be itself.

At the door I realized I'd left my umbrella behind.

I thought of going back for it.

But, instead, I stood there and watched the rain fall. Trucks roaring through puddles raised great wall-size waves. And lightning streaked across the sky while pedestrians scurried to safety.

As I watched, the feeling grew:

I hadn't left my umbrella behind. I'd outgrown such foolish things. I'd left behind a man's concerns in the same way a man leaves a child's. A storm was a place where a shadow could grow.

So I opened the door and surrendered again to the wisdom and strength of my shadow.

It was one of my better decisions. I spun like a top in the gale and crashed happily against a street lamp.

That was when I saw them: framed in the doors I'd just passed through, watching me intently.

"Hello!" I cried and waved to them.

Michiko, again in her red leather dress—no coat, as if rain couldn't touch her—just smiled. At her side was a matching red suitcase. Cotter, bags slung from both shoulders, wore a "Frisco" sweatshirt, along with a blissed-out expression.

He pressed his face to the glass. His lips moved. But Michiko, still smiling at me, raised her hand. She made two passes, up and down, just as she'd done in The Store. And Cotter whirled into her arms.

I walked off to start screaming again at The Store.

My ads came back from Mr. Blue with scrawlings on small yellow Post-Its:

Yeah!

and

Not bad but try screaming louder!

I screamed every morning, then went Underground, with long walks in the rain to and fro.

After work, I'd walk again, for the streets were deserted and pleasant at night. You could walk for blocks and blocks without seeing a sign that read "Open." The lightning and thunder and rain were all yours. Now and then you'd pass some spot that defied the town's self-imposed curfew: a McDonald's or a Burger King with a few tables filled with the homeless. But mostly you walked and saw nothing but skyscrapers closing their eyes for the night, their Do Not Disturb signs in place. You saw cars speeding north and not south along Peachtree, back to plush homes in the 'burbs . . . away from the blacks if you were a rich white . . . and to be with the whites if you were a made black.

The shadow missed nothing and grew in the rain. And when the evening walk was done, when we'd seen all there was to be seen and not seen . . . I'd take the shadow Underground for one last cappuccino. And I'd sit there, remembering Michiko, getting the chill, the big chill, in my bones.

Back home, I would sit by the window for hours, just listening to the rain.

My sleeps grew attuned to the sounds of these storms. And my dreams grew attuned to the flashes of light. If I woke, it was just for a moment, to ecstatic screams over thunder:

"EEEEEE!   HANNNNNNNK!   FUHHHHHCK MEEEEEE!"

It was like hearing old friends from the shore calling you as you went down one last time.

It was like hearing Michiko, laughing and singing:

Yes, this is Your Life!

* * *

And that is the story that I would have told . . . the ending that would have been perfect . . . if not for what happened that Thursday.

I came home around nine, same as always, soaked through and through and just chilled to the bone. I turned the key with my right hand, while lifting the mailbox's lid with my left—to confirm what I knew:

It was empty, thank God.

Except, tonight—it wasn't.

My fingers fell upon the edge of a well-fattened envelope. A flash of lightning lit up the whole sky as I turned it slowly to see what it was.

And I nearly died on the spot.

SEVEN

I'd been wrong about my phone. It wasn't a square or quaint thing of the past. It was a black and malevolent thing—and, enraged, I'd just torn its cord from the wall. It was dead, but still happily its bad black self. Still getting a buzz from its last clever trick: the brochure had arrived from Hawaii.

In the scant spot thrown by the room's only light, I read the computerized letter:

Dear Customer:

Well, here you are! The Adventure begins!

You've made the right decision in taking a chance on True Love.

Enclosed, you'll find a short brochure detailing our various services. Plus, sample listings of our lovely little ladies.

You'll note that you can subscribe to our monthly magazine (300 addresses per issue!) on a six- or twelve-month basis. At your request, we may also send addresses for just this one issue.

Or you may, if so inclined, place orders for individual listings at $20 apiece.

You may wish to consider an alternative we recommend: Extremely shy or busy men sometimes opt for a Personal

Listing. For only $200, we will send out your photograph, along with a description that you yourself write, to the first 500 ladies who write in to us.

Please note: All fees are payable by

MONEY ORDER

or

CERTIFIED CHECK.

To get you in the mood, might we cordially suggest you turn the lights down nice and low? Pour yourself a glass of wine. Put on a record with lots of warm strings. And feast your eyes on the ladies who grace the pages of this month's great issue!

Who knows . . . but any one of them might offer love's magical Click?

Aloha,
ANGEL KISS

At the form letter's close was a handwritten note:

Jack—
I sensed something special in you. And my hopes and prayers are with you! Here's a good luck charm I made for you, remembering your fondness for red.

#23

In a small envelope, taped to the base, I found a cheap silver locket. There was a small swatch of red leather within it, under a thin plastic shield.

I slapped the locket on top of the phone. Crumbled the letter and tossed it. Found myself holding my free ANGEL KISS.

Starting with the cover, there were sixteen pictures on each page. And, right off, it was evident that not all of the ladies were Asian. They seemed to come from all over the globe. Some shots were of figures about half-pinkie size. Others were passport-type headshots reduced to large stamps. I saw a beauty in full tribal dress, with a headdress the size of her torso. I saw another in a white formal gown, in blinding contrast to her hair and her skin. I saw a young lady on horseback, her bikini the size of two

Band-Aids. I saw a young girl by a palm tree, dressed like a virginal schoolgirl, one hand on her flowing black hair.

My reaction was disgraceful, but I'd been struck below the belt.

I loosened my cords, slipped them down to my knees. Sprang myself loose through the flap of my shorts. And tried growing hair on my palm till the pictures all merged into one:

Michiko, half out of her red leather dress, easing it over the curves of her hips, her Cupid's bow lips in a come-hither pout.

I lay back, winded and covered with shame.

Happy now, Jack? Wasn't that a real treat?

"I'm sorry," I whispered.

Oh no you don't, the shadow said. *You still believe way down inside that a woman could honestly want you?*

"Please . . ."

No, what you're gonna do, Jack, is allow me to teach you a lesson.

"Oh no . . ."

I mean a lesson you'll never forget. Now, put that charm around your neck. I want you thinking of Love and Romance when I shatter your heart like cheap crystal.

I marched into The Store the next morning a good hour late and with fire in my eyes. Miss Chisholm herself, I learned, had phoned in ill. And my absence hadn't been noticed.

I'd dropped off at the bank for a certified check, then stopped at a photographer's, one that looked suitably dismal.

The squat Pakistani—with still half his teeth, arranged, like his hair, into quarters—had done a wonderful job.

The passport photo was awesome.

The shadow beamed its approval.

For the lesson the shadow had set on was hard. What I needed was not just rejection, scattered No's from here and there (too short . . . too old . . . too poor . . . too dull). I needed *total* rejection—from five hundred women all over the world!

What we were going to do, then, was purchase a Personal Listing. We were going to scream a great ad in their ears. An ad that would drive them in droves to reject.

I glued my photo to the form. I studied it the way I'd study a cubic zirconia necklace.

Then I turned to the keyboard.

And my fingers flew.

The ad took me less than a minute:

> *BUY NOW!*
> *SAVE BIG!*
> *Save on a slightly used forty-year-old, who's still in good working condition. My Life is lonely and frequently boring, but I enjoy a good walk in the rain. I like quiet evenings at home with my shadow. My paycheck is small. My apartment is dull. My company may sometimes put you to sleep. But, if you insist, I assure you: I come complete, at savings, with a Lifetime Guarantee.*

Next, I printed the ad on the form, using the five lines provided. I felt sure my handwriting would push the ad over the top. I filled in my address, my height, and my weight.

I sealed the works with the certified check in a manila envelope, then ran downstairs to mail it before I changed my mind.

EIGHT

Like all good things, total rejection takes time.

I'd think, Easy does it, while walking in the rain. Give Operator Twenty-three three days to get the money. Allow her a few days to process the ad. And don't forget the mail, it's slow—five to seven days for the ad to start arriving.

Home alone, soaked through and through, I'd quietly finger the charm at my neck while thunder rolled and black rain fell and Hank reached a rollicking climax next door. It's not so long, I'd think. It's not.

And you mustn't think that I shirked at The Store. My screams acquired a new dark force. More little notes began coming from Blue: *Hot!* . . . *Bang on!* . . . *Yeah, Killer!*

No matter how you wait, though, not even the day before Christmas is *It*.

Luckily for all good boys, Santa does finally come.

On February 12th, the day I'd selected as *It*, I *felt* rejected in my soul. Surely, of five hundred, at least fifty ads had arrived.

All day long, in The Store, Underground, I was assaulted by flashes—chilling and hard as the hail: one woman after another, receiving the ad and recoiling in horror. And hundreds still hadn't received it!

So you can imagine my terror that night when I came home, triumphant . . . to find the letter in my box.

It was from Hawaii.

I stood on the step, the black rain leaking through the small peaked shelter, and tore the envelope open.

Dear Customer:

We are in receipt of your certified check/money order to cover the cost of your Personal Listing. Your photo and vitae will be sent to the first five hundred ladies who write to Angel Kiss.

Please allow six–eight weeks from your receipt of this letter for replies to generate.

Beneath the photocopied signature was a note from my old pal:

Jack!
I was deeply impressed by your unusual ad. And I think our little ladies will simply love that photo. You look like a sad Dustin Hoffman. Good work!

#23

I don't know how long I stood there.

I might have easily stood there all night, frozen with fear and despair. But a sudden squeal of tires and the sweep of the lights from Hank's van sent me scurrying into my lair.

NINE

It was as if I'd awakened, with joy in my heart, Christmas morning . . . to learn that the clock had turned back in my sleep.

What to do, what to do, what to do, I would cry. But the shadow offered no comfort at all.

My long walks at night were unbearable now. I'd lost the sweet sense of belonging on the streets, in the thunder and rain.

I found no pleasure Underground. Indeed, my very presence seemed to turn the tourists' lips. As a shadow I'd never been noticed. Now I was an open wound, stinking of rain and despair.

In The Store, the other writers avoided me completely. Miss Chisholm, seeing me coming, would spin on her heels like a shot. But the worse my isolation grew, the better the huns seemed to like it. One day they all came, a great wave of dark suits, clicking their heels, breathing fire and smoke.

"All right!" Blue cried. "Where is he? Who *is* this guy, this Pepper?"

He pumped my hand. Laid an ad on my desk. Read the head like a pearl from John Milton: " 'GOLD RUSH! SAVE 50!' " He called the others over, jabbing away at the ad. "*This* is Advertising. When I tell you to scream, I mean *scream*, kids, like this! 'DON'T WALK . . . DON'T RUN . . . STAMPEDE FOR ONCE-A-YEAR SAVINGS ON ALL OUR GOLD CHAINS!' "

And at home, late at night, through the thunder and the rain, the shadow whispered coolly:

Well? Do you begin to see? Are you starting to learn, Jack . . . to finally learn?

"Yes!" I cried.

And, "Yes!" again.

The great divorce continued, though. And day after day, though I waited and prayed, my shadow would not take me in.

TEN

There came a turning, the middle of March, that took me by surprise.

I was sitting Underground . . . when suddenly it came to

me: I felt entirely relaxed. I saw the tourists floating through the shadows of the streets—and realized that they weren't looking at me.

I sat there, for the longest time, stroking the charm on my neck. For I knew: My shadow had forgiven me.

The women *had* their letters now.

Technically speaking, I'd already failed—which is to say, succeeded.

All that remained now was closure . . . the formality of waiting fourteen little days to prove: Not a single reply would arrive.

I began to take extraordinary pleasure in the smallest things.

The pleasures of the escalators that are unique to Atlanta. Half of them are broken, or simply shut off, at all times. The shadow began to arrange it so that the ones down were the ones that I used. Day after day after day.

The pleasure of the jam-packed trains, on which I hung from the handstraps, pummeled by massive black bellies and butts.

I walked in the rain till my feet were bone-tired and my shoes were so filled I was wading. And that was when I'd double back, arriving hours after dark at my table Underground.

At home what I liked was to sit on the floor, regarding the couch Hank had left me: a nubby arrangement of earth tones and black, with his note still attached to one arm: *Paint the place!*

And you can imagine—of course you can, try—how relaxing it was to hear Hank, around midnight, shooting his load with a great rebel cry. To think, as I drifted, one hand on the charm, of Michiko.

Ah, Michiko!

Attaboy, Jack, almost home . . . the shadow would croon while I worked, while I slept. *Have you got it right now in your head, Jack?*

"Yes," I would answer.

And, "Yes" again.

"Yes!"

By the day, my mailbox grew more delightful to me. Nothing had come. Nothing ever would come. Nothing but shadows within.

The last morning of March took a life and a half.

The afternoon was an epoch.

From six to nine, an age.

I walked all day and half the night, in torment, through the rain. But when I arrived on my doorstep, I sighed. The long wait was over. I'd made it at last.

There was just that small formality of checking the box one last time.

I arranged the appropriate lump in my throat. And slowly, very slowly, I slipped my hand under the lid.

The sky erupted in white light and roars.

I went in with the thick stack of letters I'd found and sat in the darkness and cried.

ELEVEN

That was on a Saturday.

March 31st. I remember it well.

I remember thinking: I should wait till April Fool's.

I sat in the spot of light thrown from the gooseneck, lit like a clown on the stage.

April Fool's, Jack—almost . . . You thought it was over, huh? Thought you were home. But I meant what I said when I told you: a lesson you'll never forget. Seven women, of five hundred, took the time to write—to tell you how pathetic and lowdown and ugly you are.

I spread the letters before me like a losing hand of cards. And stared at them, terrified, while the hand of my watch spun around and around.

Finally, at midnight, as Hank's van squealed into the drive, I took a breath—

Come on, Jack—go!

—and opened the first of the letters.

TWELVE

Dearest Jack,
   (the letter read, the letter in rich powder blue)
   Your letter makes me laugh! You have a good *cents* of humer. (Ha! Joke! Save—Cents?) My English is not excelent but I am eger to comunicat with a kind and tender man, I mean who has ballance inside between life's busness and life's joys.
   My name is Sol Dicson and I am virgin Filipino (true!) . . .

My dearest Jack,
   (the next one read, the letter on tissue-thin paper)
   I fall in love with your pixture. It look like a sad Dustman Huffin . . .

Dear Jack,
   (the third letter began, the calligraphed one from Korea)
   I would surely like to save 20% on any man who made me laugh like you did. That was a very funny ad and your picture informs me you have gentle eyes.
   Let me introduce myself. My name is May Ling Soong. I am of mixed blood—half-Korean, half-Chinese. My age is just-turned forty, and though I feel young and look youthful, I'm told, I know many of your correspondents will be a lot younger. So . . .

Dear Mr. Pepper:
   (the fourth letter, from Poland, began)
   Greetings from Warsaw!
   I do not now if my colors will be to your satisfying. I am blonde, as you can see, not an Oriantel.
   My name is Wanda Yolinski. I become 20 in 7 more months. And my dream has always bene to live like Southren Bell. And if I get my Green Cart (hint!) I cook grits till you beging to stop . . .

* * *

Well, hello, Atlanta!

(the letter from Kenya began)

I was born myself in the Emerald City.

And, as you can see, I seem to have spent a bit too much time in the sun.

Yes, I'm black.

And, no doubt, you're wondering why a black girl, in Africa, is writing a white guy who's trying to find an Oriental bride.

Well . . .

Something "clicked" when I opened your letter and first saw your eyes. I thought, Jeez, *The Graduate.*

My name is Missy Davis. And, to explain in a nutsell what I'm doing here in Kenya . . .

THIRTEEN

I was still sitting that Sunday at my old spot Underground, with the letters and photos before me, when I felt a light hand on my shoulder.

The Jamaican girl from Barnie's had brought me a fresh cappuccino.

"Sorry to disturb you, but . . . We see you all the time and today—you just look so happy. Compliments of Barnie's."

I couldn't recall even once in my life when someone had smiled and said, You look good. I smiled back, like a fool.

As she was leaving, she told me, "That sure is a colorful shirt!"

I could scarcely believe my own eyes.

I was dressed in a wool pullover, turquoise with small scarlet diamonds. It had been a Christmas present one year from my wife. Something I'd been planning once to find the nerve to wear. This morning, still dazed by the letters, I'd slipped it on without thinking.

The shirt felt warm and comfortable. I must have forgotten my corduroy sport coat, the gold one I'd worn since the rain had begun. My hair was dry. My clothes were too. I hadn't even noticed that the long rain had finally stopped.

I'd awakened, I thought. There was joy in my heart. I'd awakened from a nightmare in which my shadow had passed through. Now I was wholly and truly awake.

I began to make my way through the photos and letters again.

Sol Dicson, Filipino, with quick eyes and a bright sassy smile. I wasn't all that certain about the virgin part. But she wrote boldly, with humor and verve.

May Ling, of "mixed blood" . . . a slender, mature-looking woman beside a fountain in some park. Her black hair was cut in a modified shag. And the eyes promised something like wisdom.

Missy Davis, the black beauty, simply smoldered on the page. Those legs went on forever, through a pair of short white shorts. And the pale blouse, though buttoned and loose, could not disguise the great swellings of breasts. She wore her hair short, almost clipped to the skull, with two great hooped gold earrings. *(Well, hello, Atlanta!)*

Or could it be Wanda Yolinski—that *click*—hale, hearty blond Wanda who yearned to be a "Southren Bell"?

I'd write her too. I'd write them all.

Seven women of five hundred . . .

I needed, wanted, nothing more.

And that was what I still believed—I did believe, I swear it—when I came home from The Store Monday night.

I believed it right up to my mailbox . . . when I saw the lid bulging from what was inside.

FOURTEEN

That night there were thirty-seven letters waiting for me.

Tuesday, there were twenty-two.

Wednesday, eleven.

Thursday, nineteen.

Friday, forty-seven.

Ninety percent of the letters came from the Philippines. The rest, from almost everywhere, including England, France, and Peru. All looking for Americans in search of Asian brides.

The women ranged from eighteen to as old as forty-six.

The photos ranged from impoverished and crinkled black-and-whites . . . to blurred color Polaroids . . . to deluxe studio settings.

Their clothing ranged from denims and T-shirts . . . to tribal dancing costumes . . . to almost nothing at all.

One wore the bottom only to a small bikini, her arms folded over breasts as round and firm as Dolly's.

Their figures ranged from hard-to-tell . . . to rather-wish-I-couldn't-tell . . . to appealing . . . to sublime.

Their black hair ranged from pageboys . . . to nearly Michiko-length falls.

Their smiles ran the spectrum from formally inscrutable . . . to quietly flirtatious . . . to Playboy-style come-hither grins.

Most of the writing was formal and strained . . . the little pidgin the girls had puffing for breath as it flapped with one wing, and that wing badly fractured. *(Please to sending leter for I wanting Amercan young loving mind and someday I come, promise true.)* A half-dozen letters were come-ons for cash: five of them for "postage" (Could I send a month's worth in advance?) . . . one of them for plane fare (The girl in the Band-Aid bikini wrote, "Fly me fast, Jack, and I fly you high!"). But a handful of the letters were as charming as May Ling's, sincere, basic English, straight from the heart.

All week long, at home and The Store, and for hours each night Underground, I studied and considered and arranged them into stacks:

NO
MAYBE
YES

And the piles kept growing with every day's mail.

Friday night, exhausted, I fell asleep around three on the couch. As I drifted, I heard screaming from Hank's across the drive. Glasses, dishes being smashed. High-pitched, furious curses and threats. Screen door springing as if kicked, then slamming shut ferociously.

"I'll call Ted! He'll kick your ass, you limpdick pothead—"

"Outtahere! Get *outtahere!* You call Ted, I'll cut your throat!"

"I'll call Ted!"

"Kiss my ass!"

"Asshole!"

"Douchebag!"

"Faggot!"

"SCRAM!" Hank screamed and slammed the door.

I remembered my wife.

I felt sorry for her.

I felt sorry for Hank.

I felt sorry for all who were still trapped and bleeding on the mine field of Western Romance. Somehow, somewhere along the line, things had all gotten so twisted and dark.

But me . . . I was removed from all of that. I'd taken a chance, and a big one, on Love.

I'd been willing to go to the ends of the earth for the real thing, the right thing, that

click.

I rolled over with a smile and slept the sleep of kings. I dreamed of Cotter, on the stairs, imploring me:

Don't . . . mock . . .

Don't mock the procession of lovers by standing alone in the shadows?

I dreamed Michiko passed her hand and my whole life was blessed.

Saturday I heard the robins singing when I woke.

I bounded up, snapped up the shades, and was instantly flooded with warm loving light.

What joyous news was mine today?

I heard the spring door squeaking and skipped across the room.

The mailman gave me two bundles.

I thanked him. Over his shoulder, I saw Hank's face pressed to the window.

I waved. And I laughed happily.

"Good morning!" I cried. Then, on fire, I howled, "The South shall rise again!"

I closed the door.

I locked it.

And I began counting the letters like coins.

FIFTEEN

I counted seventy-three.

In a bold and massive leap, I'd crossed the great divide. I was no longer well off, but rich.

I regarded the letters before me.

I fingered the charm that I wore on my neck.

April in Atlanta now.

And it was time to get to work.

To get, at last, what I deserved.

I stood back from the corkboards I'd hung on the wall and slowly rolled up my sleeves.

I had to begin somewhere.

I had to use my head.

That girl in the bikini . . . the one who wanted plane fare . . . Surely every single man of sudden, massive wealth had had a few reckless moments?

I uncapped the colored pushpins and put her up first on the board on the right. The board reserved for my Primes. Those arms folded over those Partonesque breasts, all the more enormous on that tiny little frame . . . That waterfall hair, like Michiko's, tumbling in waves over shoulders to waist . . .

Along with the pushpins, I'd bought some gold stars.

I placed one in the right corner.

Stood back to admire the view.

I put up Sol Dicson beside her. The more I thought about it, the more I liked that sassy smile, those bright aggressive eyes. (*I am virgin Filipino, true!*) And the gold chains and rings, the jade necklace? Hell . . . I felt good about Sol. I gave Sol a gold star.

May Ling, mature and elegant . . . intelligent and eloquent . . . slender and tastefully, conservatively dressed. Gold star!

Missy, ebullient and beautifully black. Gold star, gold star!

By six, I was seeing some progress.

On the right board, Primes, I'd mounted sixty-five photos.

On the left board, Possibilities, I'd mounted forty-seven.

In a pile on the floor, thirty-one all-out rejections.

I'd yet to start in on the mountain of letters I'd gotten today.

Was I daunted by the task?

Are you kidding? I was RICH.

I fingered the charm that I wore on my neck. Popped open the latch for a look at the swatch. And I smiled and thought of Michiko raising her hand behind Cotter.

And I was still smiling, remembering something that Hank had once said—*You'll be just like that Yankee doc got*—

—when three things happened, all at once.

My eye chanced upon a glint of yellow in one pile of letters I'd gotten today.

I heard a pounding on my door.

And lightning streaked against the sky.

The first two, unknown to me, would change my life forever.

But, even at the time, I knew that the lightning and thunder were nothing at all.

I sprang up to answer the door.

SIXTEEN

"Y'all wanna run that by me once again?"

Hank mimed a whack on the side of his head with his palm, as if to clear it.

I was seated on the couch in a new crimson tee and a pair of black jeans. Hank, a real Southern boy, sat discreetly apart, on the floor.

He'd come by to see how I was doing. The first thing he'd said was he couldn't come in. But then his eyes had widened. And I knew that he'd seen the two boards on the wall. On second thought, the real neighborly thing would be to drop in for a minute.

He'd been here now for five and seemed to be finding it harder by the second not to look. Which wouldn't have been very macho or cool.

I reran the question, enjoying his predicament.

"Can you help me get some of this paint on the walls? I've— never painted before."

Hank slapped his knee. His ponytail whipped. Muscles rippled in shoulders and arms under the Budweiser tee. "Well, fuck my ass," he growled. "Goddamn. What're y'all fixin' to do, boy, start *livin'* in this joint?"

"Yeah," I said. "I guess I am."

Hank chuckled, as close to a laugh as he got. He touched his left ear to the shoulder, following up with the right, as if all he were doing were ironing out a minor crick in his neck. "Ah, shit," he moaned. "I'm stiff." He rotated his neck in two small lazy circles. "I swear, these fuckin' women, boy, are just sappin' my youth through the end of my dick." He made a sharp turn to the left with his head, away from the boards, looking straight at the door. He held the position a moment and drawled, "Fuckin' New Women, boy. Jesus, they're mean." Slowly, then, and casually, he turned his head all the way to the right—and cried, "Whoaaaa!"

Hank looked abruptly, from the boards to me, and back.

He clambered to his knees. Scrambled to his feet. Marched right over to the boards. And stood there with his back to me, clenching, unclenching his fists. I heard his knuckles cracking. Saw, in a sliver of profile, a vein throbbing on one cheek. When he wheeled, his eyes were blazing.

"What the hell y'all *doin'* with this goddamn jungle bunny and these fuckin' Chinks on your wall?"

"Get out," I told him, on my feet, without a thought for his size.

"Get them eyeballs off me, boy, or you'll end up a few inches shorter. That's a goddamn nigger on your wall! Y'all slappin' your meat to a big-titty spook?"

There wasn't any part of me that hadn't started shaking. How much was anger and how much was fear I can't guess at even now. I quivered right up to him, shaking away, lips shaking, eyes shaking, fists shaking at my sides. And then I told him, my voice shaking too, "Don't you *ever* call me boy again, you redneck, narrow-minded simp!"

"Why, I'll kick—"

"Shut up!" I held the line. There was no distance between us at all. "You knock me down, I'll get back up. And every time you kick my ass, I'll get stronger and better and madder than hell.

And I will not just kick your ass, I swear to Christ I'll kill you. The name is *Jack,* you got that?"

Somehow we both did it together, backed off, neither one of us taking an eighth-inch step first. Our stances slumped. Our fists relaxed.

"Whooooo-eeeee," Hank said. "I do believe y'all mean that—Jack."

He was smiling.

So was I. "Well, I guess if all else failed, I could always call—what's his name?—Ted?"

He didn't blink. He didn't flinch. But I knew a few things about shadows and I saw one settle over him.

"Jack," he said, quietly, "now that we've got the ground rules straight and everythin's cool and we're buddies again . . . Don't ever, I mean ever, even think about that, hear?"

It would be a little while before I learned who Ted was. But then and there I knew the name was a line that must never be crossed . . . just like the pictures I had on my wall.

I saw Hank to the door. He looked at the paint cans, still piled where he'd left them.

"I'll be here Sunday mornin'," he growled. "We'll paint a spell, then have some beer and look at them *wimmen* y'all got on your wall."

"Go on," I said. "Get out of here. Before I call—Mrs. Palerno."

We were both chuckling as I shut the door.

And it was still raining when I took my seat.

And flipped through the huge stack of letters I'd got . . . to the gold one that had caught my eye.

It was brighter than lightning and richer than thunder. Righter than rain in a glorious spring.

As if in confirmation, the charm sprang open with a *click.*

I thought I felt the bright gold paper glowing in my hands. Long before I opened it, I knew in my heart:

This is *It.*

I thought it first, then said it:

"*Click!*"

SEVENTEEN

Miss Suki Hirazawa
Natsukawa Bldg.
#301
3-5-9 Komagome
Tokyo
Japan

Mr. Jack Pepper
768 Mell Ave.
#4
Atlanta, GA 30362
U.S.A.

Japan—the land where *she'd* come from!

Michiko, Michiko, Michiko . . .

I prolonged the pleasure of anticipation. I tried to imagine what might be inside, for the envelope was both heavy and thick.

Suki Hirazawa : . .

A magical, mystical, musical name!

Jack and *Suki* went together

(Click!)

the way pieces fit in a puzzle.

Jack and Suki Pepper . . .

I imagined a small slender woman, with Cupid's bow lips and black waterfall hair, dressed in a white silk kimono. I saw her sitting cross-legged before a low oak table, dipping her brush in a pool of black ink . . . pausing just a second to collect her thoughts . . . then filling a line with bold strokes of her brush.

I turned the envelope over . . . and lost my control altogether.

EIGHTEEN

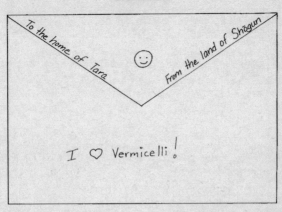

The force of personality, more potent than perfume or wine, had transformed an envelope into a living heart. Without even seeing her picture . . . without even reading a word . . . I knew all there was to be known.

She was perfectly mannered . . . and yet very bold: *Mr. Jack Pepper* . . . brushed in that incomparable flourish.

She was as romantic as I was: *To the home of Tara From the land of Shōgun.*

She was childlike—that Happy Face—and yet incredibly worldly: Vermicelli?

Vermicelli!

I swore as I opened the letter that I'd die before I lost her.

This was my karma.

Oh, *she* was my fate!

2

BEGINNINGS III
NOVEMBER, 1989
TOKYO

ONE

 Vermicelli, *vermicelli*, VERMICELLI.
VER-
MI-
CELL-
I!

It is almost like *vermilion* now.

Or *cello*.

Or *easy*.

Or *mystery*.

It is almost a word. Just a word and no more. A sum of harmless, soothing sounds, all of them in other words I have no trouble with.

My lips tremble when I speak it. True. But I speak it at last. That is fact. I worked long days and I worked longer nights, returning again and again to the page on which the V-word had been boxed.

My progress was abysmal for two unending days.

I would sit in my apartment, staring at the notebook and shivering at the memory of all I could recall: having opened it

and seen the word . . . vomiting and screaming . . . and
then, again, forgetting.

No time for food. No time for sleep. Could anything less than
my soul be at stake? Why else would *They* have taken such a
harmless and *soothing* assortment of sounds? The V-word must
be special. The V-word must be part of me in some way that
scares *Them.* It would be good to scare *Them.* To terrify *Their*
souls . . . for what *They* have taken from mine.

For two days I sat. And, again and again, stunned by the
screams and the sickness, I stared at the notebook and gathered
my strength. And slowly reopened the cover.

For two full days it continued. There wasn't a thing in me left
to bring up. My throat had grown too hoarse to scream. I had
scarcely the strength left to open my mouth.

At dawn, though, on the third day there was a miraculous
turning. My eyes were opened by the warmth of a gently rising
sun. I found myself seated right where I had been, cross-legged,
naked, on the floor. But this time there was a difference. I felt
warm all over, as if I were with Dr. C. As if I were lying
stretched out on his couch with his hand on my knee and his
eyes on my breasts and the fan's airy tongue flickering through
me again. I felt good and I wanted to

KISS

him.

And I knew, just like that, what it was: the V-word.

I knew it without looking.

It still made me ill. Just the thought and I gagged. But I knew
it could no longer hurt me. So I took a deep breath and I said it,
gagging and biting my hand.

I said it again.

And again.

And again.

Biting my hand till the teeth broke the skin. And I liked the
thick salty taste of warm blood.

By midafternoon that day I felt in the mood for a walk. I
wanted to put something colorful on, something outrageous
and—

shocking . . .

though I am, and must be, a traditional girl, as I've been told from birth I must be.

I believe that if I'd had one, I'd have put on a red leather dress.

I settled instead for a flowery print. You might think that this shouldn't have mattered, since I covered it up with my ankle-length wrap. But it is always important, if you are a traditional girl, to feel, as well as look, *pretty*.

Outside, I froze, for a couple of minutes, in the softest snow-fall that I had ever seen. I imagined the cottonball snowflakes as soothing assortments of soft, harmless sounds fluttering down from the heavens.

Vermilion . . .

Mystery . . .

Easy . . .

Cello . . .

Yes, and

Ver-mi-cell-i!

I said the V-word softly.

Gagged a little and swallowed the bile. No trouble that I couldn't handle.

I said the V-word clearly, as distinctly as if it were sculpted of ice.

And, smiling, I looked all around me.

At midafternoon on our Tokyo streets, you will always see successful men, with powerful eyes, in long fabulous coats. You will see many beautiful women, most of them belonging to these or to other rich, powerful men. But it is the men who command your attention as they strut to their limos or briskly hail cabs or march in packs to meetings where heads will roll and momentous decisions be made without batting their powerful eyes. The collected gleams of sunlight reflected in their diamond rings would be potent enough to burn down the whole town. The collected leather of their awesome attachés, outstretched, would pave the road to Oz.

I walked. And as I walked, I looked, seeing powerful men all around me. I fixed my eyes on each in turn, repeating the V-word again and again until it was said without gagging.

I am happy today. I believe I will eat.

Yes, the food will be good. I must eat and be strong.

I am filled with a glow of contentment and peace. Something has come home to me with a light certain flutter of purposeful wings.

Are *They* watching?

Good for *Them*!

What has been taken must now be returned.

What is mine cannot be kept from me.

Tonight I am going to see Dr. C. I sense that we have boarded an enormous roller coaster. And that for weeks we have been chugging up a great vertical rise. I sense that we have reached the top and that now the great ride can begin.

I sense that tonight we are going to make another spectacular breakthrough. And when we have broken through, the bottom will fall out from us. I'll scream with delight at the rush.

—Wait, I have a great idea.

—Too late. It's nearly six. The stores will all be closing. No time to find what I surely must have.

Oh, not for the men in their Burberry coats, with their powerful eyes and their sleek attachés.

No, just for him. For my sweet Dr. C, who has freed me and whom I must

KISS

or go mad.

For Dr. C, and for his eyes alone, I will buy a new red leather dress.

TWO

My hand is shaking wildly.

I am still in my overcoat. And the snowflakes have not yet all melted. I must not wait a moment, for a miracle has happened and must be recaptured while it is still fresh.

I must write quickly, with passion and speed. I must remember—before I forget!

I am lying on the couch I adore, my dress far shorter than last week's. Some "traditional" girls might object, I am sure. But, as a *truly* traditional girl, I want to please Dr. C. The dress has risen to the red panties the fan's flickering magic rides through.

"You look . . . very nice tonight," he tells me and whispers my name.

I like it when he whispers. He is a doctor, he has a degree, and he knows my innermost secrets. And yet, though he knows all our natural needs and has no trouble with our needs, there is a suggestion of shyness. I like that. Strong men with real shyness in them set fire to the hearts of traditional girls.

I say, "Thank you," the words sounding thick to my tongue. Warm and thick and salty sweet as the remembered taste of blood.

"You seem very relaxed," Dr. C says.

I am. I feel as if I am relaxing into my innermost self as the fan blows its
kisses
right through me.

"Well, why don't you start by telling me—"

"*Vermicelli*," I say.

I am sure he can scarcely contain his surprise, but his eyes widen only a little. He does just what the world's greatest doctor should do: He smiles warmly, casually, as if I've just said, say, *vermilion* . . . or *mystery* . . . or *easy*. The most natural thing in the world.

I find my right hand slipping under my panties, my fingers stroking myself, slipping in.

"It's all right," he tells me. "You must always feel perfectly free here. You can do anything that you feel you must do."

Do you see why I'm telling you? Do you begin to understand why I feel I will die if, right now, I don't
KISS
him?
Surround him and
crush
him with
KISSES?

I am writhing on the couch, unable to stop now, unwilling to stop. There is no need for fear or shame. I can be what I am, a traditional girl.

"Vermicelli!" I repeat.

"Exactly," Dr. C says. He nearly places his hand on my knee. "Yes, yes, that's very good. You have no trouble with that word, no trouble with that word at all. It is only a harmless assortment of sounds that fall like snowflakes on your ear, soothing and cool and refreshing."

My body shudders in release, my hand inside me right up to the wrist. Spent, I collapse on the black leather couch. For an instant I am frozen in painful indecision. My nerve ends, open wounds, can no longer tolerate contact with my fingers . . . and yet they scream in protest at the thought of my moving my hand. Finally, my hand slips out, glistening with juices. I shudder once more spastically. Then find myself raising my hand to my lips, fantasizing that the slickness has come from him, Dr. C.

"Feel better?" he asks me.

I nod and begin— No . . . Wrong . . . There is no beginning, I simply find myself licking my hand . . . licking and sucking the fingers . . . then chewing on them as I suck . . . as if seeking the thick, salty sweetness of blood.

For the first time since I've known him, my dear Dr. C looks alarmed. He takes my hand in both his hands, carefully easing my hand from my mouth.

I feel so good I can't stand it. I feel hungry, insatiably *hungry*.

"Easy," Dr. C says, as he lets go of my hand.

I cry "No!" and take his hand to pinion it between my thighs.

"All right," he says, "I'll . . . talk like this." Beads of sweat are glistening on his upper lip. "It appears," he tells me, "that we have much to talk about."

"Yes . . ."

"There have been some . . . *changes* since you came here last. Why don't you tell me about them?"

"Oh, yes . . . I will tell you *everything* . . ."

"That's good," he says. "That's very good. There is nothing that you cannot tell me, my dear. But first, I have something nice for you."

"Yes!"

Dr. C smiles benignly. "Actually, it's a surprise to yourself." Gently, Dr. C slips his hand from the wet vise, setting it now on my knee. His hand feels hot and sticky, almost as if it is covered with blood.

I start to rise to

KISS

him, but slump back, still stunned by my climax.

He gives my knee a little squeeze, then clasps his hand upon his lap on top of the prominent bulge. I have no trouble with his need, just as he has none whatsoever with mine.

"Last week, my dear," he murmurs, "you told me of another word that causes you to scream. You told me that it was an M-word."

"I did . . ."

"But what I didn't realize, not until after you'd gone . . . Do you see? Why, the V-word—"

"*Vermicelli.*"

"Yes. You see, it took us weeks to even learn that it began with a V. When you first came to see me, you didn't have a clue. All you knew for certain was that a word you would promptly forget set you screaming whenever you heard it. But last week you mentioned an M-word . . ."

"I see . . . yes, I am, I'm starting to remember."

"Amnesia is a funny thing. It begins with an absolute blankness. And our memories come back like a series of pinpricks, and then whole sections of the screen collapse and the light flashes through."

"It's like a roller coaster . . . and now I'm starting to fall, really fall."

My hand has slipped under my panties again. There is no way to stop myself. I need to appear in a red leather dress and just smother and

CRUSH

him with

KISSES!

"That's all right," he tells me. "Please, there is no need for shame here. You may touch yourself if it helps you relax . . . if it helps you relax and remember. You want to tell me everything and that is why you must remember."

"I must be . . . a *traditional* girl . . ." My body is writhing and bucking again. My hand has grown totally shameless and free.

"A traditional girl . . . We must talk about that. That seems to be very important to you."

"Yes—oh!" The room is lost. I cry out in ecstasy, whirling headlong down a vertical drop toward a bottomless pool of red blood at the base. I hear Dr. C, with the wind in my ears, the wind roaring with open abandoned delight.

"In time we'll talk of everything. There is nothing for you to be shamed by. But tonight we will search for the M-word. You are so close to the M-word . . . that sometimes you can feel it, can't you, start to take shape in your mouth?"

"Yes!" I cry. And, yes, I can. Though I cannot begin to imagine the word, nothing can stop the great fall I am on. The M-word must come, for I need it—tonight!

"It is surely nothing but a harmless and soothing assortment of sounds. My dear— My God, your hands! Watch out!"

I have both hands inside me now, it is starting to hurt, and the pain feels divine, I wish I could open myself up so wide that . . . whatever's inside would be free to come out. I feel his hand on my hands, and then his hand, in my hands, caught, being shaped into a fist. And then I have it inside me, Dr. C on his knees looking up through the haze.

He is surely the world's greatest doctor. Though we're falling a mile a minute, he remains calm and assured.

"It is nothing . . . It is nothing—oh!—but a harm . . . less . . . and soothing assort . . . ment . . . of sounds . . . It could be *Mary* . . . or *Mayflower* . . ."

"Yes!" I cry, delighted.

"Or . . . *money!* . . . or *mother* . . . Dear Jesus, my—arm!"

Oh, yes, it's coming, I can tell, there is something inside me that's starved for the light, and nothing can stop a good man in the grip of a traditional girl.

Here it comes—the M-word!

Wheeeeee!

"It could be . . . *meatloaf* . . . or— Help me! . . . or *mostly* or . . . *minion*—Sweet Jesus! . . . or *marriage* or—"

But that is when it happens.
And, once again, I start to scream.
The M-word has come home again.
Soon I'll remember *everything!*

BEGINNINGS IV
DECEMBER, 1988
TOKYO

ONE

A few miles from Tokyo, just before the three women in red leather struck, Jiro Watanabe was beginning his last rounds.

The *dojo,* or the training hall, of the church that he looked after might well have been mistaken for a large country resort. It was isolated, spacious, and magnificently built.

But then, the church had money. Membership was growing, though the newspapers still howled with glee. The night watchman, Jiro, was sixty. And though he himself was not a member, his wife owed her life to the church. Two years ago, Chiori had discovered a lump on her breast. Jiro had begged her to go to the doctor. But Chiori had refused him with a curt shake of her head. *"Shikata ga nai,"* she had answered. What will be will be and it cannot be helped. From the time we are born all is karma.

The lump had begun growing larger. It grew to the size of a golf ball. And, at night, while his wife slept, he would sometimes reach over and touch it. He would imagine that he felt it growing, her karma, and he too would whisper, *"Shikata ga nai."*

One month after her discovery, on a dreary autumn morning, they were having breakfast when they heard three light knocks on their door. This was, in itself, a remarkable thing. The four-room house they lived in was miles from the town. The couple had no children. And their neighbors had always been neighbors in the classical Japanese style: soundless and invisible. But far more remarkable was Chiori's bright-eyed reaction.

"Why, that must be for me!" she'd said.

And Jiro had watched his wife walk to the door as if she *were* answering a calling.

Jiro still thought of the woman in white who had greeted his wife at the door. White dress, white gloves, and a matching bonnet. In her early fifties, surely, but with a smile like a girl's. Scarcely three sentences had been exchanged, but they were exchanged so warmly that even though he could not hear them, Jiro half wondered if they were old friends. Until they cried louder, in parting, *"Hajimemashite! Dōmo."*

So nice to meet you . . . Thank you . . .

"Who was that?" he asked her.

And Chiori shook her head, sitting down, her eyes fixed on a card she'd been given. *"Saa,* life is so mysterious. She said she was driving by and she sensed that somebody was ill here. She gave me her card. There's a service tonight. I think, if you have no objections, I'll go."

Two years ago . . . two years ago . . .

Jiro knew no more particulars of this bizarre religion, the Makahari faith, than he had when the woman in white had arrived. He only knew for certain that one week after Chiori first went, the lump on her breast had decreased to half size. In three weeks, the lump disappeared.

He did not know the details.

And he did not wish to know.

Chiori had taken to coming and going with increasing frequency . . . lately five evenings a week. But she never tried to convert him. And if she'd become just a little eccentric, blessing the toaster, the TV, the car . . . she was discreet about it. Only once had Jiro caught Chiori blessing *him,* waking up to see her passing her hand in an odd little move. It had actually felt rather pleasant. And though she'd never done it since, at least while he was looking, lately he'd found himself feeling quite *calm* . . . unusually *agreeable*. In fact, one of the absolute joys of his life, now that he came to think of it, consisted of making her happy.

And nothing made her happier than these hours he gave to the church.

Jiro padded barefoot around the corner of the mats, on the watch for anything he might have missed. A speck of dust. A ball of lint. A lock to a window that wasn't quite closed.

He paused to restraighten one picture on the far wall . . . then another.

He tried not to think of the pictures themselves: that one of a woman who appeared to be climbing a wall . . . that one of a young man in the middle of a screaming flip . . . that one of an elderly man who seemed to be in a great seizure . . .

He was here because his wife had asked him.

He did not want or need to know.

Jiro bowed before the shrine with three white candles placed before a picture of the Founder.

He bowed because it was a shrine. And because one bowed to shrines. And because, to his wife, it was holy.

And because—Jiro shivered—sometimes the room gave him the chills.

Jiro checked his watch. It was just a few seconds till midnight. It made Chiori happy when he finished at midnight precisely, coming home at the same time precisely for a nice cup of freshly made tea.

Time to go.

Jiro turned to catch the light in the *dojo*'s locker room.

He'd just started to go—it was midnight—when he heard something like gas. A long steady hiss . . . yes, exactly like gas. And then a sort of rattling sound, which he could not identify but which disturbed him greatly. Not exactly a rattling, a series: at first, rather tinny, then increasingly pronounced. Like something trying to open, or blow.

The sounds came from the locker room where church members changed before climbing the walls. There could be no mistake about that. But—

Suddenly the hissing stopped.

The rattling grew ferocious . . . and then, as suddenly, the rattling stopped.

And Jiro heard three lazy pops . . . then the almost playfully slow squeaks of hinges.

Jiro thought of the tea that Chiori would be preparing to make.

Surely no one, not even Chiori, would expect a nonmember, a mere volunteer—

He was tired, he'd finished, he wanted to go. And, by the gods, this place gave him the spooks!

He was leaving, he meant it, no fooling, let them put his own picture up there on the wall, airborne like a banshee—

He'd already taken a couple of steps, and nothing was going to stop him . . . when something did.

Jiro froze in his tracks.

He felt a chill at the back of his neck.

And then the smell came over him. It was powerful, evil, and dark as the grave.

And though the odor had no sound, he imagined it hissing behind him. Like gas.

The old man turned, or was turned. What he saw before him, on the bottom row of lockers, should have compelled him to run. He could not. The doors of three lockers, each side by side, had been sprung from their latches, now inches ajar. And billowing forth from the lockers were thick clouds of blackish-cherry smoke.

Jiro wanted nothing more than to leave here and be wholly rid of this place. They were devils, certainly, the women and men of this church. Devils or witches or something much worse. But—the thing of it was . . . Yes, the thing of it was . . .

Saa, it must have been very important he see, or why would his feet have betrayed him like this, step by step leading him closer? It must have been a command from the gods, or why would he kneel there, enveloped in smoke that continued to thicken and crowd in his lungs? It must have been ordained from birth, his hand trembling like crazy yet reaching to open the first of the doors, on his left.

To see, through the smoke, the two burning red eyes.

TWO

Taro Miyamoto, local head priest of the church, received a call at twelve thirty A.M. from Yukio Daiku, his second. Daiku had just had a call from Mrs. Watanabe, whose Jiro had still not returned. Jiro always took the same route home, at an identical speed. He was as reliable as the grandfather clock in their parlor.

The call was a minor annoyance, for Taro, whose own wife had died years ago, was consoling a newly made widow, recently joined to their flock. Still, Taro knew full well the weaknesses of other men . . . especially the unconverted.

The young widow, a new member, with his member in her, writhed in her need underneath him. Taro stilled his movements to counsel his assistant. Since no one had answered the phone at the church, clearly the old man had already left. Wanting the church to be perfect, he had run, just this once, a bit late. Or, in a moment of weakness, he had stopped for a drink on the way. A man without faith was a reed in the wind—(the widow expertly squeezed down below)—even as precise a man —(the widow whispered, "Comfort me!")—as Watanabe's husband. Give the man an hour—*("Aa!")*—and be understanding— *("Aa!")*—when he at last comes home. *"Hurry!"* cried the widow, and Taro slammed down the phone.

The second call came at one thirty. Mrs. Watanabe, increasingly distraught, had begged Yukio Daiku to phone the police. Taro sat up carefully. He dared not disengage the widow's arms from his tubular waist. The slightest move might awaken her . . . and stir within her the fiery need for further consolation. Taro was sixty-eight and the last consolation had half slipped a disc. But the one thing that troubled him more than her need was the thought of police at the church. The church was beginning to prosper and grow, but it would still be many years before the unenlightened grew tired of their ridicule. Another story in the press—NIGHT WATCHMAN POSSESSED BY THE DEMONS OF DRINK AT MAKAHARI CHURCH!— this was the last thing they needed. What to do, and how to do it, without awaking the widow? Dear God, no matter what progress they made in the church, women were truly a species apart.

Taro spoke softly but sternly. Call Mrs. Watanabe now and command her to be a good wife! A loyal wife, a loving wife, did not phone the police if her poor husband strayed. When the old man returns, sheep-faced and hung over, she must fetch him his slippers and bring him his tea. When next they met, Taro would have a discreet talk with Jiro.

The third call, at dawn, awoke him from a nightmare. In his dream, he'd been strapped to a table and someone had attached a large crab to his face . . . a hairy, almost slimy thing . . . that cried out as it smothered him: "Lick me! Lick me! Comfort meeeeee!"

Taro sat up with an agonized cry, the widow tumbling back onto the roll of his belly, caressing his ears with her dainty white feet.

Dear God in heaven . . . the women . . .

Taro, looking down with alarm, reached for the receiver, already dreading the worst.

Mrs. Watanabe, unable to contain herself, had taken a cab to the church.

Yukio Daiku was with her.

And it was an EMERGENCY.

The worst thing that could happen had happened.

He hung up the receiver.

The widow regarded him coyly, with glazed-over, lascivious eyes.

Taro was no longer a man, though, a mere reed himself in the winds of desire. He was the local figurehead of a growing, mighty church.

And the church was in serious trouble.

He fixed the widow with his eyes. And passed his hand in a series of circles that sent her scurrying under the sheets.

He flicked on the radio. The widow no longer existed for him. All that existed was *trouble*.

As he showered, he caught scattered bits of a special bulletin. It did not concern him then.

But it would.

And very soon.

The report of three Japanese men who'd been crushed near three of the seediest bars of the town.

THREE

Three bodies found, each identically crushed.

Near three of the seediest sections of town.

In his car, on the way to the *dojo*, it was all Taro heard on the news.

The Yakuza . . . Of course it was . . . Some new sort of ritual slaying . . .

(Three . . .)

Taro paced the *dojo*. It was difficult to think with Mrs. Watanabe still wailing at the door . . . the fading but still-potent fume of the stench that seemed to have flooded the *dojo* . . . and, of course, the watchman's corpse.

A heart attack, that much was clear. Natural causes. No grief for the church. But the

three

opened lockers disturbed him.

He had felt, on seeing them halfway across the *dojo*, an almost overwhelming sense of—no other word, it was

evil.

The others must have felt it too. Neither Mrs. Watanabe nor Daiku, his aide, had gone within six inches of the foul-smelling lockers . . . or the corpse seated before them as if it were watching some hideous show.

Taro would not soon forget the pop-eyed, drop-jawed look of horror on the old man's face.

What could have caused it? What could he have seen?

On examining the lockers, Taro had found them quite empty.

Except for a curious thing. Discreetly mounted on the back of each was an expert reproduction of an ancient photograph: a stern-looking young woman, with wire-rimmed glasses, wearing a pure white kimono. She wore her long hair piled high. She might have been a geisha . . . except for the fury he saw in those eyes and the grim little smile she wore. The photograph gave him the shivers. As did, for no reason, the swatch of red leather upon which each photo was mounted. He removed the pictures. It seemed important to trash them right now.

Quite suddenly, he dropped all

three.

He cried out to Daiku, who bowed his head and shuffled away from the woman.

Taro told him quietly: A terrible misfortune, and that was all, had occurred . . . and *shikata ga nai*, that was that.

"*Hai, wakarimashita!*" said Daiku. It was agreed.

An ambulance would be called for . . . when the worst of the stench had been aired.

"*Hai, wakarimashita!*"

There would be a service. And Jiro would be buried, with honors, as a member.

"*Hai, wakarimashita!*" Daiku looked over his shoulder as the woman, on her knees, howled and shrieked to Jiro.

The widow, it went without saying, would be provided for. If she would agree to stop wailing, and now. And to sign a rather minor vow of lifelong, total secrecy regarding this misfortune.

"*Hai, wakarimashita!*"

Furthermore, Taro said, perhaps it might be fitting if . . . a minor exorcism were performed on her. Not so much to ensure that the demons of grief did not obscure her judgment—

"*Hai!*"

—but rather to ensure, for the widow's own protection—

"*Hai!*"

—that the spirit of evil possessing this place had not tainted the good widow's karma.

"*Hai!*" Daiku, whose eyes had drifted to the photos, could not agree strongly enough.

"*Ima,*" said Taro. Now . . . His voice dropped half an octave. Far more important than any of these things: You will find who these lockers belong to . . . and bring me the women by nightfall.

Daiku hesitated, as if trapped by the eyes in the photos. The commanding image of the stern woman on red. "*Demo—*" he said. "*Demo—*" But . . .

"*Komban!*" roared Taro.

Tonight!

BOOK TWO
APRIL–
JUNE, 1990
ATLANTA

ONE

 Vermicelli, vermicelli, vermicelli . . .

What you must understand is this, ridiculous as it might seem: I had only the vaguest idea what it was.

Vermicelli was a word as strange as it was elegant.

As such, it was a part, you see, of the golden envelope with bold strokes of the brush, from Japan.

Japan!

What I knew of Japan, on the surface, would have fit on the back of a stamp.

But what I know of Japan, in its soul,

(Michiko, Michiko, Michiko!)

ah, I could have filled volumes with that. It was a land of *qualities*, of opposites that merged. It was sublimely subtle . . . yet breathtakingly bold. It was pure and natural . . . yet blazingly erotic. It was elegant . . . yet down to earth.

Oh, you could keep your Polish girls, your flashy Filipinos. You're welcome to your cuties from China and Korea. All the best to all of them, from Timbuktu to Kenya.

This was Japan, friends.

And this was My Life.

I fingered the charm on my neck. Popped the lid. Just one peek at the swatch of red leather. Then I slipped my penknife's blade under the envelope's flap.

As I withdrew the letter, a photo tumbled to my knees.

For some time I just stared at it. The picture was so bright I feared that it might burn my fingers. You might have said over-exposure, for her features were lost in a nimbus of light. I felt that the light flooded from her.

Finally, I picked it up. Where it had lain on my knees felt quite warm. I held the picture to the light. But the highly glossed finish played tricks with my eyes. I thought I saw

Michiko . . .

I shifted position, away from the light. This time suggestions of details came through. It seemed that her hair was more brownish than black, and was neither long nor straight, but a halo of blow-away curls. The face gave the impression of full-ness. The eyes were extra brown and big, not at all like Michiko's ornate almond slits. The only half-clear thing at all was her smile, which was blinding.

I pressed the photo to my heart, unfolding the letter.

Dear Mr. Pepper,

Hi!

I hope you like my papers. I am wanting to return to you your own magical thing in my mailbox.

Yes! It's true! There was really some magical thing when I looked.

Can you guess what it can be?

Do you give up? Cry Uncles?

Very well, I will confess:

There was a sunshine ray inside, surprisably sealed in my Angel Kiss mail.

Good griefs!

How bright it be! How warm it be!

Why, it must be—

Jack Pepper.

From Atlanta, U.S.A.

Please to forgive me if I say: I'm also seeing sadness there. It's okay! I know "blue" too. But now, Mr. Pepper, the Japanese way, always wanting to repay. So here is sunshine from Japan and I hope it be as warm and bright.

My name is Suki Hirazawa. I am thirty-two years old and—

No.

I must show you something first.

Must not to hide.

It be unfair.

Please to turn paper over, but firstly—take deep breaths!

I didn't have to take deep breaths.

A spell had been cast over me and nothing could possibly shake it. Was she missing a leg? Was she short half an arm? Whatever it was, we could just work it out. I fingered the charm and I did turn the page.

Dear girl, I thought, there's no trouble at all. If there is . . .
then, it's my kind of trouble. We go together, you and I. Jack
and Suki Pepper . . .

The letter went on for six pages. I'd never seen anything like
it. The language was a living thing that seemed to just flow from
the end of her brush, each stroke expressing another of her
charms.

If Suki didn't know a word, no problem, she played it by ear.
Surprisability . . .

When a picture could do the job better, please to turn the
page again: for a full-page map, amazing in its detail, of the
street on which she lived . . . a diagram of her apartment . . .
or charts comparing temperatures in Tokyo and Atlanta.

I fell asleep reading the letter, her photograph pressed to my
heart, near the charm.

I read it all day long at work, while grinding out the illusions
of screams. How long would it take for my letter to reach her, so
that I could get one more? (Six days from Japan . . . if I wrote
one tonight . . .) I was filled, in equal parts, with joy, hope, and
frustration.

When I left The Store, though, for my "office" Underground,
something astonishing happened. I felt a tingling at my neck. If
my feet touched the ground, friends, they touched it so lightly
you couldn't have measured the impact. Across Peachtree . . .
through the station . . . down the steps three at a time, like a
shot.

I came home to find thirty-odd letters—and a parcel from
Japan, wrapped in a plain brown paper.

I heard Hank's pickup coming. I slapped the stack of letters
down without a second look. I dropped on the sofa, clutching
the parcel, a lazy orange Southern sun setting just over my
shoulder.

I heard the volatile thumpings of doors. Raised voices in the
driveway.

Hank: "Well, I'm goddamn sick of goin' out—"

Girl: "Jesus, listen to you, man. You sound like a little ole
man, sittin' at home with your lah-dee-dah fire—"

Hank: "Bitch, I'm fixin' to get me some—"

Girl: "Prick, you're fixin' to get *me* to fix y'all some grub."

Hank: "Yeah, well, y'all take a walk and flag your little ass a cab."

Girl: "Well, then, *call* me a cab and I will!"

Hank: "Fuck I will. I ain't callin' you nothin' 'cept a loudmouth and a ballbustin' whore."

Girl: "Well, eat shit!"

Hank slamming the screen door behind him. Whipping it open to roar: "I'm fixin' to get me a woman who knows how to *treat* a damn man!"

Quiet now. The sound of peace. One early April evening in a town where I'd once been a shadow. Plain box underneath the wrap. Simple royal burgundy, with a crown-shaped golden "M." Under its lid, over layers of tissue, a small card from Suki:

Dear Mr. Pepper,
   Please to forgive me for writing again. But they say it be cold in Atlanta right now! And in your passport Polaroid your complexions appear to be pale. Stay warm!

Under the tissue, I found a scarf of burgundy and silver, threaded through and through with dabs of emerald, jade, turquoise, vermilion, scarlet, and bloodred.

I wrote my first letter to Suki that night. I filled six pages easily without stopping once to consider my thoughts or play it cool with my phrasing. I wrote the way a man should write: fearlessly and openly, without a care in the world. A direct connection between my heart and my pen and the page.

I closed with a stab at a joke of my own.

I too must make a confession, I wrote. *I am—don't be embarrassed, please!—a vermicelli virgin.*

I mailed it in the morning. Special Delivery, air mail. Then I steeled my heart for a wait of two weeks.

Hours later, at my desk, I was still steeling my heart for the wait—when I started to feel it all over again: that electric tingling.

I made it home in record time.

An empty mailbox yawned at me. I sat on the stoop feeling crushed and abandoned, outfoxed by the hands of the clock.

She wouldn't receive my first letter for days, and—

"Ahoy there, y'all Jack Pepper?"

Strong Southern drawl from the end of the drive. Portly mailman coming my way, something in his hand.

"Pepper!" I screamed. "Pepper! Yes!"

"Well, I got a whole shitload o' mail here."

I met him halfway, snatched the batch from his hand.

"Say, uh," he said, "Mr. Pepper . . ."

"Jack." I started flipping through a stack of maybe forty letters. "China . . . Korea . . . Korea . . . Goddamn!"

"Say, Jack, if y'all don't mind my askin' . . ."

"Philippines . . . Philippines . . . Philippines . . . Jesus!"

"Well, Jack, don't y'all take no offense—"

"Lebanon!"

"—but ah'm gettin' *mighty* curious . . ."

"Fucking Portugal! China! Korea!"

"All these women, Jack—what's it about?"

I said, *"Love."* I held up the postcard I'd found in the stack. And I pumped his hand warmly. "It's Love . . . It's Japan!"

Somehow I survived the days, until they'd been joined in a week.

Saturday morning I woke up at dawn and with my first breath I cried, "Now!" By now she'd been reading my letter for hours. And in five or six days, the first letter would come that started simply,

Dear Jack.

By noon I'd finished a thirteen-page letter, and was just on my way out to mail it, when Hank slammed his screen door behind him.

"Hey, get your Yankee ass inside and let's slap some damn paint on the walls."

TWO

Brisk slap-a-slaps of Hank's brush on the trim.

Blurrrppp-urrrrppppps of my long-handled roller.

Hank's shirtless torso was dripping with sweat. Muscles rippled on his arms, bunching in shoulders and neck. He was a few hours into a ferocious assault on New Women.

I listened, spreading the paint slow and smooth, white latex for good Southern walls. Now and then I'd stop to towel a little more sweat from my brow . . . or slip her picture from my pocket, assured again that she was there.

". . . Predators, I'm tellin' y'all straight. Time was, when a man was the hunter. Today . . . The New Woman, basically, 's like a fuckin' snake. A creature of absolute instinct. A mere whiff of excitement or money'll have her risin' like a cobra from that ole wicker basket. With luck, a man gets his rocks off and slaps the lid down just in time."

Blurrrrppppp-urrrrrppppp.

Blurrrrppppp-urrrrrppppp.

Pause to slip another look and smile at Suki's photo. Hi.

Slap-a-slap-tap of Hank's brush on the trim.

". . . But, look again, they're like big jungle cats. They hunt us down in packs, Jack. They scent us out, comparin' notes, and they run us to ground where they want us, fleecin' us out of our money, our property, our peace of mind. They're creatures of the night, like cats—late sleepers and faithful to no one. They got cat's eyes, man, cold and bad. They preen like cats. They talk like cats. And they look weird, just like cats, when they get their fuckin' hair wet."

Blurrrrppppp-urrrrrppppp.

Slap-a-tap.

We finished our sections and crisscrossed around the table where I'd propped the boards. Hank paused there a second to pick up his shirt and wipe some of the sweat from his torso.

". . . 'Course, I dunno," he said, "'bout some foreign girls. I mean, over yonder. Mebbe it's different and mebbe it ain't." He spread the ladder before the next wall and, climbing up, continued, "What was I sayin'? . . . Oh, yeah, cats." Slap-a-slap-a-slap-pat-pat. "I got a sneakin' suspicion, y'all ever want to marry one, I mean a New Woman, and want to know what it feels like before . . ." Pat, pat, pat, slap. "Yeah, best way to do it . . ." Slap. ". . . 's to buy a Bengal tiger first and tie it up in the backyard. Support it, feed it, and give it your love

. . . then take a deep breath, try to mount it. Yeah, I think that would be just about right."

Hank climbed down the ladder and moved it over a couple of feet, stopping off once again for his shirt. And a slightly longer look at the Angel Kisses.

Blurrrrrppppp-urrrrppppp.

Blurrrrrppppp.

I stroked the wall with my roller, almost as if it were Suki.

"Sayyy, what are they like, Jack, these *wimmen?*"

Blurrrrrppppp-urrrrppppp.

I stopped for a second and told him. "They're different. Really different. They're gentle and sweet. They're *exotic.* They make you feel . . . like a man."

"Is that right . . ." Hank shook his head slowly and climbed back up the ladder. "Used to be, till a few years ago, a down-home sho-nuff Southern belle . . . was the most romantic, moth-er-fuck-in' *ex-o-tique* creation you'd find on the face of the earth. I'm talkin' your blond—no offense—Southern *ladies,* all dressed up to kill in their long, pleated skirts, with slips rustlin' like wind through the leaves underneath. Goddammit to hell, Jack—a real Southern gal had a voice like pure honey and manners to match. Darlin', they'd say, what would y'all like? Shall I suck that big ole thang of yours for another hour . . . or would y'all like to fuck me upside down? . . . Well, nothin' lasts forever. Still, what a moth-er-fuck-in' shame they couldn't've turned into some other thing than an army of Yankee piranhas."

Slap-a-slap-a-tap-a-slap.

Blurrrrppppp-urrrrppppp.

Blurrrrppppp-urrrrppppp.

I paused for a second with Suki, till aware of the silence behind me, I turned. Hank was staring at me with a truly baffled expression.

"How the *hell'd* y'all meet all them *wimmen?*"

I put Suki back in my pocket, then told him the truth with a smile.

"Wait a cotton-pickin' minute, boy—"

"Ted," I said, the magic word. Wherever he was, he sure had *some* effect.

Hank turned away, tapping more paint on the trim. "Why not

just put a fuckin' sack over your head, spin around a few times, and walk out on the street?"

I said, "Here."

I walked over. I stood there by the ladder until I had his attention. I showed him the photo of Suki, her face like a nimbus of light. Hank's eyes widened comically. He took a step down the ladder and reached. But I pulled it back with a smile.

"Jesus," Hank said. "Fuck my ass. That girl—she's really somethin'."

"Click."

We worked for an hour in silence. Then set down our brushes and stretched, Hank dwarfing me by half a foot. He allowed himself one long look at the boards.

"Jack," he said softly, "just tell me one thing. No shit now. Y'all tell me the truth. Uh, do they really do that funky shit, like walk on your back, fetch your slippers?"

"Good-*bye*, Hank," I said, laughing.

At the door, he turned. "What'd y'all say her name was?"

I told him.

He said, "Soo-kee . . . Hell, that's almost as purty as Betty Lou or Marilee."

I shut the door and locked it.

THREE

Slap-a-slap.

Blurrrrrppppp-urrrrrppppp.

Tap-tap!

Sunday, around four P.M.

"Done," Hank said. "It's lookin' good."

The first coat looked better than he did. My guess was he'd been with a cobra last night or had tried to mount a tiger.

I had just one strip of this last wall to go. I took it easy, thinking.

Hank strolled over watching me.

"Man," he said, "y'all got it ba-a-d."

"I've got it so good," I said slowly—

Blurrrrrppppp—

". . . I can hardly believe my good luck."

"Lemme see Soo-kee's picture again," Hank said.

He took the photo to the board and stood there, while I finished up.

"There's sure somethin' different about her," he said. "'Course, now, I ain't sayin—but . . ."

I took the photo from him.

"I'll see y'all next week," Hank said. "We'll slap the next coat on right quick. And lemme check with ole lady Palerno 'bout a respectable carpet. Y'all got yourself a woman now—even if she's just a mail order—"

"Ted."

Without missing a beat, he continued. "I say, even if she's a fine distance away. 'Sides, this here carpet looked like shit even before y'all set it on fire."

At the door, Hank asked, "Lemme see that picture one more time."

"Go on, find yourself some nice Southern girl."

FOUR

I was seated at my desk, attempting to get a small scream on the screen . . . something to keep the huns off of my back . . . when my phone began to ring.

I answered without thinking, "Jack and Su—Jack Pepper here."

"Mr. Pepper? This is Mary Lou, down here in Reception. There's a Western Union man who has a *wahr* for you-all."

"Western Union?" I said. "There must be some mistake." My parents had been dead for years. I had no family, no out-of-state friends. Just then I felt that old tingling again. "Ask him where the wire's from!"

"Well, my goodness! Just a minute . . ."

Everyone was watching me. I must have screamed the words out loud. At a volume Young Blue would approve of.

"Well, fancy that," said Mary Lou. "He says this here *wahr's* just come from Ja-pan!"

DEAREST JACK STOP DARLING JACK STOP YOU
MAKE ME WORLD HAPPIEST WOMAN STOP YOUR
LETTER TO SUKI FIRST SEEMED LIKE GREAT
DREAM STOP TODAY HOWEVER I PLEASE TO RE-
PORT WHEN I WAKEUP YOUR WONDERFUL LETTER
BE THERE STOP MUST GO BECAUSE MY HEART GO
QUICK STOP YOU PUT A SPELLING ON ME STOP
NOW TO JACK PEPPER I WRITE TWICE EACH DAY
STOP XXOO STOP SUKI

"Miss Chisholm!" I cried.

"Mr. Pepper!"

Dear Miss Chisholm, sweet Miss Chisholm, looked up in
astonishment from behind her desk.

I hadn't even thought to knock. Just barged in flapping the
wire and grinning ear to ear.

She leaned back with a sad, tired smile.

"I've been a fool, Miss Chisholm, I—"

"It wasn't your fault. Things are changing. I'm old."

"No," I said. "The Store's still here! And we can beat them at
their game. I tell you, we'll outfight them—"

"Jack." Miss Chisholm's shadow smiled at me. "That's very
nice, but it's too late." She held up a memo she must have just
got.

"What is that?" I asked. I felt frightened for her. You could've
fit what was left of her light on the heads of a couple of pins.

"There'll be another meetin', Jack, this afternoon at one. Sales
have gone down about twenty percent since all the screamin'
began. Mr. Blue, I believe, will be callin' for some heads to
roll."

I checked my watch. It was just past eleven. We still had two
hours till hun time.

"Miss Chisholm," I said firmly, "this isn't over yet."

"Why, Jack . . ."

"Please, ma'am. Let me finish. I've been a damn fool, like I
told you. It's true. I got tired and old and diminished. All I was,
was a shadow and I didn't care. I saw The Store changing—it
suited me fine. I saw darkness wherever I looked—it was good.

But things have changed. I've seen the light. And the South shall rise again."

Miss Chisholm said, "I do declare . . . Why, what on earth has happened, Jack?"

I waved the wire in one hand, touching the charm with the other.

"What's happened, dear woman, is that I'm in love!"

I was off and running then to send Suki a dozen red roses. And to try to figure out how we might outfox the huns.

FIVE

"Judgment Day has come," said Blue. And the huns smiled around him.

You should have seen their haircuts!

You should have seen their suits!

You should have seen old Morris, who seemed to be blowing smoke through his eyes as well as his nose, ears, and mouth.

"As of today," said Mr. Blue, "there'll be no more mercy. Turn in one ad that don't scream—and you're out. You get my drift there, Pepper?"

The question took me by surprise. My heart betrayed me. I looked down.

Blue snarled, disgusted. "You started off like gangbusters. But you sure went to shit in a hurry, bub, eh?"

"See here, you—" said Miss Chisholm. Her small gnarled hands were just shaking with rage.

"Calm. Down. Harriet," Morris Britch growled.

Morris dragged on his Havana, angling his head a half inch to Blue, who accepted his sign to continue.

"What's the matter, Jack, wax in your ears? Those grits for breakfast slid down to your ass? What's the problem—tired, boy? No stomach for the business?"

"Eat my shorts." The words came out. Licketysplit. Just like that.

Blue's eyes nearly popped from their sockets. He leaned over, his hands on the table, and managed a half snarl, half squeak. "What the hell did you just say, boy?"

I caught a brilliant flash of red from the corner of one eye. Miss Chisholm's high-necked, bright flowery dress.

I looked at Blue.

I looked at the huns.

I fingered the locket I wore on my neck.

And suddenly I knew exactly what I had to do.

"You—boy—you, Pepper!" cried Blue.

I sprang, or was sprung, to my feet like a cat, my hands gripping the ends of the table like Blue's.

"Mister," I said, "listen up. You call me boy one more time, you're gonna see me barrelin' over the top of this table straight at you!"

Pandemonium at the huns' end of the table. All eyes on Attila, whose blue eyes continued to saucer, while Morris Britch sat back and puffed, looking, you'd swear, half-amused. I figured a half-amused look from the Man was as good as a tip of the head to a hun.

"Sir," I addressed myself to Morris Britch. I stepped from the table, stood straight. My hands were shaking, but then so were Blue's. "We're not the ones who are ruining The Store. It's these yuppie carpetbaggers in their thousand-dollar suits, their polka-dot suspenders, and their eighty-dollar hairdos. They drove Macy's and Bloomie's right into the ground. The smooth ones. The slick ones. The arrogant shits."

"Go for it," Miss Chisholm said.

Morris smiled.

I went for it.

"They're laughing at your culture. They're looking down their noses. They've found themselves a place to roost until their next disaster. And when The Store's gone, they'll do what they do best—go where the money is, man, just move on."

"I've had enough of this!" Blue screamed. "I demand—"

"Sit down," Morris told him. "You ain't demandin' nothin', son, least while The Store is still mine." The old man leaned forward, elbows on the table now. "Supposin' we cut to the chase, son? Y'all got till I finish my see-gar to light a nice fire beneath me."

I looked at Miss Chisholm.

She nodded and smiled.

"My proposal, sir, is simple. Let's take what Miss Chisholm's been trying to do—but this time go all the way. The romantic approach wasn't wrong, it stopped short. It stopped short because those were our orders. I say, remove the limits. Let the huns do their thing at their end of The Store. For one week, let us do what we know how to do: romance people back to The Store."

"ROMANCE!" shrieked Blue.

Morris murmured, "Romance."

I circled in back of Miss Chisholm.

"The Woman in Red . . ." I began.

SIX

I stood before the blackboard.

I had an image in my mind, of Suki writing a letter. I saw her poised at her desk with her brush. Not thinking or not-thinking. Collecting herself. Maybe taking a breath. Then moving swiftly, surely. A direct connection.

I touched the locket I wore, once for luck . . . then I just let the chalk fly. When it stopped, I stood back and looked, blown away.

I'd divided the board into thirds.

MONDAY'S AD

WOMAN IN RED!

LAST NIGHT I SAW YOU IN THE STORE . . . AND HAD THE SWEETEST DREAMS ALL NIGHT.

WHOEVER YOU ARE, YOU'RE THE SOUL OF THE SOUTH.

I BEG YOU. MEET ME AND WEAR IT AGAIN. PUT ON YOUR RED LEATHER DRESS JUST FOR ME.

TONIGHT. 8:00 P.M. AT THE STORE. IN LINGERIE. LET ME BUY YOU SOMETHING RED!

LOVE, JACK

* * *

TUESDAY'S AD

WOMAN IN RED!

WHERE WERE YOU?

I WAITED AND WAITED UNTIL THE STORE CLOSED. I LEFT WITH AN ARMANI SHIRT AND AN ITALIAN SILK TIE, BOTH ON SALE.

I WILL WEAR THEM BOTH FOR YOU . . . IF YOU'LL MEET ME TONIGHT IN THE STORE. IF YOU ARE THE SOUL OF THE SOUTH, YOU'LL BE THERE.

ROMANCE IS ALIVE—IT IS US . . . IN THE STORE. TONIGHT. 8:00 P.M. MEET ME IN HANDBAGS. AND I'LL BUY YOU ONE OF RED LEATHER.

LOVE, JACK

WEDNESDAY'S AD

JACK! JACK! FIND ME!

I JUST GOT BACK FROM SAVANNAH—AND IMAGINE MY SURPRISE! THE SOUL OF THE SOUTH? TRUE ROMANCE IN THE STORE?

HOW CAN I RESIST, YOU DEAR, SWEET, ADORABLE MAN?

BUT, JACK, THERE IS A PROBLEM . . .

MY RED LEATHER DRESS HAS BEEN STOLEN!

WILL YOU RECOGNIZE ME WITHOUT IT?

BUT, OH, NOT TO WORRY. I THINK I'D KNOW YOU ANYWHERE, FOR YOU TOO ARE THE SOUL OF THE SOUTH!

TONIGHT, MY LOVE. 8:00 P.M. MEET ME IN MEN'S WEAR. THEY'RE HAVING A SALE. I'LL BUY YOU A RED TIE TO WEAR JUST FOR ME!

LOVE, SCARLETT

No one spoke for a very long time.

I'd just thrown the huns more words than most of them read in a year.

And I saw a few dazed looks on the huns' pale faces.

I didn't look at the writers.

I didn't look at Miss Chisholm.

I knew what I'd see on their faces.

Mostly I watched the old man puff away, stroking one tip of the family moustache.

Now and then I looked at Blue, who looked at me but did not move, just looked at me and sat there.

Finally, the old man threw up his hands and swiveled.

"That's the *damn-dest* thing I ever saw. But I dunno . . . *Red leather?*"

I said nothing. Poker face.

Blue made a sound. An airy, mirthless chuckle.

"Leather . . . Red leather . . ." Britch said. "In The Store?"

Blue leaned back, slow as Clint Eastwood around the twentieth take. He locked his hands behind his head.

"Chief," he said to Morris Britch. "Trust me. It's a *killer*. You let me and the huns—God, I like that!—you let us take care of our end . . . and put this damn genius in charge."

I said, "No."

Blue said, "What?"

I said, "Teamwork. We're a team and Miss Chisholm's in charge."

"Jack Pepper," Britch said. "The more I learn about you-all . . . Have a goddamn see-gar."

I didn't smoke, but I took it.

SEVEN

Slide show: my first spring in Atlanta.

1.

Hank and I are putting a thick second coat on the walls. Note the pale gray carpeting in place of the charred filthy mocha. Compliments of Mrs. Palerno, whoever she may be.

Hank's been going on at length, with some gusto, about the New Woman. ("Good thing marriage licenses are sold in fuckin' courtrooms. It's convenient for the state. And it helps us get accustomed to what'll be our second home.")

The April light is streaming through the open door and windows. A living thing, with both texture and weight.

"Say, wait a minute . . ." Hank's finally noticed the corkboards. He steps down from the ladder, goes over for a look. The photos are all of Suki.

Hank swallows audibly.

"Jesus, she's cute as a button."

"Ted," I say.

"Just lookin'."

Close-up of the corkboards.

Her first letter, of course, had prepared me . . . for the difference, I mean, in our sizes.

But in two of these pictures with friends, she appears so childlike I'd feel almost frightened to touch her. I find myself thinking: There's been a mistake . . . She can't be thirty-two, she's twelve . . .

But then I turn to this picture. Suki in half-profile, and in a half-sassy pose, the tight curve of her bottom through stretched denim of her jeans . . . the firm swellings of breasts under turquoise . . .

Suki in shorts by the seashore. Her legs look strong and powerful, her shoulders just slightly squared. Her face appears more squarish here. But she's smiling almost as brightly as in that first nimbus of light.

Here she is in evening dress. Those blow-away curls have been permed to the max. Her features seem more streamlined. If her hair were long and black, she would look just a bit like Michiko.

Mug shot with a steaming plate of, surely, vermicelli. So clear and sleek and shiny. So simply made-for-us. Until she comes, I will remain a "vermicelli virgin."

Suki playing soccer, her face a grim, determined mask.

Slide show of Suki . . .

And Suki . . .

2.

Jack Pepper in Miss Chisholm's office. I've just been promoted to Assistant Copy Chief, with a raise of $5000. Miss Chisholm's eye is sparkling. Even the occluded eye seems glazed over with content. Black woman in her red flowery dress. White man in a blue work shirt and jeans.

"Congratulations, Jack," she says.

"Ma'am," I start. But I am stopped as Miss Chisholm raises her hand.

"My whole world's been black and white. Well, now I'm seein' *red*, Jack. And I thank you for that."

3.

I've never had a promotion before. And I'm expecting trouble from the other writers. As I turn into our section, though, I'm blocked by a great wall of people. A crowd of nearly a hundred —writers, artists, typesetters, photographers, and models—begins on cue from Mr. Blue:

"For he's a jolly good fellow . . ."

4.

R-E-D DAY.

The new campaign is scheduled to "break" two weeks before Memorial Day.

Huge R-E-D DAY signs are everywhere. As if we needed reminding of how much work lies ahead.

What I'd scrawled on the board were just blueprints, no more. We have to stage a two-week chase between "Jack" and The Woman in Red. A chase that will be thwarted at each and every turn—until they finally meet.

The artists are busy designing the Look: ads that look like personals and spell Excitement in The Store.

The hunt's on for Jack and The Woman—the biggest local cattle call since the filming of *Gone With the Wind*.

The huns are making sure Store shoppers will see Red wherever they look. Frantic orders are being placed for red dresses of leather, cotton, silk . . . red panties . . . red bras . . . red slips . . . red handbags . . . red neckties . . . red socks . . .

The Display people are ordering red carpeting, red roses.

And on and on and on.

5.

Slide of Jack Pepper on Peachtree in spring. Horse and buggy passing by. Smiling faces, mine among them. For the first time since arriving here, I can see it—the Emerald City. Spaces between buildings, with small forests of sycamores and maples, lush gardens of gardenias, chrysanthemums, and lilies. My pockets are stuffed with new letters and postcards from the land of Shōgun to the home of Tara. And, verily I say to you, the South shall rise again.

6.

Mood-wave machine in an Underground glass. The foot-long casing is filled with blue liquid that slowly changes to red . . . as the unit tilts from side to side, the waves slowly splashing the sides.

This is where I often stop on the way to write letters to Suki. The rhythm of the waves is like our letters' interflow.

Our letters take, in crossing, sometimes ten, eleven days. If either asks a question, the reply may take up to three weeks. In the meantime, there will be up to three letters or postcards a day. And by the time the answers come, the question's been lost in the flood.

The rhythm grows in power, as do the waves of the glass mood machine.

I can't remember how or when the letters began to get sexy. They did. It may have been a chance remark on her part or on my part. Something the other picked up on. Or maybe it happened on both sides at once.

But today I've just gotten the letter that starts: *Dearest Jack, what did you do? You must be, I think, a magicster. Or how can I be in Atlanta like this, with no care for family? And I am dripping, dripping, Jack!*

The waves in the casing are redder than red. And here I am stumbling, a bulge in my jeans, to grab a cappuccino, wink at the Jamaican girl, and sit at my table to write:

Darling Suki, hurry here! You must be a magicster too. Or where has it gone to, my shyness? You can't be here, for I am there. I kiss your eyes, your adorable mouth . . .

More and more, my letters are written with sperm and not ink.

7.

Early May. Hank and I are hanging some shelves on the wall. Compliments of the increasingly generous Lady Palerno.

Hank's been coming over lately with increasing frequency. This past week it's been every night. Usually just for a coffee, a few pointers on New Women . . . and a look at the photos of Suki.

Tonight Hank's more restrained than I've ever seen him. He hasn't been "out on a date" in a week. Half of him feels worried. The other half feels relieved.

We work in silence a couple of minutes. I have nothing to tell him that he wants to hear. Nothing to give—

except what I dare not:

the envelope to "Mr. Hank, c/o Mr. Jack Pepper."

What *possessed* me to tell Suki of him? What had I been thinking of, filling my letters with stories of Hank, mountain climbing, iron pumping, six-foot-two, *young* Hank?

It's me that Suki loves, I know. But I can't, and won't give Hank the letter.

Suddenly Hank takes a murderous whack at a nail. "I swear to God, I'm sick to *death* of ballbusters and bitches. I'm tired of women with muscles. I'm tired of women with hair colored

green and purple and orange and platinum. I'm tired of women
in suits and men's ties. I'm fed up with women in blue jeans and
T-shirts. I'm sick of Ted's damn hand-me-downs. I may just cut
my dick off. I've had it up to here. I—"

"Hank."

This is, for me, a leap of faith. Whatever it is Suki's sent him
is his.

Hank stares at it a second.

"What the hell?" he says.

"I don't know."

"Hey, wait a minute."

"Go on," I tell him, "open it. I sure hope to hell we both leave
here alive."

"Hey, I never said shit to your Soo-kee."

Hank thumbs the envelope open and finds another one inside.

"Fuckin' China boxes."

He looks hard at the envelope, a small Post-It note attached.
He reads the note, detaches it, and passes it to me. As he slits
the next envelope open, I read and sigh with relief:

Dear Hank,
   You are Jack's special friend. I to you send letter from my
special friend. I hope you do like.
                                                              Suki

I look over to see Hank just grinning away.
And then he roars with delight, "Suck my dick!"

8.

Here, Hank is viewing the photo he's found.

Note the waterfall hair—it is black as the night—the headlong rush it falls in, tumbling down past her shoulders, and
down. Note the faintish red flush of the subtly bowed lips. And
the eyes, those almond slits with two earthen brown orbs. The
face is devoid of expression, yet it is hardly aloof. Rather it

seems to be too self-contained to emote for a passing effect. If
Suki is the summer sun, this woman is the moon.

I finger the charm I still wear just for luck.

I remember Michiko and smile.

(A woman like that could be—*trouble* . . .)

"Well?" Hank asks me.

"Dynamite. But Suki is my cup of sake."

"Yeah," Hank says. "Soo-kee . . ."

"What's it say?" I ask him.

"What?"

"The letter, Hank. The *letter?*"

"Oh."

Hank unfolds the single sheet.

Begins to read.

Says, "What the fuck . . ."

Reads on, scratching his head.

And screams, "CUNT!"

9.

Closeup of the letter:

Dear Mister Macho Hank:

Suki pressurized me to send along a letter.

And so I do to tell you that I send you no more letters.

*Suki tells me much about you. The smallest thing is too
much.*

*So, you have a pony's tail and muscles. Are those things big
deals?*

I think maybe you better move away to San Francisco.

San Francisco good for you! Right where you belong!

*Please to forgive my sharpness. I cannot handle the Marl-
boro Man and I am not the Stepford Wives.*

I am 100% hellcat girl.

Look at my picture. Believe what I say.

And please now to go sucking the egg.

Sayonara,
Kuniko

"Please now to go suckin' the egg! Why, that cold-hearted, arrogant, slanty-eyed bitch . . ."

It's twenty minutes later.

And I'm still having trouble not laughing.

Fortunately, Hank can't take his eyes off the letter to see. Back and forth he paces, reading it, rereading it, over and over and over again.

" 'Suki pressurized me'? Dumb cunt can't even speak English . . . 'San Francisco good for— Whoaaa, she means what I think she means, I'll slap her smart mouth silly . . ."

Abruptly, then, Hank does look up. He seems more hurt than angry.

"What the hell're y'all smilin' at?"

"Just glad she's yours, that's all."

"My ass!"

"Uh, aren't you missing something?"

Hank shoots me a quizzical look with one heavy-lidded eye. "Well, Jack. I dunno. I've read the goddamn letter about three hundred times. And I don't rightly reckon—"

"Wait. Left corner on the envelope. Tell me what you see."

"What the hell'd she give me her damn address for if she don't want me to write her!"

"Maybe she wants you to write her?"

Hank's grin is not a pretty one. He looks like a hangman at Christmas, on receiving a load of fresh rope.

"So, she wants a letter, huh? Tell y'all what we'll do, Jack. I'll go fetch my Polaroid and we'll take a couple of pictures. Marlboro Man-style pictures. Then I'll write her a letter she'll never forget."

"No, Hank," I start. But I'm laughing out loud.

Please now to go sucking the egg—what a pip!

10.

Picture of discovery.

About a mile from where I live, past shaded sleepy Southern homes, there is a small but pulsing center known as Little Five Points. I'd never guessed its existence.

It begins at McClendon and Moreland with a triangular "square": a leafy little area where Georgia-style hippies strum their guitars and read poems out loud . . . and beer-bellied bikers loll with leather-vested chicks.

From the packed square stretches a three-block row of head-shops, bars, boutiques, cafes.

Hank had brought me to the square to prove that Things are Happening here.

He looks around slyly and lights up a joint. Slips something from his fatigues.

His first letter to Kuniko.

He says, with real pride, "This is war, Jack." And then he starts to read:

Dear Lady Libber:
   Write me again like that last one, I'll fly over there right quick and show y'all what a real man is. I think your hair is ugly. It looks like the long dirty head of a mop. I think your face is silly. That hard little mouth of yours looks kind of like an asshole. I think your manners stink. And I bet you're a lousy lay. Like doin' it with a dead fish.

Bye,
Hank

EIGHT

May bloomed in a flourish of colors and scents: azaleas and roses, gardenias and lilies.

With each letter from Suki I learned something new. And I'd know it all over again: This was *It*.

Suki worked in a department store. She had two years of college. She came from a small family and believed in strong family ties. She believed that she was simple: letter after letter praised some *simple* thing or other. And yet she loved elegant things: vermicelli . . . Mozart . . .

Now and then she worried, though. In Japan she could never be traditional enough, but . . . what about for me?

I never failed to assure her: I respected traditional women. I

respected the New Woman. I believed in balance between the
old and the new. Fifty-fifty. Equals. That's what we would be!
Because that's the sort of man that her Jack Pepper was. I'd help
with the dishes. I'd help do the laundry. If she was sick, why,
I'd cook for her too.

How could anything possibly ever go wrong?

It was May in Atlanta and this was My Life.

At The Store, the fever had come to rival my own.

We were all sworn to secrecy.

Locks were added to the doors.

Miss Chisholm was given a shredder.

And each night all our work was put into a safe.

Small blurbs began appearing in the *Constitution*:

Something's happening at The Store . . .

We tinkered away until D Day. And, win or lose, old man
Britch was having the time of his life.

But we wouldn't flop and I knew it.

The Woman in Red was a killer.

Our destinies grew oddly linked, Jack and Suki Pepper's, with
those of Kuniko and Hank.

If Suki and I were like sun unto sun, then Kuniko and Hank
were like moon unto wolf.

I'd hear him howling at all hours at something she'd just sent.
Then hear the slap of his screen door as he came to try out his
reply.

> *(Dear Frigid Bitch,*
> *I had a horse when I was young. It looked a lot better than*
> *you all.*
> *The horse's name was Wildfire, which is almost as dumb as*
> *Kuniko. Wildfire was proud as hell 'cause nobody could ride*
> *her. I rode her right into the ground. You've got a great big*
> *sassy mouth. Come here and I'll put somethin' in it.*
> *The Real Marlboro Man)*

Hank was never at a loss for words. Some letters were so
damned scorching they should have been packed in asbestos.

But he never failed to be puzzled by her amazing furor. The worst thing was, she'd *started* it—his every move was *reacting*.

> (*Dear Real Marlboro Man?*
> *You want me to come see you?*
> *You want to show Kuniko who is the Big Boss?*
> *You like to play with fire?*
> *Good!*
> *I maybe do fly to Atlanta.*
> *Try to ride me into ground!*
> *I will buck you, one-two-three, from there to San Francisco.*
> *That's where you belong, "Red Neck."*
> *You better listen to me.*
> *I promise you everywhere hurt.*
>
> *Kuniko)*

Suki begged me to reason with Hank. He should send flowers or say something nice. Kuni was gentle. She really was sweet. They'd made a bad start, that was all.

I told him.

He half listened.

She troubled him. She puzzled him. She drove him up the walls. Yet it was undeniable: He was fascinated too.

How could any woman hate a man she'd never met, with such fury . . . and in the same note send along sweet greetings to Jack Pepper?

I sent greetings to Kuni through Suki: Tell her Hank is being weird, her black waterfall hair is terrific!

And Suki sent regards to Hank: Please to tell I most impressed because he can go climb the mountains.

We tried, then, in passing. But, more and more, we were filled with our dreams of meeting.

I decided to go to Japan in the fall.

Mid-May, The Woman in Red campaign "broke."

The ad read like a simple, choked cry from the heart of a man who had just seen the Soul of the South. But hundreds of hours had gone into the making of that simple ad. While it tugged at your heart strings, it grabbed for your throat. Wake up, was

what it really said. Romance and excitement? Where else but
The Store!

Monday night . . . The Store was as empty as we'd ever
seen it, and Mondays had always been slow. But the fuse had
been lit. And now patience was all.

Tuesday . . . On the train to work, straphangers were craning to read the next guy's paper. And see what the hell he was
chuckling about.

WOMAN IN RED!

they were reading.

WHERE WERE YOU? I WAITED AND WAITED

and so on. Chapter Two of Jack's thwarted pursuit.

The Store wasn't much busier Tuesday. But the faces of shoppers had changed. They wandered around, as if in a dream,
vague smiles on their faces. As if seeing The Store for the very
first time.

At six, as we were leaving, Blue and Miss Chisholm walked
in, arm in arm. Smiles on their faces that stretched from ear to
ear. They'd just come from Britch's office. And word was that
the telephones were ringing off the hooks.

Blue's eyes were twinkling. "Turn on your TVs, eleven, tonight. The huns," he said, "haven't been idle—and the old man
has pulled in some markers."

Morris Britch certainly had. The first story on News at
Eleven was this:

"Atlanta is just buzzing with the heart-tugging tale of a local
named Jack and The Woman in Red . . ."

Wednesday . . . No one was craning to read. Everybody on
the train had purchased his own *Constitution*—surely a first for
Atlanta.

JACK! DARLING! FIND ME!

began Scarlett's desperate plea.

The game was on.

We had them hooked.

Today she had spoken, The Woman in Red, and who knew what might happen tonight in The Store?

That night, on the news, we learned: About three thousand people had showed in The Store around eight.

Thursday . . . we needed control guards. Men were cruising everywhere with red roses and JACK signs. And more and more women were starting to show in sleek, lethal red leather dresses.

The Store became *the* place to be.

The weather grew hotter and hotter through May.

I was the hero of the hour.

And throughout the May days of glory, Suki's letters and presents still came.

And I never felt more sure of us, of Jack and Suki Pepper, than when I heard Hank's screen door slam and heard him padding over.

"That bitch!" he'd scream. "That fuckin' bitch!"

I felt sorry for Hank, but the fact of it was: We all got the love we deserved.

He was young, that was all. While I'd waited lifetimes, becoming a shadow, before my own life in the sun.

NINE

At the absolute peak of my glory, the Saturday Scarlett and Jack were to meet, the light of my life disappeared.

I was wearing my new bonus suit from old Britch. I'd splashed on a few dabs of Obsession and blown kisses to the Boston ferns now hanging in the corners. I was whistling something catchy as I locked the door, when I turned to see the mailman coming up the drive.

"Special Delivery for Pepper and Hank!"

I heard the slap of Hank's screen door.

"C'mon, pop, what y'all got for me?"

The mailman beamed, Santa Claus, dangling the letters before us. "Now, have y'all been good and nice—"

We snatched our letters from his hands.

I opened mine faster than Hank did.

But his was shorter to read.

And so it was that we stood, side by side, and screamed out together:

"Oh, fuck!"

TEN

Kuniko had sent back, unopened, the last letter from Hank she'd received.

She'd scrawled on the envelope:

> *Please to go to hell.*
> *K.*

Suki's bold brush strokes came at me like swords.

Dear Jack,
   Good-bye forever.
   You must not to write me again.
   I will not read any things you will send.
   I tell Post Man throw away.
   I cannot explain. There is reason. If you knew you might to forgive me. But I have a giri. That meaning obligation.
   Giri much bigger than love, Jack.
   Good-bye.

                                        Love,
                                        Suki

Hank snorted, grinding Kuni's note under one Adidas.

"Motherfuckin', cocksuckin'—"

"Oh, Jesus," I whispered. "It's over."

Hank took her letter from me.

When he'd finished, his face was of stone.

He grabbed me by both shoulders.

"Pull yourself together, boy."

Hank hadn't called me boy since the night of our Mexican standoff. But I had no objection right now.

He threw one arm around me. "C'mon, let's go have us a beer."

ELEVEN

We were on our second beer. For me, that was like half a dozen.

Hank was on a rip-snorting tirade, splendidly vile and abusive. His last speech on New Women seemed as puny and beside the point as a child's penis. This was a swaggering cock of a speech, fully erect, full of venom and bile.

It was just what I needed and wanted to hear. I was forty years old and as green as a babe. Forty years old and a bumpkin from the sexual sticks. Jack the mark.

So Hank was preaching to the recently converted. But I was only half listening.

You see, I'd never been in his apartment. And I was simply blown away. The layout was different from mine, with no dividing wall between the sleeping alcove and the rest. So perhaps the square footage was close to the same. But Hank's place seemed enormous. The ceiling was higher, about thirteen feet. And the floor was freshly polished pine without a scrap of carpeting. I'd never seen a shade of white as bright as the paint on his ceiling and walls. These were contributing factors. But mostly the room seemed enormous because it was virtually empty. No, no, that's not it. The room had been stripped of all furnishings except the purely essential. And the ordering of these essentials was as stringent and as stark as a military menu. You had the sense of daily rigid parings to the bone:

Rolled futon in the corner, upon which Hank was sitting. Folded covers at the end, intricate stitchwork of black and white.

A single long oak table between the futon and my pillow. On the table, a windup alarm. A twelve-inch black-and-white TV. A small stack of letters from Kuni. A slim vase with a single rose. And a sketchbook, its cover closed.

The walls were barren all around. Except for one painting that Hank may have done: an abstract of a woman, or perhaps a train or building—in black and white . . . but, at the core, ex-

ploding into colors. In the southeast corner, beside a kung fu
kicking bag, there were about six photographs, only one of
which I could see clearly. A blowup, in stark black and white, of
without doubt the cruelest face that I had ever seen. The hair
was worn long, with a tail just like Hank's. And the strained line
of the mouth was the same. But from a distance of ten feet, the
eyes scared me stiff and raised goose bumps. Hank's eyes were
hooded and eerie until you got used to them. The eyes in the
photo were open, wide open, and horrifying in the depth of
their utter lack of emotion. Around the portrait were a slew of
snapshots of this killer holding up trophies and sparring.

I couldn't take my eyes away, yet dared not be caught looking.

Ted, I thought. Jesus, who *is* he?

Hank went on and on, though, toking away on a joint he'd
just lit, head back and eyes on the ceiling.

"See, it's hard to accept. But there's no other way. The fact's
starin' us right in our faces. Women have drives and emotions
that are useful to all predators—hunger, fear, the love of a good
kill. But they don't have feelin's. The ones that they appear to
have—hell, all *they* are is bait. The minute your job's gone or
y'all become sick or some damn yuppie stops to dangle a diamond ring under her snout—"

POUNCE!

Purrrrrrrrrr . . .

A bright orange tabby, from nowhere, had bounded onto my
shoulder and over, landing on Hank's belly.

Hank doubled over with a "Whoooofffff!"

And then, to my astonishment, began to coddle the cat.

"Naughty Peaches. Go-o-o-od Peaches. Why y'all jumpy-
wump on Hank? Go-o-o-od Peaches. Pret-ty girl."

I couldn't have been more astonished if Hank had slipped out
for a second and come back in a red leather dress.

Hank, who spoke of women as predators and jungle cats with
cold, evil, and unfeeling eyes?

Hank cooed to the cat like a baby. Then gently, very gently,
he set the cat beside him. He crushed out his joint, took a swig
of his beer.

"Y'all see them pictures on the wall!" Hank jerked his thumb over his shoulder.

I nodded. No sense in denying.

"That's Ted, my older brother. Ted's the killer of the family, my daddy's pride and joy. He's knockin' 'em dead in New York now, I hear. Remind me to tell y'all sometime 'bout Ted and my first cat." Hank brooded a moment in silence. "That's the whole difference between us right there. That's what the ladies all see in his eyes. That's where it's at, Jack, the eyes." Hank tipped the emptied bottle over, sent it rolling with his feet. In the all but empty room it made a desolate sound. "I guess I can do the act good as any man in town. But that's all it is, though, with me, just an act. Not with ole Ted, though. Not with Ted. Now he's gone, I get his groupies and we have ourselves some high ole times. For a couple of nights I screw good as ole Ted. Till one night they look in my eyes and they see. It ain't Ted that they're seein' at all."

"Hank," I said. "You've had a lot of women since I've been living next door."

"Yeah?"

"Well, they weren't all Ted's—"

"Most. I reckon I picked up a few. But it don't make any difference 'cause the way I've been pickin' 'em up's just like Ted. And one night they look in my eyes and they know."

"So why bother, Hank? Why not just—"

Hank smiled at me grimly. He nodded at my letter. "Why not just—let my hair down, Jack, and let it all hang out? Be me? Yeah, that's a hellfire fine idea. Look what it got you-all. A goddamn Dear Jack letter, a plastic inflatable Judy, and a tube of Mister Stiff."

I began to cry.

And I felt so beaten at this point that I didn't try to hide the tears. "Jack," Hank murmured. "Easy now. Why don't y'all try to call her?"

"Can't," I blubbered. "She hasn't . . . No phone."

"Where the hell's she work?"

"Department store . . . I forget."

"Well, go back and go on through her letters and—"

"No," I said, "forget it." A faint rustle of wings in the distance. My shadow coming home to me. And riding it, smiling, the terror.

Hank slipped away for a couple more beers.

He reasoned with me like a child. Reminded me of all the other Angel Kisses waiting.

But that rustling of wings wasn't nearly so faint. And I was freezing cold inside.

Around five, when we'd finished the last of the beers, I decided to go home and end it.

I hadn't a clue how I'd do it. In fact, it was troublesome standing. But these things, I felt certain, had a way of working out.

"Jack," Hank said. So I turned at his door. "Y'all gonna be all right, Jack?"

"Hell, yeah," I told him. "These things have a way of just working out fine."

"C'mon." Hank started to get up. "Let's hop in the van, get some vittles."

"I'm fine," I insisted. "I mean it. Sit down. I'm gonna go home for a nice, a Big, Sleep."

"Okay," Hank said. "Hang in there. I'll drop around tomorrow."

"Sure."

I backed out, shutting the screen door.

I caught a flash from the side of my eye.

And turned to see a Western Union truck pull in the drive.

I screamed, "HANK!"

TWELVE

An important update from the land of Shōgun:

   DARLING JACK STOP DEAREST JACK STOP EVERY-
THING IS NOW WORKOUT STOP I SORRY IF MY LET-
TER HURT YOU STOP PLEASE TO FORGIVE ME STOP
SOON SOON VERY SOON ALL MYSTERIES TO BE
QUITE CLEARED STOP SUKI AND KUNIKO COMING
NEXT WEEK TO ATLANTA STOP JAL FLIGHT 898 AR-

RIVING MONDAY AT 8 PM STOP PLEASE PLEASE TO
BE AT AIRPORT YOU AND HANK TO MEET STOP AND
PLEASE TO KNOW I DO LOVE YOU MY VERMICELLI
MAN DEAR JACK STOP SUKI

"What the hell," I murmured.

Hank read the thing over my shoulder. "Goddamn," he
croaked. "I mean god*damn* . . ."

I stared at the wire so intensely that the words were just blurs
on the page.

Too much.

Too soon.

Too suddenly.

From the heights to the absolute pits of my soul . . . and
now higher than I'd ever dreamed.

Suki here—in two more days! In my arms . . . in my bed
. . . every sleeping dream of her made truly, finally flesh.

I felt dizzy and giddy and wholly confused. I heard a light
metallic pop and looked down at the charm of red leather.

"What's happening," I murmured.

"What's happenin'?" Hank yowled. "I'll tell y'all what's happenin', Jack. The ole South has just risen again!"

I said, "Wow."

Hank threw both arms around me. "Congratulations, bud.
But I dunno. This Kuni. Think I can get her to blow me?"

THIRTEEN

International Arrivals.

Hank's van wouldn't start, so we'd rushed here by cab, eager
to be first in line. That had been an hour ago. We might as well
have waited.

Men and women half our size nudged, bumped, edged, and
cut, hungry to meet their own kind. The crowds swirled and
eddied around us. An absolute ocean of chatters and bows,
flashbulbs exploding and presents exchanged. We waited. And
we waited. We never budged half a step from our spots, not
even when the space around us began to expand, by the foot,

then the yard. Hank in a white shirt and blue jeans. Jack Pepper in his bonus suit, cheeks scrubbed to the pink like a choirboy's.

We waited till the crowd had halved.

We waited until it had quartered.

And on.

We were still standing there waiting when the last scattered arrivals came through, like tiny drops of water dripping from a turned-off faucet.

Plop . . .

Plip . . .

Plip . . .

Stop.

We waited for a long time after the last of the lot had come through.

Finally, Hank grabbed my arm. "Let's get the fuck on out of here. We're gonna get plastered and find us some whores."

That sounded like as good a plan to me as any other.

We'd actually taken a couple of steps when both of us felt it. And felt it at once. And turned to see them coming.

Suki, little Suki, in tan khaki shorts and a Disneyland tee. A pink carryon over one shoulder. And the largest, and most nervous, grin you could fit on a small woman's face. Kuni, in a cream knit dress, her black hair tumbling over both shoulders and down. Faint crimson hue to her Cupid's bow lips, neither smiling nor not smiling.

"Jack!" Suki cried.

Ten yards now between us and both sides advancing.

"Suki!" I cried. Then, "Hi, Kuni."

Kuni smiled, quietly. And then she nodded at Hank.

Hank nodded back. *"Hi,* Suki."

"Hank," she said. "Her-ro."

I don't know how it happened.

To this day, I still don't know.

There were no words.

There was no sign.

About eight feet apart, we stopped: Suki across from me, Kuni across from Hank. And then Suki and Kuni crossed paths, just like that, Suki into Hank's arms, Kuni into mine.

Hank said, "What the . . ." but no more as Suki drew his mouth to hers.

"Wait—" I started. "What—I'm—ohhhh!" Kuni's breath smelled of cinnamon, cloves, very sweet. A pulsing of heat from the charm on my neck.

"Please to kiss me," Kuni said.

And I did.

Oh God, I did.

3

BEGINNINGS V
DECEMBER, 1988
TOKYO

 After moving Jiro's body and sealing off the church, Taro Miyamoto retreated to his limo. He had a dire call to make. The buttons he punched on the phone connected him, in seconds, to a mansion in Kyoto. The number was the hot line to the Founder's widow.

She answered on the second ring, her voice deep and gruff as a man's. And Taro again thought, The women . . . He told her of the old man's death. Of the powerful feeling of evil that had spread throughout the *dojo*. Of the horrible stench. Of the lockers—each with the same photo. He was just starting to tell her —because it was so . . . curious—of the three men found crushed in their cars, when the widow snapped. *"Shimatte!"* Damn. "Three of them?" *Hai*, three of them. "Crushed to death . . ." *Hai*, totally crushed. The widow and he talked for five minutes more. She talked, that is, he listened. When their little talk was done, he sat back and looked at the phone for some time.

Do not attempt, she'd warned him, *to pick up all three women*

*at once. Begin with one and let us see what species of trouble
we're faced with. And I don't care how you do it: Make sure that
you bring me one woman alive! And, oh yes, by the way . . .
You'd better tell one of the three men you send to . . . stay well
out of reach.*

TWO

The three men were dressed identically, in dark blue suits,
white shirts, blue ties. They looked like Sumo wrestlers got up
for Sunday service. They were among the largest and strongest
men in the church. But they had been selected as much for
other reasons. Their devotion to the church was close to absolute. They had more hours among them than any dozen members. Their faith was fierce, unquestioning. They believed what
they were told.

They'd been told that a woman, Masako, was wanted for
questioning *now*. She lived an hour's drive away, about halfway
to Tokyo.

That was all they needed, or really wanted, to know. It was all
the more an honor to be trusted with a mystery. To be told what
to do, and told simply, not as a child, needing reasons . . . but
as a true believer.

So Masako would go back with them. It was hard to remember Masako, though they seemed to remember her name. The
church had many women and the number was constantly growing. The three men found this troubling, but kept their feelings,
of course, to themselves. Still, on their off-nights, when the call
of the sake was wild, it was often difficult not to grow troubled,
out loud. And they would. For the business of Purification—was
it not, in the end, a *man's* work? Did it not require a man's
strength, a man's contempt for pain? When they themselves
were Purified, their roars and screams were heard for miles.
What demons they must have inside them! Why, even the elderly and infirm men might be seen, on good nights, rolling
around like crazed speedballs. But a woman—your average
woman—embarrassed the church and was boring to watch. The

demons that possessed them were bottom of the barrel, pathetic little amateurs.

I'm possessed by a turtle! a woman would wail.

Or: *A fox's ghost is inside me!*

Then they'd wail in their high tinny voices and jump around on their knees.

Oh, now and then a woman might try to compete with a man. There had been three women once who'd put on quite a show. They'd been off in one of the corners, each of them prone on her back, and then—the men still debated this hotly—they'd *appeared* to bounce straight off the floor, a distance of roughly three feet. But these women had not been seen now in months. Fearful, no doubt, of exposure. And the three men had gone on with their increasingly awesome back flips and wall climbs.

Still, it was odd, the men agreed, that their thoughts should have turned to these women today. They wondered if this woman might have been one of the three. They began to hope out loud as they approached her building.

And at the metal staircase, they stopped to consider a moment. They had been told to bring her. To take any *appropriate action.*

Would it not be appropriate . . . if this woman Masako were one of the three . . . to ask how she'd done it, that trick on the floor?

By the gods, it would be something, at the next Purification . . .

They would ask her nicely.

They would ask her quietly.

But they had been empowered to take any *appropriate action.* And this was something the church didn't know. The three men knew, between them, a half-hundred ways of making a man their own size talk.

A small woman would not take them long.

THREE

The men advanced, carefully, up the winding metal stairs.

The woman Masako lived on the third floor.

Despite their stealth, their synchronized footsteps made dull leaden thumps. So at the second landing, they paused to catch their breath, proceeding thenceforth one by one. Each trying to lightfoot his size-thirteen shoes.

Thhhhh . . . (ump) . . .

Thhhhh . . . (ump) . . .

Thhhhh . . . (ump) . . .

Everywhere, the curtains drawn. Small-town Sunday morning.

A simple job.

A piece of cake.

Bring a woman, and no doubt a small one, to the church for questioning.

(*Three feet* off the floor?)

Still, the men proceeded as if their lives depended

(Bitch!)

on their not making a sound.

At the top they paused before a numbered metal door. They checked the number to the left, then turned as one to the right.

Two doors down.

Not one of them could have said why this seemed important.

But

(What *was* that horrible smell in the church?)

they slid their socks on the gray metal walk. And, finally, shoulder to shoulder, they stood before her door.

The men exchanged nervous but Purified smiles.

Before their knocks had sounded, though, the door swung halfway open.

They looked at one another.

Smiled.

Asano, the soul of politeness, made a gesture to friend Buncho.

Buncho, the man in the middle, deferred. This was far too great an honor. He gestured in turn to the third.

Chaboro, on the right, fingertipped the door. It swung all the way, bouncing softly on the stopper at the wall.

"Masako-san?" he croaked. He smiled (a little) to show them how foolish it was, this playacting, as if their lives depended—

"Masako-san?"

"Masako-san?"

The others' voices, echoing, appeared to betray them as well. He looked at them. They looked at him, smiling (well, a little).

Chaboro leaned in through the doorway. The apartment was quite empty, as far as he could see. By even Japanese standards, small. Sparsely but tastefully furnished.

Typical in every way of a young Japanese woman who had passed the marriage age. Well, almost in every way. His attention was drawn to one corner, to what he'd thought was a family shrine. This time he saw a photograph, blown up to half poster-size, of a pretty but *stern*-looking woman, dressed in a kimono, with a soldier at each of her arms. The woman was smiling (a little) and the smile did not seem quite human. The smile disturbed him. The soldiers disturbed him. The mounted sword to the photograph's right disturbed him more than a little. But something else disturbed him more, something so gross he had missed it at first:

The candles on the shrine were black.

"No one's here!" Chaboro cried.

He gestured to the middle man, who shuffled in for a look. Buncho noticed the candles right off. The sword. The woman's eerie smile.

"No one here!" he echoed.

The two stepped aside for Asano, who stuck his head in from the left.

"Quite clearly," he said, "she is gone. I wonder if they meant for us to—wait for her in her apartment. Or . . ."

"*Saa,*" said Buncho. "They did not tell us to do that. Of course, she is only a woman. And perhaps she is one of those three. *Demo* . . . The church has always taught us to show respect."

"Exactly," said Chaboro. "Maybe we should call the church and tell them—*Wakaranai* . . ." I don't know.

Buncho agreed, no longer troubling to whisper. "*Hai!*" he cried. "The candles—black candles! We should call them."

Asano, if he'd tried to, could not have agreed more. He grabbed Buncho's arm and cried, "*Hai!* We must call. That is the *appropriate action!*"

The three, as one, were just turning to go when the door by

the kitchen swung open, with an eerie creak. And a high clear
voice called out:

"Irrasshaimase."

Welcome.

The three true believers turned and were blown away on the
spot by the sight. The woman Masako, in shocking red leather,
her breasts swelling over and out of the V. Her black waterfall
hair tumbling over her shoulders and over the swells of her
breasts to her waist. Her red Cupid's bow lips in that *smile*, the
same one they'd seen in the photo. And her wide Kabukied eyes
brazenly urging them in.

"Irrasshaimase," she repeated.

The woman Masako had been, as they'd hoped, one of the
three trickster women. But they were hard-pressed to remember how plain and unappealing she'd seemed to them in church.

"Trouble," they said, and they said it as one.

The woman in red, this Masako, began sliding her hands in
slow rhythmical waves over the leather that kissed at her hips.

"Irrasshaimase!" she implored them. *"Irrasshaimase,
kudasai!"* Come in, *please!*

She slipped one tiny red-nailed hand under one flap of the
red leather V. And she began to move her hand in circles like
rippling waves.

"Aa! Aa! Aa!" she moaned.

"Trouble . . ." they repeated.

Well, the thing of it was . . . Yes, the thing of it was . . .
They had been empowered to take any *appropriate action.* And
no one had said a word forbidding them to—

"Aa! Maa!"

The woman in red, this Masako, knelt on the edge of the
futon, circling her lips with her long pointed tongue.

The men's eyes darted wildly from the woman in red . . . to
each other . . . and back.

"Irrasshaimase!" cried the woman in red. *"Isoide!"* Hurry!

Down she tumbled, on her back. Her arms were stretched
out to the heavens, her bent knees spread wide as if ready for
birth.

Asano could stand it no longer. He felt himself being half
sucked through the door.

Buncho was in, in a wink, on his heels.

Chaboro was delighted. He was two steps in . . . when the others looked back.

Not a word had to be spoken.

They had been given orders: for one of the men to stay—well out of reach.

Asano winked.

Buncho wriggled his nose.

Chaboro stood in the doorway and watched as:

. . . Asano knelt behind her head, his joystick quivering, ready to blow . . . and now taken in one of her hands . . .

. . . Buncho knelt between her legs, easing the red leather up to her hips . . . slipping the shocking red briefs past her knees . . .

. . . She tilted her head back, leveling Asano's cock with a yank . . . and reeled him in through the bow of her lips . . .

. . . Buncho's trail of kisses rose until his lips were planted on the prize at the V of her legs . . .

. . . Asano, roaring with release, savagely pistoned his hips at her face . . . his eyes, wide open, turning to the spellbound Chaboro.

What happened next happened so quickly Chaboro's head turned, again and again, as if watching a fast game of tennis.

Left: Asano's eyes popped wider still, the roar buckshot with puzzled cries: *"Ee? . . . Ee? . . . Nani!"* What!

Right: Buncho echoed, his head between her legs, *"Nani!"* His hands flopped to her hips—pushing, he was pushing, but—

Left: More grunts and cries. A call for help. Then . . . What were those? Those whirring sounds . . . whirring sounds and wet, gross slaps. The room was dark. The sun was dim. Chaboro could not see at first. But Asano was no longer bucking his hips. His whole body seemed to be shaking, hands plucking at his groin.

Right: More whirring sounds and slimy slaps. And then a truly anguished scream. Buncho was pushing with all of his might, yet his face remained stuck, as if plastered.

Left: Asano screamed, "Chaboro—help!" and the woman growled, turning her head to the door. With a shifting of the light, Chaboro was able to see: the translucent, steaming mass vomiting out of her mouth in great glops. These instantly broke into myriad strands, which fed the coils lashing around Asano's breastbone.

Right: Buncho had freed his head a half foot from the horror below. His back buckled. His arms quivered. His head jerked obscenely, as the woman in red belched out globulous masses from between her legs. And the coils lashed and whipped and slapped around his skull.

Appropriate action . . .

Appropriate action!

Chaboro stood, transfixed with terror. His orders could not have been clearer. He was, at all costs, to stay well out of reach!

Yet—

Left: Asano's ample belly had been squeezed to a will-o'-the-wisp. His chest, ballooned to monstrous size, was suddenly diminished with a series of horrible cracks as the tendrils whirred and slapped and squished. Asano's face was turning as deep a shade of purple as a fully ripened plum.

Right: Buncho's head, wholly covered with tendrils, looked like some hideous turban. His hands, plucking at the coils, were pinned to the sides of his skull.

Suddenly, Chaboro heard the most frightening sound of all. A sudden cessation of whirrings and slaps. He saw the woman Masako relax, a soft slip of a girl in red leather. She looked as if she might sleep now, with two men, one at either end, frozen in yards of her glistening coils. She seemed to be fully removed from the scene.

If ever there would be a moment for taking *appropriate action . . .*

Chaboro's eyes darted to the sword by the blasphemous shrine.

He looked back at Asano, whose blackened face implored him.

Chaboro's eyes suddenly flooded with tears. They'd been sent here like lambs to the slaughter. The church must have known or the church must have guessed.

Appropriate action?

Try this!

He was already moving when, from the corner of one eye, he

caught a small sliver of movement. He stopped. The woman Masako was taking a breath that half forced her breasts out of the red leather V.

He understood, instinctively, that the real horror was to begin.

He ran, for his own life as well as his friends'. He did not trouble to lift the scabbard from its mounting on the wall. He grasped the handle of the sword and whipped it as he was whirling. The scabbard shrieked as it flew off the blade and crashed into the opposite wall.

He raised the sword over one shoulder and charged . . . as the woman in red, this Masako, expelled all the breath from her body with one ferocious *squeeze.*

Buncho's head, between her legs, exploded like a melon within the wet, glistening vise.

Asano's insides—all, it seemed—spewed out of his mouth and his ears . . . in one horrendous blast of chunks, crimson sprays, and coils of flesh.

The woman in red wasted no time at all. She rolled over to her knees, the coils retracting at dizzying speed.

The bodies fell before, behind.

Chaboro circled warily, praying for an opening.

He brandished the sword, the handle slipping grossly in his hands.

She hissed and turned . . . then sprang at him, already respewing the coils.

When he swung, his eyes were closed. Later, he thanked God they had been. He himself might well have missed through terror and confusion.

It was his *faith* working through him.

A miracle was truly wrought.

His aim was true. The angle, sure. The timing, to perfection.

The blade sheared her neck at the shoulders.

He was showered with relief.

And with wave after wave of the woman in red.

BEGINNINGS VI
NOVEMBER, 1989
TOKYO

ONE

It is the same every morning.

I always feel so refreshed when I wake. I feel as if I have been floating down a warm and amazing long river. One that is bringing me closer each night, through my dreams, to the beautiful Source. To whatever it is that *They've* taken.

Each morning my eyes slip right open. I sit up and say it with pleasure and pride:

"Ver-mi-cell-i!"

Then I proceed to the business at hand.

"Marriage," I say softly. Gag.

"Marriage." Gag.

"Marriage." Gag.

Now and then the M-word still makes me deathly ill. But I am, and must be, a traditional girl. And traditional girls must be patient, correct?

Anyday I know I'll awaken to find that it too has come home to me. And I'll say the M-word with pleasure and pride.

Already there are moments when I feel incredibly close to the Source. So close I feel that if I stretched a millimeter more . . .

Flashes tantalize me. Ghost outlines of memories, gone in a blur.

I had *friends*.

And they were *powerful*.

I can feel that so clearly—but *who?*

I had one friend who—proved no friend . . .

I have a repeated flash of somebody asking me questions. Sometimes I think it's a woman. Quite old. Sometimes I think it's a man. He's afraid. I don't want to answer them. I try to leave. I cannot move. They are about to do something dreadful —but *what?*

Sometimes I look at the dress I have bought, the mini of shocking red leather . . . and I have the disturbing flash: that I have worn it before. Impossible, I know that. I never even tried it on. One glance and I knew. I just knew it was mine.

And I knew that the first time I wear it must be tonight, for Dr. C.

It must be magic, red leather . . . or why does it do what it does to my heart?

Surely it's mine and was made just for me.

Oh, *tonight,* for certain, I will please him.

And please him.

And

KISS!

him.

BOOK THREE
JUNE, 1990
ATLANTA

ONE

 Remember one week . . . the best week of your life . . . the best you knew you'd live to see, or ever hope to want to . . . how, though you knew the days must pass, you tried to savor each moment, even as you felt the moments slipping through your fingers. It may have been with someone special who was leaving you soon, and forever. It may have been in some lost magical place that you can never return to, your last time there, your best time there.

Try to remember.

I'll never forget.

I remember the week as a liquid collage . . . a series of shifting suspensions in time: dreamy, almost trancelike states, in which I felt more like a mood than a man—the mood of a ship that has weathered fierce storms now docked and firmly anchored, home . . .

then states of ravenous hunger, when I wanted to roll up the windows and roar: I'm a lion and this is My Life!

In between the two of them, a thin layer of something like blue liquid ice: eerie little flashes . . . questions and shadows of doubts.

In and out I drifted, now in one state, now the other, now half in each with the ice slicing through.

If you can remember, you know what it's like.

If you've been there, it's like this:

We are in our cab, going home by ourselves.

And Jack and Suki Pepper are already a dream of the past. I am sitting, my arm around Kuni. The meter is ticking away as the cab snakes through the thick airport traffic. We are bathed in a shifting succession of cool shadows, glaring lights. I say nothing, I just hold her and inhale the commingled perfume of her hair, her silken skin, her soul. She says nothing, she just nestles as if married to my side. At one stop, in a flooding of shadows, I pull away and our eyes meet. And I feel then the first passing: from the dreamy half trance to the unbridled hunger. On the way I'm cut nearly in half by a whiplash of blue liquid ice. (*Suki, though . . . What's happening?*) I whisper, "Wait—" But Kuni's eyes draw me magnetically to her, my mouth seeking those Cupid's bow lips. The ice lashes once, a harsh flick (*Maybe trouble!*), but then I am home in the hunger. I thought I knew how to kiss. I did not. Kuni flicks at my lips and my teeth with her tongue . . .

then, with a move of her lips, opens mine, snaking her tongue through my mouth to my tongue, licking it, flicking it, circling it. The cab jolts forward and her tongue nearly reaches the back of my throat. And then I feel her tiny hand encircle my cock through my slacks. My cry is cut to ribbons with her incredible tongue. I am forty years old and no virgin, not quite, but never, never, not even in dreams, has a woman just reached out and touched me. A simple warm and friendly squeeze. Hi there. Nice to meechuh.

I turn, turning Kuni, my hand on her breasts. Vibrant and warm through the cool satin blouse. We sit, softly fondling each other, descending with a single splash

(*This woman's an absolute stranger!*)

into the well of well-being, content.

And here we are now. Jack's place.

(You're gonna get in trouble!)

I close the door behind me, charged with desire again, flooded with light. There is no need for candles. Or even the wine I had bought. Any questions I have can be answered tomorrow. What questions are there, anyway? From the first time I saw Kuni's picture . . . I *knew*. I see that now, I must have known. And, seeing her now, calmly breaking the board with Suki's pictures in half . . . I find myself doing the same with the image I have in my heart. The sight of her there at the airport, with her Disneyland tee and her bowling-pin legs . . . her frizzy hair and her gold-flecked buck teeth. We'd been in love with Love, I guess, swept away by the warm soothing flow through the mail. We thought we knew each other. But all along we'd been strangers. All along it had all been reversed. She was Hank's girl; Kuni, mine. And with an "X" at the airport, the reversals were reversed.

I watch as Kuni unbuttons her blouse, floating over my way. Underneath the white satin, a pale blue lace bra. Twin shadows of her nipples, larger and darker than any I've seen, on two perfect, pear-sized breasts. Standing now before me, she raises my hand to her heart, the pulse strong and rhythmic. "Do you see what you do to me?" she asks. I say, "Yes." And Kuni smiles. "Tomorrow, my darling, is—how do you say? It is—Q and A? We talk. Tonight, we are waiting a very long time. So please to be there no shyness."

My lips find hers, my tongue her tongue, my hands can't get enough of her. I slip the cool blouse from her shoulders, releasing the catch of the powder-blue bra. Her breasts are freed with a quiver, dark nipples erupting into rigid little fingers. And, oh, there it goes, the trim black skirt eased to the floor with a wriggle, her lithe body twisting against me. That satin blouse was sandpaper compared to the silk of her cool tawny skin.

I catch another flash of blue just below her navel. Kuni scissors her legs around my right thigh and I feel a rushing of moisture and heat. I want to touch it, reach the source. But her fingers encircle my wrist. I feel as if I've been handcuffed. She raises my hand to her shoulder. I'm stunned by her strength. Kuni giggles. "Why don't we become now quite shocking?"

Hours later, I lie back and start to sink through the floor of desire . . . back to the warmth of the trance . . . more icy flashes in between.

(Kuni's in the bathroom now. A dreadful sound, like retching.)

(My wrist aches where she grabbed it a second time in bed. Foreplay, I'd thought. The thing to do. But she hissed, "I don't need that!" and fiercely slipped my cock in.)

The splashes are chilling. But here I am, home. And the trance of well-being is wondrous and deep. I am dreamily conscious of Kuni slipping in beside me, nothing but her panties on, wet and hot against my hip, her fingers lazily circling my cock, tracing her nails on the scrotum. I am limp with exhaustion, I'll bleed if I come, and yet, as she strokes me, I stiffen again. "Sleep," Kuni coos, slipping one thigh over me and her panties off. She straddles me and, with a sigh, lowers her weight to my hips. I am barely conscious of her floating forward at the waist until her breasts have met my chest, her cheek nestled to my cheek, my arms around her waist.

We sleep in this position, dropping yet still farther down through the trance. In sleep, the memories are deep ocean waves: I remember the muscles of Kuni's vagina doing impossible things, now gripping, now caressing, now milking my shaft with a vengeance. I swear I could feel her vagina caressing my balls and my asshole. ("I can make magic," she said that first time, "if you close your eyes. And no questions.")

I awaken near dawn from a wonderful dream: that I am being swallowed whole by an enormous squid. I sit up, sleepy-eyed, to see her hair fanned all over my groin. Everywhere beneath her hair I feel a swirl of movement . . . like a thousand fingers . . . yet Kuni's head never moves, not a twitch. Suddenly the motion stops and I begin to undergo the agonies of withdrawal. An eternity passes. But then her head moves, first up and then down, oh deliciously down, with a pop as I slip past her gullet, and down. I feel her teeth clamp softly around the root of my cock. And, incredibly, though her teeth do not move, I feel the action everywhere: milking, pumping, squeezing, churning. I close my eyes, terrified of risking the magic by looking. It's Japan, I think . . . It's magic . . .

I hear myself scream then, thundering into a milky release. I think I hear another scream, Hank's, shrill and piercing. I wish him well, but he'll never know. Suki's a clown in a Disneyland tee, while Kuni—Oh God, Kuni!

Done, every cell of my body feels drained. And I lie breathless and beaten by love, as the rhythm below slowly slows and then stops. I think I hear a few sounds I'd really rather not: whirrs and slaps and then . . . a plop? But my ears are still ringing with Hank's scream and mine, and surely my hearing deceives me.

Kuni disengages. She rearranges her hair with a toss and gentle strokings of her hands. And then she nestles to my side, smiling, oh, she's smiling. "*Tanoshikatta,* Jack? Enjoy? Please to forgive my selfish thing, but I thought maybe a surprise." I say "Yes," and reach for Kuni, the blood roaring in my ears.

Try, you must try, to remember one lover who made a liar of your past; made you feel young and alive and on fire.

I hear then, as my mouth finds hers, another anguished scream from Hank's. But, "Darling," Kuni murmurs and her hand, around my cock, begins weaving its own spell of magic. "Jac-k-k-k," she croons, "Kuni is hungry. For Jack!"

I wake up at nearly eleven—two hours late, to my horror, for work. Kuni's in the bathroom singing "Just the Way You Are." On my way to the phone I pass by. The door's open, Kuni on the head, whistling away as she pees. I feel my face turning crimson. She laughs. "Jac-k-k-k," she says. And like a child I shuffle over, no longer hiding my eyes. Sight of Kuni peeing. Happy smile on her face. And happier still when I take my own turn, allowing her to hold my cock and watch the golden arch. "Oh wow," she says, "it's a big fire hose!" When I finish, she shakes the last drops loose, then bounces my stiffening rod once or twice. "Jac-k-k-k," she cries. I moan, the deep purple rumbling from aching balls to the crown. I yank her up—

(Splash: Christ, my wrist! Purple band around it from where she grabbed me hard last night.)

We stumble into the shower, Kuni's legs around my waist, and I switch on the water, cold, to try and douse the fire. The icy spray, instead, has quite the opposite effect. The contrast is explosive, between our heat and the bristling spray. And in a move we crash against the shower wall, paralyzed with passion, locked at the hips and unable to move. But, really, there's no need to. For Kuni and I are both screaming into each other's mouth, as it starts to happen all over again, down below where the magic is stored. And when it's over I drop to my knees, Kuni's legs around my waist, until the heat, exhausted, gives way to a spell of the shivers.

While I shave and dry my hair, Kuni showers, curtain drawn. She is singing something sweet. I turn to pull the curtain and tell her that I love her. But before I can reach it, she slips it flush tight. *Women,* I think. *Women!* There is nothing forbidden between us, except—

Over the whirr of the dryer, I think I hear Kuni retching again. I flick the switch. Silence now. Only the whispering rain in the stall. Then: "Jack? When you finish, darling, please to shut the door. Don't you know a girl, Jack, has woman things to do?" Kuni is singing again as I go, soft-clicking the door shut behind me.

My first thought is the telephone. I have to phone Miss Chisholm. I've never missed a day's work at The Store. To be two hours late—what excuse can there be? I find my problem answered in the living room, of course. The phone's cord is still shot, as it has been for months. Oh, well. Use a pay phone tomorrow. For heroes, allowance is made.

I am seated on the nubby couch, almost purring with content, the morning sun flooding the white walls and gray carpet, when Kuni comes into the room. She's wearing a long pleated dress, the hem fully covering her knees. Snow-white, with subtle finessing of lace at the throat, on the sleeves. "Oh, Jack," she says, "I love it here. Your apartment—so lovely and *big!* All my life I've been wanting . . . a place I can relaxing, yes? A man I can relaxing with."

So Love, in the end, is this simple.

By the second I sink with this woman into the well of well-being. As we sit, then as we walk, the June air warm and clear, Kuni sounds her amazement again and again.

—Atlanta's streets are broad and quiet, all of them lined with magnificent *trees.* Kuni spins, her arms outstretched, laughing and singing out, "Trees!"

—Atlanta's trains thrill her nearly to tears. Her eyes dart ex-

citedly from the carpeted floors to the orange-gold seats. She
sees, again, the abundance of *space*—room to stretch her legs,
relax.

—Le Peep, where I first saw Michiko . . . Our waiter is a
Southern gay with an accent that Kuni adores. He bows each
time he serves her and never fails to call her ma'am. "Oh, Jack,"
she cries, "the people! The people are so nice! Even gay boys
are like men!" She takes my hand, says "Thank you" . . . then
sees for the first time the welt on my wrist. "Oh, no!" she cries.
"So sorry!" Gently, she raises my wrist to her lips. "Jack," she
says, "is there the park for us to Q and A?"

Q and A . . .

Q and A . . .

We spend our lives in Q and A—believing our questions and
answers add up.

Where do you work? What's your title, your income? How
big is your family? And do you like cats?

Suki and I had played at it. We heard all the answers we
wanted to hear. But it wasn't just that our questions were
wrong. We'd been wrong all along in assuming *we* made the
decisions, when Love has a way of its own.

I feel this now in Piedmont Park. We've strolled arm in arm to
a bench by the lake, on which the willows pitch ripe leaves that
sail around the swans and ducks. The charm on my neck beams
approval and luck. Summer in Atlanta . . . How had I ever
feared it?

Kuni beside me, her head on my shoulder, one hand lightly
draped on my thigh.

"First time I see your picture, Jack . . . and letters Suki
show me . . . I know you are the man for me. But you belonged to Suki. That hurt me a hell of a lot."

I say, "How . . ."—not a question so much as a statement of
wonder.

"Did you feel too, darling?" Squeeze of my thigh. Fingertips
brushing lint off my jeans about a half inch from my hard-on.

I say, "Yes. I didn't know it— No, I didn't know I knew it—"
And I begin to ramble of my terrible bout with my shadow . . .
how Suki's photo had seemed like the sun, flooding my being

with light. I haven't even started when Kuni gives my balls a pat and looks up, smiling impishly. "They are big, like horse's. Can we do it tonight like the doggies? And can I watch you shoot?"

I begin to whoop with laughter.

"Jac-k-k-k, Q and A time. That is my next question."

"Yes," I tell her. "Doggie style, horsey style, any way you like. But first . . . Kuni, really, tell me: How did you and Suki—ahhhhh!"

This time it is no shy, sly pat but a deep circular rub down and up that has me squirming on the bench.

"Jac-k-k-k," Kuni says, "that is—how do you say—trading secret? Besides . . ." Kuni's hand is chaste now, except for one sly finger slipped under the waist of my jeans . . . then my shorts. "Suki," she says solemnly, "cannot be good for you, darling. She very sweet . . . but have bad blood. The Marlboro Man have a big, *big* surprise!"

"But wait a—Oh! Oh!—bad blood?"

Miraculously, in Piedmont Park, in broad daylight, in full view on the bench, Kuni, with only the pad of that finger, works the most sensitive spot on my shaft, and brings me to a crazed climax. She giggles again when it happens and slowly slips her finger out to lick it clean with a swirl of her tongue.

"*Oishii!*" she says. "Is good! Oh, Jack, look—over there!" On the far side of the lake a cocker spaniel is yipping away, trying to mount a bored beagle. Kuni sighs. "So-o-o cute! Please, Jack, can we go to the Stone Mountain?"

This is how it goes all week. I belong, more and more, to just two states—the well of well-being, the fire.

But now and then the blue ice, though subtler and smoother, does splash.

I'll worry, for example, about her continuing retching, almost always after sex and first thing in the morning. But then she'll return, her breath sweet, her skin flushed. And I'll know, again, it's just jet lag or nerves. And so there is no need to ask.

Or I'll find myself still curious about the details of the switch: why she kept writing those letters to Hank . . . what Suki meant when she said she had an obligation. (*Giri* is stronger than love, Jack.) Sometimes I'm close to asking. But something always gets in the way. I'll find myself looking at Kuni and be lost in a far greater question: how I would live if I lost her. Or, sitting on the emerald quad, Stone Mountain looming before us, she'll swoon: "This is the Home Sweet Home, the South."

There are questions that I do ask, for which her answers break my heart. She is doing the dishes on Wednesday when I slip on an apron and ask to help dry. She throws her arms around my neck and starts to squeeze me, hard. "Oh, Jack," she cries, "thank you! I don't need a Hank—I need *real* man."

Q and A . . .

Q and A . . .

By Thursday I will be amazed at the questions I still haven't asked her, how many details I still do not know: her schooling . . . her family . . . her hobbies . . . And I will be both amused and amazed at her skill in evading some questions. (How many past lovers had Kuni? "Oh, Jac-k-k-k, you embarrass me! If I ever had real lover, why am I needing another?")

I will be no more amazed, though, than I am by their pure unimportance.

I know this woman, I feel, in my soul. If not in the particulars, then in her absolute essence.

Kuni *is:*

. . . seated across from me now on the couch, working it out with the soles of her feet while watching *Marcus Welby*. And when I come, she turns to watch, squealing delightedly, "Good for you, shoot! Oh, I wish I had a willie, Jack!"

. . . walking the length of my tiny apartment, as if she's been caged all her life and set free . . .

. . . brushing her beautiful waterfall hair, as if putting the finishing touches on a priceless work of art . . .

And nightly, when the lights are low, and our clothing lies in long trails on the floor, and we crash on the mattress, rutting in flames, Kuni is:

amazing me, her magic so exquisite now I no longer dare to describe what I feel. And when I wake to my favorite dream, Kuni's hair around my hips, I close my eyes. I must not see. I feel drained and exhausted . . . but somehow enhanced . . . as if I've been able to give her, somehow, a piece of my soul.

"Jack," she says, on Thursday. "Do you really love me, just a little-bittle?"

Q and A . . .

Q and A . . .

By Friday, two days before Kuni must leave, I begin to get the hang, at last, of Q and A.

Who cares about past lovers?

So what if I still haven't quite got around to learning the basics about her? I'll learn.

What to tell them at The Store? I never phoned. I don't know why. And now I no longer care.

I believe that in my life the only thing I had more of than plans were useless questions.

But now there is only one question.

And on Friday I finally ask it at Six Flags amusement park. We're on the giant coaster, a few yards away from the crest of rise one . . . when the question breaks free.

And I ask her. For a second, I fear she might jump from the car. She throws her arms around me. And just as we top the curve, beginning a headlong descent, she cries:

"Jac-
   c-
     c-
       c-
         c-
           c-
             c-
               c-
                 c-
                   c-
                     k-
                       k-
                         k-
                           k-
                             k!"

And all of us are screaming then, screaming with delight.

TWO

It's Saturday night and the evening is going to hell in a hurry.

We're in the Strada restaurant, across from Hank and Suki, on the girls' last night in town. Hank hasn't said six words all night. And the few that Suki has said I wish I hadn't heard. I can't understand a word that she tries not to strangle in that coarse and ugly voice. I pity Hank. I bless my luck. She's a cartoon of a woman in her pink Snoopie T-shirt. Her oversize breasts look absurd on her frame, like apples on a kewpie doll. There's nothing there, no elegance, no charm, no sensuality. Not even a spark of the boldness that, in her letters, once set me on fire.

Tonight Suki seems almost evil to me. I see the reflection of evil in Hank—his eyes so bloodshot and so bagged, his expression so anguished and haunted—I can almost believe she's a warlock or vamp. I remember his screams. They were nothing like ours. Seeing him, I hear them now for what they must have been: tormented cries from hell. (*Bad blood* . . .) I'll try to help him. Sure, I will. But right now I'm too angry. Because it might have been *me* there, if not for that curious twisting of luck.

I want to drive my happiness home like a hot stake through her heart.

Guess what? We're getting married!

I clear my throat. I swallow. "Uhh . . ."

"Just a minute, buddy." Hank looks up so slowly I think I hear his neck creak. He doesn't look tired, he looks aged and bled. "I'm goin' . . . back with Soo-kee."

Kuni responds with a shocking-sounding burst of Japanese.

"Watch your mouth," Hank growls at her.

"*Baka!*" Kuni sputters. Then she hisses and spits it again and again.

This is too much for Suki. If frogs can shriek, that's what she does.

Next thing you know, all four of us are starting to go at it, when—

　　　　　　　dren-n-n-n? Chil-l-l-l-
　　　　l-　　　　　　　　　　　l-
　"Chil-l-l-　　　　　　　　　l-
　　　　　　　　　　　dren-n-n?"

The waiter arrives with a low silver cart, and a good imitation of Mitchum. I can't remember the movie and nobody else seems to care. But the tension has been broken.

Calamari is served up for Kuni.

Chicken parmigiana for me.

"And for the *little* lady— By the way, how's Snoopie, eh?" The waiter walks around the cart. I crane my neck to see. (For Suki, when she ordered, just pointed at the menu, too embarrassed to speak it out loud.) Triumphantly, the waiter produces a large silver bowl . . . from which he removes the lid, steam billowing up in a cloud. He picks up a pair of tongs. And begins laying great batches of steamy coils on her plate.

I'm ready to say something nasty when—

Kuni gasps and drops her glass, her eyes riveted on Suki's plate. She lurches from the table then. And scrambles out the front door to the street.

I throw twenty bucks on the table and run, Kuni's purse under my arm.

"Jack!" Hank calls.

I turn around.

"Good luck, buddy. Watch yourself," he says.

"You too," I say, looking at Suki.

"I'll drop by tomorrow mornin', before we take off for our plane."

"Sure."

Outside, I see no trace of Kuni. The street is dark and empty, except for a couple of punkers standing at an alleyway, watching—

Oh, Jesus, not Kuni!

They're gone like a shot when they see me. Smart move. I can see my arms swinging. I feel my lips drawn.

I round the corner. Stop cold in my tracks. Kuni's kneeling, back to me, puking in sickening splats. Worse—Oh, God, let me die if she dies—after each splat, I hear slurpings and sucks—as if—as if—I don't know!

I cry her name, start to her.

Kuni throws her arms up. "No!" Then, "Ohhhh! Jack—" SPLAT!

I'm on my way, not scared, not me, but before I'm halfway there, she crumbles, her face to the pavement, and—

SLURRRRRPPPPP!

"Kuuuuuu-niiiiii!" I wail.

"Jack . . ." Kuni kneels up shakily, as if testing her strength by the inch. She shudders once, then she's upright. "Jack, please to stay where you are."

"Kuni—"

"Please. I been sick. Don't look."

"Can you get up? Are you okay?"

"Jack, darling . . ."

"Yes!"

"Please. I think okay. But—maybe . . . If I make sick again, you run."

"What?"

"I say, *run.*"

"I won't leave you!"

Kuni is silent a moment. Then, "Darling, please to run—for help?"

But there's no need at all to run.

I can see it, by the inch: Kuni coming back to me. A little wobbly at the start. But when she turns she's smiling, then waltzing ahead to my arms.

To my surprise, her breath is sweeter than I've ever known it. Very sweet, very fresh, just a little starchy.

"Tonight I will make you in heaven," she says. Then she leads me, in tow, with an iron-gripped tug.

The alleyway was poorly lit. The spot where she knelt was some twelve feet away. My glimpse lasted only a second. I know there is some explanation . . . and yet, when I looked at the spot she'd been sick on, I swear:

I saw nothing at all.

THREE

Kuni's in the bathroom and refuses to come out.

All the way home we'd gone on, arm in arm, over and over

the plans we had made. She'd go back . . . We'd work and save . . . We'd get hitched in Japan after New Year's . . .

I'd just shut the door behind me when I remembered something.

"Hon," I said, "when you're back in Japan, check on something for me? To help speed up your visa, maybe get your physical sometime in the fall?"

"Physical?" Kuni said.

"Sure," I said genially. "You know, for Immigration. Blood test, some X rays—"

"What!" Kuni dropped her handbag. She looked at me, I swear to God, as if I'd just ordered her shot.

"Kuni," I said, "easy—"

"X rays?" She shrieked the word.

"Hey," I said, "it's just routine."

"You want to give me cancer!"

"No!"

She was off and running, though, before I could stop her, locking herself in the bathroom, where she's been now for nearly an hour.

"Kuni?" I cry. I expect no response. I've been calling her name with no answer nonstop.

But this time she does answer.

"Yes?"

"Darling, please come out of there."

I hear the water running, patter of hands lightly splashing her skin. I think I hear Kuni taking a breath.

And then here she is.

She looks all right—well, better, but . . .

"Darling, what is it?" I ask her.

"I'm fine." She takes my hand. "Come, fucking time."

In my life I've never seen a more dreadful smile.

She tries to lead me. But I pull away, watching her shrug as she goes. She stops in a sliver of moonlight, slipping out of her dress like some overworked whore. She unfastens her bra, lets it fall to her feet. Sits on the edge of the bed, which she pats.

"Jack, please to quickie, yes? Kuni's plane leave early time." She lies back, slides over to the center of the bed, bends her knees, and spreads them wide. "It's okay. Come here and shoot."

"Go to hell," I tell her.

I spend the rest of the night on the couch.

FOUR

I'm having a terrible nightmare: of being chased, pell-mell, through The Store, God only knows what on my heels. I run screaming through Towels and Linens, through Carpeting and Furniture, and everything I see is red. I've just toppled a few hundred pieces of Mikasa's red casual china . . . when I hear the pounding at my door.

I bolt up, find myself on the couch, half-naked and sweating grossly. I wonder what I'm doing here, where Kuni is. Then I recall.

"C'mon, Jack! Get the door, we got a plane to catch!"

There, I'm half-blinded by the light.

"How they hangin'," Hank drawls. "Christ, y'all look like death warmed over."

I feel worse, seeing him grinning away like some kid off to camp. Bags over his shoulders just stuffed to the seams . . . but nowhere near as heavy as the bags he's got under his eyes. He's telling *me?* She's *killing* him!

"Jack, y'all losin' weight?" he asks.

"Hank, look, I'm tired. Okay?"

But now that he mentions it, I hadn't noticed before. My new jeans—the Mature Fit—have slipped, in my sleep, to my hips. And, shirtless, I look down to see my belly half flat for the first time in years. I wonder how many calories you burn when you make love.

"Hank," I say, "good luck. But—"

"Here." He brandishes an envelope I slip open the screen door to take.

"Suki's number's in there, 'kay? And I wrote an address for y'all to send the rent to. I'll be gone about a month. I put fifty bucks in there for y'all to look after my cat."

I say, "Sure."

Hank offers his hand and I take it.

"Call me, Jack. We gotta talk."

"Watch yourself," I whisper.

"*Me?* I'm fine, bud, I'm worried 'bout *you*. —Hon, say bye to Jack now." Suki peeks around his shoulder, her head half lost in the swell of his biceps. Neither one of us can hold the glance.

I watch them walk off arm in arm down the drive to where their cab is waiting.

I shut the door and turn to see Kuni dressed, her bags at her feet.

"Please to call me a cab?" she asks softly.

I start to shuffle toward her, wracked with confusion, pain, and guilt.

But Kuni leans over to pick up her bags. "Please to call me a cab, Jack." She means it.

I point to the cord that I pulled from the wall.

"Fine," she says. "I walk to train."

"Will you please just tell me what—"

But Kuni brushes by me, a little lady from Japan with a wall three feet thick all around her.

At the door she stops and turns. "I go to Japan now and you have your life. One month, two month, all memories gone. This week is only dream."

"You're wrong!"

But Kuni is already gone.

And in my heart I feel it too strongly to deny:

The week is already becoming a dream.

FIVE

I'd been rich in chances. Now the last is gone.

I once covered two corkboards with photos of women. No more Angel Kisses now.

If I relax, the surface of this room grows porous . . . until I can see through the pores to the past. Beneath the virgin white paint on the walls, the chipped and fading original coat. Beneath the pale gray carpeting, the scarred and moldy pine. Past the

hanging, potted ferns, crannies where spiders, like fates, spun
their webs.

I'm *home.*

I feel myself begin to drift.

And I know this will be a good dream.

Back in Le Peep, they've been waiting for me.

Michiko is wearing her red leather dress, her black waterfall
hair tumbling over her shoulders, her breasts swelling over and
out of the V. She moves her hand. And Cotter slumps, grinning
like Dan Quayle.

His lips move.

I can't hear him.

But then I don't have to.

It's my dream and I know I am cursed for all time with two
words I could not understand:

Don't . . . mock . . .

Don't . . . mockknock . . .

Knockknock—

"Jack!"

I am on the shadow line strung between dreaming and waking. I know that voice. She has come back. Everything hinges
on holding the line. Breathe too deeply, step too quickly, and I
am over, forever, the line.

Mockknockknockknockknock!

"Jack!"

If I can just hold the line up to the door . . . My eyes are
half-closed when I turn the brass knob.

For balance, as I pull the door, I push out with my heart,
thinking, Dream.

I open my eyes.

Love is real.

Magic works.

"Jack," Kuni cries, and then she's in my arms. "Save me,
Jack— Oh, marry me!"

Behind me, Peaches is hissing and spitting up a storm.

And I think happily, Women!

EPILOGUE

Kuni's taken a room at the Hyatt downtown. We're giving
Peaches a couple of days to get used to Kuni's scent, her clothes
in the apartment. And Kuni needed a couple of days to have her
own space and relax. She was up three times ill that first night
she came back. But last night, when I stayed with her, she
couldn't have been more relaxed. Or more magically loving in
bed.

Tomorrow night Kuni moves in.

We haven't set a wedding date. Sometime in a couple of
weeks. Next week I'll start looking into immigration lawyers.
Maybe we can find a way around the dreaded X rays. At least we
can put them off until her nerves have settled.

Meanwhile, I've returned to The Store. It was tense the first
couple of minutes. But Jack Pepper created The Woman in Red.

Tomorrow a meeting is scheduled. The time's come to top
that campaign. Turn me loose.

I've been taking this time, in the morning, for an hour or two
before work, to finish these notes that I've kept all these
months.

More and more, I've come to feel that I should publish this
journal. I see the lonely everywhere, on the streets and Underground. I see men and women possessed by their shadows,
believing the light of their lives has been lost.

I believe that what I've written—

Wait.

(I heard a series of long steady rips and a guttural growl in the
bedroom. I went in to see Peaches raking her claws through one
of Kuni's dresses. The cat looked like she was smiling. Should I
put her back in Hank's place? No. I can't. I gave my word.
Some stubborn part of me rebels. These two little ladies will just
have to coexist.)

I believe that what I've written would be of use to millions: a
defense guide to whupping one's shadow . . . and a real-life
fairy tale with a happy ending. The price was high, but worth it.

In time, if this is published, I'd like to call it *Angel Kiss*. I believe we're watched over by angels, every step of the way in our journeys through life. I believe they were angels, Michiko and Cotter, reaching out from the heart of the light. I believe that the angels we are sent need one thing only to fill us with light: an opening, however small and shaky, in our hearts. The English used by angels is as simple as a child's:

Don't . . . mock!

I believe, if I live to a hundred, I'll be haunted by those words. I believe it will be my life's mission to try to understand them. I believe I will die, though, in failure. Because angels are angels and we're incomplete. But a man could do worse than aspire.

Don't . . . mock!

I tell you, there are angels. We ignore them at our peril—and spend our lives as shadows, or end being crushed like that "Dead U.S. Doc."

(Memo: Ask Kuni about that someday. *Why* are the cops over there being mum?)

The love we want . . . the love we crave . . . the love we imagine we can't live without . . . If only we had enough patience and faith, we'd see that these are nothing, compared to the love we deserve.

I've got mine!

4

BEGINNINGS VII
NOVEMBER, 1989
TOKYO

ONE

Dr. Alex Coburn, who still had twenty-six minutes to live, waited nervously for his last patient. And their last session together.

The Roppongi Clinic, of which he was director, had been fully booked for years. The clientele was corporate: primarily, American men and their long-suffering wives. *My husband has blond hair, blue eyes. Do you know what that means here!* Dr. Coburn knew full well, his own hair gold as Kansas wheat, his eyes a remarkable blue. As knew his lover Tomiko, who'd insisted, before moving in, that he henceforth restrict his practice to men.

He'd agreed, and gladly, for in five years in Tokyo he'd not met six women who had half her charms. (His hot bath, drawn . . . His dinner, cooked . . . His tense back, trodden by her tiny feet . . .)

How, then, had it happened so quickly—just weeks—an intended act of mercy that had gotten so out of control? One look at his hand and his hangdog expression after last week's session, and Tomiko was already packing. *Choose,* she told him. *Her or*

me. Oh, he'd chosen, then and there. The new patient had to go.
But he wondered, as he'd wonder until the moment he died,
about her:

the amazing woman who had burst into his office that cold
stormy night. And sat in tears across from him, crying "Please to
help me!"

She'd looked, at first, preposterous, her face wholly obscured
by her shades and her scarf. She'd looked more like a coat than
a woman, the coat was that long and that full. But underneath—
ah, underneath! He'd found himself facing a childlike creature
with waterfall hair and red Cupid's bow lips. Dressed like a
schoolgirl in loafers and knee socks . . . pleated blue skirt and
a virgin-white blouse. Supple curves beneath it all, but posture
very prim.

He'd thought of Tomiko and started to tell her . . . but
heard himself saying instead: *Relax, my dear, and tell me. What
seems to be the trouble?* By the time the young woman had
finished her tale of a word she could never remember, he had
wanted her so badly that—

He'd miss their sessions, Alex knew. At least, he'd miss the
challenge. He'd never met a man or woman so uniquely—troubled. And, yes, he'd miss— Dear God, he'd burn for the sight of
her lying there, there, on the couch . . . in those schoolgirl
skirts that grew shorter each week . . .

His left hand, freshly bandaged, involuntarily shuddered.
(Felt like she had my damn hand in a vise!)

But with still a few minutes before she arrived, he flicked on
his recorder, continuing his notes.

". . . In short, after weeks of treatment, I find myself unable
to reach a definite diagnosis. Her next therapist, however, may
wish to consider a tentative hypothesis. It would be counter-
productive to start with the cure that the patient was seeking.
We may never learn why these two particular words affected her
so bizarrely. If there were any connection a logical mind could
discern between *vermicelli* and *marriage*, it would surely be
well worth pursuit. Alas, there seems to be none. We must be
doubly cautious of zeroing in on just one of the words. The most
obvious choice being *marriage.* At thirty-one, the patient is well
past the age here. But in all our conversations, she has not

betrayed a scintilla of guilt. She insists she lives alone by choice and is quite happy. And I believe that she believes that this is an absolute fact."

Alex paused for a Camel, his sixth for the day of the ten still allowed by Tomiko. He inhaled deeply. Good-byes could be tough. He thanked God for Tomiko. And Camels.

"I believe that the analysis that will be most productive will start with a single, most salient point: the patient's bizarre ambivalence toward the Japanese imperative—of being, as she puts it, a completely traditional girl . . . while showing up in miniskirts designed to drive the therapist out of his fucking mind! And if that fails, she'll take his hand and stick it up her—"

Jesus! Alex switched off the recorder.

He reversed the tape, finished his smoke, and started over, calmly, with another cigarette.

". . . of being, as she puts it, a completely traditional girl . . . while displaying, in our sessions, almost sluttish—"

He reversed the tape again.

". . . of being, as she puts it, a completely traditional girl . . . while manifesting symptoms of, er, *untraditional* needs."

He heard the front door open, close. Then the clicks of high heels on the just-polished floor, not her usual shy semishuffle of pumps.

He flicked off the recorder.

Sat upright and straightened his tie.

His wrapped hand started throbbing in rhythm to her clicks. As if each step were freighted with some urgent sense of mission.

And he was not surprised at all when, instead of stopping, as always, to knock, she swung his door open and stepped boldly in.

"Good evening," she said. "I must *kiss* you."

Dear God.

He said, "Child, sit down. I—"

"Come," she said. She unbuttoned her coat, the black wrap she'd been wearing the first time she came. Then off came the oversize shades, the great scarf. He caught a subtle flash of red . . . and then it came at him in waves . . . as she eased the wrap over her shoulders . . . and it slid down her arms, past her hips.

Tonight she was wearing a sweet little nothing of shocking, oh shocking, red leather. And her breasts swelled dramatically over and out of the sides of the red leather V.

"Come to me," she urged again. Her eyes, which looked Kabukied, were half-closed and glazed over with lust. "*Isoide*, please—please to hurry!"

He did.

He half bolted, crazy for trouble, around the table and into her arms. She writhed hotly against him, lips just out of reach, her breath hot and sweet, almost starchy.

"Dr. C?" she asked him sweetly. Her voice was as high and as clear as a child's.

His own voice barely whispered, "Yes?"

"Do you really like Japanese women?"

"Oh, yes!"

"Am I a sufficient traditional girl?"

"Yes, oh, yes!"

"May I please to be your love slave?"

"*Yes*—oh, Fusako!"

She shook her head, writhing against him, her body a bedful of snakes. "*Chigaimasu*," she said. "Wrong name!"

"But you told me—"

"*Iie*, my name be not Fusako. I was always fearing *Them*. Not tonight, though. Not no more. I think my red dress be a magical thing."

He leaned over to kiss her, but she was too quick.

"Who *are* you?" he moaned, in a fever of need.

"I *Michiko*," she said. "Dr. C?"

He groaned. "Yes?"

"I really have to *kiss* you."

"Yes!" he cried. But her hand held him back.

"Watch first. This is scary!"

"What?"

She giggled.

His eyes widened . . . as her adorable Cupid's bow lips slowly opened as wide as the muscles allowed. Far and away, in the back of her throat, he caught a flash of something, a slimy and translucent blob, rising and gathering speed as it rolled along her tongue and—

OUT!

He felt as if he'd been splashed in the face with a huge plate of spaghetti.

There was the sense of spreading, first . . . and then the subtle sense of wrapping . . . and then a revolting, and pell mell, collage of slaps and whirrs and sucking sounds.

He began to pluck and tug at the coils now nearly encasing his head. He tried, and tried, but could not scream. His left hand was pinned, fingers over his nose, with only a sliver to breathe through. And then his right hand was attached to one cheek.

The whirrs and gooey slaps went on. In seconds, he no longer heard them—his ears flattened back to the sides of his skull and wrapped with thick layers of slime.

He felt the coils tightening, by the inch, around his skull. He felt the small crunches of hundreds of bones . . . then massive cracks in the last of his hope.

His last conscious thought was Dear Jesus, she'll squeeze my brains right through my ears.

And she did.

TWO

Dr. C, poor Dr. C, how can I ever thank him?

Thank him for the gift of life.

And thank him for my freedom.

I thank him for the memories, taken with the spell *They* cast, and locked inside two little words. The memories that only required a touch of red leather to release them. The memories that come back to me with every breath I take. And feed, and feed, the hunger.

The hunger to tell *Them* again and again:

The hell with traditional girls!

Dr. C, dear Dr. C, I thank you for the memories.

Let me close my eyes and remember it all.

Eleven months ago.
The day after the night of red leather.

THREE

I remember . . . I remember . . .

The other two were gone, I knew. I knew it the instant I opened my eyes. Although the room was very big and only lit by candles, I knew where I was. The mansion in Kyoto.

They'd come that night while I was sleeping, still drunk from my first feeding. I felt as if I had been drugged, but I remembered nothing, not even the dream of a struggle. My body lay spread-eagled on some sort of table, bound feet and hands stretched as far as they'd go. I didn't feel frightened so much as confused. Something was wrong with my eyesight. I seemed to be looking through some kind of mesh. Gradually, it came to me. My head had been caged; and, most likely, my hips.

Around the edges of my vision, I became conscious of movement. From the shadows that surrounded me emerged a small circle that wished me no well. No faces yet. They kept at bay. But I could see their robes, all white, except for one black robe, by my feet, at the table's end.

These were the elders, I guessed, of the church. I'd never seen the robes before. Our own local rituals were really rather casual: with us, the possessed, wearing pairs of loose sweats and Miyamoto Sensei in his regulation suit. So this would be, then, a gala event . . . with the full artillery. *Shikata ga nai*. There were things worse than death—like being a slave to all men.

The circle shrank with light shuffles. A command was given, and I was half-blinded by flashes of light as gleaming swords were raised. Everywhere except ahead, where the black-robed shape stood calmly.

I waited, prepared to join my two Sisters—hating the fourth who'd betrayed us and run. The false friend who would not be our Sister.

The black shape advanced, one hand upraised.

I felt my breathing quicken. I knew the gesture very well and fought against my bonds.

"Shimpai shinaide," the voice said. Relax. Beneath the black cowl, two reptilian eyes regarded me shrewdly and wryly. I didn't have to ask to know who my Inquisitor was. I had seen the photographs of the Founder's widow. The photos had done justice to her awesome ugliness—the hollowed cheeks, the wrinkles—but not to her real, undeniable force. She held her hand straight as a sword . . . the only weapon in the room that struck my heart with fear.

Could it be they weren't going to kill me at all?

Could it be they were going to—

No!

"Gently. Rest easy," the old woman said. "We do not wish to harm you."

"Lie!" I wailed, thrashing with all that I had. My strength was lost with a pass of that hand. I hardly even saw the pass, the widow was that strong, that good. I slumped back, trembling with fear and rage.

"It's true," she said, "your friends are dead. I can't tell you how much that grieves me. My husband always meant for us to be one happy family. And in any family, when someone has a problem—"

"Lies!" I took a breath. I was going to blast a hole through the top of the cage—

Again the hand moved, up and down. And the hot sticky mass was stillborn in my throat. I gagged. The hand moved. The mass dissolved, sliding back down my gullet.

"Your friend Masako killed two of our men before they could wish her good morning. Your other friend, Yasuko, chose, when caught, a suicide Mishima would have sold his soul for. She wrapped herself up in whatever you've got . . . or whatever it is that's got you . . . and—" The widow squiggled her nose in distaste. "This time we'll have none of that. Come, my dear, we're *family.*"

"No!"

Another pass, at a sharp angle, above. I felt it slice like a blade down my length. I knew what she was doing, but was powerless to stop her.

(Splitting me—splitting *us*—me and my Sister within me—my soul!)

The widow's hand was still, thank God. But her expression made it clear: The walls would soon ring with my screams.

"I think you'd better tell me, child, what it is that you three have been up to."

"You taught us how! The church!" I cried.

"And what is it we taught you, child?" Her voice was low and almost sweet. She moved her hand a little, in a pass I'd never seen.

The answer flew out, on its own, like a shot.

"You take the demons out!" I cried. "We put a—spirit *in!*"

I saw the sword blades tremble, sending a rippling shimmer of light.

"You *put* a spirit *in* you? *Saa* . . ." The widow reached her left hand within the folds of her robe. Slowly, she held up the thing she'd retrieved. A photograph roughly the size of her palm. Too dark to distinguish the details. Too vague through the mesh of the caging. But I could see clearly the swatch of red leather on which the photo was mounted. I knew it was Sister. I moaned.

The old woman smiled terribly. "So, *this* is the spirit you girls have put in."

I closed my eyes. I would not look. Let them cut me in hundreds of pieces. If I closed my eyes and focused, I might resist the widow's power—

"Aieeeee!" I screamed, tormented. The shock had been massive, obscene in its power. I smelled the frayed ends of resistance sizzling like singed hair.

"This is, if I am not mistaken," the widow said congenially, "the last photo of Sakai Ito."

"*Hai,*" I answered. Yes, oh yes, that was her—my Sister.

"Executed—1923, for crimes against the State."

"Lie! Lie! Oh no—oh don't!"

This time the smell of smoke was real. Even the hair in my nose felt enflamed.

"My dear, my dear, my adorable dunce. You mustn't fight me like this, *ne?* We're family and I will help you. But don't think for a moment, though, we've taught you every trick *we* know. I know a few that my husband did not. And I warn you, you'd rather not learn. Your spirit is formidable. But it is no match, I

assure you. Now, if I am to help you, you should start by help-
ing me. What on earth possessed you"—the widow chuckled at
the pun—"to wish to be possessed by the vengeful spirit of a
rabid bitch?"

I answered, hopelessly, "Freedom," feeling condemned as I
did. My Sister retreated within me.

"Freedom?" the widow said, looking quite stunned. *"Dekinai*
. . . Surely it cannot be . . . You *put* the spirit in you to assist
in these—feminist murders?"

"Men crush women!"

"And so you . . . crush men?"

"Freedom! Freedom!" I cried.

I saw the swords around me quivering wildly in the men's
hands.

The widow's hand circled their circle, calming the men's
troubled spirits.

"Well," she said. "I must say you've certainly captured my
interest. Something new under the sun, after all. You must try to
relax, dear. I know this will hurt. But before we exorcise you, I
can't resist a little chat with the powerful presence inside you."

There was scarcely a second to think or prepare.

"Hajime!" the widow barked. And begin it did, with a low
rhythmic chant and the stomping of feet and mesmerizing
passes of the old woman's hand. I felt within me a great welling
up, a massive force displacing me and filling the void with itself.

"I command the spirit," the old woman cried, "now possessing our daughter Michiko to rise. Vengeful and unhappy spirit,
by the powers of light that flow through me, I command you
and you will obey. Show us your presence and make yourself
known. I call you up in the name of the gods!"

The chanting and stomping and swaying went on. The old
woman topped the din with a long chain of shrieks of the names
of the gods.

The presence within me continued to rise, higher with each
name she shrieked. Until it reached my throat, my lips—
and then I was lost in the rush of the Voice.

FOUR

Mimimimi-chichichichi-ko-chi-ko-chi-ko-chi-ko!

I awoke to the voice of my Sister, whose voice was alarmingly faint. Even so, the echoes painfully bounced off the walls of my mind. Far more distressing, though, were the bitter cold and dark. And the confusing sensation that my whole world was upside down.

How long had I slept?

What had happened?

Michiko-chi-ko-chi . . .

Stop whispering! You're supposed to help me.

We're in trouble.

I know that! I can't move a muscle and I'm—hanging upside down! I'm blind!

I'm very weak, Michiko. They made me tell them everything. Then they really went to work and tried to—exorcise me.

No!

I tried to fool them, make them think— Aa, maa, they'll be back. The old woman won't stop till she's certain I'm gone.

But—

You'll die if you don't let them take me. For now.

Please!

I'll be back. Don't fight them. This time I'll leave just the tiniest part. No larger than a single cell! That much, perhaps, I can leave you. So small even you will not know it. Perhaps for a very long time. But I'll be waiting for you, until you find a way. Remember me and I will come.

I hear footsteps!

Yes, it's time. If you love me, obey me. Don't fight them.

Good-bye?

For now. But, Michiko?

Yes?

I said I told them everything. But there is just one small thing that I—neglected to tell them. They do not know of—the other.

The fourth. The false friend who would not be our Sister.

For one wild instant I felt fully repossessed, strong enough to burst my chains—

No! Please, you must wait and endure.

But how will I remember?

Trust me, you'll think of a way.

Key's clink in the heavy door and forceful clicks of tumblers. And then the slow, eerie creak as the door swung on its hinges.

Light slaps of wooden *getas* on the concrete floor.

Rustlings of robes.

And men's whispers.

Blindfolded, naked, I hung from my feet, my hands outstretched and chained to the floor.

"Are you awake, my dear?" The widow's voice. "I'd hate to start without you."

I nodded. Just enough strength left to lift my chin to my chest.

"That's good. I'm going to take off your blindfold. I believe I'll leave the taping we've placed on your mouth and—up there —in place. The tape has been blessed. You can't fight it."

The widow took the blindfold off.

The light, dim though it was, only candles, was too sudden for my eyes. I winced.

"Look now."

I blinked.

"Look deeply in my eyes."

I tried.

"As I thought. Our little friend is still hiding in there. Oh, she's a sly one, your Sister."

Upside down, the ancient face looked almost unbearably wizened and sly.

I said nothing at all with my eyes, except Sorry . . . and Forgive me . . . and I love the church.

The widow chuckled mirthlessly. A dry sound, like rustling leaves. "Your demon is quite intriguing. Who could have guessed, back when she was alive—fierce, unyielding woman— she had such a sly sense of humor? Through the years, I've come to feel that in confronting demons we are distracted by their powers—from their *personalities*. That, I believe, is the place to begin. And so, to truly exorcise your funny little friend, I think that I must *exercise* my own rather bizarre sense of humor. After our last session, I half despaired of matching her wit. What could possibly be funnier than a mad dog feminist's effort from beyond the grave to gain immortality . . . by crushing men as they crush women? But luckily, my husband's spirit visits me still on occasion. And, though you'd never guess it from those ghastly solemn photos, his humor was quite off the wall. I wish you could be in on it, instead of being the punch line. But, of course, salvation first!"

The old woman clapped her hands.

Slaps of *getas* drawing near. And then, involuntarily, my nostrils started to twitch; my taped-shut mouth to salivate. It must have been days since I'd eaten. And the steam I smelled first was a meal in itself: the clean, starchy fragrance of—

What?

I saw one of the men hand the widow a platter covered with a silver lid. I looked again, more clearly. It was Taro Miyamoto. And he was smiling terribly.

The widow set the platter down. She inhaled the fragrance, winked, and slyly pulled off the lid.

"Do you know what this is, child?"

Oh boy, did I ever! My eyes feasted on the heaping mound of steaming, shining—noodles!

The widow chuckled. "Ah, but not just any noodles, *ne?* No, look more closely. See how clear they are, almost translucent. They look so soft, and yet so strong. The way the name itself sounds."

Vermicelli, I thought dreamily.

"Very good. You see, already *vermicelli* makes you think of the demon within you. But, trust me, when we're finished, only one word—*marriage*—will fill you with half as much horror. You will never marry. Or live with any man. There will be no chance for you of ever undoing our spell. For, since your demon is cunning itself, we won't just exorcise it . . . but banish, and forever, all thought of its return. The words will fill you with such horror they shall not exist in your mind. Until you hear them. And you scream. And then forget them all over again. You will remember nothing of the church or Sakai Ito."

I waited, regarding the upside-down plate with its steaming and glistening . . . coils.

Good-bye, good-bye, dear Sister.

(I'll be back!)

"Hajime!" the widow roared.

The real exorcism began.

FIVE

Three weeks have passed since my *release*.

My Sister and I, we are partners again, as if we were never divided. I feel as strong as the night I fed her with that first *kiss*.

No, I feel more powerful. She's grown infinitely slyer and more cunning in our sleep.

There is, of course, no question of our staying in Japan. In the weeks since Dr. C's death, the newspapers haven't been idle. No rumor is too wild to fly. Some people are trying to link Dr. C with the three unsolved Red Leather Murders!

Let them talk.

Let them look.

The police are the least of our worries. Dr. C never knew my real name till that night. After that first visit, we always met, alone, at night. And no one ever saw my face.

The police will be eager to drop this, still ashamed of their failure last year.

But, as for the church, there is nowhere to run. It is only a matter of time here. They will tell the papers nothing. They will tell the police even less. But they will be relentless in the spreading of their net.

I write these lines in Shizumi, where I wait for the letters to come, as they must. For Dr. C's last gift to me was the tabloid I found in his lobby. My Sister said *Look*. And I noticed the ad:

ANGEL KISS
AMERICAN HUSBANDS FOR JAPANESE GIRLS

I phoned them from my apartment that night. And Operator Twenty-three just couldn't do enough.

"Little girl," she said, "I just *know* what it's like for a sweet thing like you to be stuck with—those men."

"But no," I cried. "You can't, you can't imagine what it's like!"

"I know it must be hell on earth with their damn 'Bring me this, girl,' and damn 'Bring me that.'"

"Oh yes!" I was crying, real tears in my eyes. "It's hell, it is! I need—"

"I know. You need an American man!"

I said, "Yes!"

I wired the money the next afternoon.

And five days later the parcel arrived, with the thick batch of Personal Listings.

Operator Twenty-three had placed her first choice on the top. "You'd be a damn fool, honey," she wrote, "if you let this one get away!"

I didn't even have to look through the rest of the packet she'd sent.

His name is David Cotter.

He lives, I'm afraid, in Atlanta—which is about three thousand miles from where we want to be. But he is blond and blue-eyed, and he has a warm, kind, gentle face. I think we'll have no trouble with him. In his ad, he specifies he hopes for a Japanese woman. And we know what men want when they specify *that*.

I must be, once again, a traditional girl. For just a little longer.

His letter will come—it must come!—anyday.

I must only survive here one month, maybe two.

And try to survive without *feeding* till then.

Two or three letters, that's all it should take. We will reach San Francisco by summer. Home of the new Asian love slaves. Hiroshima of feminine freedom.

And in San Francisco we'll figure out a way to settle a very old score.

I saw her, our betrayer, the day that I left Tokyo. I may have seen her many times during the year that I slept. But *They* erased my memory, along with the memory of all I had been. I saw her at the station, a hundred feet between us. And I realized, with horror: She must have seen me countless times and, knowing I couldn't see her, thought: There, but for the grace of God . . .

Yes, there she was, on the platform, reading the news like some innocent child. I started to feel rage and hate welling up. We were meant all along to be four, and not three. *There, but for the grace of God!* If she hadn't lost heart, if she hadn't lost soul —the others might not be dead.

I started to rise from my seat on the train. But my Sister told me gently: Wait. She is not nearly as free as she thinks. Revenge is ours, but let it wait.

So I sit here and wait for his letter to come, my blond, blue-eyed lover of Japanese girls.

Soon, San Francisco!

BOOK FOUR
JUNE, 1990
TOKYO

ONE

Tuesday, 4:00 P.M.

I'm bein' watched.

That much I know. And it ain't make-believe, it's a certified fact.

Reminds me of a joke I heard that throwed me for a loop once. Ted and me was in a bar the week after he got back from Nam. Some college kids—real Yankee snoots—was raisin' hell one or two tables down. I forget what it was they was talkin' 'bout—the Illy or the Oddy or some other Greek fag pome. But college kids can't drink worth shit. They kept makin' less sense as the minutes went on.

Well, Ted was plain crazy before Nam. Since then things seemed to be snappin' inside. He looked like he was listenin' to some screechy caterwaulin'. Finally, one of 'em started to bang a spoon on the side of a jug.

Rinketytinketytinketytink!

And I heard Ted's teeth grindin' like some rumble from the grave.

College boy leaned back and said they was forgettin' somethin'. In the words of so-and-so, even paranoiacs (or was it schizzophrennies?) got real enemies. And the whole damn table started hootin' and drivin' Ted into a fit.

Next thing you know, Ted's over there, every college boy's nightmare come true. "Y'all wanna tell me," he says, "what the *fuck* is so damn funny."

College boy says, "Sorry—"

WHAP! Ted gives him an open-palm shot in the head and there's six of 'em there and they're all scared to death. Ted would've whipped all six of 'em just to let off some steam *before* Nam. But tonight—

"I asked y'all a question, boy. What the *hell* kinda language y'all talkin'?"

"Well, you see," the kid says, "it's a joke—"

WHAPBAPBAP! Another shot on the top of the head and two lightnin' quick slaps on the ears.

"It ain't shit," Ted tells him. "Y'all see me laughin' over there?"

Well, some local good ole boys managed to calm Ted a little. The college boys lived to fight their books another day. I told Ted the joke was shit. And I laughed like the devil to show him. That was when Ted broke my nose—I mean, for the third time —and our real problems began.

But the point is—I'm damn sure I had one—oh yeah: I never did draw a bead on that joke. And in a shot I forgot it.

Till now. Today the joke come clear to me. And for a second I wished I could see 'em again, those college boys, and say Guess what, I fuckin' finally got it!

Even paranoiacs or fuckin' schizzophrennies got real enemies 'cause—shit, it's harder than hell to explain a good joke. But I got it, all right, and it sure made me laugh.

I'm bein' watched. I know I am. And I don't mean just here and there, but absolutely everywhere.

They been watchin' me since I got on the damn plane. Japan Air girls comin' by, checkin' my hair out and checkin' my legs out, and lookin' at Suki and gigglin'.

But it was a real long flight and we was busy anyway. Yeah, we was busy practicin' the patience of the saints—I mean, communicatin' around her fuckin' handicap with the English language. She can write okay but can't talk it worth shit, which says somethin', I'd say, for their schoolin'. We had a pad of paper out and we was writin' words down, sometimes drawin' pictures, just like we done all week.

Now and then, when we got stumped or started to think, Oh my God, what the hell, I'd poke her or she'd tweak me and one of us'd say *Black Man.* And then we'd be laughin' it up like two kids, rememberin' the night I screamed.

Yea, the Black Man is usually good for a laugh, 'least what I *thought* the Black Man was. What or who the Black Man is, though, I ain't got a clue. And Suki can't, or won't, explain. I gotta meet him for myself to clear up the mystery of what she calls her Bad Blood.

So we was talkin' on the plane. And I was busy thinkin' how beautiful she was and how we could finally *do* it—after we took care of business: the Black Man and Suki's Bad Blood. And, bein' busy, I reckon, I didn't notice all that much that I was bein' watched.

I sure noticed it, though, at the airport. I just stood there slack-jawed, in some kind of daze. A hundred thousand midget Japs was lookin' at me, all of 'em, and chatterin' in chicken-scratch.

Gai-jin! Gai-jin!

Foreigner!

I didn't know which way to go. I couldn't read the fuckin' signs 'cause they was all in chickenscratch. And I wanted the Japs to stop lookin' at me and pointin' at my hair and makin' pictures with their hands of the difference in size between Suki and me.

Gai-jin! Gai-jin!

I just wanted one fuckin' sign I could read, so I could take her by the hand and say, C'mon, girl, follow me. But I just stood there turnin' and lookin' at 'em look at me, and point at me, and laugh at me.

Gai-jin! Gai-jin! Gai-jin!

Suki couldn't move me, my damn feet was nailed to the ground, which kept turnin' as I watched 'em all watchin' and laughin' at me. Finally, she did somethin' weird. Goddamndest thing I ever seen. She called my name and waved her hand—up and down, like some blessin'. Whatever it was, it relaxed me. And I let her lead me off to the chickenscratch signs that spelled Customs.

I was watched there real good while they had a high time with my baggage. Two fuckin' midgets, nine feet between 'em, rifled my socks, lah-dee-dahed at my shorts, and giggled at my back support like it was a girdle.

In the cab, when that was done, Suki moved her hand again and that relaxed me somewhat. But the cabdriver was watchin' me and watchin' Suki bless me. And I would've sold my soul right there for even a couple of minutes alone in some place where no one was watchin'.

Tokyo that late at night should've been a spectacular show of ebony and neon lights. It should've been somethin' special. Christ, it should've been funny as hell! I mean, the very thought of me in Tokyo with Suki—

It would've sent Ted into some kind of fit. And if my mama could've knowed, it would've freaked her sober. But she's been gone a long, long time and fuck her *with* the Colonel.

Tokyo—Sweet Jesus Christ! I'd never got past Lexington. I was a world traveler now, here on a mission with Suki. Here to learn what I gotta learn before she'll consent to a pokin'.

So I should've been *excited.* But all I could think of, wherever I looked, was: Watchin' me, they're watchin' me. I thought I seen 'em watchin' me in every passin' car or cab. The driver was watchin' me hard in his mirror. And it looked like he was watchin' still when we got out of the cab.

I can *hear* 'em watchin' me, though I don't speak no chickenscratch. I don't gotta speak it. It all means the same damn thing, for all the bowin' and smilin' they do. Every word I hear's the same, whether they're sayin' it straight in my face, gigglin' it behind their hands, or mutterin' it under their breath as we pass.

Outsider.

White nigger.

Look, a white nigger with one of our girls!

Suki drawed me an amazin' map so I could get around a bit while she's off nine-to-fivin'. And I tried like hell one mornin'. I

held on to her map like a life raft. But most streets here ain't got
no names, and those that do's in chickenscratch. And the numbers are all out of sequence. Still, I done pretty good for a
couple of blocks—till it hit me again, like at the airport. Twenty
school kids, 'cross the street, all wearin' blue plastic raincoats
and hats, pointed at me, all at once, and started yellin':

Gai-jin!

I took a left . . . and then a right . . . and then, for all I
knowed, I was in fuckin' Yokohama. But I wasn't askin' no Jappo
for help. I walked on, gettin' loster and loster, till I stumbled by
chance on the way. And when Suki asked me "How go day?" I
screamed "Fuckin' wonderful!"

I reckon Suki's kinda pissed underneath the worried. She
reckons it's the same for me as it was for her in Atlanta. There
ain't no way to make her see, not till she knows more English:
That's the home of the free and the land of the brave. How's she
gonna understand what it's like for *me*—to be watched, 'cause
I'm white, like a nigger!

I tell Suki I'm powerful sorry, I really do love her to pieces.
But I ain't ready for Japan. I just wanna get this over with. The
Black Man, the Bad Blood, whatever they are. I'm gettin' so
horny sometimes I can't walk. And I can't stand it no more,
bein' watched.

I feel like goin' to the window now.

I know it. I just feel it. There'll be a little crowd out there
waitin' for *gai-jin* to show. Maybe I'll yell out the window, Why
the fuck don't y'all learn some English!

Goddammit to hell, I'll just do that.

Good for a laugh.

She'll be here in an hour.

TWO

Wednesday, 10:00 A.M.

Jesus Christ almighty, that college boy sure had a joke and a
half.

They're watchin' like nobody's business.

I went to the window yesterday, full of piss and vinegar.
'Least till I looked through the curtain. Like one of them scenes
like you see on TV. One guy stops cold and looks up at the sky.
Next thing, there's a whole crowd around him, all lookin' up but
not knowin' at what.

'Cept there wasn't one guy but two guys.

And they wasn't walkin', they come in a cab.

Pulled right up across the street. Two of 'em, two big ole boys,
got out, both rollin' their shoulders. They said somethin' to the
driver. I seen his finger pointin' right here at Suki's buildin'.
Then he stuck his head out and I knowed his mug right off—the
Jap cabbie we had from the airport. Then, licketysplit, he was
lookin' at me and pointin' and jabberin' away.

And then the two fatsos in tight navy suits set their slanty
eyes on me.

The cab pulled away, but the fatsos stayed put, foldin' their
arms, lookin' at me real good.

A couple of kids joined the party. Then a half a dozen, yellin'
Gai-jin! Gai-jin! while the two fatsos took swats at 'em and tried
to scare 'em off. Then there was a dozen lookers, includin' ole
women and peddlers.

I was startin' to feel the steam blow through my ears when I
seen Suki comin'. She looked at them and looked at me and
covered her mouth. And then she started runnin'.

I got away from the window.

An hour later when I checked, wasn't no one there.

Took Suki half the night, two dictionaries, and six sheets of
paper to explain what the fuss was about. She's sure the two
fatsos was government guys and she's gonna lose her apartment.
I done what I could to relax her. Hell, she don't need the apartment, since I'm takin' her back to Atlanta right quick. Right
after Bad Blood and the Black Man. I guess that helped a little,
but Japs fill their women with powerful shit. And Suki was still
in a state. So, mostly what we done all night was simply sit and
cuddle. Suki didn't pressure me none to get out and wander.
And I didn't pressure her to stop feelin' the shit she was feelin'.
I guess that's what love's all about. I can't say for certain. I
never knowed about love until now. But then love never
knowed shit about me.

I never kept a journal. So I got no trainin'—what to put in and leave out. But since meetin' Suki, the one thing I learned's that I been a liar my whole goddamn life.

So I figure I'll put in whatever I please, 'long as it seems like it's truth. And right now the truth is this: I gotta break and slap my meat. I'm so horny now, shit, I can't breathe.

1:00 P.M.

What I done was, I went to the window instead. But real carefullike, just like I promised.

Hank, please to not do trouble thing, Suki begged me last night, on her knees.

Part of me wanted to laugh like I should, a big strappin' ass-kickin', red-blooded boy. But then I felt it meltin', the laughter, in my throat. And I found myself seein' the matter from Suki's point of view. The way she explained it last night.

An apartment in Tokyo is hard as hell to come by. Even a dump half the size of a closet costs three times as much as a penthouse back home.

What they got all over Tokyo, which is like a deck of cards goin' every which way—what they got all over, like diamonds in the heaps—is the Tokyo dream, known as Housin' Estates.

An Estate's a concrete compound made up of rectangular blocks, each ten to fifteen stories high and holdin' a few thousand families. Everythin' is subsidized and so the rent's dirt cheap. Only way to get in, though, is to have a family—and to win a fuckin' lottery.

Well, Suki won hers fair and square. But she ain't got no family, 'least not livin' with her. So she lied and told 'em the apartment was for her grandpappy and her.

And this worked out fine for a couple of months, until they started checkin'. Once a month or so at first. Lately, two or three times. Sometimes callin' on the phone, sometimes showin' at the door. And grandpappy's where he's been all along, happy as shit in the country, where we're soon bound to meet the Black Man.

Suki's had to lead 'em all on a slippery chase: Honorable grandfather's out for a walk, or shoppin', or playin' bingo.

So the sight of the blue-sighted fatsos was the last thing she needed to see.

And so I went for a look on the sly, keepin' my promise to Suki.

Saw, far and away, some industrial barges plyin' up and down the ole Sumida river.

Watched the Great Golfers a second or two. On the roof across the street, they've set up a drivin' range, Jap style. A hundred little Nippers in Arnold Palmer caps and pants stand on tiered decks in the cage—and drive balls into a net about ten yards away.

Not much action on the street. Mostly cars passin' by as they do all day, their loudspeakers blowin' out these tinny little melodies and sing-a-ling announcements.

I walked around the window for a look-see from the other side.

And there they was, the boys in blue, arms folded and watchin' me.

If they're there when I go to the window again, I'm gonna do somethin', but I dunno what.

2:00 P.M.

I just done somethin' stupid. I guess it's cabin fever from bein' cooped up every day while she works. I was gettin' around to the business at hand. I ain't been laid now in more than a month, and so I was happily pumpin' away—

Well, that'll be enough of that. I don't read no dirty books and goddamn if I'll write one.

I was gettin' close, real close, to obtainin' a little relief when the phone begun to ring. I guessed I'd best just let it be, with Suki's situation. But it wouldn't stop. It kept ringin'. So I figured it might just be Suki. Or someone who knowed his own someone was in, in which case the phone would keep ringin'. Or—

What if one of the fatsos was on it?

I was thinkin' like a wuss, but with all the ringin' I couldn't scarcely remember my name. I stood there, holdin' my hands on my ears. And the phone just kept ringin' and ringin' away.

Then suddenly it come to me.

I knowed who it was on the phone. It was Jack!

Well, I was in a right merry ole mood as I picked up the phone and said, "Pepper!"

What I heard next stopped the ringin' in my head right quick.

"*Gai-jin,*" this voice said. It was fatso for sure. A real fatso-type voice. Then a whole bunch of chickenscratch, like a general snappin' out orders.

I'd had all I could take.

I roared, "Damn it to hell! Talk fuckin' English, boy—I ain't no Nip!"

This took the starch right out of him. Generals love givin' orders, till they get throwed the finger and fuck the salute.

"*Gai-jin,*" he said. "Risten."

"No," I told him. "*Y'all* listen. I'm a goddamn guest and I want some respect!"

"*Gai-jin—*"

"An' I'll tell y'all somethin' else. This here ain't fuckin' Russia, dig? That girl won this place fair and square and y'all know it."

"*Gai-jin! Prease!*" Somethin' new in his voice. Like he needed to say somethin' bad. So I took a breath and I waited. "*Gai-jin-san,* you . . . mock a . . ."

I couldn't catch the rest.

I said, "Run that by me one more time. I ain't quite sure I got your drift."

He said, "Sol-ly . . . Eng-rish . . ."

I said, "Repeat your question."

"Ahhh . . . You are . . . mock a—"

Mock a *somethin'*. Hi-ki? Hock-ey?

"Look," I told him. Real friendlylike now. Almost like I was his brother. "I didn't mock a nothin'. Y'all got my word on that. This here's a wonderful country and I'm surely glad I could visit."

He thought about that for a second, his own head surely ringin' now with English, like it should be spoke. "*Gai-jin . . .*"

"I'm still here."

"You no mock a—"

Holly?

"Absolutely not," I said. "Never did. Never will. I don't mock shit, like I told y'all before."

"You—never mock a—"

"No!" I yelled.

"Gai-jin-san . . ."

"Yes," I sighed.

"Prease to—reave apartment."

"Hey, please to suck my dick," I snarled.

"Must reave. We come. We take you—"

"Hey!" I screamed. "Y'all do just that! I'll tear your fuckin'
heads off and shit right down your necks!"

I slammed the phone down hard as I could. And this time the
bells sounded pretty.

I looked out the window, but no one was there. For an hour
or so, I sat by the door with one of Suki's choppin' knives,
waitin' for them to come get me.

Then I rested a spell.

Then—

I started to say there ain't nothin' to do. But that'd be a lie.
There is. Suki's got about two hundred tapes, from Mozart to
Elvis Costello. She bought me some good waterpaints, hopin'
someday I'll start paintin' again. And my fans are out there
waitin' for *gai-jin* to go for a white nigger walk.

Oh, there's things to do, all right.

But this is where I always end: at the low black table on the
fresh *ta-ta-mi* mats . . . tryin' to figure out how come it's me,
and not Jack, in Japan.

5:00 P.M.

I gotta work that out right now, or everythin' will go to shit.
Saturday, when she quits work, we're headin' for the country-
side. Take care of the Black Man and Suki's Bad Blood. Get
away from the fatsos in blue. And then we're gonna go, she says,
to the best Love Hotel in Japan.

But it won't be right, it can't ever be right, if I don't get it
right in my head about Jack.

I seen them pictures on Jack's boards and felt my damn stomach just go upside down. My daddy the Colonel was shakin' my
guts. And Ted, he was shakin' away at 'em too. I got sick as hell,
like they taught me.

But I seen the changes in Jack even then. His shoulders wasn't half so hunched. Had some spring in his step when he come up the drive. And I wasn't just seein' the photos—I was seein' Jack seein' the photos with fire and hope in his eyes. And I didn't like what I was seein', not just 'cause their skin had got colored all wrong. Women wasn't supposed to do what I seemed to be seein' them doin'. I mean, puttin' fire and hope in the eyes and erasin' a hangdog expression.

So I couldn't stop myself from savin' a poor hopeless sinner like Jack. From the photos I couldn't stop seein' myself. By spreadin' the gospel accordin' to Ted: Women's this . . . and Women's that . . . I was twenty-fuckin'-six, and I didn't have one opinion that wasn't accordin' to Ted.

Good ole Ted.

If I hadn't seen them photos first, Suki's picture might've left me cold. What them women and their pictures done was give me enough rope to hang from. Enough time to run out of excuses. Enough time to hear how tinny the gospel accordin' to Ted sounded next to the fire and hope in Jack's eyes. Jack, whose shoulders wasn't so hunched. Jack, who was gettin' that spring in his step. Jack, who just smiled, ignorin' the gospel, seein' pictures of women, not niggers and Chinks. Jack, whose ass I could kick to New York, puttin' his face right on up in my face.

That first shot of Suki was one sorry snapshot. But things was changin' when it come and I felt like I'd had my eyes splashed with the sun.

Suki.

I swear to God I resisted.

I swear on my life I attempted to save the ole gospel accordin' to Ted.

I tried as hard as a human can try to avoid goin' over there night after night, hearin' Jack tell me how great Suki was, seein' him standin' up taller and straighter, seein' his eyes filled with more fire and hope.

And, on my soul, I swear: When Kuni's letter come, I tried, I surely did—

Bullshit.

She was knockout gorgeous, yeah. But I knowed lots of

women with hair darker and longer than hers was. And I knowed lots of women with sexy secrets in their smiles. I was tryin' to see her with hair more like Suki's. I was lookin' in her eyes for somethin' that might fill my own eyes, like Jack's.

I guess it got to be fun in a weird kind of way, swappin' them letters with Kuni, like we was bickerin' lovebirds. But there wasn't no feelin' and never would be. I never seen a woman's face I just wanted to punch more than hers. And if Kuni'd ended up stayin' with me, I'd've hid every knife in the house.

So I was writin' to Kuni and fightin' with Kuni and findin' excuses to mosey to Jack's.

But I never thought, I never dreamed, that things'd get all switched like this.

I was lookin' at Suki from get-go. That much I know for a fact.

Jack must've been lookin' at Kuni—'cause at the airport he looked like he'd got a lifetime supply of True Love.

And Kuni, arm in arm with Jack, was like a different woman. She looked like she had her own lifetime supply.

Suki, though . . . What about Suki? She crosses her heart she was lookin' at me. But there ain't no doubt she loved Jack at the start. And maybe she still kind of loves him. She still ain't took his pictures down. We got Pepper photos all over one wall. And she keeps a whole shitload of letters from Jack inside a small red box. Now and then I'll see her stop to touch the box when she's passin'.

All I know's the switch begun with some kind of *giri*, which means an obligation. And Suki wouldn't talk of that—in fact, she seemed ashamed of that—but once we got together, it all worked out fine.

Of course, I mean after I screamed.

It *is* gettin' better and better each day. And I believe in a couple more days, when we solve the riddle of Suki's Bad Blood, it'll be clear road before us.

But, man alive, that first night—when she told me that she was a—

Whoops, here she comes.

More tomorrow.

THREE

Thursday, 10:30 A.M.

We gotta get out of this city. We scarcely slept a wink all night, 'tween goin' to the window and lookin' at the goddamn phone.

Last night she come in, that big smile on her face, glad to be done with her day at the store, but lookin' proud as always 'cause she figured she done so much good. Japs *love* work. And she called out, same as always, *Ta-da-i-ma!* (I just come back.) It's a major ritual y'all gotta do in Japan or be damned. So I yelled *O-ka-er-i!* (Well, come back and come in.) And, God almighty, the look on her face. You'd've thought I was a cat that upped and started talkin'.

She run over to where I was sittin' and hugged me, one of her boobs pressed so hard to my eye I feared the nipple might blind me. Right through her Shetland sweater.

Then I started to tell her 'bout fatso.

She went certifiable in a quiet Suki way, pacin' in circles and touchin' her hair. She begged me, Tell me in plain English exact-ry what fatso said.

And I tried. "Mock, that means make fun of, right?" Here I done a fatso voice to give her the clear picture. *"Gai-jin,* he says, you mock a somethin' . . . and I tell him, Hell I do, I don't mock a nothin'."

"Wa-ka-ra-nai!" Suki wailed. That means, I don't follow none. She collapsed at the low shiny table, cuppin' her chin in her hands, gazin' at me with the most sorrowful expression.

"He from Housing, yes, Hank?"

"No," I said. "I'm sure he ain't. Hell, he didn't give a shit—"

"What he say?"

"Wa-ka-ra-nai!" I barked at her. Then I wanted to die when she jumped. "Jesus, Suki, I'm sorry as hell. But all I do all damn day long is wait to meet the Black Man. I can't go to a movie, I can't watch TV, everybody's watchin' me—and, I ain't never pressured y'all, but . . . I wanna sleep, I mean *sleep*, with y'all bad."

"I know," Suki said. She took my hand. "Soon," she whispered. "Tell me, Hank."

I took a breath. I tried again. "*Gai-jin*, he says. He says Listen. He says they was gonna come get me 'cause I mocked a somethin'."

"*Na-ni?*" Suki urged me. What?

"I can't remember!" I cried.

She said, "Shhh." She gave my hand a little tug and nodded her head to the bedroom.

I never felt so relieved in my life. Why the hell we gotta wait till I meet the Black Man? I ain't scared about Bad Blood. If anybody's got Bad Blood, it's gotta be Kuni, not Suki. I come here 'cause she asked me to. But there's a time for everythin'. And right then it was time for us. Some gay nigger used to sing 'bout sexual healin' or somethin'. I always thought the song was just your usual nigger jive sex shit. But I could hear the music now. That nigger sounded like some angel singin' in my ear.

We got up, Suki half my size, leadin' me real gentlelike— when the damn phone started ringin' again.

It wasn't no friend on the line, that was clear. I guessed it must be fatso, from the look on Suki's face. I stepped up to get a listen, but Suki flashed her hand at me. And I stayed where I was, where I couldn't hear nothin' 'cept this low voice on the phone, not so much speakin' as buzzin' out words.

The buzzin' went on, low and even, Suki starin' at the phone and noddin' at it fiercely.

On and on the buzzer went, low and slow and even, Suki cryin' Yes and No and No, not mock-a-somethin'.

A man can only take so much of seein' his woman get buzzed into bits. I was fixin' to give the ole buzzer a real three-alarm *gai-jin* blastin'—when Suki bowed, thanked the buzzer, and put down the phone.

Suki looked up. The light caught her right flush. She looked white as a ghost on Stone Mountain.

I run over just in time.

"No trouble," Suki gasped. "Mistake!" And then she collapsed in my arms.

I laid her out real gentlelike on her soft futon.

I wrapped some ice up in a washcloth and pressed it to her

forehead, holdin' her, protectin' her, and hopin' we live till the Black Man.

Goddammit, there's the phone again!

11:30 A.M.

I looked out the window first. The fatsos wasn't there. So I knowed it was one of the fat boys in blue. Or the ole buzzer biddy that phoned here last night. Or some other asshole from their mock-a-somethin' church.

These guys must be all stone deaf or worse than fuckin' Krishnas.

So I picked up the phone and I started to yell. "Cocksuckers! Sons of whores! Fuckin' fish-eatin', slanty-eyed Nips!"

"Hank . . . for God's sake . . . Hank . . . Hank?"

The line had some crackle in it, which I hadn't heard through the yellin'. And the voice sounded tiny and real far away, with these little echoes around it. English, though. English! It just made my heart sing. And I looked at Jack's pictures and started to laugh.

"Well, fuck my ass," I said. "Hey, Jack!"

More crackle and a waitin' spell, like my voice was bouncin' and echoin' off of the crackles to Jack.

"Hank . . . can you *hear* me . . . please?"

"Jack, speak up a little, man. I can't hardly hear y'all."

Like talkin' underwater in a pitch-black metal tank.

But crackle-echo, back come Jack.

"Hank," he said, but damn it if he wasn't talkin' softer. "It's Kuni . . . I think . . . Hank, she's crazy . . . She's—"

A long burst of crackle then. I went at him with an echo blast. "I can-not fuck-in' hear you all!"

Crackle-spitz! the damn line went. Then he started cryin', these echoin' sobs, and honest to God, they just tugged at my heart.

"Hank . . . I think . . . I swear she'll . . . kill—"

The rest got lost. Another blast, the worst yet, of that crackle-spitz.

Then, "Oh! Oh no . . . She's here!"

I could hear ole Kuni fine, even over the echoes and crackles.

"Jack!" she screamed.

The line went dead.

I was in a powerful funk of worryin' and grievin'. I tried to phone Information back home. Took three Jap operators. And then all the circuits was busy.

What the hell was happenin' there at—*somethin'* o'clock in the mornin', their time?

I tried again and got right through. I asked 'em to connect me, on account of it was urgent. They gave me Jack's number and slammed down the phone. So I started tryin' to dial direct. This time it took me six minutes to learn Jack's number was out of service.

Shit, I thought, I should've knowed. I could see that cord he'd yanked plain as day now in my mind.

All right, I thought. Calm down. Relax. Ain't no one killin' no one. Jack Pepper ain't got it in him, for one. And Kuni, she ain't much bigger than Suki. Hell, even Jack can handle her.

They're just havin' a spat.

(*I swear . . . She'll kill—*)

Where'd he call from?

My place.

Yeah. She wakes. He's gone. She's on the rip.

I decided to phone 'em at my place and try and help 'em patch things up.

I got through quick as a whistle this time, me knowin' my number and all.

It didn't do me much damn good.

The phone just kept ringin' and ringin' away.

1:00 P.M.

I wish I could write Jack a letter.

Or take his pictures off the wall, his eyes look so accusin'.

(*Kuni's crazy, man . . . She'll kill—*)

I thought hard about phonin' the Colonel to check. Just have a look in and make sure all's okay. I reckon he's got it by now, the old man—the letter I sent him to say I was gone. But I never had the guts to tell him just where it was I was goin'. I ain't never had the guts to tell him squat but Bye that once. And he laughed and said Boy, you'll be back sure as shit. And, same as always, he was right.

So I couldn't phone the Colonel yet. 'Sides, the minute he showed on the doorstep, I'd be caught in another damn lie. Jack would say, *What! You're the owner? But who the hell is ole lady Palerno?* I can hear the Colonel laughin' from twelve thousand miles away: *Boy, ah believe y'all have had the mis-for-tune to deal with the greatest mistake of my life—flesh of mah flesh, blood of mah blood, that liar, that coward, that loser—son Hank.*

I gotta tell the Colonel soon. But I gotta get things straight here first. This notebook's the only damn place I can go.

I was gonna call Ted. Put it all on the line. Scream my damn socks off if I had to: *Goddamn your soul, we're brothers!* That's what I'd have screamed. *Y'all broke my nose and broke my heart 'cause I couldn't get through to the Colonel, not once, on account of the fact I could never be Ted. Y'all owe me, motherfucker!*

I would've phoned. I swear it. I ain't puttin' no lies on these pages. But what could Ted do, bein' up in New York? Nothin', 'cept laugh his damn ass off. *Ja-pan!*

I keep hearin' Jack sobbin'.

And Kuni screamin'.

They're all right. They gotta be.

Probably just like that damn call last night, me hearin' the buzzer and ready to blow, thinkin' we was in real trouble.

Jesus, what a joke.

2:00 P.M.

I tried Jack at my place a couple more times. But why the hell'd he be there at their time of the mornin'?

I need a little somethin' here to take my mind off Pepper.

Maybe I can cheer me up by recollectin' the buzzer.

That sure was a good one!

Suki put down the phone and she fell in my arms, groanin' *Big mistake.* I sat by her, nursin' her and holdin' her like we was doomed. An hour later, when she woke, I said, "Tell me straight." And she proceeded to tell me, with sign language, a pad of paper, and two dictionaries, 'bout—

Where the hell's that piece of paper?

Here.

The Ma-ka-ha-ri church.

Suki don't know nothin' about 'em, she said. They're into mesmerizin' or exorcisin' fox spirits and such. She don't know no one in the church. But, accordin' to the ole buzzer—the high priestess herself, in Kyoto—they was certain she was one of 'em on account of that hand thing she done in the cab. She seen Kuni do it once . . . and Kuni seen someone else do it . . . and the two of 'em thought it was funny as hell.

So Suki tries it in the cab. And, sure as shit, the cabbie just happens to be one of 'em. And he tells it to someone else. Who passes it on. And the two fatsos come.

"So, why they call!" Suki cried. "Why say you must go?"

I put my arms around her. It felt nice to have the tables turned, me bein' able to put her at ease, first time since I come to Japan. They was tryin' to scare *me*, I said. They don't want no *gai-jin* pokin' 'round in their funky religion, watchin' 'em just like they been watchin' me.

Suki started to come right around.

Sure, she said. Sure. That must've been it. 'Cause we looked out the window and no one was there, just like no one was there all this mornin'. And the phone ain't rung once since the buzzer last night. So the word has been spread: We are cool, all hands off. We ain't mockin' nothin', not even their damn Ma-ka-ha-ri.

Suki was glad, in a tense kind of way. And gladder still they wasn't any fuckin' Housin' assholes. And it was lookin' good, real good, us makin' it till Saturday. But she still wasn't Suki, not by a long shot, and I couldn't get her to talk 'cept to say: That church is heap big powerful. And it wouldn't do, no, it just wouldn't do to have 'em mad. *Big trouble.* Then she started to bawl 'cause she'd got me in trouble, and here in Japan causin' trouble is the ultimate capital crime. She was just so goddamn cute I feared I might fuck her right there on the spot, and the hell with Bad Blood or the Black Man.

So I tickled her rib and she tickled me back and I whispered, "Black Man!" And then she was fine, laughin' and rememberin' how she made me scream.

Maybe I can cheer me up, just like I done Suki, if—

—Jesus, what was *that!*

2:30 P.M.

Christ on a crutch, I am edgy as hell.

I could've swore I heard—somethin'. Like a scratchin' at the lock.

I got up, real quietlike. Then, when I couldn't hear nothin', like in the fuckin' movies, I stood there awhile without movin'.

That didn't make no damn difference at all.

Stone-cold silence was the only thing there was.

Pussy, I thought. Sit your ass.

And I did.

And I didn't hear no scratchin'.

No, what I heard was—whisperin'.

I stayed cool and level-headed. Hell, ain't I the fearless Colonel's son? Ain't I ole killer Ted's younger brother? So I looked at the door and I reasoned it out. Couldn't be them Ma-ka-ha-ris, 'cause we settled that shit on the phone just last night. Couldn't be the Housin' assholes. I believe a Jap official'd cut his goddamn dick off before forgettin' to smile and knock.

So there couldn't be no whisperin', 'cause—

Then I felt it, through the door. There *was* someone standin' there, waitin' and watchin' me through it!

I charged to the door with a war cry. I didn't care shit if I lived or I died. I run to the door and I whipped off the chain and I didn't want no damn cleaver, not now, I wanted to kill with my hands or be killed. 'Cause by the day, and by the inch, they was cuttin' me down to Jap size.

I yanked open the door and I screamed.

I screamed, "Shit!"

Weren't nobody there at all.

I'm gonna remember the Black Man right now and have me a helluva laugh.

Soon as I fetch me a beer.

FOUR

3:00 P.M.

Okay, that's good. Jap beer ain't bad. Ain't got no kick but it's good for a buzz. A buzz'll do. It's all I need. Ain't no one scratchin' at my door. Or—

Oh, shut up.

The Black Man.

Yeah. Hell, be more fun rememberin' than fartin' in a metal tub.

We was in our own cab from the airport that night, back home in Atlanta. Both of us, I reckon, was in a state of shock. Suki sat two feet away, starin' at her folded hands. I didn't rush her and we didn't talk. But I figured it was fine to look. And I was glad it was, 'cause I couldn't've stopped if she told me.

I remembered Jack's face at the airport when we turned and there they was. I thought he looked right horrified, with Suki got up in a Disneyland shirt, short little legs stickin' out of her shorts. And when she grinned, he seen the gold. And her eyes was as big as they looked all along, but her nose was tiny, flat, almost like it once had got busted. So I guessed Jack'd be wearin' by now one of them cat's meow expressions. But me, hell, I was doin' the same, just lookin' at her in the cab. And seein'—somethin'.

Somethin'.

We pulled up in the drive. Saw the lights on at Jack's. And heard the moanin' and groanin' as we walked 'round the cab, past his window.

I shut the door behind us and switched on the light. And I seen Suki's eyes light up, love beams spreadin' through the room. The room with nothin' in it, 'cept a handful of photos, a table, a rose. (Fuck Ted, I *like* flowers.) The room with my last paintin' I kept meanin' to get back to. The room with the futon I roll every mornin', not 'cause I'm neat—'cause my back needs the fluff, the back that's still bad where Ted kicked me. The room it tries my sanity to try and keep simple enough, nothin' there to remind me of—nothin'.

She was walkin' 'round the room just like she was in Disney-land.

And I was gettin' embarrassed, thinkin' of Ted and the Colo-nel. And Jack, screamin' next door like he's dyin'.

I undone a couple of buttons, to give her an eyeful of superpumped pecs.

Suki kept on walkin' 'round, touchin' things and whisperin'.

So I rolled up my sleeves, 'cause my forearms is fierce, and I squared back my shoulders and called her. I opened up the ole growl in my throat, the lie that's my voice since Ted kicked me there too. After breakin' my nose and alignin' my back to his own satisfaction.

Suki just said, "Please to wait." She walked over to the paintin' I still ain't got the heart to complete. Abstract of my mama hangin' from the rafters. Looks sort of like a train. Or plane. Or anythin' I please. Yeah, abstraction's just great for a liar like me.

Suki kept on lookin' at it.

I thought Damn it to hell, I'm the man here, I'm king. If a man's with a woman, then they gotta fuck. That's what I was thinkin'. That's how I was raised.

So I walked over big and tall, ripplin' with muscles and male-ness. I grabbed Suki's shoulder and spun her around. Her eyes lit up again, with shock. But before she could open her mouth to object, I leaned over and opened it for her with mine. Then I started workin' my tongue through her mouth and pawin' at one boobie while she's punchin' away at my chest.

I pulled away, fixin' to give her a modified version of Ted talk. Just enough to get on with the fuckin'. After that, there wasn't nothin' I wanted to do more than cuddle, which I never done with a woman before, and which I now felt powerfully pos-sessed to wanna do.

I never got no Ted talk out. I dunno how she done it, but Suki wiggled and slipped from my arms. I was used to women fightin' me and used to women yellin' No, 'cause the Colonel and Ted always told me they got a big problem with Yes. Some-thin' biological that changes a Yes into No in their throats. And that's one of the reasons they're women, not men.

Suki looked real angry, though. Somehow her eyes just

stopped me cold. She had her little fists balled up and all her features screwed real tight. Like she was concentratin' hard enough to bust. I figured she was fightin' to be the first woman since Eve to say Yes. History made in Atlanta.

But then the words started comin', low down.

"I—I—I be—I am—"

Oh shit, I thought. The virgin trick. They warned me, the Colonel and Ted, about that. Said Reach for your cock on the spot or you're done. A cherry's more lethal than bullets, they said.

"I am—" Suki croaked.

I growled, "Listen—"

But she waved her fists at me. She took a breath. And then she wailed:

"Hank—I am—black man!"

And that, of course, was when I screamed. I wanted to puke, but I was too damn sick. I'd just stuck my tongue down some nigger man's throat!

"You bitch!" I screamed. "You—bastard!"

"Hank—"

Suki looked, you'd've thought, almost puzzled. And this made me even madder—I'd got tricked by an *uppity* nigger.

"Junglebunny! Fag!" I roared.

"Jung-uh?" Suki wondered. "Fack?"

I heard Ted roarin' in my ears. I growled, "Boy, don't sass me. If y'all are a man, not a woman—"

"I *black man woman!*" Suki cried.

My fist was just shakin' with anger. It was bad enough kissin' some damn nigger man. And an uppity one, Jesus Christ, that was worse. But I had me a *liberated* uppity nigger whatever. And I'd kill before havin' Gay Lib in my house.

I grabbed her, or him, or it by the shirtfront, barkin': "I'm gonna kick your black ass, boy!"

"Hank, please!" Suki begged. "Please to not make hurt you!"

I threw a lot of punches in my twenty-six years of existence. But this one was somethin', a class of its own, like somethin' shot out of a cannon, high over my shoulder and down for that face. A punch to cleave a donkey's skull. Or stop a chargin' bull.

But Suki didn't bat an eye.

Suki didn't flinch.

Not till the final moment, no more than a hair 'tween my fist and first bone. I caught a blur of movement, kind of like a corkscrew. Next thing I knowed, my fist was headin' to punch a hole through the back wall. Then the floor. And my whole world went upside down, my feet kickin' and tryin' to stand on the ceilin' to stop the world from turnin'. I spun ass over teakettle, landin' with a ferocious crack, half on my shoulder and half on my back.

I screamed in pain. I screamed in shock. No one had ever throwed me. Ted pitched me through a window once, but the window was open and he pitched me straight. But I just been throwed upside down and around by a damn nigger queen I was fixin' to kill. I screamed. And I would've kept at it, 'cept I hadn't no practice with landin' like that and my breathin' just wasn't worth shit.

Suki rolled me on my side. I felt my knees bein' drawed to my chest.

"Hank, please to *listen*," Suki said.

"Nigger . . ." I said, groanin'.

"No!" cried Suki. "Japanese!"

"Your daddy—" I started, then run out of air.

"Father, mother, *Japanese!*" Suki sat down, cross-legged, hands loosely restin' on knees. "Hundred percent Japanese. I try to tell, I *black man.*"

"So, some Jap nigger—"

"No!" Suki cried.

My head was spinnin'. I sat up. My shoulder felt fucked up real proper.

"Please to look me," Suki said.

I tried to, but how could I? "I thought you was a *woman*, man." And then, huffin' and puffin', I looked down in shame.

"You thinking . . ." Suki muttered. Under her breath, more or less to herself. "You thinking I . . . Oh-ho! Tee hee!"

That wasn't no man's laugh I heard. But—how could it be a woman's? The Colonel said a woman's lungs wasn't equipped for a laugh like a man's. Their lungs was built for screamin' when they didn't get their way. Ted said when a woman laughed, it was more like a nervous reaction, to cover the fact she was thinkin' of fixin' to do a man serious harm. Or she'd be laughin' 'cause he was, same way she'd pat some poor idiot dog. I reckon I believed 'em 'cause I had no reason not to, never havin' heard one bust a gut true like a man.

I looked up and seen Suki rockin' with laughter, like some bean-bottom Buddha.

I didn't feel threatened and didn't know why. To tell the truth, like I promised I would, I felt somethin' like warm all over.

Oh-ho-ho, I joined in. "What?"

Tee-hee-hee, oh-ho-ho. "Hank, you thinking—" Tee-hee-hee-ho—

Ha-ha! "What?" I asked her. Ho-ho!

Tee-hee! "You thinking I be—she-boy?"

A-ha-ha-ha-ha-ha! "Yeah!"

"I be *woman*—ab-so-rute-ry!"

Well, we was both rockin' and laughin' away. But Suki still had some explainin' to do. And I still had a horrible taste in my mouth.

"Suki," I said, "tell me straight. Y'all are a *natural* woman?"

"Ab-so-rute-ry," Suki said. She fluffed her curls, lookin' wounded.

"And y'all ain't got no nigger blood?"

"Look me," she said. "Listen."

I did just that and did both hard.

"No nigger," she said. "Black man." She said it real slow this time. Sounded more like *boo-rock-uh men-uh*.

"Let me get this straight," I said. "A black man *ain't* a nigger there?"

"No!" she said. She shook her head. "*Boo-rock-uh men-uh*, yes?" she cried.

"Okay," I said. "Black man. Black men."

"*Ate a,*" she said, or it sounded like, next.

I nodded, repeatin' and waitin' for more. "Black man ate a . . ."

"Fishman," Suki told me. "Hammerman. Leatherman."

I put it together, slow, real slow, almost slow as Suki, makin' sure I got it right. "Black man . . . ate a . . . a man who's part fish?"

"Fish-ing man," she told me.

"Black man . . . ate a . . . *fisherman?*"

"*Hai.*" Suki nodded, a dark cloud settlin' over her face. "Fisherman. Leatherman."

The riddle confounded me truly.

Suki herself was an absolute Jap and a certifiable woman . . . but in the village where she come from some nigger ate a fisherman. And then a leatherworker?

"Bad Blood!" Suki cried.

So, the blood of the village was tainted?

I never seen a more hopeless expression than the one she was wearin' right then.

She told me she wanted to sleep on the floor and look for a hotel tomorrow.

I said Wait, no big thing, 'long as she wasn't no nigger.

Suki pointed at my neck. "Red neck. Big thing."

Suki slept on the floor, wouldn't take the futon. I sat in the corner, cursin' her riddles and mule-headed ways, till I closed my eyes and was out just like that.

When I woke, she was standin' there ready to go.

I didn't care if she throwed me again. I run over and grabbed her, my eyes a disgrace, hot tears coursin' down my cheeks. I spun her 'round, pulled her to me, cried "Stay!"

"Cannot," she said, right against me.

God help me—and fuck Ted—I fell to my knees. I buried my head, not a thought in the world, about half on her belly and half underneath. It was soft there and, Jesus, she surely smelled good.

I cried, "Don't—"

She said, "Hank," brushin' my hair with her fingers.

"Stay with me," I begged her. "Please. I ain't never heard a woman laugh. I—"

Suki said, "Hank."

And I looked.

She was smilin', but cryin' like I was. I mean, just the tears and no soundtrack.

"Suki stay, but make conditions."

So I agreed not to ask her no more about the mysterious Black Man.

I agreed to fly here and have a look-see for myself.

And I agreed that one of us had to sleep on the damn floor.

But I *negotiated*. And we started swappin' nights, with me on the floor and then her on the floor. And I kept negotiatin' till we was almost side by side. And then, one on the floor, and one on the futon, we started holdin' hands at night. And then she let me kiss her. And I never kissed a woman, never, I wasn't fixin' to poke. It was a new experience. I liked it as much as I liked Suki's laugh.

And so, here I am.

And it did cheer me up, recollectin'. But the Moment of Truth is arrivin' real soon.

One more day.

We can make it.

I just got one problem left.

Lemme try to work it through.

5:00 P.M.

All right, I think I got it.

Suki throwed me.

Fair and square.

And I gotta admit, when she throwed me there wasn't no way I could rise.

And yeah, okay, I reckon Suki could throw me again.

If we was *playin' fair*.

That's what I just got worked out.

Martial art shit works just fine, 'long as everyone plays by the rules. Ted won lots of trophies and laughed about that. The street was what he liked the best. And Ted was my cruel, mighty teacher.

I kind of like it, actually, the way it all works out. She can throw me like a man if we're funnin' in the house. But on the street—I'm the Man.

That's a balance of power, I figure. And men and women need one if they're gonna be in love.

I hear footsteps.
Suki's home.

FIVE

9:00 P.M.

This here is a domestic scene.
First time we ever done this.
We're both seated at the low table, on Suki's fresh *ta-ta-mi* mats.
My belly's just a-purrin' with gratitude to Suki. She cooked her heart out all week long. And I'd've died before I told her how sick I was gettin' of seaweed and rice. But I'll be damned, she seen right through my rubbin' my belly and tellin' her Yum. Tonight she come home with some Kentucky Fried. And I was so damn happy she could've pickled my dick on the spot.
So here we are, with just one day to go.
Suki's sittin' there across from me, a mystifyin' but beautiful sight. What she's fixin' to do is called *sho-do,* she says. I'm bein' privileged to watch her tonight, since *sho-do* is Suki's great passion. And she never let no one watch her before. So I'm bein' Suki's reporter tonight, 'cause privileged moments in life are so few.
This here is the Get Ready phase.
Suki's got this coal-black stick in hand. Looks like a chunk of sealin' wax. Nearby's a slatelike inkstone, a trough at one end filled with water. Suki keeps moistenin' the end of the stick and rubbin' it slow on the surface. The inkstone's now a shade of black that makes Kuni's hair look like blond.
Suki keeps workin' away at the stone.
"Su-mi o su-ru," she just said. "Must to have consist—sist—"
"Consistency?" I asked her.
"Hai." And then she went back at it, gettin' that pitch liquid gurgly thick.
I wonder how the hell long that shit takes.
—I just asked her.
Suki smiled. "'Mericans."

"Jesus," I said, "y'all got a red neck?"

Suki laughed, dippin' and rubbin' away.

"C'mon," I said, "how long? That's weird. Y'all got all the black ink a body could want."

Suki sighed. "Must do," she said, "until heart be quiet."

"Oh."

That ink gets any blacker—

Whoops! Here we go. The Action phase.

Suki's takin' out a large square of black felt. Here comes a sheet of paper. And a pitch-black paperweight. She's squarin' the felt on the table, fiddlin' with the corners till she gets it— There we go. Just right. Okay, here we go again, squarin' the paper sheet off on the felt. Fiddly here, fiddly there. Now here comes the paperweight. Now a small sheet of paper that Suki unfolds, studies a second, then sets on the floor.

It really is amazin' how white that sheet of paper looks, stuck all by its lonesome there in a black sea. The tabletop, the felt, the weight, even Suki's sleeves . . . all black. I find myself pullin' my hands and this page back, so as not to whiten the scene.

Suki's dabbin' the tip of her brush in the trough, now spreadin' more gurgly black on the stone.

I ain't never seen her this quiet before. She takes a sip of air, shuts her eyes, and holds the sip. Looks like she's resettlin' the air farther down.

Her eyes open. She don't see me. I see the brush begin to rise, like it's levitatin'.

She's sittin' there, froze like a statue. Ice that's ice but on the verge of bein' totally liquid, at once.

It's a weird country, Japan is, and—

Wow!

One second, Suki's arm's outstretched, the brush hangin' over the paper—and then it plunges like a sword. Her brush is dancin' all over the paper, fiber drinkin' up the ink, the brush skippin' on like a stone over water in whirls and gnarls and—

Chickenscratch?!

She ain't even drawin' a picture at all!

—Wait a minute. Somethin's wrong. Suki's brush has stopped

skippin' and dancin'. She sets it down. Looks kind of like she's comin' to, out of a deep fuckin' trance.

Suki sighs and stretches. Gives me a big Suki smile.

"No good," she says. "Still my Bad Blood."

Better cheer her up some.

9:45 P.M.

Tried.

But didn't have no luck. There's just one of me against thousands of years of Jap weirdness.

Suki's over there watchin' the news, Suki style. She's got the volume off, just lookin' at the picture while she stretches, breathes deep, and does splits.

Here I am, glad for the balance of power—and Suki's all broke up inside 'cause her chickenscratches just looked like chickenscratches. I told her they looked beautiful. I put a wonderstruck look on my face. What else could I do? What can anyone say to a woman who thinks chickenscratches is art?

I feared for Suki's sanity.

As, I guess, she feared for mine.

"No, *no*," she said. "Can't see?"

"It's fine," I said. "It looks just great."

Suki sighed and shook her head. She picked up the paper she'd put on the floor and laid it out before me.

"See?" she said. "*This* be Good Blood."

I lost it then. And I ain't proud. But here I gotta tell the truth. I could not *believe* my eyes. I started yellin' at her: The fuckin' Good Blood picture looked exactly like the Bad! She wasn't even makin' her own chickenscratches—she was only copyin'! And—

What the hell was she smilin' about?

Suki said, "Someday you try. And I promise understand. Maybe painting true begin."

Yeah, right.

Sure it will.

Anyway, she looks relaxed, stretchin' and watchin' TV.

And—

10:15 P.M.

I just seen a white nigger's face on the tube.

Face looked a little familiar.

The screen cut to more white niggers then, two flaggin' their fingers at Japs in blue suits, the Japs smilin' and bowin' and shakin' their heads.

Cut to Jap announcer. The absolute essence of solemn.

Then the top of the screen broke into little squares. First, these three powerful-lookin' old farts. Then two Jap women's faces, alongside a small blank square with a question mark inside.

I told Suki to crank up the volume.

She did, leanin' over and pressin' one cheek to the rug.

"What the hell they sayin'?" I asked her.

"Shh." Suki didn't move a bit, just sat there collapsed at the middle and listenin' with one ear.

The screen changed to a weather report.

Man, I thought, that first white nigger surely looked familiar.

Suki still didn't move. She just sat there, collapsed, like she was thinkin' now with that top ear.

"Uh, hon?" I said, just to speed her along.

Goddammit, I knowed that white nigger! I seen his face back in Atlanta. The news.

Suki sat up, swung around.

And then she shrugged and said, "Murder. Now sleep."

11:45 P.M.

Suki's brushin' her teeth now. It's somethin' to hear. Like the sound of a scrub brush on freshly laid tiles, with long stretches of passionate garglin'.

Should've wrote this while she soaked. The soakin' part's good for damn close to an hour. And refluffin' her curls takes forever.

One more day.

Just one more day.

We meet the Black Man and fix her Bad Blood.

Anyway—hurry up.

So, Suki says *Murder. Now sleep.*

Just like that!

I said, "Wasn't that that Yankee doc, got all crushed up here a few months ago?"

Suki said *"Hai,"* while her eyes said So what.

I said, "So, what's the story?"

"What?"

I asked her what the news said.

"Aa." She shrugged again and she tried to explain while touchin' one ear to her knee.

American officials are demandin' the doc's body back.

Jap officials are still holdin' same, along with autopsy reports.

And no one's sayin' diddley 'bout speculations in the press of certain—similarities to three murders some eighteen months back.

"Them three guys on the TV?"

"Hai." Suki folded behind, flat on top of her legs. Then she folded her hands on her belly and chilled.

"Well, look," I said. "I gotta say you're takin' it all just remarkably well." I felt edgy as hell, but I couldn't say why. Crushin' just seemed so damn funky.

Suki turned her head my way, I guess matchin' my words with my eyes.

"Japan way be different, Hank."

"You're tellin' me?" I snorted.

"Not be better. Not be worse."

"Meanin' y'all don't give a shit."

"Meaning," she said, "ways be different." With her hands on her belly, and still watchin' me, Suki pulled herself up to an angle of some forty-five degrees. I figured she had cold steel cable for guts, for her face didn't show any effort at all. Holdin' it there, she said, "Doctor, others, not my world. How can I make feeling for strangers?"

I exploded. "Jesus Christ, four guys gross-out murdered!"

Suki lowered herself about fifteen degrees, addin' I guess some more tension. "I care my world, my home," she said. *"U-chi . . .* Home world . . . Japan way."

"Who do they think killed that doctor's ass?"

"Wa-ka-ra-nai," Suki said.

Yeah, right. I don't know.

"All right, who killed the other guys?"

"*Wa-ka-ra-nai.*"

Her eyes pleaded with me. But I wouldn't give up.

"Tell me who them women was."

Suki sighed, sat up straight, then swung around, crossin' her knees.

Then she told me the goddamndest story 'bout a hunt in '88 for three women in red leather dresses, seen leavin' three bars with them men on TV. Some kind of ritual slayin' was thought, 'cause all three of the women was made up the same. Right after the killin's, two girls disappeared, their apartments burned flat to the ground. Cops begun to wonder and started showin' their pictures around. But without the red dresses and makeup . . . Cops retouched the photos. Now folks started sayin' Yeah. Then the TV had a field day, addin' wigs and makeup to dozens of photos of Jap girls. And, sure as shit, every one of 'em was surely a woman in red.

"But only two women," I said, "disappeared?"

Suki shrugged. "*Hai.* Two."

"That's pretty damn mysterious."

"Hank, life be mystery. That not my world, not your world."

"Still, maybe that third girl—"

"No!" Suki throwed her hands up. "Different. Japanese men, maybe Yakuza kill. Doctor, he *American.* And how can woman crush big man?"

I said, "Yeah." The whole thing was beyond me. And Suki was clearly upset. And I didn't even wanna think about three little girls who could crush—Jesus Christ!

I said, "Hey, it's a copycat kill."

She said, "What?"

I explained.

She agreed and clapped her hands. "Coffee cat kill," Suki said.

—There she is. She's callin' me.

I just thought of somethin' wild. Bet Jack'd get a crazy kick— him doin' that Woman in Red for The Store—if I wrote him a letter and told him that tale.

Maybe I will.

Maybe later.

Right now I'm fixin' to cuddle away.

SIX

Friday, 11:00 A.M.

All right.

I'm gonna do it.

I put it off pretty good all week long. And I come up with some real fine excuses.

But now I'm gonna do it.

On my life.

No turnin' back.

I'm goin' *out* that door.

I am.

Let 'em watch, let 'em hoot, let 'em do what they like.

I can take any shit they throw at me.

I'm white and proud of it.

I'm goin'.

I mean it.

I'm goin' *out* for a walk.

Here I go!

Noon

I'm gone in a couple more minutes.

For sure.

I'll just sit and see if Jack calls. Must be two or three A.M. there now. Give Jack another half or so, 'case Kuni's on the rip again.

I'm sure glad I thought of that.

Would've been awful if I was still here and had to think I was too scared to go out.

Thirty minutes, Jack. Call.

Or my ass is out that door.

1:00 P.M.

All right. That's it. They're sleepin'.
Charge!

2:00 P.M.

I was goin'.
Truly.
I was halfway out the door when this chill come over me.
I stepped back in. I closed the door. I felt afflicted in some way I couldn't draw a bead on.
So I come back in, slippin' my shoes off again. I thought, This is her world and I'm part of her world. I seemed to be seein' things in a new light. Them *ta-ta-mi* mats sure looked invitin' as hell, palest gold I ever seen, so clean so looked-after it was hard to believe they weren't livin'.
Light rippled through the windows and I thought I seen a shimmer of pale green in the gold. Suki told me, my first night here, how the mats was when she come, the just-cut straw as fresh as grass, the gold sometimes hummin' with light. She said she was sorry, the fragrance was gone. But she's wrong and I did see a hummin' of light. And when I stepped I felt the fibers sinkin' underfoot.
I went to the slidin' screen of rice paper and balsa. Now, on the *ta-ta-mi* mats, I seen the screen too in a whole different light. It ain't flimsy at all, but a whisperin' strength. The rice paper's stretched taut as the head of a drum, and one shade of ivory this side of transparent. On the base, the scrollin' don't look carved but embroidered.
I turned in a circle and looked all around, really seein' it for the first time, Suki's world.
The low black table where she sits and sews and works and writes and eats. Three drawers left and right, each side. In it goes, and out it comes, Suki's world just as she needs it. Nothin' on the tabletop, not even a lone speck of dust.
Small marble stand against the wall, Princess phone on top of it. Big jumbo cushion beside it, patched and repaired with a

rainbow of threads, like the more she sits on it, the more chance to color it up.

The room is empty, 'cept for these.

No, it ain't empty—it's spacious and clear.

Behind the screen, her bedroom thumbs its nose at the notion of size. The futon, when it's laid out, leaves one foot on either side. When it's rolled, like this mornin', I can take about three steps without bangin' into a wall. I couldn't fit a paperclip on top of Suki's dresser. But the top don't look cluttered somehow in the least. This room is Suki's private world. And everythin' is in its place, every bottle, every lipstick, every photo, every doll. Like some livin' design that's just growed through the years, as Suki grows more into Suki each day.

I remember the night Suki come to my place. I remember watchin' her walk 'round and 'round. I believe she thought she was seein', in my simple space, a reflection of hers.

But there's this peace to Suki's clean. I had mine beat into me, first by the Colonel and later by life. My neatness is like a gun, wardin' off the things I can't seem to forget.

(Why couldn't mom stick her head in the oven or pop down a bottle of pills? I swear to Jesus, hangin's *gross!*)

—Hey, there it was again. I seen it in the bright noon sun, a green shimmerin' over the gold. The straw still smells like fresh-mowed grass, if a body'll just pay attention.

I gotta tell her about this.

I'm gonna show her that I ain't no wuss.

I can do it.

Sure I can.

I'M GOIN' OUT FOR A WALK!!!

4:00 P.M.

They was watchin', all of 'em, Japs to the left of me, Japs to the right, watchin' and whisperin' *Gai-jin.* If the fatsos was there, they was well out of sight, but I didn't care, they was fat, that was all, and I'd tell 'em up front their blue suits was just shit.

I took a left, I took a right, Suki's map beamin' the way in my mind. I walked like a lord of the earth, although I didn't feel much like one. I didn't show 'em nothin', 'cept what I wanted to show. My eyes told 'em, loud and proud: I ain't no nigger.

Gai-jin!

Two blocks up, another right, whereupon I found myself on an amazin' thoroughfare, somewhere in between a street and a Yankee thruway. I believe that thoroughfare defied every known law of physics. Not one inch of sidewalk wasn't covered with Jap bodies. Yet, from the moment I stepped onto it, not one of them bodies so much as brushed mine. Like our bodies had bubbles around 'em, preservin' each separate space.

I was thinkin' I should hang left soon.

But I wasn't gonna let 'em see me lookin' at my map.

And I couldn't've looked at it there if I'd tried. My eyeballs had suddenly gone out of whack, dartin' every which way.

Amazin', just amazin', towerin' scrapers of steel and smoked glass and Blade Runner-chic department stores, all side by each with these rickety huts and sleazoid pinball parlors.

Amazin', just amazin', the traffic on the street so thick the fuckin' walk seemed empty. Buses, trucks, stretch limos, cabs, Toyotas, Datsuns, Hondas, rickshaws, and a thousand bicycles, all burnin' rubber, just screechin' away on every square inch of the road—then stoppin', all together, without a squeal, without a hitch, each time the lights turned red.

Amazin', just amazin'—

Gai-jin!

Gai-jin!

Gai-jin!

—I was totally lost, but I thought: What the hell.

I took a left, a right, a left up a deserted alley.

I leaned against the wall and wished I had a jumbo joint.

And then Jesus, I thought, I ain't toked in two weeks. Not since the night she arrived. In eight years there wasn't three nights runnin' that I wasn't stoned.

What was happenin' to me?

I took Suki's map from my pocket. It was long past bein' useful, with the street signs in chickenscratch, the numbers out of sequence.

Somehow that seemed mighty funny.

I laughed.

Then I cried, "Yo—To-ky-ohhhhhh!"

"*Gai-jin-san,*" a voice said. Fingers touched my elbow.

I guessed it was fatso, but I couldn't see. I was laughin' so hard my damn eyes was a mess.

"*Gai-jin-san,*" he said again, tuggin' at my elbow.

A small guy, maybe my age, wearin' the Jap uniform, an off-the-rack navy suit.

"*Gai-jin-san* is lost?" he said.

"Oh yeah," I said, wipin' my eyes. "Them's the words. Ain't that a hoot? I'm shit lost in Japan!"

"Please to slowly speak," he said. "Cannot understand too fast."

I clapped his shoulder. "That's all right. I am truly impressed by your show of concern. But I got me a map."

Which I showed him.

He took it from me. He opened it up, bowin' and tellin' me *Do-mo.* That's Thanks. Then he begged me to show him exactly where the *gai-jin* wished to go.

I pointed at the station. I intended to give him a real hearty laugh. But what I heard myself sayin' was "Jesus, I'm *lost.*"

"I must to help you," he said.

He sure did.

If anyone was readin' this they couldn't tell by my writin' that my ass is on the train, which barrels along, licketysmooth, over glass.

And all the while, overhead, these loudspeakers is singin', not talkin', the news. It don't sound like chickenscratch. It sounds like somethin' a choir might sing. And I find myself translatin' almost like I understand:

We humbly beg your forgiveness, our most esteemed honorable travelers, for this unthinkably rude interruption of your rail-bound reveries. We only wish to remind you, with a song in our hearts and a lilt in our voice, that the next stop coming up . . .

Somethin's happenin' to me.

All I can hear is the music.

There's children at the windows now, countin' the stops to Shin-ju-ku for me. A small crowd of blue suiters is watchin' while the *gai-jin* writes.

I can't look up. I dunno why. Why didn't they warn me, the

Colonel or Ted, that my whole world could break, like that, on the Ya-ma-no-te line in Tokyo, Japan?

4:45 P.M.

I'm in the cafe of the store where she works.

A cafe's a *kis-sa-ten*. The waitress helped me learn that word, 'cause I let her squeeze my muscles and give my tail a tug.

She's over in the corner now, watchin' me good with a few of her friends.

But I don't mind 'em watchin' now. And I don't mind 'em gigglin'. It's a nervous reaction. I'm nervous myself. Skin is a curious, puzzlin' thing.

I should've brung my camera. I'd like a picture of them girls. But mostly what I'd like's a shot of Suki when she seen me.

Took some doin' findin' her, this bein' another Blade Runner-type set and just packed with the beautiful people. Even the counter girls was dressed to die for and lipsticked to within an inch of their lives.

Suki never talked about her work, 'cept to say she helped folks, some kind of Public Service. I wasn't real sure where to start.

So I sprinkled on some *u-chi* dust and mosied on up to Perfumes, where there was a harem of Japanese foxes.

At the counter I bowed, nice and low and polite, nearly bangin' my head on one knee.

The girl behind the counter never heard of Suki and couldn't rightly figure what Public Service was.

But I had me more powerful *u-chi* dust on. Her and some six of the women, all bowin' and smilin' and sayin' *Aa so,* took me to another counter, where Suki was a stranger too and Public Service was pure Greek.

I made a good haul there, though, collectin' two salesgirls and nine shoppin' foxes.

Took us two more counters before Suki's name rung a bell.

The Handbag girl's almond eyes lit right up. "*So, so! Pa-bu-rik-ku Sa-bi-su Ga-ru!*"

I said, "Yes, ma'am. *Pa-bu-rik-ku.*"

And off we went, with our army in tow.

We arrived, at the back of the store, at a bank of elevators.
And I stood there, feelin' excited and proud, wonderin' which
floor Public Service was on.

To my left there was a ding and I looked as the doors slowly
opened.

And there was Suki, on the job.

She was wearin' a navy-blue blazer and slacks, a white blouse
with black bow tie, and spankin' white gloves. Lace cap clipped
onto a couple of curls. On her face she had this smile, this tiny,
contented, and proud Suki smile, as she bowed, with this elegant wave, directin' the passengers out.

Public Service Girl.

She still hadn't seen me. I thought I ought to run, on account
of she might feel embarrassed. But when she straightened, our
eyes met. And I seen her pride in what she does. And her joy
that I been for a walk.

—And here she comes now, 'cross the room.

We're gonna do the town tonight!

SEVEN

Saturday, 2:00 A.M.

Our last night in Tokyo.

We was almost home.

Hell, five more hours and we'd've been gone, off to meet the
Black Man.

Don't look like we'll make it now.

We gotta face the facts.

We got the door locked, the bolt slipped, the knob propped
with that dresser that weighs half a ton.

That may slow 'em a bit, but it ain't gonna stop 'em.
Not if they're determined to come. I believe they're determined
to come.

Suki's sittin' cross-legged, hands on her knees, her eyes glued
to the door.

Me, I gotta write this down. If they come, ain't nobody who'll
see it. But that don't matter. It's for me. What it is, is the sense

of completion. 'Cause somethin' happened to me here, in crazy, neon, jumpin', sprawlin' Tokyo, Japan.

We done the town and done it good.

Then they done us, the cocksuckers, as we was headin' home.

We was leavin' Shin-ju-ku 'round midnight, wobbly from much *sa-ke*. The streets was still teemin' with drunk—*Japanese*, most of 'em wobblin' like we was. But the teemin' was thinnin' from hours ago and here and there the neon lights was callin' it quits for some shuteye, like us.

We took a left.

We took a right.

Then I forget which turn we took, but we was away from the crowd. *Street's* a little fat, I reckon, for the stretch that we was on. But *alley* sounds a little thin.

What the hell, call it an alley. Life's short.

Suki took me by the hand, guidin' me and hurryin' me. For the air, of a sudden, was feelin' right cold. A light breeze was jostlin' the jumbo red lanterns and pluckin' at the tails of dragonlike banners hangin' outside of the shops. Here and there a face peeked under the fringes of closed curtains, hearin' the clops of our shoes on the road. But we wasn't their world, so they didn't look long.

We wobbled along to the center, where I must've been struck by a sliver of moon. I throwed my arms around Suki and kissed her so hard we was gaspin' for breath.

"Marry—me!"

I heard those words and guessed they come from my mouth. Suki smiled. "Tomorrow—ask."

And I knowed what she meant.

"I don't give a shit—" I said.

"Hank." Suki tugged my arm.

"—'bout no goddamn Black Man—"

"Hank!" Suki really tugged my arm.

I looked where she was lookin', at the far end of the alley. One of the fatsos was standin', arms folded, half fillin' up the exit with three hundred pounds of blubber.

"*Hank.*" Suki tugged again.

I was growin' rapidly to dread those little tuggin's. I knowed

what I'd see, but I turned and I looked. And, lo and behold,
there he was, fatso two, blockin' the opposite end.

"Goddammit to hell," I told Suki. "I was havin' a wonderful
day. Fuck this shit."

The first fatso called out somethin'. And it was clear from the
tone of his voice they was back now to snappin' out orders.

"What'd he say?" I snarled at Suki.

"He say we must go them."

"Fuck."

"Go them, he say. Not be hurt. Only talk."

"That a fact?" I asked her. "Give that fat pig a message from
me."

She said, "What?"

"Tell him the real hurtin's gonna begin if he don't get out of
our way."

She didn't tell him nothin'.

So I told her, "Tell him!"

"Cannot," she said. "That—very rude!"

"Y'all know what trouble is?" I growled.

"*Hai*, Suki know," she said.

"Then y'all know we're *in* trouble."

"*Hai.*"

"Well, I'm the man here and I'm gettin' us out. Tell him to
move!"

She said, "Why? He no move."

I said, "I got no time to argue, girl."

She said, "Suki protect—"

And I screamed, "Y'all got elusions of grandness, or what? I
don't know how to break the news, but the top of your head
hardly comes to my belt!"

Suki smiled grimly. I heard her crack her knuckles and then
seen her startin' to rotate her neck. Then I seen fatso two start
to waddle our way. I swung around to see the other fatso comin'
too. They was takin' their time, puttin' on a good show, hands at
their sides now and swingin' real loose.

I grabbed at Suki's hand. "C'mon!"

She snatched her hand back, pivotin' 'round, pressin' her
back against mine.

"Back-back," she pleaded. "Stand back-back. Suki no let hurt you."

Yeah, sure, back-to-back! I swore, if we got out of this one alive, I'd teach Suki the rules of the street.

The two fatsos was closin' in.

Thirty feet on each side.

Twenty-eight feet.

Twenty-six.

And I remembered all too well the fate of Strongarm Custard. No back-to-back Little Bighorn for me.

"Stay here," I snapped. "Just stay out of his reach. I'll be back in a couple of seconds."

"Hank," Suki begged me, "wait."

"That ain't my style," I told her. "Charge!" And then I strode off, muscles ripplin' and blood-gorged, a snarl on my face, my lips droolin' with rage.

"C'mon," I yelled, "you big fat sack of shit!"

Fat boy stopped, in a crouch, sixteen feet between us.

Suki screamed, "Hank—*su-mo!*"

Well, I might've been a Roman off to fight the Christians, my wife callin' out to me, *Honey, your lunch!* I was off to prove my manhood by fellin' this great wall of blubber, this goddamn *su-shi* wrestler—and there *she* was talkin' about raw fish! Who could figure women? We was made to love 'em and not try to figure why.

Su-mo! I shivered, disgusted.

Then I put up my dukes and advanced on my guy, my crouchin' *su-shi* wrestler.

About ten feet away from him, I knowed just what to do, 'cause ole Ted was a powerful teacher and a sly and evil human. I throwed up one hand to distract him and screamed. And as he blinked, I lightnin'-streaked to a trash can and frisbee'd the lid at his face.

While he was blockin', I shuffled right in. I feinted with a strong front snap, then whirled and shot my leg back straight, lookin' up for half a second to see how Suki was doin'.

I ain't sure what happened next. I mean, how what happened happened.

The kick was good, my aim was true.

But, in an awful flash, it come to me: My foot hadn't connected with nothin'.

I looked back where I should've been lookin'. And the *su-shi* was gone. Just my leg in the air. I heard Ted screamin' *Move it!*

I was slow, though, *sa-ke* slow. From the corner of one eye, I caught a racin' silver blur as fatso, now squarely behind me, smashed the lid down on my knee.

I heard myself scream. When my leg hit the ground, my mind flooded with red and my vision was nothin' but squiggles and stars, hot pain roarin' up my leg and out through the top of my skull.

Then I thought, for a second, a wave must've struck, ripplin' all over my back and my butt. Then washin' around and around me.

Fatso had his arms around me tight.

"*Gai-jin!*" he cried. "Risten!"

I kicked back at his shins. If he had shins, they was miles in back of the blubbery wave. The circle I was locked in kept tightenin' and tightenin'.

I had so little air left I must've been tryin' to breathe through my eyes. I couldn't see nothin' but squiggles and stars—and red pulsin' flashes of Suki dodgin' fatso two.

"*Gai-jin,*" mine said, "prease, we talk!"

I had a squiggly starry flash of Ted sittin' and yawnin' and pointin' thumbs down.

I bowed my head down to my chest all the way, and leaned over a little to draw fatso in.

Then I snapped my head back like the tail of a whip and skull-smashed him hard as I could.

Fatso screamed. The circle broke. I slipped right through and spun around and I was swingin' as I did, my skull-cleavin', mule-fellin' roundhouse, sockin' him flush on the ear. And through the squiggles and the stars, I seen a gushin' from his ear and knowed it wasn't water.

My uppercut's my next best shot. Truth told, they don't come sneakier.

But fatso, still gushin', was sneerin' as he stormed into the punch.

He throwed his arms around me, spittin' a mouthful of teeth

in my face, and he didn't waste no time this time in crushin' the breath from my body.

He screamed somethin' at me, his face in my face, while he tightened the blubbery vise. I don't know what the hell he screamed, but it wasn't *gai-jin* and it wasn't *please*.

My left arm was useless, pinned high by his ear. My right arm was plain out to lunch at my side.

I butted him, smashin' his nose again good. But he was through screamin'. He laughed and he squeezed. Then he done the grossest thing I ever seen any man do. He blowed his busted snout at me, sprayin' me with blood and snot.

And before I could recover from this devastatin' shock, he butted me back, flattenin' my nose, like we was at some fine to-do, swappin' party favors.

I believe I would've died if fatso hadn't done that. I might've checked out with a horrified squeak while he squeezed the last breath from my lungs.

But fatso hadn't reckoned on one major factor. He had no way of knowin' that I had made a solemn vow—right after Ted busted my nose that third time—I did swear before God if it got broke again, I'd pull out all the stops.

I butted him back, only angled and higher, sinkin' my teeth in his nose with a chomp.

Fatso roared as he tightened that ole *su-shi* vise.

I screamed in pain. I yowled for air. I lost the damn nose altogether.

Fatso, clearly attached to his nose, kept his head back now. I couldn't get in, not for nothin', to chew on that savory prize.

Fatso got a rhythm goin' with his squeezin', like a snake.

Crush, he'd go, with a roar as he *crushed*.

Then he'd pause to take a breath, watchin' me under the hoods of his eyes.

Then *crush* he'd go again and howl.

Two more crushes, I believe, would've had me wheelchair-bound, my backbone crushed to carrot pulp.

But then two things happened that brung me to this table, where I can wait with dignity for the bastards to beat down the door.

Suki screamed behind me and I heard an awesome crash.

There was a grand awakenin' in every cell and foll—folla—Shit, them things your hair sticks into. I come to, everywhere at once. We'd never see no Love Hotel. We had that much comin'. Life owed us.

Then, in my newly revitalized state, my mind clicked in on somethin'. As fatso leaned back, tankin' up on more air, the vise relaxed a little. I thought Jesus, I thank thee, and started to wrestle my right arm in from the side.

I got it trapped between our thighs when—

"Ban-zai!" fatso screamed, really leanin' into it.

The next crunch was it. Not much doubt about that. I hung loose while he snapped, popped, and crackled my spine. Through the pulsin' red squiggles and stars, I pictured Suki naked in our Love Hotel.

Another scream behind me. Hers. And then another crash.

Then fatso's crushin' faded to another leanin' back, a breath.

This time I was ready. I leaned in with him, and as he was breathin', I snaked my hand in, with a twist as I snaked, until my fingers clenched around two massive *su-shi* balls.

These I proceeded to squeeze for dear life.

I done some bad Ted-bashin' here. And God knows, there's lots more to be done. But I gotta give credit where credit is due:

Ted, thank y'all for grabbin' me that one time by the nuttos. Y'all taught me how inspirin' it can be for a man with his balls in a vise. A man feels inspired to throw up his arms and rise up on tiptoes and sing like a girl. A man feels inspired to beam through his eyes a warm flood of respect and goodwill. A man feels inspired to be your best friend and go quickly and gladly wherever he's led.

All this and more my new friend fatso felt truly inspired to do.

I led him backward on tiptoe, right into and half through a wall. His eyes rolled. His mouth started bubblin' foam. I let go of his balls. He looked grateful as hell. But before he could breathe half a sigh of relief, I got down to business just like I been taught.

I started rainin' blows on him, not one of 'em lightened with even the ghost of half an ounce of compassion. I hit him Ted style, everywhere—the nose, the mouth, the ears, the skull, the solar plexus, then square on the heart.

I watched him fall hard to his butt, then keel over, makin'
these horrible sounds in his throat.

Shit, I thought.

Then, Fuck him.

I whirled, takin' off for the next guy.

I got about two steps before my knee just exploded with pain.
And I found myself fallin', facedown, to the road.

"Suki!" I cried.

I was down, though, and good.

Then, through the squiggles and stars, I seen that the scene
wasn't quite what it seemed.

Her fatso's shirt was torn to shreds and blood was streamin'
down his skull. Suki dodged him easily, Lady David 'gainst Go-
liath. She'd pivot or shuffle right out of the way, once with a
swat to the back of his head.

Finally, fatso roared and went into his low-down *su-shi*
crouch, arms out like he's holdin' a barrel.

Suki thumbed her nose.

Come on.

Fatso shuffled side to side, splashin' his sizable self.

Suki waved.

Come on, come on.

He come at her, all right, like a tidal wave.

Suki didn't bat an eye. I thought she might be froze with fear.
But she was smilin' and she looked relaxed.

Then, in the final half second, I seen a suggestion of movement: Suki steppin' in lightly to meet him, with a lazy half turn,
her arms risin'.

Fatso almost had her—when she turned into a corkscrew,
hands, hips, everythin' spiralin' in and around and then down,
while lettin' rip with this deafenin' scream.

Bodies wasn't meant to fly the way that fatso's done. He shot
over Suki's shoulder and crashed into the wall, feet side up,
with his back. Then he dropped with a scream, and a crack, on
his neck.

Suki lorded over him, cryin' *"U-chi! U-chi!"*

That boy wasn't goin' nowhere, though, judgin' by that crack.
And the fact that his head and his body was goin' in radically
different directions.

I scrambled up and started limpin' Chester style to Suki.

I grabbed her hand. She wouldn't budge. She kept jabbin' her finger at fatso.

"Goddammit," I told her, "c'mon, girl."

"*U-chi!*" she wailed. "*U-chi!*"

I throwed my arms around her. "Please. I gotta meet the Black Man."

Suki come to. But I still had to drag her. She kept lookin' back, whimperin' "*U-chi!*"

We was exitin' the alley when I seen my fatso crawlin', still clutchin' his heart, 'long the wall.

I dropped Suki's hand.

She howled, "*U-chi!*"

I gave her an open-hand crack on the cheek and said, "I said snap out of it. I wanna know what's goin' on. And I wanna know fuckin' *now.*"

"*Hai,*" she said and touched her cheek.

I hauled fatso back in the alley, my knee screamin' with every step.

I sat us both down, my back propped on the wall, my legs wrapped 'round his arms and chest. I twisted his head up, half turned it to mine, lockin' it there nice and tight with one arm. Like I was fixin' to kiss him.

My knee was still screamin', but I liked that fine. I scissored him tighter and looked at his nose, nicely embellished with chew marks and blood.

"Tell him talk or I'll eat it," I said.

She said, "*What?*"

And he said, "*Gai-jin!*"

"Tell him," I growled. "Tell him now!"

"Hank—that gross!"

"Tell him I will chew it off and spit it in his mouth."

Suki told him in what sounded like a high-fallutin' fashion, full of much bowin' and 'scuse me-type words.

But fatso got the message. He shook his head, strainin' fiercely.

"Tell him *now,*" I said. "I'm gettin' powerful hungry."

I leaned in, face-to-face. His breath was hot and quick and

bad, but I didn't flinch. I just looked at his nose, prayin' to Ted for the strength to go on.

Suki bowed and 'scused herself, and bathed him in another flood of genteel Japanese.

Fatso screamed some word at me, sprayin' my face with his spittle. He bucked and reared. But I tightened the locks, re-anglin' his head till I heard the bones crack.

"What'd he just say?" I asked Suki.

She shook her head.

I asked again.

"He say—*ba-ka*. Sorry! *Ba-ka* very bad."

"What's it mean?"

Fatso screamed the word again.

"Girl," I growled at Suki.

"Hank, come. He no talk."

"What the fuck's it mean!"

"That be our worst insult. Meaning—highly silly."

Well, playin' time was over now. I been called a lot of things. But I didn't really cotton to bein' highly silly. Which, I guessed, in Japanese, meant like *motherfucker*.

I reached inside my small bag of smiles and come out with the cruelest I got.

"So," I said, "I'm silly?"

Then I done what I said I would do.

And while fatso was yowlin' and spittin' it out, I told Suki to tell him I'd chew off both ears.

She looked at the nose by her feet and she gulped. Then again, they *had* messed with her *u-chi*. She bowed and told him. Considered a second. Then gave him a shot in the ear.

Fatso sang a mad high song.

Suki put it, as he sang, into somethin' resemblin' English.

The song of how our fates was sealed the night she done that hand jive. Which wasn't Ma-ka-ha-ri style. Which would've been terrific if it hadn't been wrong quite that way. But it bore an unhappy resemblance to the hand jive of three certain women who broke from the church some time back.

Three women who'd concocted some new kind of Black Magic.

Three women seen leavin' three Tokyo bars in spectacular red leather dresses.

The church, fatso sang, caught two with somewhat disastrous results.

(Two women and a question mark on the TV screen.)

The third one they managed to capture alive.

And there wasn't no trouble, no trouble at all. The dead men was forgotten. The two women too. The third woman in red was *reprogrammed,* stripped of her magical powers.

Till, of course, that Yankee doc got his head squished like a melon.

Now the hunt is on again, but that woman's nowhere to be found.

And what if them three women is only the start of a new renegade church?

"What's that woman's name?" I barked.

Fatso screamed that he couldn't remember.

I thought I heard a siren whoopin' in the distance.

I licked at my chops and I twisted his head and I started to snap for one ear.

Fatso screamed *Michiko.* Yes, it was *Michiko!*

Siren comin' closer. I still had a lot of questions, but no time to ask 'em: like how three small women could crush three big men, Black Magic bullshit aside.

I loose'd my legs, which delighted my knee. I lumbered up behind him, then topped him flat on his side with a boot.

"Tell him," I told Suki, "to give that high priest bitch a message. Tell him they fuck with our *u-chi* again, I'll go there and bite off *her* nose."

That siren now wasn't two blocks away.

I grabbed Suki's hand, started tuggin' her off. She stopped only once, to give fatso a kick in the groove where his nose used to be.

And, so, here we are.

It's three A.M., with me here at the table and Suki still watchin' the door like a hawk.

If we can live a few more hours we might make our train.

But we ain't seen the last of these mothers, that's sure. Don't know what they've got in mind if they ever catch our asses. But

I guess the pain'll fall like rain and the droplets won't feel much like flowers.

I'm gonna close this book now.

I'm gonna go sit by the door at her side.

If I check out, if this is it, I guess I die a happy man. But I'll die wishin' on my soul that I'd told her of Ted and the Colonel. And how my mama hanged herself. And how close I was actually gettin' to turnin' my back on the money no washin' can rid of the blood.

Hell, there's worse things than dyin' without gettin' laid, though part of me still wonders what.

I come here and got civilized.

And *now* I gotta die?

Life's cruel.

I guess what I'd like to do now is sit quiet, like Suki, and just watch the door.

Japan.

EPPYLOG

Saturday, 7:30 A.M.

Not havin' writ no book before, I got no way of knowin' if an Eppy can go in the middle or not. But this sure seems a good place to put one, so I'm puttin' my Eppy right here, as I please.

We waited till four. No one beat down the door.

We waited till five. Not a peep in the hall.

And gradual, as the sun started to rise, we begun to wonder if . . . Then we begun to hope. Then we begun to really feel that we was gonna make the train and finally meet the Black Man.

And we was almost out the door when the phone begun to ring. Suki tugged at my arm. I said "I wanna know," then marched to the phone like the Colonel, snappin' it up with a barked "Talk to me."

For a second I didn't hear nothin' but crackle and spitz on the line. Then I heard that welcome voice, echoin' over the static.

"Hank??? . . . Hank? . . . Is that you?"

I cried, "Jack! Bless my soul! Hey, bud, how they hangin'?"

In due time, when the last of my echoes got through, Jack rippled a series of echoes to me.

"Hank . . . Listen . . . Everything's   *fine* . . . Heaven . . . I'm in . . . *heaven* . . ."

"Great!" Then I started to tell him that we had to fly. I was cut off by more echoes that must've got stalled in the wires.

". . . my letter . . . Forget it . . . Hank . . . Don't read . . . Peaches will be . . . fine . . ."

I said, "What the hell is wrong with Peaches?"

Pause for the rush of Jack's echoes to stop.

"Don't worry . . . Hank, Peaches . . . fine . . . Oh man, I'm in . . . heaven . . ."

I started to tell Jack I'd call him tomorrow night at—

"Hank!" Suki whispered.

I waved and started to tell Jack again.

"Hank!" Suki urged me.

"Six," I told him. "Six P.M. Be there. Gotta go."

I hung up, turnin' to Suki.

"There no telephone," she said.

Oh well, what the hell.

Jack's fine.

The cat's fine.

Kuni's fine.

And here we are.

For now, we're seated side by side on the Shin-kan-sen. A.k.a., the Bullet Train. On the open stretches, on our way to the north of Japan, the Shin-kan-sen appears to reach about the speed of light. Ain't nothin' but blurs out the windows, meltin' impressions of rice paddies, hills.

Girls with trays slung 'round their necks waltz smoothly up and down the aisles, peddlin' fish and rice balls.

Most of me wants to get out of this country while we're still able to *git*.

But I am the Colonel's son. And I can't abide bein' fucked with.

I gotta know who them church bastards are. And who they're thinkin' *we* are.

There's more to this than beats the eye.

But, for now, I close this book, satisfied that all is well, at least, with Jack and Kuni.

What the hell did he mean that my cat *will* be fine?

Easy.

Everythin' is fine.

I gotta comfort Suki now. The farther north we get, the more her stomach's tied in knots.

Put my arms around her.

Yeah, the Black Man scares me too.

But we're rollin' on air now.

For now, we'll be fine.

And that wraps up my Eppy.

Bye.

Oh. Wait. I forgot:

To Be Confuckintinued.

BOOK FIVE
JULY, 1990
SEA OF
JAPAN/TOKYO

ONE

 We arrived in Mi-zu-ya-ma, far and away to the north of Japan, in the early afternoon. The Shin-kan-sen only goes part of the way, so we'd made the last legs of the journey on a train as slow and rickety as the Bullet Train was sleek and smooth. At the station we caught us a taxi that looked like a Japanese Lovebug and cabbed it the rest of the way.

I ain't sure village is the word for Mi-zu-ya-ma. We was in and out of whatever it was before the cab's wheels had spun six times around. I seen what might've been a bar that held about three people. I seen a market of some kind with fish in a window and produce. And then Mi-zu-ya-ma was lost in our dust.

Suki squeezed my hand. She kept squeezin' it tighter and tighter as we sped, country style, six miles an hour, to where the ole Black Man was waitin'.

The driver knowed Suki, who'd bowed back and smiled. But her mood had growed tighter and tighter, along with her grip on my hand. Now there wasn't no sound in the Lovebug at all, 'cept for the bumps of the wheels on the road and the small crunches of bones when she squeezed.

A mile out of the village, the road narrowed to a width a flea couldn't fit on between passin' cars. And the road become as choppy as an ocean in a storm. The Lovebug took some fearsome bumps, and the three of us bounced off and back on the seats, me smackin' my head on the ceilin' each time. But the Sea of Japan was now comin' in view, and the mountains, they was loomin'.

This was where she come from.

And nothin' this lovely could be all that bad.

The Lovebug stopped at the top of a hill, a row of houses lined up below along the sparklin' sea.

I didn't have to ask to know why we was stoppin' here: to give me time to 'climatize to the horror comin'.

Suki paid the driver. I watched her, with a sigh, wonderin' again how to tell her I been lyin' for years about money. And I ain't the poor boy I made out to be.

We started off slow down the long dusty slope, like we was floatin' through a dream, the sea air growin' stronger, the mountains so high they was kissin' the sky.

When we got to the base I was drinkin' the air in like fresh country moonshine: a potent brew of seaweed, fish, and kicky mountain air.

I said, "Ohhhh."

She pointed left to one of the *u-chis* that looked pretty much like the others, 'cept there was a timber yard between it and one neighbor.

The Black Man's house had a porch that apparently went all the way around. Some kids was runnin' 'round the porch, while an ole woman rocked in her rocker. Seein' us comin', she called somethin' loud and really started rockin'.

A washin' line run from the roof to a tree. It was loaded with undies like I never seen. And a woman with a bamboo pole, loadin' on the undies, dropped the pole, pressin' her hands to her hair. She cried, "*Aa!*"

Suki didn't say nothin', but picked up the pace. The kids scrambled 'round to the front of the porch, the bigger ones jumpin' up onto the rail.

Suki didn't say nothin'. We walked on to that house where the Black Man was surely residin'.

We was twenty yards away—when, like that, from 'round the back, this blocklike figure of a man, shirtless and tanned as a nigger, come struttin' with a string of fish over his barrel chest like a vest.

Suki muttered somethin' that started with an "o."

Then again: *"O-tō-san."*

She let go of my hand and forgot about me. There was tears in her eyes, but she started off slow, till she couldn't walk slow any longer. And I knowed by her tears and the way she was runnin': *o-tō-san* was her daddy.

As she was runnin' to him, *o-tō-san* slung the fish off and held the line hitched to one finger, arms stretched wide in welcomin'.

Suki cried, *"O-tō-san!"*

She almost jumped the last three feet into her daddy's arms.

The kids tittered and clapped on the railin'.

The bamboo woman beamed with joy.

But somethin' was stuck in *o-tō-san*'s craw.

He set her down, barked somethin' fierce, and started jabbin' at her curls. Before Suki could answer, he throwed his fish down, grabbed a handful of blouse and a handful of skirt, tilted her lengthwise and carried her off.

They all howled with laughter.

Then, by degrees, the laughter stopped.

I took a breath and moseyed toward 'em, wonderin' who was the scareder.

TWO

My ass was installed in a rocker, one of the six on the porch. And I was then subjected to tail-tuggin' and skin-rubbin' and muscle-squeezin' by one and all.

The roll call on the porch was this: grandma, the ole rocker woman . . . grandpa . . . papa's brother, a widower . . . and his four kids.

We was havin' a whale of a time on the porch playin' with an atlas—when the screen door opened.

Out come papa.

Out come mama.

Both with these real foxy grins.

Then out come, grinnin' sheepishlike, the new improved version of Suki. That girl's hair must've been washed with acid and clipped with garden shears. Half dry, the results looked revoltin'. It wasn't brown, it wasn't black, it wasn't straight or curly, but everythin' and all at once, just goin' every which way.

But already I could see the drift of where her hair was headin'. A few more days and washin's, it'd be a jet-black pixie shag like the kids was wearin'. So I didn't laugh, I smiled at her, knowin' it hadn't been cut but restored.

"*Ii de-su ka?*" Suki asked me.

Is it good?

I said, "*Ii de-su.*"

THREE

I guess that was six days ago.

It don't take much time here to lose track of time.

I don't wear a watch no more.

There ain't no newspapers.

Ain't no TV.

So I can't keep a diary proper, on account of I don't know the date.

But I heard tell once 'bout a book that might be just the thing now. The book was called a Comin' Place—kind of like an attic for stuff a man wants to recall.

And someday, I know, it'll be hard as hell to remember how the Black Man ever could've caused such woe.

The Black Man.

Boo-rock-uh-man, she said in Atlanta.

Or, that was what I heard.

The Black Man . . . ate a . . .

She'd been tryin' to tell me. But then she stopped cold, insistin' I come here and see for myself. 'Cause, though *bu-ra-ku-*

min don't mean black man in the sense that I was worryin', a *bu-ra-ku-min*'s like a nigger here.

Bu-ra-ku-min = *e-ta* = fisherman, tanner, or butcher.

The *bu-ra-ku-min*, or the *e-ta*, are outcasts to Real Japanese, such as are found in Tokyo, Osaka, and Kyoto.

By and large, they're built much stockier.

Their skin, as a rule, 's a bit darker.

Their faces, a little bit flatter.

Real Japanese can spot 'em across a crowded room. Or class 'em by their accents the minute they open their mouths. No *bu-ra-ku-min* has a chance in hell of marryin' up from their class, 'cause background checks is thorougher than fuckin' CIA checks.

A *bu-ra-ku-min* can't get no good schoolin'.

And the only city jobs open is like pickin' litter off the tracks or drivin' elevators.

We was walkin' along the great Sea of Japan, the surface speckled with fishin' boat sails, when Suki told me this and more: how she walked out two years ago, determined to take the big city by storm and leave her Bad Blood behind her. She told me how she got that job, beggin' 'em to take her, to let her serve Real Japanese. She told me of the lottery and how she swore, on winnin' it, her beggin' days was done with. She started to tell me of Kuni, who was shoppin' one day at the store. How one thing led to another, till Kuni was takin' her shoppin' and makin' her hair brown and curly. Next thing she knowed, Suki's writin' to Jack, sayin' she *loves* vermicelli.

Suki shuddered, recollectin'. "First time I taste in Atlanta— too gross!"

She nodded her head at the Sea of Japan. Breathed the fish-sweet air in deep. And pointed at one mountain loomin' over all the rest, a cloud 'round its peak like a bracelet.

"Fu-ji-san," Suki said.

"Suki-san," I answered, touchin' her hair, her real hair, her black hair.

"Hank," she said. "This me. Right here. I try hard, but—"

"Yeah. I know."

"I am *bu-ra-ku-min*," she said, soft and fierce.

"Yeah."

"You can't *see?*" she asked me, touchin' her cheek with one finger.

I pressed that finger to my lips. "I see just fine," I told her. "Your skin excites me silly, girl."

"You don't *care?*"

"I care for *y'all.*"

We was alone by the Sea of Japan. A gull screamed as we started to kiss, the water pantin' at the sand.

We dropped to our knees, tumbled onto our sides.

I guess we was fixin' to do it right there.

But a man's only as good as his hard-on.

'Sides, I'd gotten attached to the notion by now: our first time like uncorkin' some bubbly in that Love Hotel.

So I done the next best thing to pokin' Suki by the sea.

I whispered "I love y'all" real soft in her ear.

And she hugged me and whispered in mine.

FOUR

Suki says it's Thursday.

I'll take her word for that.

Tomorrow we'll be headin' off by train again for Tokyo.

Our Love Hotel is waitin'.

In Tokyo we'll also fetch a Ma-ka-ha-ri book. I can't get them three women in red from my mind. Or figure the connection between exorcisin' foxes—and the head-to-toe crushin' of bodies.

Well, we're leavin' tomorrow. We'll see what we see.

For now, I been learnin' *Ni-hon-go* and set down what I learned in this Comin' Place book.

U-chi

House. My house. My world.

The house is in the ole plain country manner, with a back porch around and a sweepin' peaked roof. Past a slidin' screen door, the main room's covered with eight mats, from under which the smell of pine, freshly waxed, comes waftin'. There

ain't a stick of furniture, 'cept for a long wood table. There ain't
one ornamental lick, 'cept for an alcove in one wall with urns of
ancestors' remains and such shit.

The beddin' comes out of cupboards at night, with foldin'
screens for privacy. But by day there ain't a clue that five out of
nine people sleep in this room.

The grandfolks sleep in a small room in back.

Upstairs, Suki sleeps with her parents.

And my ass has been installed across the hall in another blank
room the size of four *ta-ta-mi* mats.

But the house part, that's the easy part. The hard part's un-
derstandin' how true it is, what Suki said, 'bout the *u-chi* not
bein' a house but a world.

Ko-tat-su

This next word sheds some light on that. The *ko-tat-su*'s that
big ole wood table—some ten feet long and two feet high, with a
latticed wooden frame and a parquet top.

But it ain't just a table, it's more like a spine, 'round which
the family gathers and huddles to keep warm. Most nights the
table's covered, when the night wind starts to blow, with a gi-
gantic homemade quilt that covers the legs of all bodies around.

On winter nights, hot coals get loaded into a brazier fixed
under the top.

The *ko-tat-su* weaves a mighty spell.

I could feel it myself that first night when we ate, one leg
touchin' papa, one leg touchin' mama, my hips snuggled to
grandma's and Suki's. The quilt covered our parts so there
wasn't no parts, not under the *ko-tat-su*, where the warmth
melted all things together.

Yap-pa-ri Ni-hon-jin ja nai to . . .

Unless one's Japanese . . .

The first night was the first time I heard it, though I heard it a
million times since. I was given the guest spot of honor, with my
back to the family shrine. The *ko-tat-su* was laden with dish
after dish:

—a jumbo lobster, shockin' pink, on a bed of ice . . .

—prawns laid tail to whisker in these see-through, ribbed corsets . . .

—octopus and eel parts, sliced and diced like works of art . . .

—rice balls . . .

—*su-mo* balls . . .

—massive bowls of steamin' rice . . .

I was gawkin' at my plate, wonderin' where not to begin, when I heard these slurps and crunches that freaked me somethin' fierce. I looked up, discreetlike, not wantin' to be rude, to see:

Papa with a bowl of soup, things jumpin' in and out of it, the tail end of somethin' slimy squigglin' out of his mouth.

Grandpappy, beside him, was chompin' through that lobster shell, the lobster bein' so pink, I now seen, on account of they hadn't quite cooked it. Its claws was swingin' to and fro. I thought I heard it screamin'.

I don't think I could've been more shocked if I'd seen 'em both eatin' boiled babies.

Papa roared with laughter, spittin' half of that squigglin' tail in his bowl.

"*Yap-pa-ri Ni-hon-jin ja nai to* . . ." he told me with a wink.

And all around the table the clan nodded, repeatin' the words: *Unless, of course, one's Japanese* . . .

—such food'll be revoltin' . . .

—the house'll be too small and cold . . .

—life by the sea'll be too much hard work . . .

It was clear, then and there, our balance of power was missin'. So, through Suki, I made an announcement: I'd go fishin' with the boys at the crack of dawn.

Yu-ka-ta

Short cotton summer kimono, the clan's bein' blue and white. Mine comes up to my knees and my elbows.

That first night was powerful chilly. But after dinner I retired with the men of the house to the porch—where the drinkin' begun with first slap of the door.

In a couple of minutes the slaps of the door was like somethin' in a cartoon—the women rushin' in and out, the men roarin' for more, lots more, seaweed and booze.

It all started off nice and civil, the *gai-jin* their great guest of honor.

But as the *sa-ke* and beer flowed, I might as well've been under the porch.

Their jokes was beyond me and they didn't care.

The loster I got, hell, the louder they roared.

By degrees, I come to feel a sort of *underpinnin'* to the whole festivities.

Now and then, for no reason at all, papa-san would pat my knee, an ugly shade of purple. Or grandpappy would squeeze my arm, makin' a wonderstruck sound. Or uncle would look at my eyes and my nose. And they'd repeat the magic words:

Unless one's Japanese . . .

I took some pride in bein' the last man to pass out.

Gam-bat-te

Hang in there.

I heard that roared the next mornin'.

Over and over again.

The sun was just risin' and my head was splittin'. I wasn't real sure where I was. Real gradual, I made my way from my futon to the floor and stumbled to the window to see an astonishin' sight.

O-tō-san and Suki was danglin' upside down from bars attached to the branches of trees. They was doin' these vertical sit-ups. On the ground, the other men rewarded each with a punch in the gut and a great cry of *"Gam-bat-te!"*

They was just wrappin' up as I got there, droppin' down to their hands and flippin' onto foot.

Papa grinned. *"Goo-du mo-ru-nin-gu."*

"O-ha-yō," I said.

He jerked his thumb back at the bar.

"Yap-pa-ri Ni-hon-jin ja nai to . . ."

Papa looked at my knee, the yellow-purple just about matchin' my nose.

He conferred with grandpappy, who then conferred with uncle, all of 'em noddin' and talkin' real low. Then papa said somethin' to Suki, puttin' his hand on her shoulder.

Suki bowed and answered, *"Hai."*

She turned and bowed to the other two men, who bowed back and bowed to me and started to walk off with papa.

"Hey," I said to Suki. "I was goin' fishin'!"

"Papa worry for your leg."

Suki took me by the hand, tuggin' me off to the house.

"Shit," I muttered. "I wanted to go."

"Gam-bat-te," Suki told me.

I-so-ga-shii

Busy. Like, real busy.

After breakfast—toast and eggs, in the *gai-jin*'s honor—the clan wasted no time in goin' into overdrive. Before the last chopstick had half hit the table, they was off and runnin'.

The table was cleared.

And the dishes was done.

And the kids was whooshed off to start sweepin' the porch.

And then mama was off to go scrubbin' some walls.

And then Suki was dustin' and straightenin' things.

And then grandma was scurryin' hither and thither, gatherin' this and fetchin' that.

And then Suki run off to start drawin' my bath.

And the kids, finished sweepin' the out, swept the in.

By the time the bath was drawed, I was too winded from watchin' to move.

So I was beamed up by these scurryin' bees, their hands so light they felt like wings, liftin' me, coaxin' me, leadin' me to the joy of their life, the hot tub in the back.

The water was hot as a kid's first wet dream, the steam risin' so thick it brung tears to my eyes.

But, gradual, I found myself inhalin' the steam with some pleasure. And then with a measure of pleasure. And then with unmeasured delight, my hands splashin' the water on shoulders and neck.

I don't remember driftin' off. I must've been out for an hour or so. When I come to, the water was tepid and I felt relaxed all over, like a million fairies had opened up my pores, cleaned 'em out, shut 'em up, kneadin' the knots from my muscles.

I heard, from somewhere in the back, somethin' like a hammerin'.

And then there was a chantin' in rhythm with the blows.

I lumbered up with a yawn and a stretch, my knee still high from all the heat. I limped along to the back, where I found the whole clan in *yu-ka-tas* and headbands emblazoned with red suns.

Mama-san and grandma-san was kneelin', kneadin' rice and water into a thick creamy paste, which they'd set on a wooden block in clumps the size of softballs. These Suki proceeded to flatten with swings of a great wooden mallet, the kids foldin' the sides to the center and flippin' the clumps between swings.

Suki seen me between swings. "Make rice cakes," she said with a big Suki grin.

"*O-ha-yō!*" the kids cried.

"Rice cakes," I said. "Why not buy 'em?"

Grandma said, without missin' a beat, "*Yap-pa-ri* . . ."

I finished it with her, my favorite line. *Unless one's Japanese* . . .

I went up to my futon and rested my leg till Suki come up and we went for a walk.

"Happy?" she asked.

"Sure," I said. "'Cept . . ."

"What?"

"I don't think they like me."

Suki assured me they like me to death, but life in the country is *i-so-ga-shii*.

I said, "Fine, but tell your papa I wanna go *fishin'*."

Show him that I'm a real man.

"*Hai*," she said, then tugged my hand.

It was time to go home and be *i-so-ga-shii*.

Suki's hair, washed out again, was almost black and brushed shag flat, with only a few stubborn curls poppin' up.

I said, "I mean it. Tell him."

"*Hai.*"

Ma-da- yo-i no ku-chi da zo

Word for word, It's the mouth of the evenin'.

Or: Hey, bud, the night is young.

The men took turns yellin' this when I upped and walked out of the second big bash.

But I'd had enough of the party and split, sick of 'em roarin' for *sa-ke* and beer, sick of the women all runnin' like slaves, sick of 'em ignorin' me and cuttin' up in Japanese like I wasn't there.

But mostly I was sick to death of the other thing I sensed last night, that there was somethin' *on* I couldn't draw a bead on.

"Hank?" Suki asked me.

"Y'all tell that man I'm goin' *fishin'*!"

Ma-da de-su

Not yet.

The next mornin' I was awakened by a powerful series of shrieks from the yard.

The room was still about pitch-black.

I was goin' *fishin'*, though. I was gettin' my ass on that boat, that was fact.

I quick-limped to the window to tell 'em, and seen:

Suki and papa-san sparrin' and grapplin', shriekin' as they punched and kicked. Fists, elbows, feet, was flyin', some of 'em parried and some of 'em used as launchin's for powerful throws.

I yelled through the window, "I'm comin'!"

But when I got down she was waitin' alone.

"*Ma-da de-su*," Suki said. "Papa say tomorrow."

"Yeah. What's goin' on here, Suki?"

She throwed her arms around me. "Papa think you *very* nice!"

FIVE

Suki and me just been out for a walk. Herewith the lesson continues while the women is all makin' noodles.

Three little words

The day went like the day before, the hive hummin' from git-go.

The night went like the nights before. The booze flowed like the nights before, in the same quantity, at the same speed. The men roared like the nights before, the women rushin' in and out, it seemed, in the same order. The jokes sounded the same and each man laughed the same, just as often, just as loud, as he done the nights before.

I sat there shiverin' in my *yu-ka-ta* and, just like the nights before, I felt that underpinnin'—like they was lookin', in their eyes, over a wall at my knee and my face, then climbin' back down, three invisible men, to discuss me, unheard, on their side of the wall. I begun to wonder, just like the nights before. But, unlike the nights before, my head was startin' to pound.

I had a strong jaw. I touched my jaw. Women simply loved my jaw.

My cheekbones was finely chiseled. I touched my cheekbones. They felt fine.

I touched one eye. My eyes was fine. My eyes was strong and hooded.

I touched my nose. My menacin', macho, and much-busted nose. My nose was mine. I liked it fine.

I touched my nose—

and *seen* 'em.

Papa shook his head again. He said somethin' that sounded like "*San-nen . . .*"

Grandpa agreed, with a shake of his head. This time I caught "*San-nen ka-ta . . .*"

Uncle looked sadder than both men combined as he studied my nose and my knee.

And this time I caught it all: "*San-nen ka-ta ho.*"

Nose.

Knee.

Knee.

Nose.

I glowered at papa, then uncle, then grandpa, while touchin' my knee, then one side of my nose.

"*Mot-to sa-ke!*" uncle cried, pointin' at my glass. More booze. Papa clapped his hands and roared.

Then I clapped mine, roarin' "No!" and stoppin' the three women cold at the door.

Oh-oh. Crazy *gai-jin-san*.

"Hank?" Suki said, at the door. "What wrong?"

"Y'all know damn well what's wrong," I said. "Kindly send the other ladies back into the kitchen. And get yourself out here right quick."

This took a little doin', but Suki was very persuasive. I knowed that she knowed. And she knowed that I knowed.

And the fireworks was to begin.

She took her place beside me.

The three men didn't say nothin'.

She just said my name.

"Tell me what *san-nen ka-ta ho* means, please, if y'all would be ever so kind."

"*San-nen* . . ." Suki's voice broke. "Who say *san-nen—O-tō-san!*"

Papa throwed up his hands, his red face nearly glowin' in the dark. He said Sorry to Suki and Sorry to me, bowin', bowin', bowin'.

"*O-tō-san!*" Suki cried again. I couldn't catch the rest.

"*Yap-pa-ri* . . ." papa pleaded.

Right. Unless one's Japanese.

"Hank," she said, "it nothing. Only proverb."

"Please tell me what this proverb *means*, if y'all would be ever so nice."

The three men looked down, like three kids caught at school.

Suki said, soft, slow, "Warrior only show feeling—one time in three year."

I nodded, touchin' the side of my nose while the boys counted their toes with real feelin'.

"Your daddy thinks *you* all done this to me."

"Hank—please to understand. Cannot tell the church to them. I make worry. They be old."

"I see," I said. I touched my knee.

"Cannot tell you fight for me. Or I make papa *giri*."

"What?"

"That be equal obligation. *Giri* very difficult. It—"

I said, "Tell 'em and leave out the church part. Just tell 'em I fought like a man."

I was able to follow the tellin' by the men's reactions, rangin' from low grunts to gasps. When Suki got to the nose part, the three men sat bolt upright.

"*O-wa-ri,*" Suki said. "Ending story. Now okay."

I half thought we was fine, for a second.

But Suki's papa waved his hand and snorted out somethin' that sounded real crude.

Suki tugged at my *yu-ka-ta.* "Come."

"What did your daddy," I asked her, "just say?"

O-tō-san answered for himself, jabbin' his finger and fuck the polite.

"*Bull-lu shit-tu,*" papa said. No white pussy defended his daughter.

I said, "Is that a fact."

Suki tugged at my *yu-ka-ta* twice. But I shook my head and pointed to the rocker by her daddy's side.

She shuffled over, her head down, sayin' my name one last time.

The men started rockin' their rockers. They inched forward on their butts to get a closer watch.

My rocker started movin' too.

Rumpasqueak.

Rumpasqueak.

Ted, I thought, don't fail me now.

I set my right hand on the arm of the rocker, got a good grip with three fingers and thumb, leavin' the little one loose. I reached across with my left hand, encirclin' and raisin' the finger. I raised it slow and raised it smooth until it had nowhere to go and I could feel the joint protestin' Man, don't do this crazy thing.

San-nen ka-ta ho.

My forehead felt half-bathed in sweat, my knees was almost knockin'.

I couldn't stop the shakin'.

And I couldn't stop the sweatin'.

And my voice, I knowed, betrayed me.

But them wasn't the rules of the game here and now. Savin' face was everythin', the only thing they cared for. And so I put all the strength I possessed into guardin' the passes all over my face and lettin' nothin', not a trace of feelin' anywhere, slip through.

"Tell your papa he owes me a *giri* if I show him *san-nen* true," I said.

Suki told him true, for sure. A cloud of black and red begun darkenin' *o-tō-san*'s face. And his eyes was flashin'.

"*San-nen ka-ta—*" he begun.

But before he'd got quite past the middle, I yanked the finger back clear to my wrist.

I imagine the thumb would've made lots more noise. But the crack, while not quite deafenin', was truly obscenely disgustin'.

Papa's face showed nothin'.

Or grandpa's face.

Or uncle's.

I knowed if mine showed anythin' I'd see the reflection in theirs.

I had to get out of my body and fast, 'cause my finger was screamin' and I couldn't think how to guard all the passes at once on my face.

I let go of the finger, which flopped to half mast, then stuck there, crazy-quiverin'.

The quiverin' didn't matter none.

It wasn't my *u-chi.* It wasn't my world.

I didn't trouble with the tears. Who could tell 'em from the sweat pourin' down my cheeks?

I just knowed it would freak papa proper if I broke that finger fresh without even usin' my hand.

My finger stood there screamin' and shakin' like a leaf.

I seen the start of a faint smile form on papa's lips. I knowed my face was a hare's breath from truly beginnin' to crumble.

I thought: Finger, I command y'all, circle on over, and all by yourself, touchin' that nail to the back of my wrist.

The finger screamed *I can't, I can't.*

With my mind, I yanked at it, screamin' at it *Up! Back!*

I was proud of that finger. That finger had soul. It screamed and fired rockets, yeah, but it climbed and continued to climb.

That finger got half upright, stretched tight as the string of a bow.

Then what I done was let it go.

It shot down like an arrow and cracked on the way.

I had it now, that finger.

We got a rhythm goin', like one of them piano clocks that tick-tock without tellin' time. My finger, havin' learned the moves, shot down and up in its own song:

Crick!

Crack!

Crick!

Crack!

Suki started babblin', with grandpa and uncle in tow. But so far I'd only succeeded in wipin' that sly smile off papa's face.

Crick!

Crack!

Crick!

Crack!

Up and down my finger whacked, my *yu-ka-ta* soakin' up the sweat along with the gorge that I hadn't choked down.

Crick!

Crack!

Crick!

Crack!

That finger sung, and continued to sing, while our rockers rumped and squeaked, everyone freakin' 'cept papa.

I started singin' to myself to keep my mind from driftin'.

Oh, Suzanna—
Crick!
Doncha cry for . . . me—
Crack!

I made it through one chorus, my voice itself crickin' and crackin'.

Then Suki's lips was movin'.

Then grandpa-san's and uncle's.

Then they was singin' soft and low the handful of words that they knowed, slappin' the arms of their rockers.

And papa's lips was tryin'—but no sound was comin' out.

"*Gi-ri,*" I said with a crick and a crack, wavin' my left hand like Lawrence Welk's wand.

"Ohhh . . ." papa started.

Crick!

Papa croaked: "Su-san-nuh . . ."

"Good!" I made the next word with my lips.

"Don't, uh . . . cry!" papa howled.

And we was off and runnin', slappin' the arms of our rockers.

When the tune was over, the men laughed like three devils. Then suddenlike, all at once, they remembered the tale told by Suki. They rubbed their noses, horrified, their rockers froze cold between rocks.

Crick!

Crack!

My finger stopped.

"*Yap-pa-ri gai-jin ja nai to . . .*" I gasped.

Unless one is a *gai-jin.*

And then I passed out.

SIX

And so this mornin', crack of dawn, they come knockin' at my door to take the *gai-jin* fishin'.

I rolled over with a groan, draggin' my hand out from under the quilt. They'd reset the finger—while I was out like a light, praise the Lord—and bandaged it real pretty.

I yawned and waved the finger. Fact was, I hated fishin'. And now I didn't have nothin' to prove.

"*Ma-da de-su,*" I told 'em.

Not now, guys, maybe tomorrow.

I spent the mornin' writin'.

After lunch I walked and spoke with Suki by the sea. She told me *o-tō-san* can't figure me none, but said I was like samurai as he carried me into the house. While they was settin' my finger he sung so I wouldn't cry out in my sleep.

We had a high time on the porch after dinner. And, at my request, the women was allowed to join us. When, of course, they wasn't takin' turns fetchin' us this thing and that. Mostly what we done was sing, for the clan had a powerful yen for old songs, of Southern and Western persuasion.

They knowed the tunes.

I taught the words.

We started with "Home on the Range."

By evenin's close, I knowed we had us a genuine balance of power.

It was time to obtain the clan's blessin'—I mean, for the upcomin' pokin'.

I looked at Suki, called her name.

"*Hai?*" she said, her face shinin'.

"Does your papa-san and mama-san know where we're headin' tomorrow?"

"*Hai,*" she said. "It be okay."

Papa asked her what I said.

Suki bowed, translatin'.

"Boone-san," he answered. First time he ever used my name. "*Ii de-su. Wa-kat-ta?*"

It is fine. Understand?

"*Ii de-su,*" the others said in a resoundin' chorus.

SEVEN

It's definitely Friday and we're on the Shin-kan-sen, on our way to Tokyo and to our Love Hotel.

Across Japan, Suki says, there's some ten thousand—four thousand of 'em bein' in Tokyo alone. On account of apartments and homes is so small. The Kentucky Fried hotels of sex.

The Love Hotel to which we're bound is famous through all of Japan, Suki says. And the room we'll be in for the night is the prize, a magical spot for new couples. She reserved it weeks ago, payin' the nine thousand yen.

I gotta tell her soon about the Colonel and the dough.

And she's got somethin' on her mind regardin' her and Kuni.

But this weekend is ours. After all we been through, we got this much comin'.

—I wish she'd put that thing away. Jack's letter, rerouted,

was slapped in our hands as we was leavin' the house. She's starin' at the envelope like it's holdin' some terrible curse.

I should've throwed it in the trash.

We ain't supposed to read it.

And we ain't *gonna* read it.

Man, I dunno why but it gives me the creeps.

EIGHT

Suki's in the Minnie Room—I swear, there's a Minnie and Mickey—brushin' her hair, maybe scentin' her skin, doin' whatever a woman must do to equal herself to this place.

I reckon that'll take a while.

I ain't sure it's possible.

The lightin' is mood-sensitive, the mirrored walls and ceilin' throbbin', now in amber, now in pink.

I'm writin' at a marble desk with Snow White and the Seven Dwarfs hand-painted all over the legs.

We got a Pluto vendin' box that sells condoms and dildos and sex toys.

And there's the main attraction: the five-step climb up Dumbo's head, with a greased slide down his trunk to the bed. I sure love them Prince Charmin' sheets.

To the right of the bed, on the wall, there's a box shaped like some fairy-tale castle. If a couple breaks all records for changin' the lights in this room, somethin' wonderful's promised to happen.

I ain't sure I want to know.

—Sounds like Suki's finishin'.

Sorry, Jack. Every man for himself.

NINE

She come out in this long silk kimono. It was a fine misty yellow, with silver and mint julep threaded into small clusters of pines. Over her heart, in gold, a heron hovered, wings spread to the full.

Them is the colors I seen by the sea when her mama packed it.

I wish to God I had the skill to paint the way it looked last night, that mood light throbbin' pink to red and then the red to scarlet.

I couldn't get enough of her.

I tried, but I just couldn't.

I lost count of the number of times we slid, laughin' and pantin', down ole Dumbo's trunk onto that wavy and rollickin' bed.

We was like kids in some X sex cartoon, tryin' this and tryin' that, throwin' more coins in ole Pluto's machine.

Our last time was our best time, the mirrors all around us blazin' with rocketlike flashes of color.

When we come, the record box erupted in a trumpetin':

We're off to see the wizard!

Make 'em scream when they come, Ted would say, and they're yours. If Ted was here I'd tell him No, love 'em proper and they whisper Wow. That's the thing.

Suki's off shoppin' for books on the church. We're on the city outskirts and she's travelin' by cab. I reckon she'll be fine.

I'm in a little *kis-sa-ten* not far from where we spent the night.

I got a table in the back, overlookin' a rock and moss garden.

I got Jack's letter before me.

I know I gotta read it.

But I keep hearin' two things Suki said as we was leavin' Disneysex.

I was struttin', real cock o' the walk, her hand in my hand, and I said, "I believe I have just learned the meanin' of *no inhibitions.*"

Suki smiled, kind of sad. "No sex uptighting," she agreed. "But same thing in other way."

I asked her what she meant.

She pointed to a cherry blossom tree. For a few weeks every year, Suki said, the blossoms just blaze, a perfection of light. And all across the country families and lovers will gather, sittin' on blankets, to watch. The blossomin' is cherished 'cause it's gone in the wink of an eye.

Like the freedom lovers know before they get hitched in Japan. Before they end up in a couple of rooms, the husband sewed into his navy-blue suit, workin' six days a week, fourteen hours a day, while the woman sits home with her babies, *i-so-ga-shii* 'round the clock.

The second thing she told me was, "In Tokyo, if look can see them seeing me *bu-ra-ku-min*."

And when I looked I surely did, thinkin' before they was just seein' me. But seein', really seein', now that their eyeballs was callin' her nigger.

So I sit here in this *kis-sa-ten*, lookin' all around me. Mostly what I see is suits sittin' together in pairs and in packs, and talkin' low in urgent tones while lookin' at their watches—and bein' served and served and served and bowed to by the women.

I'm gettin' my girl out of here.

But first things first.

Jack's letter.

TEN

Dear Hank,

I'm in hell. And Kuni's the devil herself.

Words can't describe how crazy or ugly and vile it's getting.

Usually, I hear them before I turn onto the drive: Kuni screaming at the cat, Peaches yowling and hissing at her. Now and then I'll find them growling softly at each other—hackles up, eyes blazing, bodies coiled and ready to pounce.

Each night it's the same. When I open the door, the cat half flies across the room and jumps into my arms. And Kuni's off and running on one of her hellish assaults.

I can't begin to imagine what happens here while I'm away. Even the memory of how it began is growing vague in my mind.

This much I seem to remember. On our way home after dinner that night, we were skipping along like a couple of kids, planning for our wedding. We'd already set the date: January in Japan. I reminded her that she'd need X rays . . . and Kuni went out of her mind.

She left me cold, just packed and split.

I was left with nothing, you off with Suki and me here alone, not even knowing what hit me. How had it happened, that switch at the airport? How had the change seemed so naturally right? Nothing had ever seemed righter to me.

Hank, I'd been in heaven every minute she was here. In bed or out of bed, I'd never known anyone like her. And, in bed, on my life: the kind of magic no woman can fake.

She was gone, though.

X rays!

I went over to your place and picked up the cat. I fell asleep on the couch, Peaches purring and sniffing around. I was in a deep, deep sleep when the pounding began on the door.

She'd come back!

She threw her arms around me. "Save me!" she cried. "Marry me!"

And I was so happy and lost in her arms, I was hardly aware of the growls at my side. No more, I guess, than Kuni. Until we heard this incredible hiss . . . and saw Peaches, hair up like a porcupine's quills.

Kuni gasped, "Get rid of it!"

I don't know which of the two looked scared more.

"Get rid of it!" she begged me.

But I couldn't.

And I wouldn't: I promised you I'd look after the cat.

And—I'd been a wimp all my life around girls.

I took a stand.

I told her No.

It looked like she might go again . . . until I had this brainstorm. I put Kuni up for a couple of nights in the downtown Hyatt.

Give her time to settle down.

Give Peaches time to get used to her scent.

Kuni was fine in the Hyatt. She was loving and gentle and . . . Kuni again.

Meanwhile, Peaches was coming along. At least, I liked to think so. That first night she got so crazy—hissing at the very space where Kuni had been standing!—I locked her in the bathroom. I hung a few things in the closet—Kuni's raincoat and some dresses—and let Peaches out in the morning before setting out for The Store. And, by and large, from there on, Peaches appeared to be fine—with one notable exception, when I heard growling and ripping, and turned to see her swinging from Kuni's favorite dress.

Women, I thought. Ah well, somehow we'd work it out.

And, in my heart, I thought we would . . . right up till the minute we got to the door.

I said to Kuni, "Be nice to her, dear."

And Kuni said sweetly, "Yes, darling, I will."

As we walked in, the cat came out, eyes a baleful yellow.

"Smile," I said.

Kuni tried . . . then screamed "You bitch!" and went after the cat.

That was the moment, I think, of the *snap* of all restraints within Kuni.

That was the sense—of a snap . . . then a leakage of little dark things . . . then a flood.

Little remarks, at first scattered, then strung together and cracked like a whip while she was unpacking and pacing the room.

The apartment was too small. She'd feel like a prisoner, trapped in this hole.

The furniture was ugly.

My TV was black-and-white.

My phone was old and didn't work.

And everything I had was cheap, including the clothing I wore.

I was too stunned to argue. God help me, I sat there and took it. For in between the blasts and snaps there'd be these spells of *sweetness*.

Once she stopped, her fingers to temples, looking shocked by the state she was in. "Oh, darling," she said. "Please to— Wait, I can show!"

Kuni scrambled through a suitcase, digging for something

through skirts, slips, and tops. She came out with a small pocket planner and showed me this last week in June.

"There," she said. She turned the page, showing me July. "And *here*," she said. "And that be all. Please to wait for Kuni —please!"

What in God's name was she saying—five more weeks of mad abuse? Before I had a chance to ask, she was off, unpacking, snapping at the hissing cat, alternating blasts at me and everything I owned with declarations of her love.

Finally, in tears, she crashed, insisting she sleep on the couch.

I fell asleep, in tears myself, not knowing what I'd gotten into.

But in the morning, when I woke, she was sitting beside me, my coffee in hand. In her other hand, the calendar had a dark X through last night.

"See, darling?" she asked me. "Soon!"

She saw me off with a hug and a kiss.

I wagged a finger sternly. "The cat stays."

"Yes, dear," she said.

"Be nice to it."

"I promise."

"And be nice to me tonight."

Kuni giggled. "You're the boss."

"And don't you forget it."

I took off, thinking Whew, that's that. But halfway down the drive I heard her screaming "Fuckbitchcat!"

I'd just settled into my desk at The Store when the phone rang shrilly.

She'd found my savings passbook and learned what I had in the bank.

They heard her screaming two aisles away.

I sat there and took it while Kuni went on, calling me failure and jerkoff and bum. And while I sat there taking it and reasoning and crying, I tried to reassure myself:

It's like she's in a state of shock . . . She's sick in some way I can't fathom . . . If I could only find a clue . . .

The day at work was hellish. I couldn't think, or write a word. Over and over again in my mind the horrid tapes replayed: Kuni's screams, her digs, her jibes. And while the tapes played, on my console I pictured her chasing the cat through the house with a knife.

But, rounding our block, I heard nothing.

Turning onto the drive, not a sound from the house.

On the stoop, not a peep.

I stepped in. There she was in a yellow housedress . . . table set, candles glowing, dinner cooking on the stove.

She ran over to give me a hug.

She smelled divine. So did the place, of soap and pine and incense.

"Oh, Jack," she said. "Please to forgive me that call. I only want us to be happy. I don't mind if we be poor."

"Kuni," I said, "will you stop that?"

"I don't mind you wear Fruit of the Loom."

"I said *stop.*"

"Jack, look, come over here." Kuni tugged me by the hand. She was smiling, but to tell the truth I thought she looked kind of crazy. She showed me our summery dinner. "I find bargains in that store. Spam and rice and Boston beans."

"Christ almighty, Kuni— Wait." I'd just remembered something. I asked her, very slowly, "Kuni, where's the cat?"

"*What?*" That loopy smile disappeared. Her eyes turned hard as flint stones. "I cook you *dinner.*"

"Where's the cat?"

"I scrub—I clean!"

"Where *is* it?" I snapped.

She snapped back, twice as hard, "On my knees—scrub-woman! Poor people can't have maid!"

"Listen, you—"

"Look!" she shrieked. She whipped open a drawer to show me: Every bag in the place had been flattened and stacked. Loose rubber bands were in a box; paperclips, another. "I waste nothing! Poor people must eat!"

And I shrieked back, for the first time. "Where the *fuck's* the cat!"

She came to, abruptly.

She shrugged, pointing over her shoulder, and went back to cooking our poverty stew.

She'd pointed to the bathroom.

The Kuni-clean door was shut tight.

With a lump in my throat, I called "Peaches?"

"Hrumph!" Kuni snorted.

"*Peaches?*" I called, my heart starting to thump. I couldn't walk over there slowly enough.

"Cuntcat," Kuni muttered.

"Peaches!" I cried. I stopped short at the door, terrified of what I'd find.

Then I heard a muffled sound that scared me even more. And thumps.

I ran in, calling the cat's name again . . . and what I saw sent cold chills up my spine:

There was a box in the bathtub, the top weighted down with a suitcase.

Inside the box I found the cat, trussed up in a pillowcase, masking tape over its mouth. Its fur was matted flat with sweat. And its eyes were terrified.

I dropped down by the tub, the cat in my lap. My shoulders were shaking with anger and grief.

Kuni cried, "She make me! She give Kuni Evil Eye!"

"Don't you *ever* touch this cat again."

"Jack—"

"Or I'll put your nasty ass out on the street."

"Jack—"

"I mean it."

"Evil meat!" Kuni wailed, jabbing her finger at Peaches.

It would take me a book, Hank, to story this week. The nightmare goes on and gets worse by the day . . . with those scattered lulls and spells of something close to clarity. When Kuni's like Kuni. And then we can talk.

And money, money, money is what it all comes down to.

Money—and the cat.

I'm bending over backward. I've compromised on everything to help Kuni through this bad sickness.

Kuni's handling the budget.

I get an allowance: two dollars each day for the subway, sixty cents for one coffee at lunch.

I read used newspapers now, not new.

I eat poverty stew in half portions.

I shampoo every other day and change my shorts when she gives fresh ones.

I'm trying, man, I'm trying. But goddamm it to hell, the cat stays—I'm the man!

I haven't slept with Kuni, not once since she moved in.

I feel exhausted and beaten and crushed.

Last night was the worst ever. I came home to find splinters of glass on tabletops and counters—to keep the cat from jumping up, costing us more Lysol.

We had a terrible, lung-bursting row.

But this morning, when I woke, Kuni was there with her calendar.

"Wow," she said. "We made it."

Another day survived.

Now only all of July left to go!

I took the afternoon off work. I had to talk with someone.

God help me if she calls at work and finds out I'm not there.

God help me anyway.

I just can't escape the memory of the week we spent together. If I could only find the key to the real cause of her sickness . . .

Please don't think too harshly of me.

I promise you: Somehow I will protect that cat.

It's Friday. Maybe if we just hang on . . . for just another day?

> Desperately,
> Jack

P.S. Send me a number a.s.a.p. for dear "ole lady Palerno," in case of an emergency.

ELEVEN

Suki come, all excited and proud. She'd found two good church books in English.

"Please to check out," Suki said. "Look see what I fetch *you all.*"

I gave her a smile that died on my lips. And my eyes didn't do me no better.

"Hank," she said. "What bugger?"

"What?"

"What bugger you?"

That got a smile. "I believe y'all mean what's *buggin'* me?"

"*Hai*," Suki said.

So I showed her.

We drunk a lot of coffee in that tiny *kis-sa-ten* while she read Jack's letter, sometimes strugglin' with the words, sometimes unable to read through the tears.

We kept sittin' there after she'd finished. We stared at the moss garden hard.

Finally, I took her hand. "Come on. We sure got us some talkin' to do."

We had us another room booked for the night, a bit more economic but not slackin' on the effects. This room was done up galactic, with our bed as the moon under planets of lights. And a film of a rocket that launched when we come.

The rocket only took off once.

And we didn't set any records.

The lovin' was needy and hungry and quick.

And then we stayed up half the night talkin' of Jack's letter and what Suki knowed about Kuni.

The thing Suki needed to tell me, and couldn't until we was lovers, was this: It begun as a *giri*, or debt, like she'd said. On account of Kuni was her friend and helped her transform from a *bu-ra-ku-min*.

Kuni, like Suki, was over the age by which a girl's supposed to get hitched.

Kuni, like Suki, had started to wonder about gettin' out of Japan.

And Kuni, like Suki—on readin' Jack's letters—started to think: Maybe *him*.

At the start, Suki said, Jack was her Prince Charmin'. It was Romantic and Storybook Love, and the writin' of letters was heaven on earth, with her as a Kuni-type Princess. An opera-lovin' ex-o-tique.

But from the start, Suki said, she'd been tryin', her own way, to *tell* him. She sent pictures of her playin' soccer, mountain climbin', swimmin'. Jack never seemed to notice these, only pictures of her in her Kuni-type clothes. She asked him again and again, Suki said, how traditional he felt a woman should be. In her heart what she wanted was balance—not bein' a Libber like Kuni, yet wantin' some measure of freedom. Jack told her again and again not to worry. He'd help with the dishes and help clean the house and other things that Suki found somewhat horrifyin'.

She wanted some freedom—but which? And how much?

And meanwhile, in his letters, Pepper was tellin' her things about me.

And soon Kuni was tellin' her more things and showin' her Marlboro pictures.

She would've married Jack, she said, although she was feelin' attraction to me.

That's the way things are done. She had *giri* to Jack.

But one night when the girls was together, Kuni done somethin' that shocked her, somethin' that ain't often done in Japan: Kuni called her marker in.

They was sittin' in Suki's apartment, helpin' her work on her accent—when Kuni started sobbin'. She dropped to her knees and begged Suki's forgiveness, but really and truly, she just *needed* Jack. She couldn't survive, not no more, in Japan, and she couldn't live with a Marlboro Man. She needed, she just had to have, a gentle, lovin', sensitive, *liberated* American Man.

"That was it?" I asked her.

Suki bawled, "So sorry. I only want everyone happy."

"We are. But—Kuni *wanted* Jack?"

"*Hai.*"

"Kuni *wanted* a lovin' and sensitive man?"

"*Hai.*"

"Then what the hell's she up to?"

"*Wa-ka-ra-nai!*" Suki wailed.

I asked her to think about somethin'. In the year she knowed her, had Kuni ever acted—

"*Ki-chi-gai?*" Suki asked. "Kuni not be crazy. Never. Only your letters make angry."

Only me. Otherwise, Kuni was always *ya-sa-shii*, meanin'
gentle and perfect in manners and kind.

So what was the deal with the X rays?

And why the hell'd she pick on my cat?

Suki tugged at her hair and cried, *"Wa-ka-ra-nai!"*

X rays is completely routine in Japan. The people don't cotton
to pets as a rule, and got no real feelin' to speak of for cats—but
cruelty to animals? It just ain't Japanese.

"What'd she do for a livin'?" I asked.

Suki paused. *"Wa-ka-ra-nai."*

For the first time since I met her I knowed she was lyin'.

I didn't say nothin'. I just kissed her cheek.

"O.L.," Suki told me. "She be office lady. Typing, serving,
telephone."

She was lookin' at the ceilin', though. So I didn't say nothin'. I
just kissed her eye.

Suki turned, fiercelike.

"Waitress," she hissed. "She be waitress! Okay?"

There was nothin' to say, so I held her.

"If more trouble," she said, "Suki show you."

I said, "Sure. Her job don't matter."

"Kuni not crazy, I promise!"

"Shh," I said, and then we slept.

We're on the Shin-kan-sen again, back to the Sea of Japan.

Suki's sleepin' by my side, Jack's letter in her tiny hands.

We shouldn't've read it.

He warned me.

They're fine.

Goddamm it to hell, the cat's fine!

Meanwhile, my work's cut out with these books on those
crazy church bastards.

But first things first. Tonight I'm tellin' the truth about Ted
and the Colonel.

TWELVE

It's late. And I'm drunk, not with booze but relief.

I never told a human soul the things I told these people. I

spent my whole life runnin' from a past that come back like a whimperin' pup the minute I opened my arms.

After dinner we gathered, the women included, at my request, on the porch. And once our rockers got squeakin', nobody moved for the hour it took.

I couldn't tell 'em of the South and the things a man starts with, right off, in his blood. The ole rebel cry that sounds fainter each year, like somethin' played at a funeral. Memories passed, in the blood, of grandpas in their fine white suits and grandmas in high-neck dresses, sippin' juleps on the porches, talkin' real nice to their niggers. Memories of niggers, their mouths filled with piano keys, their eyes shinin' with gratitude, 'cause they had a real home with nice folks.

I couldn't tell 'em of the South and how, wrong or right, truth or lie, a man's *born* with the sense he's been stripped of his crown. The New South now belongin' to Yankee carpetbaggers —and New Niggers with axes to grind.

I wished I could've told 'em how our blood's just bubblin' from spank one with a crazy, dyin' hope that we'll all rise again.

I told 'em instead we was three at the start, my mama dyin' in givin' me birth. Me and my brother, with six years between us, and my daddy, who we called the Colonel—or else.

I told 'em I was without memories of the first couple of years of my life. So, all in all, I guessed the years was fairly uneventful. All I remembered, really, was the general impression of bein' in the presence of twin almighty powers: a mountain of a man in white and a hell-raisin', strappin' boy mountain. I thought I remembered 'em wrestlin'. I thought I remembered 'em yellin' for real. But I had no other memories. And if I had no memories of anybody holdin' me, or singin' to me, or payin' me mind, I also had no memories of the sort that was soon to begin.

I told 'em the Colonel remarried when I was either four or five. And we moved into a beautiful house like somethin' from *Gone With the Wind*. There was only two niggers, but that was okay. The livin' was easy and we was now rich.

My new mama kissed me the day we moved in. I remembered the curious smell of her breath, like somethin' that the Colonel drank, mixed with a lavender mouthwash. I remembered thinkin' Jesus, how come she ain't my grandma, 'cause her neck's all wrinkled up like a fuckin' turkey's.

I remembered her settin' me down then and throwin' her arms around Ted, who looked over his shoulder, disgust on his face, the Colonel winkin' merrily.

I remembered seein' that wink more and more, the Colonel takin' off with Ted, her on the porch with a julep.

But what I really remembered, after we moved in that house, was the sense that I'd only just opened my eyes and was suddenly stuck in a war.

The Colonel and Ted, they both bloomed in that house, baskin' in the luxury of bein' real lords of the land.

I knowed my new mama was feelin' lost too. But she had herself a right powerful crutch, leavin' me, a small boy, with no crutch against Ted.

I told 'em how Ted seemed to grow in power, size, and cruelty, not by the year, but by the day, like he was bein' watered by the power of that house.

It was war for affection. And war for attention. War for the right to just breathe. Like every ounce of air I used subtracted from his power.

At first the war was waged with slaps, on the top and the back of the head. Then with punches, some fierce, to the gut. If I got a hug bigger than he got. Or if the nigger shined my shoes a half second longer.

I'd cry and tell the Colonel, who'd shake his head, disgusted. And then they'd go off huntin', or wrestlin' in the yard, my new mama watchin' 'em, rockin' away.

They growed and growed, the two of 'em, in cruelty and stature—Ted sproutin' vertical, the Colonel horizontal.

I remembered how sometimes my mama fought back. She'd see 'em out there funnin' and throw her iced drink at the porch. "In the bedroom! Now!" she'd roar. And the Colonel would turn with this shit-eatin' grin. "Duty calls," he'd say to Ted.

But mostly what she done was rock, watchin' the two of 'em growin'.

And mostly what I done was hide and try to grow up big enough to keep from gettin' whupped. I growed by painful inches. And continued to get whupped. I found me a cat that I kept in my room. The cat took good care of me when I got whupped, lickin' my tears away, purrin'.

And in the shadow of my room, one day I begun drawin' pictures.

The pictures surprised me. They come with real ease. They was crude and childlike. But from the start I knowed certain things—like how to use shadows to make a form true.

I drawed Ted and the Colonel. The Colonel in white. The Colonel half-naked and wrestlin' with Ted. Ted slidin' down the banister. Ted comin' out of the shower, buck naked, with three inches at least more than me.

I told 'em how Ted found that one and pitched me out a window, after fixin' my nose, back, and throat with his boot.

And I told 'em how, from that day on, I tried to make it water me—I mean the house—with its power. I couldn't beat 'em, not hid in the shadows, so I tried to join 'em by bein' more Ted.

I got out there and wrestled and got my ass whipped.

I hit back and they loved it, the Colonel and Ted, blood spoutin' again from my nose and my mouth.

I set drawin' aside 'cause I wasn't no faggot. I yelled at the niggers and fought in the streets.

White trash and proud of it—'cause we was fuckin' *rich* white trash.

I told 'em how we found my mama swingin' one day in the attic.

Eston, the kitchen nigger, was screamin' "Lawd God! No! Mas' Boone!"

And the Colonel went runnin', with us on his heels.

We smelled the shit first from the base of the stairs.

And there she was, still swingin', her fat tongue like some horrible slug stickin' out.

The nigger, spooked, was useless.

So the Colonel said to Ted, "Cut her down. She's gettin' ripe."

Ted, then seventeen and bigger than the Colonel, whispered, "We got us some talkin' to do."

"I said cut her down," said the Colonel.

Ted smiled. Then he moved so fast I didn't know quite what was happenin'. He popped the Colonel twice hard in the mouth, swung around behind him, and hauled him off by the hair, screamin' and thumpity-thumpin' downstairs.

Twenty minutes later, as I was still sittin' there watchin' her swing, I heard footsteps comin' behind me.

They seemed too soft to be any man's steps who'd yet figured into my life.

I sat there watchin' the ole woman hang. And then I felt, real gentlelike, these fingers in my hair.

I looked up and Ted was smilin', Christ, almost like a brother.

He had a satchel slung over one shoulder, a shotgun in his right hand.

"I think y'all will find the Colonel agreeable now to a talkin'," he said. "Go on down and get what's yours or blow his fuckin' head off."

I asked Ted what was happenin', where he was goin' and—

"Fuck if I know. Maybe I'll go in the army and do me some killin' the way a *man* kills. But I've had it to here with the Colonel's bullshit. Now, go on down there and take your share. And fuck his damn comin'-of-age shit."

Ted left me there with that corpse on the rope still makin' its creepy half circles.

I looked down at the shotgun he'd set by my side.

My share of what? What was *comin' of age?*

I run down to fetch the Colonel, 'cause we had to cut the body down. The ole woman was dead and this just wasn't right.

He had his boots up on his great cherry desk, his bulk leanin' back in a black leather chair. He was puffin' on a cigar and caressin' a bottle of rye on his lap.

I said "Sir!" I was twelve and my heart was breakin'.

"My soul," the Colonel said. "That boy is an absolute ripper. He'd've done it, just like me. Blowed my fuckin' head clear off."

"Daddy," I cried. "Colonel—mom—"

The Colonel wheeled his chair around, chucklin' softly to himself.

The niggers cut the body down while I was off bawlin' away.

At the readin' of the will I learned what the *comin' of age* was about. On account of their special agreement, Ted's share of the inheritance was flowin' as of then: an allowance of twenty thousand a year, a million when he reached thirty. Wherever he lived and whatever he done.

My allowance would start when I turned twenty-one. Providin' I lived in Atlanta and helped manage family affairs.

I was the Colonel's new nigger. And I couldn't describe to the clan the next years. Except to say the years was filled with my efforts to please him, my runnin' away, and my shame-faced and teary returns. I got myself throwed from one school, then another, and got into some powerful scrapes with the law. But none of it impressed him none. He'd bail me out, then turn his back and get on with his principal genius: the unendin' multiplyin' of the ole woman's blood money.

No one knowed any more just how much the blood money was up to. Or the scope of the Colonel's investments.

But by the by he found a way to get my ass totally out of his sight, no longer bein' reminded of Ted. Or where the blood money derived from.

I was given a few of his slum holes to run. And this, at eighteen, I proceeded to do for a free apartment and four hundred dollars a month. I dealt with the Colonel by phone.

Like clockwork my allowance come, hand-delivered, cashier's check, the day I turned twenty-one.

And there ain't no doubt: In four more years a check for a mil will arrive.

I told the clan Ted served in Nam and come back a lunatic proper. He busted my nose over nothin' again, then demanded I put up my dukes like a man. Which I done, 'cause I'd growed in the years he was gone. I screamed at him to try it. He looked at me and looked at me, bobbin' and weavin' before him. And Ted, who wasn't scared of nothin', certainly not my bad self there and then, done somethin' so un-Ted-like it took my breath away. Ted the unbeatable, Ted the unconquered, whispered "Tired" and shuffled off. Soon after, he moved to New York.

So here I am, I told the clan, your future son-in-law. A fuckin' millionaire-to-be with no skills but the one he's still scared of. Can't paint or I might be a faggot. Yeah, I told 'em, here I am, the great muscle-bound, nose-eatin' *gai-jin*, who can break his own finger and thump it and sing, but can't admit to anyone where he comes from, who he is. I just work for this "Mrs. Palerno." A real happy-go-lucky and fun-lovin' guy.

When I was done, we sat a spell and nobody said nothin'.

I'd told the clan near everythin', 'cept what happened to that cat. Which I found I couldn't do, scared I might jinx Peaches.

I waited while *o-tō-san* chewed over the story I'd told him.

Finally, he looked at me and said somethin' in Japanese. Soft and straight and tender.

Suki translated. *"O-tō-san* humbly ask what you want."

"Your daddy," I said, "'s a smart fella."

"He *o-tō-san,*" Suki said.

"Tell him I'm askin' to marry your ass and tell my ole man fuck the money."

Suki smiled and started to tell him.

But *o-tō-san* raised his hand. He looked straight at me and said *"Hai."*

I scratched my head. "I thought—"

"Papa no need English," Suki said, "to hear your heart."

Good night.

THIRTEEN

Monday mornin'. Bright and early the postman delivered a short note from Jack, resignin' the joys of the heaven he's in. Kuni, the good Kuni, 's come back again. And now she's makin' up to Jack for all the woe she caused him.

Jack says he never knowed a woman could do the things Kuni does in the sack. She don't care about money. Just bein' with Jack is all she really cares for. Jack figures it was just a breakdown that week, the shock of changin' countries. He says Kuni looks five years younger.

I dunno.

I just dunno.

I can't help feelin' that somethin' is wrong in some way that's worse still than it looks.

Let's see what the mail brings next.

Right now I got me two church books to read.

FOURTEEN

Here's what I got to show for two days fuckin' work.

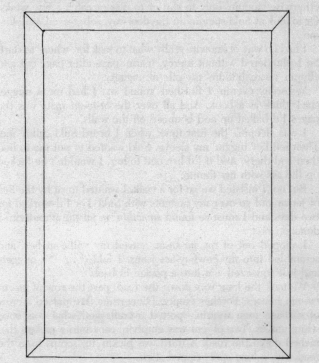

That's a portrait of the *gai-jin* in a snowstorm of bad luck, with his thumb clear up his ass.

That's right, I got nothin'.

For two days I plundered them books on the church, scarcely pausin' to eat or to come up for air.

I read 'em like the Colonel, tearin' out pages and clippin' out parts, stackin' the nuggets I'd clipped by my side.

The family looked right horrified. But nobody troubled the *gai-jin*, who was clearly engaged on a mission from God. The more I thought about it, the less I could abide the thought of women crushin' men.

I didn't bathe. I didn't shave. I ate what they left at the door, otherwise stoppin' only to shit or to piss or catch a few winks. Or to look at Suki standin' in the doorway, sober-eyed, watchin' me.

I had no way of knowin' really what to look for, where to start. So I plundered without mercy, tearin' page after page out and clippin' away, buildin' my pile of nuggets.

Yesterday evenin' I finished 'round six. I had me a nugget stack thick as a book. And all over the *ta-ta-mi* mats was the pages I'd balled up and bounced off the walls.

I was sleepin', the first time, when I heard Suki callin' me. Then felt her tuggin' my sleeve. Suki wanted to put me to bed then and there. And if I'd listened to her, I wouldn't be fucked up the ass with my thumb.

But no, I insisted we go for a walk. I wanted to sit by the Sea of Japan and go over my nuggets with Suki. For I'd worked for two days and I must've found *somethin'* in all the plunderin' I done.

I slipped out of my *yu-ka-ta*, waved my willie at her, and scrambled into my cowboy-ass jeans. I folded up the nuggets and just squeezed 'em into a pocket in back.

We took the long way down the road, past the row of *bu-ra-ku-min* houses. Porches empty. Dinnertime. We passed a crew of garbage men wearin' spotted overalls and what was once white gloves. Two of 'em was emptyin' cans into a pickup that inched down the road. A third was pickin' up scraps from the road with a long spiky-tipped stick.

They bowed to us.

We bowed to them, holdin' our breath till we'd passed.

"Them boys is workin' late," I said.

"Volunteer," Suki said. "Fishing time all day."

We walked a stretch, then took a turn that led us on down to the sands. Fifty yards, we found a bench, where I sat Suki down and said, "I know I got somethin'. I gotta have somethin'. Ain't nothin' left of them books— Oh my God!"

I sensed it first. A great lightness where the weight of the nuggets should be.

Then I felt it with my hand, the shockin' absence of nuggets.

I looked down the beach, rainin' curses on life and my idiot brain.

Suki was tougher. "Hank, hurry!" she cried, and she was off and runnin', with the babblin' *gai-jin* in tow.

We searched high and low for them nuggets, retracin' every step we took.

But finally, at Suki's house, we heard that garbage truck shift gears and roar happily off in the night.

We went back to our bench by the Sea of Japan, sea gulls laughin' overhead, and we sat there till the light was gone and the air was just too cold to breathe.

Suki prodded me hard to remember.

I tried. But I hadn't read none of the nuggets clear through. All I done was plunder, clip, on catchin' the hope of a glitter.

The harder she prodded, the surer I felt that all of them nuggets was fool's gold.

"Please to tell all can remember!" she cried. "Tell now before forgetting-time!"

What the hell. I tried. I said:

—In nineteen-fuckin'-somethin', the Ma-ka-ha-ri church was formed by somebody or other who come to be known as *O-Sensei*. The Supreme Teacher. The Savior. Who come from some village, went up to some mountain, and had his ass spoke to direct by the Lord.

—In nineteen-sixty-fuckin'-somethin', when *O-Sensei* croaked, membership was somethin' like about a hundred thou.

—Today, under his widow, the ole croaker bitch in Kyoto, that figure's now close to a mil.

—The Ma-ka-ha-ri's claim to fame is the hand jive that caused us such grief. With the official hand jive, they claim they can exorcise all kinds of evil spirits, as well as heal diseases and enhance the taste of food.

—Bodies and things collect poisons, they claim—the air we breathe bein' filled with chemical pollution and also the sins of past lives. What the hand movin' does is melt poisons and shock the spirits and sins to the open. Where Ma-ka-ha-ri counselin' can melt 'em the rest of the way.

—There's spots everywhere in the body where the poisons

congregate. The hand jive begins with the forehead—behind which, on the head of a pin, a man's Primary Soul does reside. The hand jive sends in spirit rays, which melt down the primary poisons that serve to protect the real demon within. The demon, thus unprotected, is set up for terrible zappin's all throughout the body.

—The church has got sworn testyments to the curin' of cancer, the meltin' of gallstones, the sproutin' of thick hair on cueball-type heads. And, for every one of them, there's ten oaths of the fixin' of toasters and cars, all with them magical moves of the hand.

—What's mostly done at meetin's is these funky exorcisms. Not some Hollywood pea soup or head-spinnin' shit. We're talkin' spirits of badgers and snakes, foxes and birds, or some grandmother's ghost. Whose possession is causin' one poverty blues or to be a bad husband or wife. And whose departin' is evidenced by a body bouncin' on its knees or climbin' the walls like a monkey.

—My head was spinnin', just tryin' to remember the nuttier nuggets I clipped. But I remembered a long one on the women these days in the church. More and more women, exposed to the West, are losin' their sexual balance, it said, afflicted by *Sexual Karma.* While dreadin' becomin' Ole Misses—unhitched at twenty-five—they find themselves equally dreadin' the future that waits as a wife in Japan. The church teaches that men was created a half-million years before women and didn't need women to breed with. They done women a favor by lettin' 'em be. 'Cause men was yang, and women ying, and yang was the cream of the crop. So the young women go to the church to get fixed, to have their karmas realigned and all the poisons melted that's causin' the dread of submittin' to men. Then they can lead right happy lives, with periodic meltdowns.

"*Ba-ka!*" Suki snapped. "Crazy church!"

I let the rest of the dust of them nuggets blow in the winds of my mind.

"So them three women broke from the church," I said. "And it ain't hard to see why. Well, all right. But how the *hell* could any woman crush a growed man's body by meltin' somethin' *in* him or exorcisin' somethin' *out?*"

"Black Magic, they say," she said under her breath.

"Black Magic, my ass," I said. "Ain't none."

I asked her again where she learned it, that jive.

Suki pounded her knee and cried out to the sea. There wasn't no connection. None. A year ago this crazy story showed up in the news: some husbands claimin' their church wives was meltin' 'em into submission. Kuni moved her hand and laughed, and Suki rolled her eyes.

"So you're sure Kuni wasn't no member?" I asked.

"No way!" Suki cried. "Kuni say they crazy."

"Do that hand jive once again."

Suki done it with a sigh.

But, really, I didn't feel nothin'.

I guessed I'd been imaginin' my feelin' relaxed in the cab. Or, who knows, she got lucky and, by accident, melted me down in one spot.

Suki tried it again.

I said, "Cut that shit out. We got nothin'. Let's eat."

On the porch I asked the men if a woman, any woman, could crush a man all by herself.

They was still laughin' when I left for bed.

—Oh, Jesus Christ almighty.

Don't pull no funky shit on me.

Suki's yellin' loud downstairs.

Says we got us a great jumbo letter from Jack.

Tell me things ain't took a turn for the worse.

FIFTEEN

Dear Hank,

God forgive me, but Peaches is dead.

For two wonderful days it was heaven, better than I can describe. There was no sweeter or more loving woman on earth than Kuni all through Sunday night. She existed to please me, she loved me completely. For two mind-blowing, beautiful days.

The two days began Friday at midnight, in the midst of our worst-ever row. Suddenly, Kuni shuddered and gave this long sigh of relief. She looked as if she'd been stretched on a rack and just then the screws had been loosened.

"Midnight," she whispered. "Saturday!"

She rose to fetch the calendar. She drew a big loopy X through the day, showing me proudly the week we'd survived.

"Oh, Jack, we're gonna make it!" She told me this over and over, kissing my eyes, cheeks, and mouth. "I was so bad, I said such things! I'm gonna make all up to you. I promise my life, Jack, I make heaven now."

I followed her, in a stunned trance, which fell from me in layers as our clothing hit the floor and the witchcraft began with her hands and her mouth.

For two days it went on.

For two days and two nights.

Forty-eight hours of laughter and love.

Hour on hour of sweetness and light, with Peaches herself, out of hiding at last, purring and watching, amazed.

Sunday night, around ten, Kuni started to feel tired. She asked if she might spend the night on the couch. For if we slept together little sleeping would get done. I said fine, I only wanted her to feel relaxed and well. Tomorrow, I said, I would ask for a raise to help ease the burden of money. And she told me again, for the hundredth time, that money meant nothing, no problem at all, as long as we just had each other. It had been a sort of seizure, what she'd been through, that was all. Cars and houses all around us, advertisements everywhere for everything she'd dreamed of.

She asked me again if I loved her.

I said Yes till my tongue started tying in knots.

She asked me if I trusted her.

I managed one last whispered Yes before we made love on the couch.

"Trust me," she said afterward. "If I be sick again, trust me."

She held up the calendar. "July, Jack. Only July and we're free. We're gonna make it!"

I gave her a hug. "You bet your life we will," I said.

She drifted off, in seconds, with the most radiant smile.

I was out in record time myself, the second I let my eyes close.

It seemed I'd barely shut them when the fireworks began. An explosion of hisses, yowls, and lights. I bolted up, thinking: I'm dreaming, please God. I saw the alarm flash one minute past twelve.

And then Peaches bounced off the table, howling, all claws, on my lap.

I screamed. And then I screamed again, seeing Kuni charge in with the broom overhead. She swung the handle like a bat, clubbing the cat through the space of my thighs.

I wrestled the broom from her. She looked insane. Her shoulders heaved as she struggled for breath.

"Kuni," I cried, "for God's sake!"

"You're a *stupid* man," she said. "You have no paintings, not one, on your walls. Do you *know* Monet? Have you *heard* of Turner? Jackson Pollock—who is *he?*"

"Kuni—this is—"

"*Crazy?*" Kuni shrieked at me. "Who is Kurosawa?"

"He—"

"Who is Tanizaki? And Pasternak? And . . ."

She went on with her crazed litany—some of the names half-familiar, most not, the assault itself so demented I didn't know how to respond.

Finally, exhausted, Kuni snorted in disgust, called me "brain-defect prick," and went back to bed.

I tossed and turned for most of the night, all senses on a red alert for the next swing of the broom.

But she was sleeping soundly when I left for work, unshaven and nearly too tired to walk. On the pillow by her head lay her little calendar with a dark X through Sunday.

I left a note: *I love you. But this will not go on. Get your act together now. And keep your hands off the cat!*

If I gave in on the cat I was beaten, I thought, in some irreparable way. Peaches stayed!

I was sleeping at my desk, in growing despair for my job. I hadn't written a word all last week. And I was too addled to think.

The phone rang.

"Jack?" she said sweetly. "It's me, darling."

I looked at my watch, yawning. Noon.

"Jack," she said, "so sorry. I didn't mean such things I said. I love you, darling. You know that. I only need little more time."

I said, "Yeah."

She said, *"Please*, Jack. I'm begging—July?"

I said, "How's Peaches?"

Kuni sighed.

I repeated the question.

"No problem," she said. Then she hung up the phone.

I don't know how I knew. Some indefinable something in her tone or in the words themselves.

I highballed it home by taxi in a lather of hysterics.

The dead silence I heard as I ran up the drive terrified me in my soul.

Through the screen door I saw the apartment in shambles, Kuni calmly sweeping up some shattered dishes off the floor.

In the center of the living room, the heavy oak dresser had been overturned. I shuddered at this new sign of the strength of Kuni's rage.

"Hello, darling!" she sang to me, going right on with her cleaning.

"Where's the cat?" I asked her.

Kuni shrugged and swept on.

"Where's the cat?"

Kuni turned, set the broom aside, and lifted the back of her T-shirt. Thick tracks of hellish claw marks ran, on both sides of her spine, from her shoulders to her waist.

Kuni turned, facing me. She was smiling terribly. "I warn you cat make Evil Eye. I tell you Peaches evil meat."

"Where's the fucking cat, you cunt!"

Kuni laughed and swept on. "No more problem," she said.

I found Peaches under the dresser, a pop-eyed, bloody fur-cake. And

SIXTEEN

There was six more pages of Jack's crazy shit. I quick-read them last six, then tore 'em to shreds.

It seemed evil to me, not just crazy and bad. It seemed evil, and biblical evil, Jack's tale.

Kuni's on the rip again, screamin' and stormin' all over the place.

But not about money now. Hell, money's fine. Money's the least of their worries.

Now it's Jack's brain that sets her off—not just what she knows that poor dumb ole Jack don't—but the size of his brow and the way his brain works. Jack's brain, Kuni swears, is the size of a pea. And the few thoughts that's in it is stupid as hell. Jack's face is dumb as a cow's, Kuni says. A mile off, it's plain as day there ain't nothin' at all goin' on in his head. He can't open his mouth without drivin' her nuts, sometimes in tears of frustration and shame, on account of the rest of her life's to be spent with an absolute moron like Jack.

On and on that letter went, Jack writin' down such things she said I'd've cut my throat before confessin'.

The worst of it was, the man knowed, as he wrote, how disgustin' it was, that damn letter.

He was cunt-struck, and knowed it, but he couldn't stop—rememberin' and hopin'. Rememberin' her bedroom ways and hopin' her *witchcraft* would come back again. He couldn't believe Kuni killed the cat cold. He seen the terrible scratches and knowed Kuni, fightin' for life, *tipped* the dresser. (Uh-huh.) Mainly, these Mondays through Fridays, Jack's paralyzed with amazement. How, he asks me—how, *how*—can any human bein' *say* such incredible things to another . . . stop a spell . . . apologize . . . point to her fuckin' calendar . . . then start up all over again? The part that ain't dead-paralyzed goes into, like, a state of check each time he tries to fight. He's checked by compassion for poor little Kuni, away from her loved ones and in a strange land . . . checked by the fear that she might be right sick . . . checked by the gnawin' sensation that it's like a riddle, her sickness, and if he could just ride his white horse to the key—

Goddamn that poor pussy-whipped bastard to hell!

And goddamn that spoiled cunt Kuni!

My cat is dead.

My cat, my cat.

It *was* an evil letter. And it's had its evil way. Them sunny days of our love by the sea and the songs on the porch with the clan—these are gone.

Now the air seems filled with sick and guilty unspoke things. That should've been me there with Kuni . . . Me, I'd've knowed what to do . . . If Suki had knowed Kuni better, she would've sensed that the woman ain't well.

Either way, we lost it, the two of us, there on the porch. When I tore the pages to pieces. And Suki wailed *"lie"* again and again.

The men was off fishin'. The women and kids, though, gathered at the screen to watch, grievin' 'cause we was their *u-chi*. And when we seen 'em we both was ashamed.

I looked at Suki.

She nodded at me.

It was time for Tokyo, to learn us some more about Kuni and fast.

We bowed to each other and then to the clan. And we sat side by side in our rockers and rocked.

We're on the Shin-kan-sen now, on our way to Tokyo.

I can't escape the feelin' that some dreadful secret of Kuni's is waitin' to spring like a jack from its box.

But—

San-nen . . .

Yeah, hang in.

Feelin' sleepy.

Close my eyes.

No, don't.

Cat dream. All these years and it's come home.

SEVENTEEN

Ted and me is in the yard, at the start of my new macho act. I'm ten and still puny, but startin' to water myself with the power that comes from that house. My drawin's behind me. I'm startin' to strut and cuss like a man at the niggers. I want my fair share of the Colonel's rough love.

We're in the yard, Ted choppin' wood, more muscles in one mighty arm than six from any circus. It's scary, the look in his eyes as he chops.

Ted don't seem to know I'm there. And I'm wishin' to God he could see me—when the kitty I'd loved in my youth, at age nine, comes over strokin' my leg with her fur, bawlin' for food and attention. She's always mewlin' these days. Always tryin' to play with me, like things is the same and I'm still only nine.

The ax goes up.

The ax comes down.

Ted's swingin' with tempered steel fury.

"Goddammit to hell," I yell, "I wish the fuckin' cat was dead!"

Ted stops swingin', mops his brow. He smiles, sweetlike, at the cat and scoops her up one-handed.

"Gooooooood kitty, attagirl." Ted sits the kitty on the stump he's been splittin' logs on. His palm presses her down to her belly, her head hangin' over the edge of the stump.

There ain't no warnin'.

Not a word.

The ax goes up and comes right down before I know what's happenin'.

And Ted holds up this spazzin' *thing*, blood spurtin' out of its neck everywhere.

He throws it down beside the head.

"That's the difference between us, boy," Ted says.

EIGHTEEN

I drifted off after settin' that down, thinkin' I'd word-whammied it, 'least long enough for a nap.

I woke up in a fever, Suki moppin' my forehead and whisperin' "Shhh."

She took the notebook from my lap and read the scene put down there.

She smiled at me, sad, real sad. "Too bad Kuni no have Ted."

"Oh yeah," I told her. "Fuck me if that wouldn't be *some* show."

Maybe when we're done with this I'll let her read the rest someday. Maybe the reason for writin's to help men and women shut up off the page.

I dunno.

I do know we're pullin' into Tokyo.

"*Gam-bat-te,*" she tells me.

Endure.

I say Yep and leave the refuge of this Comin' Place.

NINETEEN

Twilight. We took care of business in what was left of the day. We're to see Kuni's place of employment tonight, 'round when she would've been workin'.

Suki don't want to show me this restaurant or bar. She gives me these looks while we sit here and wait, like she knows in advance I won't see what *she* sees, 'cause *Yap-pa-ri* . . . I ain't Japanese.

I told her again a few minutes ago: I just wanna see for myself.

"Cannot, I thinking," Suki said. "Waitress, Water Trade—High Class."

"We'll see what we see," I said.

And here we wait.

The first thing we done on arrivin' was drop by at Kuni's buildin'. Suki'd never been in the apartment itself, which didn't surprise me somehow all that much. But she knowed what the address was, havin' walked Kuni home a fair number of times.

It was maybe a mile from her place. But the buildin' was miles from Suki's in style. A two-story affair with a fresh coat of white on cedar-trimmed stucco walls. Flower beds in full bloom under four windows in front. The walk was paved with a rainbow of stones, some shimmerin' like sapphires and rubies. To the right of the walk, on a small emerald lawn, was a circle of salmon-pink gravel, with a Japanese in coveralls arrangin' large rocks in some pattern.

We told him we come to see Kuni.

He was sorry as hell but—she wasn't at home.

We asked if we could wait a spell, knowin' the answer to that one.

Aa so, so, so. He was twice as sorry, but—Kuroki-san wasn't expected today.

We fretted and tugged at our earlobes and *So'd.* Then we had a great idea. Could we come back tomorrow?

Aa so, so, so, so, so, so! The ole man was three times as sorry. But we didn't get nowhere till six times, when he knowed there was no other way.

He was powerful sorry to tell us that Kuroki-san was in Atlanta. And he didn't know when she'd be back.

We said good for her, we'd come back in a month.

He throwed his hands up. He was licked. He said she'd phoned last week to say she wouldn't be returnin'.

But what about her things, we asked.

The ole man looked mighty embarrassed. It seemed most of her stuff had already been packed, like she'd been *plannin'* to move all along.

We said we had somethin' to send her, if he might just be kind enough . . .

It was clear we was ruinin' his day, just makin' him think of his troubles. He said that, to tell the whole sorrowful truth, she'd phoned him back again today. Said don't send her stuff to Atlanta. She thought she might be movin' on. Maybe to San Francisco.

That was all we was goin' to get from this boy, and right then all I wanted to know.

We said if he was certain' the packin' was all done . . .

Everythin', he said, 'cept . . . And there was somethin' in his eyes.

We thanked him and he thanked us and all three of us made the best bows in the land. Then we asked him for just one last favor, to help speed us along on our way.

It would help us remember Kuniko, and the wonderful times we all shared, if we could take one photo, from the outside, of her place. (It'd also help us learn which fuckin' apartment was hers.)

With a sigh, he walked us 'round. He positioned himself by the window of the bottom right apartment, the only one with shades pulled.

He said cheese in Japanese, but we hightailed it with a bow before he got the picture: We didn't have no camera.

We debated, but not long, where we ought to spend the night. In the end we decided on Suki's, where we're waitin' for darkness to fall.

She was homesick for *u-chi*.

I had calls to make.

And we're both tired of runnin'.

But despite all the growin' I done here, I still dreaded phonin' the Colonel.

I copped out was what I done, attemptin' to call killer Ted in New York. Lotta good he could've done or would've if he could've.

Ted's machine was so much like him, though, I almost felt like we'd talked:

"I ain't in. Here's the beep. Y'all know what to do."

I said "Ted . . ." Then I hung up.

I hadn't no choice now but makin' the call I'd even worse dreaded makin'.

I got Eston, the ole kitchen nig—

Jesus Christ, can't I even say nigger no more? But if Suki's a *bu-ra-ku-min* and that don't mean shit . . .

I got Eston, the ole kitchen *Negro*.

"Mas' Hank? Bless my soul!"

The Colonel wasn't in, he said. So I left a message and told Eston to scribble Urgent in red at the top. I was in Japan, I said, and left him Suki's number. Tell him, I said, he can keep the damn money if he'll check on Jack Pepper's apartment. I said, "Eston, understand this, hear? Somethin's wrong at Pepper's place. There's a woman livin' there who ain't in the lease. And she's *nuts*."

"Mas' Hank," he cried. "I'd surely go, but they done took my license at eighty. Can't drive."

I said, "Send the Colonel. It's his kind of trouble. Tell him pack a gun, in case."

Eston said he missed me dear and wished I'd come around.

I promised to look him up when I got back. And felt sorry as hell it had been so damn long.

Negro.

Yeah. Ain't as hard as I thought.

—It's gettin' close to show time.

There she is doin' that *sho-do* again, workin' the ink to a gurgly pitch.

She's doin' the short form, I reckon, on account of we're off now in minutes. But there ain't nothin' hurried about it. She's upped the pressure of the brush to shorten the thickenin' time. Her body's loose, she's real relaxed, her heart can't get much quieter. She sets the brush down for a second. Resquares the snow-white paper. Picks her brush up. Takes a breath. Works it down to her *ha-ra*. And winks.

Her brush drops down like a sword to the white.

It's different this time, I can see. It ain't like she's drawin' or tryin' to draw. Her hand looks like it's tracin' shapes that was sleepin' just under the white. And as her hand passes, them shapes is called up—dragons, rare birds, livin' things. I can't read a word of it. But this time I don't have to. Somehow I know: This work is true.

Suki sets her brush down, the trance-look fadin' from her eyes.

"Good Blood," I tell her.

"Love Blood."

She's packin' a flashlight and what tools she's got. Just in case the Water Trade don't fill my heart with glee.

Let's go.

5

BOOK SIX
JULY, 1990
SAN FRANCISCO/
TOKYO/
ATLANTA/
KYOTO

ONE

Michiko stirred. The early light amazed her every morning here. How cool and clean and fresh the air! How filled with the promise of what they might do, the church they might build here in time. And how hard to hold back the hunger . . . for the next great leap forward in power.

Slowly, she awakened to the sense of *something* in the light. An airy presentiment of good luck taking wing.

She had no way of knowing that seventeen hours away two strangers were entering the bar where she'd worked.

She could not have guessed that three hours away a man she'd met once had just minutes to live.

She knew only, as she stirred, that today, without doubt, would be *special*.

Michiko pulled the covers back, lazily eyeing her ripening breasts. Her darkened nipples stiffened as one hand drifted dreamily down to her still lusher bush.

"*Aa, maa,*" Michiko moaned. It was difficult, waiting.

Soon, her Sister told her. *Soon.*

"But I'm hungry!"

Patience.

Michiko, circling her lovebud, cried "Come!"

He appeared in the doorway in seconds, a gaunt and spectral figure, lightened daily by the pound. He was wearing an apron and chef's hat.

Michiko spread her knees and smiled.

"Come over here. Make yourself useful," she said.

Cotter took off his chef's hat. "The omelette . . ."

"Let it burn," she ordered.

He unfastened his apron. Said, "Yes, dear."

"Good boy."

She waved her hand. His shriveled cock sprang to a length she might make some small use of.

She waved again and he fell to his knees.

He remembered, vaguely, nearly warning poor—Jack?—in Atlanta, after seeing a book on that Japanese church, their hand movements much like Michiko's. He reheard himself, in that lull from her power, murmur "Jack—Don't—Ma-k—" before his resistance was melted away.

The flash was brief but troubling. Good thing he hadn't spoiled Jack's fun. Warn him? Goodness. Warn of what? Once you got past the resistance and did what you were told . . .

Michiko's fingers, in his hair, burrowed his face to her womb.

"Please me," she said. "Please me!"

He lapped and slurped and tried to breathe and yipped happily, pleased to be pleasing.

TWO

They entered the place between shows.

The room held forty-odd tables, a third of these flanking the strip to the stage. As friends of Kuni's, they'd been seated at one of these choicely placed tables.

Suki's eyes were wonderstruck; Hank's, filled with disbelief. The room was all silken plush. An art deco symphony of beige tones and pinky grays and rich amber lighting. A voluptuous marble nude fountain gurgled perfumed water, while *waitresses* serviced the tables in white tux tops with gold glitter lapels, fishnet stockings, and transparent panties.

The first "champagne" was on the house.

Pure 7-UP was Hank's guess.

Still he sipped slowly as Suki had urged. The Water Trade was designed for the milking of corporate pockets. Suki guessed the tab for each man here would run a hundred thousand yen. The annual corporate tab, she had read, came to four and a half trillion yen.

Hank nodded, eyeing the blue-suited men, the elegantly whorish girls. He tried to picture Kuni here, men copping feels to the left and the right.

She'd bullied Suki to get what she wanted—a gentle and loving American man.

So what madness then had possessed her—

Just then the houselights dimmed, the runway lighting brilliantly in a rush of neon. On stage beneath a mirrored light appeared a clownish figure with a mop of orange hair. She wore a skimpy corset with gold lamé cones over pendulous breasts. Striped wool stockings stopped just short of her thick and flagrant bush. An X-rated clown Dorothy from a Japanese *Wizard of Oz*.

The clown smoked a cigarette, from her mouth to start with. Then, as she strolled down the runway, below.

In her left hand she held a red lunch box. Swinging it, she pussy-blew a cloud that half covered two tables. She passed the butt to a blue-suiter who licked it and smoked for his life. Then she smiled and licked her lips, producing from her lunch box a tampon with a long, thick string.

She loaded the tampon inside her as if she were priming a cannon, lassoing the end of the string as she strolled.

A few steps on, she squatted in front of a blue suit. She said something to him. He stuck out his fist, around which she wrapped the thick string. She screwed her features hard and tight, backing away till the string was drawn taut. From the lunch box came an apple, which she quartered and cored on the string. Hard and clean.

"*Oishii!*" the clown cried, tossing the bits to the crowd.

Before the laughter faded, she loaded a long plastic trumpet
inside.

She reangled her pelvis, twice-deepened her squat, and
pussy-blew an astonishing toot.

"Open stage," Suki said as bedlam spread throughout the
room.

The lighting on the stage had dimmed, but Hank saw the
shadowy movements of men lugging mattress-sized props.
Then, clearly, the nubile forms of three tuxedoed *waitresses.*

The stage was slowly flooded with pulsing waves of soft pastels. In harmony, the disco swelled from heartbeat to deafening
roar.

The three girls danced demurely while men at the tables
around him engaged in games of Rock, Scissors, and Paper.

He looked back at the stage. The girls' jackets were gone.
Their small hands popped trick catches of their salmon-colored
shirts, which floated over their hips to the stage.

"Jesus," Hank said. "This all mean what I think?"

Suki whispered for him to be quiet. Her eyes flashed, a
shocking mixture of sadness and defiance.

Yappari Nihonjin ja nai to . . .

Stockings and panties were gone when he looked. The girls
lay down in chorus, raising and slowly spreading their legs.
These they swayed from side to side, their vulvas lit from small
lights on the stage.

The winners of the hand games were queuing at the runway.
The first three unbuckled their belts as they climbed.

Hank grabbed Suki's hand.

"C'mon," he growled. "I seen enough."

THREE

As they were leaving Shinjuku, Jack Pepper was humbly enjoying Atlanta's hottest day in years. A hundred thirty and
climbing.

His pleasure was diminished, true, by the great elm that
shaded his place in back.

But one had to look on the positive side. There were two of

them in an apartment scarcely adequate for one. Two of them
together twenty-four hours a day since the loss of his job at The
Store. It had been pleasant to sleep at his desk. But home was
where his heart was.

The doors, the walls, the ceiling dripped, seeming to moan as
they sweated.

Books drew moisture, spongelike, their spines and covers
glistening.

Clothes wilted on the hangers, gone bad in minutes, post-
washing.

The carpeting wept for the fan that Jack still stubbornly
would not connect. Oh no. They *were* poor, just like she'd said.
So let them burn like poor people.

Jack wished he could have written Hank to tell him of the
heat. His last letter had been—it was hard to recall. Sometime
last week, he was certain. Because there'd been an Interlude—
another magical respite. Again, as if some inner clock had gone
off at midnight.

More of her wizardy, mind-blowing tricks, twice better than
last week's. But something, sparked within him, and fanned by
the glorious heat, would not die.

He'd found himself *happy* to say she'd been right. They *were*
poor and he *was* dumb. His small brain was probably damaged.

Again and again she'd denied it, dropping his jaw by the inch
with her tricks.

Still, never far from Jack's mind was the knowledge that Monday would come.

Ah yes, the *other* midnight!

"We're gonna make it," she said Sunday night. She showed
him the number of days they'd survived, fourteen X's in two
rows. Almost halfway there!

He drifted off, lightly centered between paper-thin layers of
low-level sleep.

Suddenly, then, an explosion of light and one of her unearthly
shrieks.

"Well, what's the matter with you! Maybe forty years old puts
one foot into grave? Midnight, and sleep like a baby? Jack Pepper shoots willie and whole world be good." Kuni jabbed her

finger at him. "You satisfy me too, like man! You give Kuni *orgasm!* Give Kuni satisfaction!"

She came at him like a wave, across the room and into bed, where she tore off his shorts and snarled, "Fuck me! Get it up! I want some too! Come on, are you a *man?*"

Kuni left him lying there, in a miasma of shame.

That had been three days ago.

Increasingly, he found himself caught up in their lunatic rhythm. Another weekend coming up. Himself the World's Greatest Lover again. Just two more weeks of X's in Kuni's little book. Two more five-day nonstop assaults on whatever the week's evil buzz was, once sex was no longer a problem.

He'd been fired Tuesday, the barometer steadily rising since then. Now and then he could nearly outscream her. But he had no invective to match hers. By the day her body grew more beautiful and powerful. She was awesome in bed. He was forty and—Jack.

Sometimes he howled in agony, when Kuni, underneath him, yawned as he labored away. It's okay, she'd say. Just shoot. I use my finger later. (Stop!) Your prick's too small. (Stop, oh stop!)

Mostly now he liked to sit, on short breaks from sexual humblings. Today he was readin' a comic he'd found: *Vampire Biker Bimbos!* He found the plot hard to follow, his brain being as small as it was. But he enjoyed the pictures.

He heard her snicker. Looked and saw: Kuni, naked, sheened with sweat, her body sleek and dangerous.

"Wimpy," she snarled. "Pussy man."

Jack shrugged and returned to his comic. The pages were soggy and dripping blurred ink, but he wanted to understand *something.*

Like—what was her name? That woman . . . That vision he'd had, in red leather . . . Michiko . . . He remembered now . . .

This was surely the comic's best frame: Blond Vampire Biker Bimbo embracing a sister brunette . . . while in the background, sight unseen, the wounded Biker Priest crawls . . .

Michiko and Cotter again on those stairs, rising slowly out of view . . . Cotter with that blissed-out grin, handing the words from on-high: *Don't mock . . .*

And here we go: The Biker Priest—

"American vampires are sissies," she said.

Kuni, her voice hardly Kuni's at all, a new low and remarkably sane, strong.

Jack nodded, his overworked, pebble-sized brain engrossed in the next lurid panel.

"Come to me," Kuni said.

"Later, dear. I have a headache," Jack said.

"*Look at me,*" Kuni said.

Jack sighed and set down the comic and looked.

He saw Kuni as he'd never seen her.

Oh, Jesus, he thought. Jesus, help me!

FOUR

Hank shut the window behind him.

No one had troubled to lock it; for theft, in Japan, was unheard of.

Suki waited for him, looking haunted in the moon's pale silver light. Their presence violated every known stricture and code.

Perhaps in time he'd understand. It would be nice to know how Suki could have sat there, seeing the same things that he saw—and have no reaction at all. Yes, of course, it was Japan. And their thoughts about sex were, well, different. Maybe the men had no options. Maybe the women weren't seen as whores, but as high-class Service Girls.

Maybe.

Lots of maybes.

But here they were, so just see what was what.

"Flashlight," he whispered.

She nodded morosely and reached in her bag, producing a small light that cast a strong beam.

He danced the spot along the walls. Not even a picture remained. What furniture there was had been set against one wall to make way for the boxes. These formed a massive pyramid that took up a third of the room.

"*Asoko,*" she said. "Over there."

He aligned the beam with her finger.

A door.

"Bedroom," she said.

Private place.

Suki opened the door; it did not make a sound.

The bedroom looked as neat as the main room. Futon neatly rolled. A small dresser.

Hank started to lose it. He stood in the door frame, darting the beam here and there, growling "Bitch."

She hadn't left a clue.

Suki stepped past him and into the room. She ignored the white beam's angry dance, calmly viewing the room in its natural light.

When she turned to the wall with the dresser, she gasped.

"Suki?" Hank said.

"*Koko.*"

Here.

He walked over beside her, raising the beam to the corkboard hung over the dresser.

The first item captured by the spot brought a gasp even greater than Suki's.

He shifted the spot and said, "Oh boy."

One more shift and he whispered, "Bingo."

FIVE

Come to me . . .

Kuni, her wonderful plans gone to hell—the plan for the husband, the baby, the house—regarded the unhappy man on the couch with an almost tender expression.

She'd known the risks and known the odds of her desperate game from the start. But what other choice had she had? Was five weeks an unreasonable time?

Five weeks—with whole weekends between them!

She'd made a mistake, a bad one, in Japan. But . . . Couldn't mistakes be corrected? By what law should a single sin destroy a life forever?

She'd been immune to the babblings of her *co-waitress* Michiko. The Makahari church? Hrumph! Japan was full of holy flakes, none more worshipful than new Old Misses. No creed was too crazy as long as it offered a chance to change *Sexual Karma*.

Well, none of that for Kuni. She'd made the right sounds while her own flinty eyes sought a more earthly escape.

American lovers were easy to find. Alas, they were all either married or single and in no real hurry to leave.

Still, Kuni had been a survivor. And would surely have found her own way. If the bubble-brained, giggly Michiko hadn't walked into the club that one night, not looking at all like Michiko. Her eyes, dark and smoldering. The sense of a powerful presence within.

Kuni, stunned, said hello and how was it going, the church.

Michiko laughed. (Whose laugh was *that*?) "Oh, that. No more for me. I've found something—better."

What?

Michiko said no more that night. Or the night after that. Or the next. But then . . .

"*Saa*," she said coyly, "maybe you're not ready, *ne*?"

"But your eyes—they look different!"

"They are," Michiko answered.

"And your voice—that's different too! And the way you walk—"

"*So, so*. Everything is different now. Before I was weak, now I'm strong. And, it seems, by the day I grow stronger."

"But *how*?"

"Come with me after work. And maybe I'll just let you see for yourself."

Aa, if only Kuni had been a bit less curious!

Michiko took her home that night to meet her fellow Sisters. Inside, black candles burned beneath a blowup on the wall: a stern-looking woman in wire-rimmed specs, wearing a white silk kimono. That was Sister, they explained. Japan's first New Woman, executed by the State for attempting to set women free. Captured one night in her war dress, red leather, while preaching to a frenzied crowd. Found guilty and beheaded. But she was back and with them now, ready to lead the New Women again . . . now that the Way had been found.

Kuni sipped her tea and wondered when it might be best to

leave. Still, it was undeniable, the power that beamed from these three women's eyes.

"But . . . What was the Way that was found?" Kuni asked.

Michiko answered that the church, as useless a church as there was in Japan—fixing toasters and TVs!—had provided the first spark of insight. Instead of exorcising imaginary spirits . . . what if a *real* spirit could be put in, a source of incredible wisdom and strength?

Kuni nodded, thinking now was the absolute best time to leave. Still . . .

"She . . . is like a devil, then?"

"*Iie*, like a Sister!" the three women answered as one.

"But . . . Is the possession—quite painful? And are you always possessed?" Kuni asked.

"It is like a gentle wind passing through your body first. Then it's the sense of . . . a Sister. Always watching over you."

"*Saa*," Kuni said. She nibbled at a rice cake. "That doesn't sound so bad. But what," she asked sensibly, "exactly does she *do?*"

The three conferred, backs to Kuniko.

When they turned, Michiko smiled. "We think you should speak with our Sister yourself. She is happy to answer all questions."

Kuniko felt her mouth go dry. Hand shaking, she set her cup down. "*Aa, maa.* I don't know. Surely I'd like to get out of Japan. But possession's a serious thing!"

The women chuckled happily.

Again, Michiko assured her. "Sister isn't like that. She is a Sister and she wants to help. But how can she exist in a house where she's not wanted? She only wishes to talk, and no more. She can't stay till she's been invited."

"*Dōmo*," Kuni told the three. "Thank you for having me here for this talk. I'll certainly give this some serious thought! But I think, for now at least—"

She'd just started to rise from the table . . . when Michiko waved her hand to stop.

"I think not," she told Kuni.

And then she moved her hand again. And all the lights went

out. Or rather turned a shade of black that seemed like the essence of light.

Kuni couldn't see a thing. Yet when had she needed the use of eyes less?

She felt a sense of bounding joy simply in being a woman.

And then she heard a low sweet voice.

Kuniko-san?

Yes?

Don't be afraid. I only wish to speak awhile. I've been sleeping for so long! I wish to tell you some wonderful things. Then I'll request your permission to leave a small magical gift. And I'll go.

Sister introduced herself. She repeated the tragic history recounted by Michiko. And Kuni felt her spirit swing from raging indignation to almost unbearable sorrow. As if the tale embodied the lot of women everywhere, through the whole of time.

They crush us, Kuniko-san. Crush us! Crush us and crush us forever, five ways!

And, hearing Sister count the ways, she saw her life as a chain of black slides. From the start, every move, every step, had been fixed. Deviate, and a woman was crushed.

She was crushed economically.

She was crushed intellectually.

Sexually, physically, spiritually—crushed!

Her spirit swung, and continued to swing, the sorrow feeding the will to . . . crush back . . . until the swings were too broad to endure.

Well, thank you for having me here! Sister said.

Wait, Kuni begged. There's more—

Of course there is. There's more, much more. But we mustn't overdo it, not on this first visit. Sisterhood must start with small baby steps.

These last words were spoken in a breathless baby voice.

Oh, cute! Kuni said. I like you—you're funny!

Well, it takes a good Sister to know one. But now I think . . . Before I go: Kuniko-san, may I please . . . leave just a small gift . . . inside you?

Sister's voice was thrilling. They *had* had a wonderful visit. And why not a gift from a newly found friend? No harm in that.

She liked gifts. But . . . Some last reserve of cunning still glowed in the almighty black.

Kuni asked softly: Inside me? What kind of gift would it be?

Trust me. I promise you'll like it.

Kuni hesitated. Will it change the way I look?

Sister giggled. *Well, yes, it will make you prettier.*

Oh, I'd enjoy that. But . . .

I must go. One more question.

She had a lot of questions. But one more? Think. A good one!

I beg you to take no offense, Kuni said.

How can I, when we're Sisters?

Well, let's say—I mean, just make-believe—What if, for some reason . . .

The spirit finished for her, tenderly and sadly. *Kuniko-san, hear me well. This is a gift you may return if it does not please you. I will tell you when and how and I will ask no questions. Tell me your decision now.*

Yes, she said.

And they'd been right. It was like a gentle wind coursing through her body. The sense of being flooded with warmth and strength. And Sisterhood.

When she came to, she was outstretched, her head propped on Michiko's lap. Her body ached, everywhere, from her vagina to her throat. Her elbows ached. Her noggin ached. And yet she smiled proudly, having visited some secret place where only real Sisters could go.

Michiko said adoringly, "Sister really likes you!" She pointed across to the opposite wall, which seemed to have been cannon-shot.

"Whooooosh!" Michiko told her. With her hand she made a sweep to indicate trajectory.

"Me?" Kuni said, astounded.

And the three Sisters giggled.

"Rekōdo furaito," Michiko said.

Record flight. Oh boy. What had she got herself into?

She learned. She saw her Sisters smile . . . yawn . . . open their tiny mouths wide as they'd go . . . and roll out the silvery balls that split into legions of glistening strands . . . these lengthening in a slow, sinuous dance. She felt her own throat start to throb. She wondered what was happening. Or only thought she wondered. For there wasn't a thought of resisting, only the wonderful sense of release . . . as her own mouth smiled, yes, and opened as wide as it could. It was better than sex, even then at the start, skimpy little tendrils engaged in their eager-to-please little dance. A small first taste of Sister's power. To what end, though, she wondered.

She learned. Her Sisters peeled off their skirts, urging her to join them. When Kuni hesitated, Michiko smiled knowingly. "Kuniko-san, you are amazing. On stage you are quite shameless . . . and yet you won't play with your Sisters!" Kuni thought about that while watching the three lose their panties. She'd certainly seen them all naked before. Why shouldn't she relax? Besides—*aa!*—she was feeling—*maa!*—rather hot below. She tore the zipper of her skirt, attempting to remove it. Soon the four were in a row, each holding hands with a Sister. "Raise your knees," Michiko said. "Now what," Kuni asked her, feeling the workings within. Michiko said, "Now the real magic begins!"

She learned. There was much to learn. The others themselves were beginners. When they were not *waitressing,* they labored to perfect their *gifts.* The speed with which the coils were summoned. The lengths to which they might be wrought. The pressure perfection might bring to bear. They began shattering bottles. They progressed to vases. Chairs. The growing proof of Sister's power was so mesmerizing that Kuni forgot to ask what it was for.

She learned. Sister returned, as she'd promised, when the moon was full again. Again she told the Sisters how women, from the start of time, had been crushed by men. Now men had become so firmly entrenched in all major positions of power, even the best of revolts would require centuries of sustained effort. But how could this be when women were crushed not in one or in two but five ways? No woman in her brief natural span had a prayer of escaping all five. A much longer life span was needed, to start. And the gift that she'd brought was the Way.

Kuniko learned that energy was the elixir of life, the gift being the means to replenish their stores. Sisterhood would begin by reversing men's sexual slavery. For no man alive could resist the gift's spell. At climax, when his guard was down, his concentrated energy was theirs for the taking. If they were cunning and they learned . . .

Kuniko learned. They all learned, while awaiting their Sister's next visit. They practiced on each other, shamelessly (were they not Sisters?). They formed merry daisy chains, kissing and licking each other, and then covering each other with glistening coils, feeding on and being fed, as they shrieked with pleasure. They came to call it *kissing*. And then they began to Go Out. Their first adventures were cautious, with scarcely a squeeze of the gift—then, by the night, more reckless. Afterward, when they met, their respective glows proclaimed which of them that night had kissed best of all.

She learned, though, as they all learned, that kissing just wasn't enough. The pleasure was exquisite. And yet it left an emptiness that could not be denied. If kissing brought the energy and energy bought time . . . to what end, Kuni wondered. Had anything really been changed? Or would they live forever now, forever to be crushed? Michiko told her, "Patience. Sister surely has a plan. I'm sure on her next visit we'll be told the rest." Maybe, Kuniko thought. But what does Sister really want?

She learned, on Sister's next visit, that the gift in itself was no more than a toy. Unless it was backed by real power. The power of Sister's full presence inside. Sister's birthday coming up. And all they had to do to make the gift complete was awaken Sister on her day. Awaken her by kissing . . . once—just once!—the *real* way: wholly crushing the life from a man. For they might live forever, true, on feedings as she'd shown them. But for Sisterhood to rule the world, she needed to be with them, Sisters in their *souls*.

Kuni had learned enough, she thought. And so she ran like hell. She learned, three days later, that they'd gone through with the mad gory plan. Three men crushed. By three women in red, Sister's battle color. She learned to live in terror, not of the police—she'd done nothing—but *them*. But then two Sisters disappeared. And when she saw Michiko, weeks later, on the street, Michi passed her, dreamy-eyed, as if Kuni were only a shadow. The police did not come. And the church did not come.

And her new friend Suki was clearly no church spy. (She'd passed the test, laughing with Kuni at the church's ridiculous hand moves.) And though the gift itself remained, the hunger could be eased somewhat by kissing as before.

Sister came just one more time. Not a happy camper, but understanding in her way. *Aa, maa*, apparently Sisterhood wasn't for Kuni. *Shikata ga nai*, though. It couldn't be helped. All the best and so on in all her future endeavors. But wait, Kuni wondered. What about the gift? *Oh, that.* Sister considered a moment, agreed that a deal was a deal. And yet, at the same time, a gift was a gift. Moreover, Kuni had used it. And so she should offer a gift in exchange, of at least equal value. Kuni shuddered, wondering what such a gift might be.

She learned. The fair thing, the fitting thing, would be, in rejecting the gift, to display a comparable power. Yes, that would be highly instructive. Let Kuni prove able to crush a man . . . half as well as Sister . . . *without* the aid of the gift.

To crush a man . . . *half as well* . . .

The riddle confounded her: like a scale, one note short, played over and over again. To crush a man in any way . . . even a part of one finger— *Aa, maa!* Half as well? No, not even a hundredth for her!

She accepted, finally, that it was her fate: to hover between Sister's hunger and her own thwarted desires. Men couldn't get enough of her, yet sex was empty in itself. And kissing, though she craved it, only enflamed that more powerful itch. She might go weeks without kissing . . . then find herself, in a frenzy, close to cracking the spine of some poor hapless male.

The riddle was unsolvable. She'd thoroughly resigned herself . . . until the day she learned: Michiko was back, with a vengeance. And limbo was certainly heaven compared to a run-in with *her*.

Enter then Jack Pepper, a world away from the Sisters. And, as Suki sang his praises, a vision grew in Kuni's mind: a man so soft and gentle he might . . . just might . . . be crushed, so to speak, in a way *other* than Sister's. To crush a spirit in five ways was *half as good*, she reasoned, as crushing an actual body. And so, fair was fair, she'd be free of the gift.

This would leave her with just one last riddle: what to do with the broken Jack Pepper. If he could be fixed, she decided, she'd stay for as long as it took. Then she'd go . . . free to love, and be loved by a *man*. If he couldn't be fixed, then she'd stay, as she must. At least the hunger would be gone.

No plan she had ever conceived approached this one in cunning. It should have worked, it was that good. It should have taken just five weeks: five days of each devoted to one symbolic crushing . . . weekends off to replenish her strength . . . just enough safe kissing to put him securely back under her spell.

It would have worked, she was certain. But from the start she had learned how easily things could go wrong.

X rays, of all things! To be denied, at the start, the safety net of marriage. Threat of deportation. X rays. Wonderful. The gift revealed in black and white.

And—how cruel the gods had been—the presence of the cat. Peaches *knew*, and that was that. No way to stop the Evil Eye. What Jack could never understand was how the cat's instinctive hate triggered and increased the hunger. After a full day with Peaches, Kuni found herself dreaming of cracking Jack's back. What else to do? *Saa*, the cat had to go.

She hadn't counted on the heat. The hunger seemed to thrive on it, instead of dwindling by fifths every week.

But the biggest surprise, all in all, had been Jack. Who could have guessed at his anger or his rebellious streak? Mostly, as she'd hoped and prayed, Jack felt too stunned to reply. But now and then he amazed her with an outraged fit of childish pique. And it refueled the hunger she fought with her soul to defeat.

She'd crushed him economically.

She'd crushed him intellectually.

It was Thursday and he might survive the remains of his sexual crushing.

In two more weeks she would have won her desperate contest with Sister—symbolically crushing him in all five ways.

But the summer heat was far too great. And the hunger kept growing. It couldn't be stopped.

And so she repeated, rubbing the still-swelling mounds of her breasts:

"Come to me."

She saw the horror in his eyes, shot through with fascination.

She felt the powerful rhythm, within her vagina and throat, the hunger releasing—*aa, maa!*—Sister's gift. Loose ends of the coils twitched and lengthened by the inch.

They'd had this date from the beginning.

He rose, shoulders quivering, and, to his credit, came. About three feet away he stopped, mesmerized by the dance of the coils.

"You wanted it, Jack," Kuni said, her voice thick. "Well, have it. Have it! Have it!"

She took a breath and squeezed it down. And as her *hara* tightened, the gift fulfilled her wildest dreams.

She captured Jack around the waist and then around both arms, chest-high. She squeezed, hard, and as he screamed, she swung her body savagely, bouncing him off the left wall. She reeled him in. Took a breath. And, with a manic backward jerk, shot him up, head through the ceiling.

"Oh, Jack!" she screamed. "I like it! Wheeeee!"

She bounced him off the wall and door as if he were a rubber ball and she were wielding the paddle. More and more, with each swing, the left wall resembled a painting. Streaks and dots and massive splats of red, red, glorious red. And what was that —an eyeball? Wow!

"Have it!" she shrieked. "Have it, Jack!"

SIX

Ted Boone parked the rented car half a block away, not wanting to ruin his surprise. He stretched, his legs still creaky from close quarters on the plane. He stripped off his T-shirt and fanned himself with it, enjoying the sight of his muscular self.

Home again.

Atlanta.

Even here, in the sticks: Hank's exile from the Colonel. Sycamores and elm trees, gardenias, chrysanthemums. He closed his eyes and breathed the South.

Surely his last visit.

Home.

Afternoons were still the best for clarity and calmness. Morn-

ings were always confusing. But nightfall was when the real
nightmares began. No longer himself then. Which wasn't so
bad. But no longer aware that he wasn't, not when an evening
had reached its full tide and the crippling headaches began.
Demons pounding in his skull. Voices, millions, screaming. So
many of them, all at once, with no way to know which was his.
No need for a doctor to tell him. The tumor was no longer
fooling around.

But there was no confusion now.

The voices were sleeping.

The hammers were still.

He felt absurdly happy that one of the voices last night had
been Hank's. Message on the phone machine. Only one word—
his own name—but Hank's voice!

He felt a childish impulse to chuck everything he stood for.
Charge up the drive, and who cared if he squeaked, calling out
his brother's name.

Hank! Get your ass out here, look who's come home!

Be like Christmas to see a big smile on Hank's face. (Jesus,
look at you all! Is that a fuckin' pump or what?)

Instead, he walked in measured strides, his coolest Ted walk
ever, hip-sprung, great arms swinging loosely.

(Hank . . .)

Until he got fifteen yards from the drive and the screaming
started.

He froze, instinctively crouching, neck hairs bristling, fingers
clenched.

"Have it! Have it!" some cunt screamed.

And then came these bloodcurdling, god-awful *thumps*.

Ted started running, no thought in his mind except Jesus,
don't let it be Hank.

He rounded the drive, saw Hank's van, and cried "No!"—his
mind on fire, night again, and all the voices screaming.

"Have it! Have it!"

Thump and scream.

Wait. Ted whirled. Not Hank's place. There. And, oh, Jesus,
what was that?

Through the screen door—night for sure, the demons playing
with his head—sight of a naked woman, full-breasted Oriental,

swinging this guy with some horrible glop spewing out of her mouth and her pussy.

Then, just like that, she dropped him, a crushed and bloodied sack of meat, sucking back the slimy strands into their respective holes.

Suddenly she turned. And, seeing him, her eyes half popped.

"Hank!" she screamed, maniacally.

He'd never run from anything.

Not even in the war, with his heart in his throat and his shit in his pants.

What the hell.

Why start now.

Good a way as any.

Bye.

Ted made his way in with a kick that took the door clear off its hinges.

SEVEN

Home again. Suki's apartment. The booty from Kuni's place lay spread before them:

His photograph, used as a dartboard . . . The piece on San Francisco—*The World's Hottest Melting Pot*—her X's through the pictures of Asian women and white men . . . and BULL-SHIT! SLAVES! scrawled in red.

His mind kept slipping into thoughts that might well have been Kuni's:

I'm thirty and I'm stuck here, an Old Miss with ambition and brains . . . I do a dozen men a night, then read of Asian chickies in the California sun . . . I got no way to get there . . . Not till I see Jack Pepper . . .

We're gettin' close . . . Come on, cigar . . . Maybe a man she could handle?

Hank looked over at Suki, who'd emptied Kuni's leather attaché. One look at Hank's picture as dartboard, with penciled horns and devil beard—and, on the spot, all thoughts of *uchi* had been erased from her mind. He couldn't have stopped her from stealing the case, or deprived her of the pleasure, here, of snipping the paltry brass lock. She'd rifled through it, Colonel style, tossing mere personal papers without a care where they fell: checkbook . . . calorie counter . . . pay stubs . . . dog-eared copies of *Think and Grow Rich* and *I'm Okay—You're Okay* . . . postcards of San Francisco . . .

On the table before her, a few scattered pieces held some promise of fitting the puzzle: a framed antique photograph of a stern-looking woman in wire-rimmed specs . . . a floral-covered address book . . . a pocket-sized notebook, a few pages filled with Kuni's precise little *kanji*.

Suki set into the notebook. As she read, she shook her head, making a series of low baffled sounds. There wasn't all that much to read. But the entries, minimal, affected her profoundly. She closed the notebook, shuddering.

"*Kichigai*," she told Hank.

"What?"

"Crazy talk, Hank. I don't like. She say somebody—Sister—say man crush woman in five way."

Hank snorted, rolling his eyes. "My ass. Not here in Japan, they don't."

"Money rule. Mind rule. Sex rule—"

"Crush . . . What else she say there?"

"Nothing." She turned the page. The rest was blank.

Hank growled, "Hit the address book."

Suki blinked, at a loss, then followed instructions and gave it a slap. "*Baka!*" she cried. "Stupid book!"

"Uh, darlin'?" he said kindly. "Please pardon my English. I know it's a mess. But hit it means, like, read right quick. And let's see who she knows."

"*Aa sō. Sumimasen.*" Suki bowed. Then, saving face, said: "I fixin' to fetch y'all some heavy info, dude!"

"Real good," Hank purred. "Y'all are my radical woman."

"Radical," Suki said. She'd be sure to look this up later, he knew. Right now, though, she was all business again. She searched the same way she did *shodo*: regarding the book for a moment, adjusting her heartbeat and focus.

Suki opened the book to the middle, the M's. She said "*Sō*," satisfied, as Hank had guessed she would be. No number was listed for the Makahari church. She showed no disappointment.

She set the book upon its spine, fingertips pressed to the covers at top. She eased the pressure gradually and the covers spread, the pages almost sighing as they relaxed into clusters. Numbers most frequently dialed.

She turned to the first of these natural spreads. Ran eyes and fingers down the page.

"*Iie*," she said. "Nothing."

She closed the book and tried again.

The fourth time they struck pay dirt. He could see the muscles tightening subtly in her face.

"What name," she asked, "that church man say?"

"What?"

"Nosebite church man! Headcrush woman!"

"Easy," Hank said. "Easy." It was seldom easy to understand her English. But when she got really excited . . .

Nosebite church man . . .

Headcrush woman . . .

The woman the church guy said run from the church and crushed that doctor's head to shit . . .

What the hell was her name? He'd forgotten—no, wait . . .

"Mi—" he started. "Mi-somethin' . . . Mi-ka . . . Mi-chi . . ."

"Michiko!" Suki cried. "In here!"

In his heart, he knew: Somehow Kuni *was* connected. But if he accepted *that* . . .

"Shit," he said, "there's other girls that's got the name Michiko."

"*Hai.*"

"And even if this is the one . . . Well, see what I'm sayin'—"

The telephone rang.

Suki answered. But he knew who would be on the line.

"Hank," she said.

He took the phone. For the first time ever, not a crackle or spritz on the line.

"Boy," the Colonel told him, "y'all get your ass home and right now. There's trouble at your damn apartment house. I got me two dead bodies here and one of 'em's your brother."

Hank reeled and fought the tears, his heart hammering wildly.

Ted . . .

"Go fuck yourself," he managed. "I'm goin' to Kyoto."

"What!"

"I'm gonna go to fuckin' church."

And then to San Francisco.

EIGHT

Fantasy in green and blue: Kyoto in midsummer.

Set against a piercing and translucent blue, the dripping green of moss gardens . . . the thick dark emerald of towering pines on narrow-stairwayed temple slopes . . . the jade of bamboo, ivory-barked, shot through with summer light.

From peaked rooftops sky-blue carp banners fluttered in a lazy breeze, while Bach and Handel, just as blue, wafted from small *kissatens.*

Along a shaded walkway beside a rose-banked, broad canal, painters sat before their easels, artist berets above uniform suits. Heartbreaking beauties in snow-white kimonos strolled beneath blue parasols. Past noodle shops and small boutiques. To the stairways that climbed the steep green slopes of hills. Through the branches of pines. To the temples to pray for whatever such great beauty prayed for.

The seats of the limo they rode in were blue. The church driver, farting silently, discreetly pushed a button, releasing a sweet mist of extract of pine.

The driver stopped before they reached the center of the town. His uniform was very blue. He whistled softly to himself, blue echoes from a *kissaten.* He studied the congestion. Festival, he told them. Summer's best, tomorrow. The narrow lanes ahead were clogged with floats and shrines on great wooden wheels.

He apologized to both of them. The widow, though, was waiting. And it wouldn't do to keep her. He asked them as humbly as a man could ask if they would mind buckling their seatbelts.

The gold that rimmed one foretooth glittered greenly in the light.

My brother's dead, Hank thought.

"Let's go!"

"*Gambatte*," Suki whispered.

"Yeah."

They fastened their seat belts with synchronized clicks.

The driver thanked them and thanked them again.

The widow would be very happy, he said.

Life was good when the widow was happy.

He farted, out loud this time and at great length. He flooded Hank and Suki with a potent spray of pine. Checked his mirror. Waited. Then wheeled the limo around on a dime and started burning rubber beneath the blue Kyoto sky and through the lush green of the streets.

NINE

The widow spoke in English, a gift in itself to Hank's ears. Her voice was as gruff as he'd guessed from that buzz. It might have been cloned from his own stricken throat. But her face, a small minefield of wrinkles and folds, was somehow oddly appealing. The widow's robe was as black as her hair. Her small gold medallion stood out in blinding relief. It was studded with sapphires and emeralds.

The widow continued to thank them. For the wisdom shown in calling to break their dreadful news. For the courage shown in coming here after her wretched behavior. She really had just wished to talk, though. They'd never been in danger.

The widow saw Hank's expression and smiled. "You may leave anytime," she repeated.

"Oh, I do know that," he growled. He looked again out the window. Saw, through the sheer gold-flecked curtains, the limo driver smoking, butt parked against one fender.

Hank crossed the room in a couple of strides. The great oak doors were open. The hallway, empty. Not one guard.

He quick-scanned the room again. Almost entirely Western. Cluster of black leather chairs and a sofa around a low black table. The widow's desk, rosewood and brass, with wall-to-wall cabinets behind it. Wall-to-wall champagne rug . . . except for a bare strip, two feet wide, from the desk to the opposite wall.

The strip was freshly polished pine. At the edges ran broad tracks, with a high-backed chair on bearings about three feet from the desk. At the end of the tracks was a backdrop, thickly padded and shaped like the chair.

"Would you like to try," asked the widow.

"Try what."

She pointed calmly at the chair.

"Trust me," she said. "It is harmless. I know our reputation. I know that people talk and joke. I only wish to show you. Whatever you think of our teachings, you should understand: The power my husband discovered is real. And these women have mastered that power."

Hank waved his hand impatiently. He plopped his frame into the cushy black chair and crossed his legs, folding his hands on his lap.

"Don't tell me, honey. Show me."

The widow circled in back of her desk. Her waist scarcely came to the top. But she seemed, unaccountably, taller to Hank.

He willed himself to hold his smile.

He saw the widow close her eyes and raise her hands slowly before her. She began to move her hands as if she were sculpting a ball in the air.

He could not say for certain exactly what he felt. Except that with each shaping arc he imagined himself feeling lighter, as if she were sculpting the ball with his weight.

The feeling was hardly unpleasant.

In a way, he almost hoped the widow would continue.

Instead, though, she turned both palms toward him.

She did not breathe.

She did not blink.

She moved her hands with astonishing speed, one hand shooting back to her shoulder, the other shooting out.

He felt as if he'd been hit by a truck.

The chair rocketed back on its tracks, fifteen feet, crashing into the black leather backdrop.

Hank slumped back. His jaw went slack, the muscles that

worked it beyond his control. He gripped the armrests to steady his hands. His hair was on end everywhere.

He looked over at Suki. Saw she had passed out.

"Are you all right?" the widow asked.

He turned to the widow, carefully now, and with a real show of respect.

"Ma'am," he said, "I believe I can say y'all have my unflaggin' attention."

TEN

"Our story begins," said the widow, "in 1923 . . ."

They were seated on the couch, the leather soft as butter. The widow, almost girlishly, sat cross-legged on a chair, leaning over to whisk the green tea to a froth.

"Prior to the Great Kantō Earthquake, the New Women's movement in Japan had almost gasped its last breath. Bureaucracy. Bad timing. The apathy of the housewives the New Women were trying to save.

"Oddly enough, the earthquake revitalized the movement. There was a sense of urgency that had been entirely lacking. The fatal wrenching open of a flaw in the earth's surface opened the eyes of all women—to the flaws and imperfections of the world they lived in.

"Women were forbidden, after marriage, to own property. Women had no legal claim to the children they had borne. Women could not vote or join political organizations. Nor could they listen, secondhand, to reports of political speeches. Grounds for instant divorce still included disobedience, sterility, jealousy, excessive talking, aggressive behavior in bed, and so on.

"I will spare you my thoughts on these matters. I am an old-fashioned woman, reared in an older, and dying, Japan. And yet here I am at the head of a mighty and still-growing empire. My way was my way. I believe in Japan. Japan first—and then men and women.

"If I had been living, though, in 1923? If I had seen what the women of that time saw, still reeling from the earthquake:

women homeless, women starving, on their knees scrounging for garbage to eat? I can't say my thinking would not have been changed.

"No single story, it is said, so fired the hearts of the women as the tragedy of Yoshiwara. Twenty thousand prostitutes burned to death in brothels there. And thirty thousand more were crushed by falling bricks and cornices."

The widow stopped to turn the bowl in a ritualized series of moves. She raised the bowl and bowed to them, then half filled their tiny blue porcelain cups.

Hank sipped the tea. A sip would do. The bitter taste would last for weeks.

"Oishii!" Suki said.

The widow was delighted. "Green tea," she said, "was the ultimate blessing given to us by the gods."

"Let's get on with the story," Hank snarled. "Cut the crap. Just tell me what I need to know to get me that cunt Kuni's head."

"Boone-san, you need to know the nature and depth of the rage at that time.

"You need to know that no one responded to the tragedy with more fury than this woman, whose picture you have brought. Her name was Sakai Ito. None of the speeches she gave has been saved. Her name has been all but forgotten. But I remember hearing, as a young girl in the thirties, tales of Sakai Ito storming the streets in a red leather dress, preaching that women were doomed in Japan to spinsterhood or whoredom. Why? Because all women were crushed by all men, exactly as the whores were crushed in the dreadful earthquake.

"Her speeches drove crowds into frenzies. Authorities were so alarmed that she was executed with dozens of other New Women that year. The story I heard—just a legend, I thought— was that, as the blade fell, she vowed she would return."

Suki made a strangled sound, leaning her head on Hank's shoulder.

He treated himself to a sip of green tea, which seemed, unexpectedly, sweeter.

"Shall I continue?" said the widow.

"This goin' where I hope it ain't?"

"You bet your bippy," she told him. "Now, then . . ."

ELEVEN

"I suppose, in a way, they're like vampires," she said.

The tea was long gone, the sun setting.

"Three bitter and unhappy victims of the Water Trade learned, through a stroke of horrific bad luck—at least from our perspective—to put a spirit *in* them by perverting the faith of *O-Sensei*. The spirit they chose was mad, bad, and hellbent for revenge. The instrument of her revenge—or what she pleased to call her *gift*—was a substance as astonishing as it is revolting. I have seen it, as I've said. And I have seen its effects. You must believe me when I say I do not exaggerate. It's as supple as pasta . . . elastic as rubber . . . with the strength of tempered steel. And they are easily able to crush a grown man, your size, head to toe.

"Except for that last nasty habit of theirs, they really *are* like vampires. They prolong their lives through energy in its purest state—orgasmic. In this sense, of the two, they are the sophisticates. The victim lives. No marks are left. And if they do not live forever, I suspect they will live for a very long time.

"The women believed," said the widow, giving her spine a slight stretch, "that their first physical crushing was a onetime offering. To bring Sister's spirit inside them.

"I learned in my talk with the spirit that none of the women suspected what Sister really had in mind."

"And what might that be?" Hank growled.

"The plan was a stroke of mad genius. The women would alternate feedings: sexual for energy . . . with physical crushings to increase their power."

"Run that by me once again?"

"Women were crushed, they'd been taught, in five ways. Now, Sister taught them, their strength might grow through decades, maybe even centuries—if they returned the favor. Their victims would be perfect specimens of men who crushed women in one of five ways: the very rich . . . the very strong

. . . and on and on and on. Each time they wholly crushed a man whom Sister had selected, they would absorb his *essence.* His real power would be theirs. With patience, luck, and timing —and with time on their side, they could wait between kills— there was next to no danger of their being caught. One day their power might be absolute. In any case, that was the plan."

"I'm still waitin'," Hank said softly, "to see where our Kuni fits in."

"I can't answer that question," she said. "As I've told you, she wasn't a member. And there were only three murders that night, none after Michiko was caught. In my heart, at the time, I feared the three might have exposed more women to the madness. But . . . Sakai Ito, Boone-san, is a sly and powerful spirit. However I questioned, I could learn no more. Michiko nearly died in the interrogation."

"Almost," he said, "ain't good enough."

"I quite agree. We can only assume that Kuniko was just half converted and broke away before that night. The gift, though, remained and it cried for release. Perhaps she resisted. Whatever. She lost. But now, I fear, the worst is to begin. Sister is *doubly* hungry. And what I fear the most is this: She's grown too hungry to care for the plan."

"Y'all tellin' me she *likes* to kill?"

"I think she was born to kill."

"Well, maybe she'll soon meet her match. How's your hand jive, widow?"

"No! No!" Suki cried. She backed away in horror.

"Tell me," the widow said, "what is on your mind."

Hank stroked Suki's hand until she slapped his hand away.

"Well, ma'am, it's like this. I got me a crazy ole demon named Ted. Just supposin' we put him inside me . . ."

TWELVE

Michiko smiled and could not stop, watching the news at eleven.

Sister was like Santa Claus, making you wait on, on the edge of your chair.

But, like Santa Claus, Sister delivered the goods.

Michiko turned the volume up. She passed a hand at Cotter, who'd just clattered a dish in the kitchen. He flew five feet into a wall and crashed hard to the floor.

"Sorry, dear," he whimpered.

"Shhhh!"

Michiko smiled at the screen, rocking as she listened.

Picture of a fortyish man wearing a hangdog expression. She remembered him, she thought. Wait . . . Yes!

". . . stunned by the brutal slaying of Jack Pepper in Atlanta and . . ."

Picture of a long-haired jock, fuck-me-girls look in his eyes.

". . . Ted Boone, Atlanta native and son of well-known businessman . . ."

Fat cat in a linen suit. Puffy-eyed and shaky-voiced.

"She killed mah boy . . . By God, she'll pay!"

Cut to the apartment, in a bloody shambles.

". . . But who was the mystery woman, thought to be Asian, perhaps Japanese? And what is the connection . . ."

Cut to newspaper ad: blonde in red leather dress.

". . . between the campaign for The Woman in Red, devised for The Store by Jack Pepper, and . . ."

Photos lined across the top: three powerful, rich-looking faces.

". . . three Japanese men who were slain the same way—by, it was rumored, three women in red? And . . ."

Oh, look! It's Dr. C!

". . . Dr. Alex Coburn, crushed this past November . . ."

Cut to anchorwoman's face. Foxy Chinese, her hair long like Michiko's, making the most of her moment.

"This is Connie Fong. Tune in tomorrow evening at ten for a special report on the original murders and the three women in red. Remember. They're still out there. A word of caution to you men here in San Francisco . . ."

Pull back to reveal Miss Fong wearing, instead of a no-nonsense suit, a voluptuous red leather dress.

"Who knows? Perhaps in red leather a girl . . . simply can't control herself? And now, Ron Dee, back to you. How's the weather looking?"

Click.

Michiko turned off the set with her toe. Dropped her head back on the top of the couch. And slipped one finger dreamily under her panties to play.

Well, what do you think? said her favorite voice.

Kuni's in America. Oh, Sister, I've waited so long!

I know. And soon, soon, she'll be here. She can't resist San Francisco.

We can kiss her, can't we? If I don't kiss, really kiss, someone soon—

We'll just have to see about Kuni. Wouldn't you like a new Sister?

But she betrayed—

Now, now. Let's see.

But I can't wait—I'm hungry! Now!

My dearest adorable Michi. Dear ally, dear comrade, dear Sister. In another day or two, if I know San Francisco, we'll be lost in a sea of red leather. Then we can do whatever we please.

Sister, Michiko said shyly. May I ask you a small favor?

Anything. We're Sisters.

Well . . . If it's true what you say—and you've never been wrong . . . If we can move without fear, then—

What is it, Michiko?

Well, it would be wrong, I think, to let such a stroke of good fortune pass by. Maybe we should wait a while longer with our new church. I'm truly incredibly hungry!

You know something? I'm glad you asked. I've noticed, since we came here, a diminishing of interest in building a new church. To tell the truth—it's very odd—after all these years, what I myself appear to want really more than anything . . . is to have a little fun!

Do you mean what I hope you mean?

I mean, we'll paint this damn town red and kiss until we drop!

Oh, Sister, I'm in love with you!

And I with you. Forever. Now, then, we'll need our energy. Let's give Cotter a nice little kiss for old times.

Oh, not him! He bores me! He's nothing now but skin and bones!

Feed me, Sister! Feed me!

Michiko slashed the air and shrieked, "Get it up! I need you!"

The man, David Cotter, jerked, then tumbled over on his back, hands flailing at his zipper. He began to shimmy, on his back, across the room to her.

"Yes, dear," he moaned. "Yes, dear!"

6

BOOK SEVEN
JULY, 1990
SAN FRANCISCO

ONE

The widow's warning to Suki, remembered on the plane as she studied his sleep-twitching figure:

I have succeeded, in a way, as you can see at a glance. But I can't say for certain how well the possession has taken or how long it will last.

I sense a fierce resistance in this young man's soul.

I have two fears, I must tell you. The first is that neither his body nor his mind will survive a prolonged state of siege.

My second fear is greater still. If the spirit is exhausted, then God help you both. For only a spirit of equal ferocity can hope to beat Sakai Ito. Remember, there are now two Sisters.

I have placed a spell that will not last over the spirit within him.

Soon, soon, all too soon, the spirit will start to awaken.

The effects will be alarming. Sometimes terrifying. But you must never weaken, not for a moment, if you love this man.

Move quickly and move calmly and let the siege run its course if you can.

If the body, the host to the spirit, is threatened, then you must protect it. There are two ways to protect it. And each of the ways has its dangers.

The first way is to call the name of the man he was. This will have, instantly, a magically soothing effect. The effect, however, is not without its price—for it may weaken the spirit, the source of our only real hope. Use the word sparingly, only when you must.

The second way is a word that is even surer. If the danger appears to be mortal, you may fully awaken the spirit by simply calling its name. But then there is no turning back. Hear me well: Never, never, never, even think this second word until it must be spoken. I suggest separate bedrooms, for if you should whisper this word in your sleep . . .

Finally, for God's sake, see that he wears sunglasses. Or he'll be shot like a dog on the street.

TWO

On entering the city, the spirit began to awaken, quietly, with a growled menacing yawn. And Suki began to share the widow's understated fears.

She thought of the presence beside her as *it*.

Yet the word seemed far too cruel, since it still looked so like Hank.

She resolved to try, then, to think of it as *he*.

He began to crack his knuckles, methodically, resoundingly. He rotated his neck and his shoulders, his mighty biceps twitching as he cracked and popped away. His attention was distracted then by the cabbie's photo. He leaned over to study the picture, his lips toying silently with the long difficult name.

He turned his head to Suki, glancing at her coolly from behind his mirrored shades.

"Who the fuck are you-all."

"Master," she said, as instructed. The word had a bitter taste, yet seemed to neutralize him.

He shrugged, returning to the offending picture.

"Pa-pa-dou-pou . . . Hey, *boy*." He rapped on the shield
with his knuckles. "Where the *hell* are you-all from!"

THREE

It was cold here in midsummer. But he had taken his shirt off
and walked, taller and straighter than Hank, glorying, it seemed
to her, in the looks he got.

His attention span, she realized, was shorter than a child's.
He'd long since forgotten the scene in the cab: the driver demanding, at gunpoint, they leave. Himself, a drooling Fury,
banging on the shield, daring the Greek pig to shoot. Nor did he
remember her desperate calling of *Hank*. The word, called, had
stilled him, just as the widow promised, and then instantly
passed from his mind.

The effect is not without its price, the widow had solemnly
warned her.

But no serious damage appeared to be done.

He rapped her arm. "Where are we, girl?"

"San Francisco, Master."

"Oh."

They'd been walking now for blocks. Finally, they'd reached a
landmark Suki could identify. Union Square. The crisp shrub-
bery trimmed with a slide rule. Kyoto's sky a dismal gray beside
the San Francisco blue. Macy's just behind them. I. Magnin.
The St. Francis. Clanging bells of streetcars, packed with smiling tourists, in merry processions up fairy-tale hills. And everywhere the eye could see, the soft glory of muted pastels.

Suki carried the luggage. He needed his hands—one to drape
the T-shirt over one muscle-bound shoulder, one to snap his
fingers or point at things that caught his eye.

"What kind of houses is them?"

Suki set the cases down, giving her shoulders a rest.

"Victorian style," she told him. "San Francisco fame to claim."

"What kind of people lives in 'em?" He started looking
through the square, as if to spy the residents.

"I don't know, Master," she answered. "Maybe office men."

He said, "Is that a fact." His attention focused on a young

man in white shirt and bow tie and polka-dot suspenders. The youth was nibbling at his lunch, enjoying a book on his lap. "I say Yuppies lives in 'em. Goddammit, I hate Yuppies! I think I'll kick his fuckin' ass."

"Master—" Suki started.

His attention, again, was distracted. Across the square a bag lady with a loaded shopping cart whistled, hitched her skirt up, squatted and pissed on the walk. Nearby tourists scurried off, looking over their shoulders with horrified eyes.

"What's this place again?" he asked.

She told him, "San Francisco."

"Can't say I care for the people. Where to?"

"Find hotel now, Master."

"Good."

FOUR

As they rounded Geary onto Powell, he grabbed her shoulder, pointing somewhere across the street.

She caught a flash of a red leather dress before a cable car clipped off the view.

Cars honking.

Bells clanging.

Somebody yelling, "Yo! Woman in red!"

And then he was shaking her shoulder again.

Behind them now: red leather handbags and shoes . . . and, stopping traffic at the light, a voluptuous redhead in leather like blood.

At Powell and Post his attention was caught by the headline in red from a newspaper box: RED LEATHER MANIA?

He slipped a quarter in the slot. Tugged at the handle. Rattled it.

"Where's my fuckin' paper!"

"Master," she said. But it had no effect. His whole body stiffened in angry clusters of muscles.

"I won't be cheated," he announced. He started to turn in a circle, looking for the source of this latest insult. "I won't be fucked with. I won't be fooled with. I won't be laid a hand on!"

His fists had clenched. His lips were drawn. His eyes, again, appeared to blaze through the mirrored lenses.

His attention was caught by a movement of blue.

Two policemen, to the right, advanced cautiously, hands at their clubs.

"Cops," he snarled. "I'll kill 'em."

"*Hank.*"

His shoulders slumped. His fists relaxed. He appeared momentarily dazed. Then he smiled happily. "Hey, boys, what's cookin'?"

The larger of the two said, "Sir, what seems to be the problem?"

"Officers, this damn machine has just et my quarter."

"New in town, sir?"

"Surely am. And I would like my paper. Now."

The officer removed his club. Tapped at the sign that read 35 *cents.*

Suki moved quickly. She slipped in a dime, fetched the paper, and bowed.

As they were leaving he asked her, "Where the fuck we at again?"

"San Francisco, Master."

"Shit, let's go to San Diego."

FIVE

The widow had given them money. More than enough for a month. If they survived, there'd be much more: fifty thousand American dollars for each of the women in red.

Their immediate need was to find a hotel.

But who could have guessed at the labor involved?

Time and again they were told the same story: not even a room for the night. And increasingly she came to dread the scenes that occurred when he opened his mouth. He wanted to know where the doormen were from, the desk clerks and the bellboys. He wanted to know why rooms were rented to African princes and Muslims and Jews.

He could not be made to see that if he would just put his shirt on, walk softly, speak respectfully . . .

They continued their trek along Post Street. The last doorman, an elderly black in Elizabethan garb, had slipped a few words in her ear: *Get him off the street, girl. Get him down from whatever he's on. I know a bed and breakfast place* . . .

They were almost there now. Her shoulders ached. Her legs, though strong, could not continue much longer.

He slapped the paper on his leg, his attention focused now on the beggars everywhere. Men and women, old and young, huddled in doorways with small signs. They had AIDS . . . They were Vets . . . They needed bus fare out of town.

His agitation grew and grew, until the cables of his neck looked ready to explode.

"Get a fuckin' job," he growled.

Suki set the bags down. She looked at him and hated him and yearned for even a second with *Hank*.

She murmured the word. The hot tears would not stop. She scarcely heard him call her name.

Then he was with her. He said it again, stroking and kissing her hair. "Suki, darlin', what's them tears? Hey, hey, c'mon now."

She sniffled. "Please to put on shirt. You big scare everybody!"

He wondered what his T-shirt was doing in his hand.

"Jesus," he said, slipping into the tee. "Wasn't we just at the widow's?"

"Tuck shirt in," she told him. Sternly now. They had to go. No telling how long he'd be here as he was.

"Sure, okay, don't snap at me." He tucked it in neatly and straightened his belt. Finger-brushed his hair for her. "Better?" he said. And he smiled, Hank's smile, the left side only rising.

"Behave self!" she told him.

"Sure. Gee, y'all are touchy."

"No be rude!"

"*Me?* I swear."

Suki sighed, stooping to pick up the luggage.

He cried out in astonishment. "Y'all *mind* if I carry the bags?"

SIX

They had little trouble finding a room at the Continental. The thirty-room Bed and Breakfast was slivered between two fat sleep-banks for blue bloods. It was homey and cheap, but they got through the door.

"How y'all doin'?" he asked them. "It's a pleasure to be in your city on this fine, *fine* summer day. And, by the way, I gotta say, why this place looks as clean as a whistle!"

He praised the climate. Praised the rugs. And praised the paintings on the walls, of kittens and fox terriers.

He was especially taken with the blond desk girl's red headband.

Suki wondered grimly how long this spell would last. She remembered the widow's instructions about getting separate rooms. But how was she to do that now when the balance within him had shifted?

"Together room," she said and paid for a couple of nights in advance.

She took the key and turned to see him standing by their luggage. He bowed, politely opening the elevator door.

She thought they were going to make it. But he was undone by the jolt of the lift starting up. As it began to rise, so did the spirit within him.

He rattled the grill of the door like a cage and roared, "Where the fuck am I now!"

Just once more, she promised. Just get him to the room, that's all.

Danger, warned the widow.

Saa . . .

"Hank," she said.

This did the trick.

He turned, looking stunned and exhausted.

"Hey," he said. "What's cookin'?"

SEVEN

He slipped off his mirrored shades. His eyes, no longer blazing, looked wholly out of focus. He looked at her, but not at her. He yawned, asked "Seattle?" and lay back and closed his eyes.

The room was the size of her own in Japan. A double bed, neatly made, with a handsome, if frayed, printed quilt. In the corner, where she sat—just a small nightstand between them— the rose chair had some life in its cushions. Scarcely room for him to walk between the bed and the dresser. But the room was clean and warm. And now, at last, there was time for her to sit and think.

Kuniko and Michiko . . . One or both of them certainly here . . .

How would they find each other?

If Sister was inside them both . . . could one half find the other, as the old widow had feared?

Saa . . .

Where would they live?

There was no way to know.

Besides, not necessary. Surely the widow had been right again: The women would be drawn to him. For he was the soul of Oppression.

She heard a low junkyard growl on the bed. She looked up in time to see the promised siege beginning. He began to roll from side to side. And as he rolled, his tortured voice divided into sides.

Left: "Little pussy boy!"

Right: "I fuckin' hate your ass!"

Left: "Can't do nothin' . . ."

Right: "Oh, God—Oh no—Please, that's my cat!"

She whispered, "Shhh!"

He tossed and turned.

His name, that forbidden word, cried out to be spoken.

But already she could see the price.

She closed her eyes and instantly felt herself starting to drift. She let go.

EIGHT

Suki was having a wonderful dream.

There'd been a double wedding. Kuni and Jack were as happy at last as she'd always dreamed they would be. In thanks, the two had taken them to their favorite Love Hotel. It seemed a little odd, of course, having Kuni and Jack in the room: Kuni in her wedding dress, the two men in long-tailed black suits. Only she was naked. And yes, come to think of it, she did wonder vaguely why they were holding black candles.

But who said a honeymoon had to be traditional?

She climbed the ladder up Dumbo's great head. Sat astride the well-lubed trunk. Waved to the friends she loved best in the world.

She felt the trunk ripple behind her, coaxing her slippery descent.

"Wheeeee!" they cried.

And Suki laughed.

Until she saw the waterbed—now a huge mass of slithering, glistening coils.

She awakened with a cry.

Thank God, she thought.

And then, Oh no.

The room was dark. She'd been sleeping for hours. And he was no longer with her.

NINE

Michiko shimmied into the red leather dress she had bought.

The fit was uncomfortably snug at the bust, her breasts had grown so full and ripe. She'd have to have a new dress made.

Tonight, though, she was hungry and would rather die than wait.

Tonight!

Put the boots on! Sister begged. *Oh, Michiko, please hurry and put on the boots!*

Michiko giggled softly. Sister was both Santa Claus and a half-dozen tots at the tree.

Put the boots on, boots, please, boots!

Playfully, Michiko toyed with the lid of the heavy white box.

Hmmm, she thought. I don't know . . . Do you think we should really go out in red boots?

Miiiii-chiiiii! Boots! Boots!

Welllll, you have been good to me. And tonight's a special night.

Boots! Boots!

I guess it can't do any harm if I try one boot on . . .

Boots!

Michiko set the lid aside. Parted the folds of the red tissue wrap. Inside, the soft and supple sheaths coiled about stiletto heels, opened lushly, at the cuffs, into full-lipped scarlet mouths.

Michiko sat on the edge of the bed, her skirt rising up to red panties. She licked her lips and slipped one tiny foot through the soft, loving warmth of one mouth.

The leather kissed her ankles.

The leather lapped and licked her calves.

The leather encircled her knee with its tongue.

And when the leather reached her thigh, the mouth began to wetly pant, throbs of air that pierced her through.

BOOTS! BOOTS! Sister begged.

Michiko fell back, winded by the rush of desire and power.

She saw him standing at the door, looking more dead than alive.

Panting, she slashed the air hard with one hand.

He was there on his knees, gasping "Yes, dear!" to slip her left foot through the next scarlet mouth.

Miiiii-chiiiii! Sister wailed. *You promised lots of lipstick!*

TEN

Kuni was in torment here, the worst she'd ever known.

She could not eat.

She could not sleep, no more than minutes at a time before coming to, in a fever, torn between the need to kiss and the revulsion she felt at the thought.

Something had gone wrong, she knew, and gone wrong horrifically.

She could not control the voices.

Sister's she could understand. Having kissed, she was possessed, with that voice and that spirit inside her.

But Sister's voice was only one. And it seemed tormented too, crying in ciphers that tore at her soul: *Bad kissing . . . Wrong kissing . . . Crush the crushers, that makes strong . . . He was weak . . . Strong kissing quick . . .*

Jack's voice perplexed and haunted her. It was at once quieter and stronger than she'd known: **Kuniko, I adored you . . . I used to watch you brush your hair, a hundred strokes, and count each stroke . . . I fell in love with the small things: the way you laughed, the way you moved . . . I fell in love with qualities: sincerity . . . tenderness . . . good humor . . . charm . . .**

The third voice, to Kuni, was by far the most distressing. Because it was her voice, at least in the tone. Yet the thoughts were an absolute stranger's.

This stranger's voice was speaking now in the Japan Center, where she'd come craving some small touch of home.

Kuni sat at a single wood table in an open food court. Her cold noodles lay untouched before her. She sipped green tea and stared and stared at a young couple two tables down. Japanese girl, in her twenties, wearing a gray Berkeley sweatshirt. Blond American boy in a samurai tee.

San Francisco, the voice said. **I don't know where the slaves are . . . They're free and they look happy . . . Asian women, American men . . . Everywhere I look I see—**

Three mixed couples came her way, the girls happily chatting in unpracticed slang:

"C'mon, let's book."

"Hey, you guys, why don't we hit North Beach and—"

"Uh-uh, no way. I got this major sugar rush for a Double Rainbow!"

Freedom here was like a game and not, as she'd thought, a cruel war. And love seemed like a bowl of tea, with each side adding sweetener to its satisfaction. The men added black hair,

the longer the better . . . a more compact and less threatening
frame . . . a touch of the exotic in the slanted almond eyes
. . . and, in the musical voices, the illusion of submissiveness.
The girls added fair skin . . . a soft loving manner . . . that
gratified look the men had in their eyes . . . a taller, more
athletic build.

    **Oh, Kuniko, remember the airport? Darling, when I saw
you . . .**
                         Boots!
    Gentleness . . . Sincerity . . .
      Bad kissing!
      Feed me quick!
   **I remember our first night . . . I shut the door behind
me . . .**
   But if I'd been born here . . .

Kuniko sat, in misery, the voices overlapping.
   She saw a Japanese girl in black leather jacket and blue jeans,
a cycle helmet in one hand . . . in the other, freshly cleaned, a
white and pink kimono.
   Kuniko, in a white print dress—a traditional girl, even now,
in her soul—envisioned herself on a Harley. Not a big one.
Lady size. Just one small touch of freedom.
   A great shadow covered her table.
   Kuniko blinked back the tears and looked up.
   Bodybuilder. Scruffy. Bearded. Neck lost in the gorges of
shoulders.
   He looked her over, his eyes lingering frankly on her rounded
and Sister-filled breasts.
   "Hey, baby," the man said.
   Kuniko felt her throat constrict, then slowly swell with hun-
ger.
   She nodded, smiling, a little.
   He parked, leaning over the table, arms crossed. He tensed
his arms till grape-sized crowns popped from his stacked biceps.
   "I got a stash of real fine blow. And twelve inches like you
never dreamed of."

Oh, Kuni, how I loved you . . .
Kiss!

Kuni's eyes, grown heavy, dropped. She saw the noodles on her plate throb and slowly start to snake.

"Hey, chick, what's it gonna be?"

The walls of her vagina throbbed, her throat felt full to bursting.

She looked up. There was still time. She could bolt from the table or warn him, cry "Run!"

Of course, if she'd been born here . . .

BOOTS!

He slipped one hand under the table, under her skirt, to the side of her thigh.

And over his shoulders, she saw it . . . the display in Shibumi, a tiny boutique: mannequin wearing a biker-type cap of shocking, oh shocking, red leather.

"Wait," she cried. "I be right back!"

She half stumbled, in a daze, gone crazy for red leather.

ELEVEN

Tracking him was easy. A six-foot-two shirtless hulk who looked breast-fed on steroids tended to get noticed.

"That way," said the desk girl. "About twenty minutes ago. He on drugs?"

A Korean deli owner, putting out his garbage, scowled at Kuni. Spat "That way."

A wino on the next corner nodded, sobbing "That way."

One block up she stopped again. An old man walking a poodle shook his head in disbelief. "You look like such a nice girl. Should've heard him screaming: Where's the gay boys? Where's the dykes? Sent him up toward Polk Street before he knocked me on my duff. I'd get a move on if I were you. A real rough part of town."

At Leavenworth she heard the screams and she broke into a

fierce, all-out sprint. Three buildings up, a pair of blacks blocked the walk, seeing her coming. She picked up speed, fists clenched and ready, flashing murder with her eyes.

"Fothermuckers!" Suki screamed. And "Move, move, move, move, move, move, move!" in rhythm to her strides.

They moved.

At Larkin, the screams now so clearly his own, she charged across without looking. Heard the squeals of brakes, blared horns. And took off, her feet on fire.

A half block up, the crowd had grown too thick for her to pass through. Suki made a small lane for herself in the street and charged through the horn-blasting oncoming cars.

At Polk, outside a seedy bar, a wall of men circled the entrance. Men in Stetsons, hard hats, baseball and biker caps. Men in leather, black and red: vests, chaps, jackets, miniskirts, and hot pants. Men with arms as large as his. Men with breasts as full as hers. This was surely a strange part of town.

She made her way with urgent cries and tuggings at their elbows.

She made her way with screams and shoves.

Finally, she reached him. And, struck dumb, she stood and watched like all the men around her.

He'd just finished banging his head on a pole, his mirrored shades shaken loose to the walk. With a moan, he collapsed to his knees.

His left hand was attempting to butt him again on the pole— when it flew, none too soon, to block a hard shot from his right.

Left!

Right!

Left!

Right!

The two hands engaged in a furious dance of feints, blocks, counterblocks, punches, counterpunches . . . now the left, now the right, crashing home on his chin or his mouth.

"Master!" she cried. "Master!"

But he could not hear her. Not over the screams of the crowd —"Go, man, go!"—and his own divided cries:

"Stop callin' 'em queenies and faggots!"

"I talk it like I talk it, boy!"

"The right word's ho-mo-sex-u-al!"

"Bumboys! Porkers!"

"Yaughhhhhh!"

"Grrrrr!"

The left hand gripped him again by the hair. And, with a yank, flipped him onto his butt.

They saw his eyes.

The laughter stopped.

His features relaxed for a moment into a wounded, haunted look that broke her heart completely.

Then he screamed, loud as a siren:

"OH, GOD, NO! I'M WEARIN' SNEAKERS! WHERE THE HELL'S MY FUCKIN' BOOTS!"

The right hand grabbed him by the throat.

The left hand shot, eagle-clawed, to his balls.

She knelt at his side and she cradled his head, whispering "Hank" till he stopped.

His body slumped against hers.

"This don't look at all like Kyoto," he said.

TWELVE

Perry's, the granddaddy of San Francisco's singles bars, was ruefully showing its age.

A half-dozen women were sporting red leather: two blazers, one headband, one handbag, one skirt. They looked like they might be half willing, if the right man passed a blood test.

But Jay Citro, forty, Wells Fargo V.P., remembered how it used to be. Before AIDS and *Fatal Attraction*.

On Friday nights at Perry's, once, the air had been charged with the heat of the hunt.

Now it was like a museum. Soon they could mount him like a trophy over the bar, stuffed with his three haunting questions:

When was it his drinking got out of control?

How long had it been he'd been sleeping alone?

Had sex the way it used to be gone out of style forever?

Jay was making bedroom eyes at his brandy snifter when he heard a low whistle behind him. And then the man beside him gasped. Far and away at the end of the bar, the mirror flashed red like a siren.

Jay set his drink down shakily. He still hadn't seen what the fuss was about. At five-nine he found himself dwarfed by Turks on tiptoe, some themselves standing on stool rungs to see.

But this was like the old days.

The way it was supposed to be.

The air, charged with musk again, stiffened the leaves of the overhead ferns. And sparks flashed off the buffed brass rails.

Sparks flashed within him too as a stiffening like the old stiffening grew.

He brushed aside two younger Turks in cheaper suits than his. He squared off, center aisle, and would have died before giving an inch.

Oh, baby, come to me.

The woman in shocking red leather, breasts swelling over and out of the V, came at him, licking her lips as she swayed. Her black waterfall hair reached the hem of her skirt, which barely covered the source of her musk. And the high red leather boots folded lushly, inches away, around her honey-colored thighs.

Yes! Yes! You are mine! I'm worth ninety thousand bucks and I've got a goddamn Ferrari . . . I'm a senior V.P. with Wells Fargo . . . I've got Oriental carpeting, a Jacuzzi, a certified Dali . . . Fuck forty years old, fuck the love handles too . . . I've made it with women so perfect the only thing missing was staples . . . I'll make you beg for mercy . . . I'll fuck you till you scream for more . . .

The woman stopped before him.

She winked one outrageously mascaraed eye.

Then she grabbed him by the tie, turned and half ran for the door.

THIRTEEN

She awoke in the chair she'd used to block the door.

He was seated on the bed, dressed and with his shades on. He had his wallet in one hand. He'd retrieved it while she slept, upending her purse on the bed.

She took a sip of air and waited, wondering how this would go.

"Where's my stuff," he asked her. And it wasn't Hank who was asking. "My credit cards . . . My license . . ."

She saw her carryon under the bed. If he'd looked there, he wouldn't be asking.

"Mugger men," she told him. She should have trashed the wallet itself. But the taking of money was not in her blood.

"How many?" he asked her.

"No could count." What was the limit of his pride? What was an acceptable number?

He fingered the egg that had grown on his forehead. Probed at the deep purple welt on his neck. Winced, touching the finger he'd broken again.

"Six?" he asked her. "Seven?"

"More."

"Niggers?" he asked.

"Yes. And—Dayglows."

"*What?*"

"Italian men. And China men."

"I whup their asses good, girl?"

"Fight like warrior in big book. They run like children, cry for help."

He counted his money and laughed like the devil. "Hell, my fuckin' license expired! Some town. Where'd y'all say we was again?"

She told him.

He said, "Should've knowed. I'm starvin', let's get us some grub."

FOURTEEN

A buffet was set up in the basement beneath a maze of steaming pipes.

He whistled as he loaded up with toast, eggs, sausages, hot cereal, and coffee. He wondered where the *grits* were and the greased *white bacon*, but he did not complain.

Suki took half portions, longing already for pickles and rice, bean curd soup, real breakfast.

The room was half-filled. Mostly travelers, young, looking tired and not at all flush.

He nodded to several. Stopped to tell a red-eyed boy to get a job. And made his way in loping strides to a corner table.

He ate like an animal. Not even papa and grandpa combined could have rivaled the sounds that he made.

About halfway through, though, he stopped, looking over her shoulder.

Without a word he stood and loped to snatch the news from some boy's hand.

The victim cried in protest.

And she was reaching for money to pay when he slapped the news down and she saw the headline:

TWO BODIES FOUND CRUSHED

And, to the right, the subhead:

GRIM SUSPICIONS OF WOMEN IN RED

"Hurry eat," she urged him.

"Why?" He stared at the headline and smacked, slurped, and crunched.

"I buy boots," she promised.

"Oh." He stuffed his mouth with eggs and toast, chewing on the offer. "I want pointy steel toes on the boots."

She said, *"Hai."*

He took a long sip of coffee. "And—"

He regarded her through mirrored shades, smiled almost sweetly. "Be right back," he told her. He was out of his chair before she could react.

"Where go!" she cried after him.

He looked over his shoulder and sighed.

"Christ, can't a man take a piss in this town?"

Twenty minutes later he still had not returned.

She thought she knew just where to find him.

FIFTEEN

Eight TVs in ten had been tuned to the special called "Murder Most Red."

The fever, till now slowly spreading, was fanned . . . and, with the morning news, went wild. San Francisco style.

By nine a dozen heads had rolled in the top department stores for failing to raid the South's sexy campaign. Overnight some dead hick was a fucking hero. By ten a hundred more heads, just barely attached to their necks, were screaming into telephones for dresses, hats, skirts, shoes, boots—anything made of red leather.

The switchboards, lit, stayed lit without time to blink between calls.

Boutiques that had, the week before, run Going Out of Business sales were fielding calls in a frenzy. Chapter Thirteen might be struck from their books.

Phone lines were overloaded to Sausalito, Berkeley, Monterey, Santa Cruz . . . anywhere a girl might drive to get the real thing, in red leather.

A hundred women phoned in sick to jobs throughout the city: lawyers, nurses, cosmeticians, lady cops, and typists. By noon almost half of these were in L.A. to shop.

The day was young. But it had been a long time between fevers. And San Francisco, from the start, had found fever the best state to be in.

SIXTEEN

Michiko sent Cotter off with a list that would keep him busy all morning.

She felt a powerful hunger to grow in the chief way she had once been crushed.

She'd need:

The Wall Street Journal . . .
The New York Times . . .
The Economist . . .
San Francisco Business Weekly . . .

Brochures from half a dozen banks, with detailed information on interest rates and I.R.A.s . . .

She had ten thousand dollars cash from last night's entertainment: five hundred from the man's wallet, the balance from the wall safe she'd opened with a kiss.

There had been a woman once to whom ten thousand dollars had seemed as remote as a million.

But nothing was beyond her now.

Michiko parted the curtains, her naked body blessed with light. Her womb and throat began to throb, constrict, and fill with music:

Michi!

Oh, Sister!

Aren't we good together?

Yes!

Let's kiss a politician, ne? Someday we'll be President!

Then we can kiss a reporter! If we know how to use the press—

Oh-oh, we're forgetting: Kuni kissed a weight lifter and surely by now she's incredibly strong. If only— No, too risky . . .

Michiko squealed with pleasure.

Oh, Sister, no, it's too good to be true! Are you thinking what I'm thinking?

Tee-hee! A double-header?

Wheeeeeeee!

She started dancing through the room. She cupped her high, heavy breasts in her palms and bounced them, watching them ripple. Her throat gave first, and easily, the mass slipping through like an oyster, that smooth, and splitting into slick, lengthening strands. Then came the powerful churning below, just like giving birth to a Sister.

Michiko danced until she was covered with long and glistening coils.

She dropped like a stone to the carpet and rolled, moaning: "I love you!"

SEVENTEEN

Tenderness . . . Gentleness . . . Oh, Kuni—

Stop!

Kuniko looked under the bed in her room, easily lifting the frame with one hand.

Again he wasn't under there. But she wasn't about to give up. He was *here*.

And not in her head, as she'd thought.

She'd come home, her spirit *pumped* from the powerful kissing she'd done. Sister purring with content; the voices finally stilled.

She'd closed her eyes.

Drifted wonderfully down into a well of well-being, content. She belonged to Sister now and Sister would take care of—

Help!

The word had gone off like a bomb in the well. A cruel and brutal awakening:

Jack had, somehow, gotten out!

Kuni? Honey? Over here! I'm in the bathroom—let me out!

The voice so real. So clear. So his.

"Jack?" she'd cried.

Oh, Kuni, I really, really loved you!

She'd never imagined such strength as she felt. And the gift inside her was itching again for release.

But had he been in the bathroom?

Oh no, not Jack, though she hoisted the claw-footed tub from its bolts.

Tenderness . . . Gentleness . . .

Somehow, when she hadn't been looking, he'd gotten into the dresser!

I used to watch you brush your hair . . .

And on and on, all through the night, Jack called her from the chandelier. The hall. The radiator. He'd grown that cruel and quick and sly.

Now, though, Kuni had him.

The closet—she'd forgotten it!

Wouldn't it be just like Jack to hide *there* and pitch his voice all through the room?

"JACK! JACK!" Kuni screamed, the coils spewing from her throat.

She half tore the door off its hinges. But the closet was empty, just luggage and towels.

Sick in her soul, Kuni fell to her knees as the voices, all of them, beamed and echoed everywhere:

> **Of course, if I'd been born here . . .**
> Oh, Kuni, how I loved you!
> **If I'd ridden a Harley . . . been raised to believe that I, as a woman, was equal . . .**
> *BAD KISS!*

EIGHTEEN

The Polk Gulch begins at the Polk Gulch Saloon, where Suki had found him the last time.

The bars open at dawn and by ten, when she came, the Gulch was like an open wound roaring for a rubbing.

Men danced and kissed defiantly in the windows of "Creamy's" and "Cruisers," while sullen packs of Hispanics and blacks, some wielding clubs, rapped the windows. Across the street, two thuggish whites with baseball bats yelled "Niggers! Spics!" And in every other doorway was a haunted figure, huddling in a cardboard wrap or stretched out in a puddle of urine.

He wasn't on the corner.

But no need today to ask for help.

She heard the screams two blocks away.

A block away she saw the crowd.

She found him bleeding profusely from nose, mouth, and a wound on his skull. His left fist, catching him under the ribs, lifted him clear off his feet, up the pole. Then the right came crashing down in a thundering blow on his skull, and he sank. Down but not out, he continued, while the left and right voices had at him in turn:

"Pig, they ain't dykes—they's women!"

"I had enough of your shit! I will kill—"

"That's just—the way—they is!"

"Eat shit!"

She could not determine, though, how much of the damage he had done himself.

For, in the crowd around him, outside the Sukkers Likkers Bar, a vicious half circle had formed. Three heavyset women in leather and jeans, and a baby-faced blonde in a shocking red dress, jeered at him and threatened him and kicked his legs and arms. Something spattered on his head. A balloon from above, filled with urine. And then began a cruel rain of eggs and fruit and garbage.

She could not bear to watch this.

She heard the widow begging *No! Not yet, the time is wrong!*

But part of him, however small, was still the man she loved. And anything was better than seeing that part suffer.

Babyface spun in a wheel kick, stiletto heel headed straight for his eye.

Fuck the widow, Suki thought.

She dove, knife hand chopping.

And Baby, kneecapped, went sprawling with a shriek.

The bull women pushed their sleeves up.

Suki caught his left fist as it crashed on his cheek.

"Ted!" she cried.

"What?"

She cried, *"Ted!"*

He said, "Who?"

She screamed, "TED!"

His body went rigid. He shot to his feet.

He said, "Yeah."

He said, *"Yeah."*

And then, "YEAH!"

Together, they were awesome.

NINETEEN

(Once the word is spoken, there can be no turning back. You must never attempt to oppose him once the spirit possesses him fully. Within limits, though, he can be managed, if you are lucky and sly . . .)

Crowds parted before him like waves at the prow of a powerful liner.

He gave no sign of noticing. He now existed on a plane where such things were his due.

"I'm the man," he said, "I'm the *man*," as they walked, blocks between them and the sirens. He wore his Atlanta Braves T-shirt, confident now of his bulk.

"You are strong, Master."

"Yes."

"You like god."

"Yes, I am."

Get him farther up Polk. Time to figure this out: How could she find an apartment *today?* One look at him in this condition, and the Continental would phone the riot squad.

Suki found the spectacle perversely fascinating. His eyes would be perfectly focused ahead, his stride calm and purposeful . . . when suddenly his whole attention would swing to something that offended him. And he'd announce in a cold, lifeless voice, as if he were taking dictation:

Niggers in suits . . . Had to stop, it was wrong . . .

Men in dresses . . . Had to go . . .

"You are strong, Master."

"Yes."

"We have work."

"Yes, we do."

"Come, Master."

"Hey, who's the *man*."

"Master, you."

They were crossing California Street when he heard a commotion behind them.

He turned to see a taxi blocked by a crone with a walker. Driver leaning on the horn and pounding on the dashboard.

"'Scuse me," he said. "Be right back."

Suki groaned.

He left the driver, yanked from the window, collapsed in a heap on the roof of the cab.

He carried the woman to safety.

Cheers and honks behind him.

Whistles.

He approved.

He bowed to the woman, saluted the crowd.

"The South shall rise again!" he cried.

(Within limits, though, he can be managed . . .)

She backed away from him, sniffling, looking sadly at his feet.

"What's your problem?" he growled.

She said, "Sneakers . . ."

"MY GOD!"

He stared in horror at his feet.

Suki rolled the dice again. She had to keep him *busy*.

"And real man, I thinking, wear leather."

He leaned over, hands on hips, his lips stretched tight and quivering.

"That's a mouth and a half on your face, girl. I do swear I'll reduce it to size."

He seemed prepared to do it now.

(Within limits, though . . . if you are lucky and sly . . .)

"Real man work," she said calmly. "Then play."

She pointed at a paper box, red headline screaming of Women in Red.

"Well, gimme some *money!* I got stuff to buy."

She felt his eyes boring into her back as she led the way to the bank.

She came out with a thousand from cashed traveler's checks.

He took the money, snarling. "Be here at three o'clock sharp. I'll kick your ass if you're late."

TWENTY

Within an hour she had learned that APARTMENT FOR RENT signs meant nothing.

She'd walked eight blocks, both sides of Polk, jotting down numbers from overhung signs.

Three calls connected to answering machines that requested a number at work to call back.

The other calls connected with voices that droned like machines: Make an appointment . . . Fill out the forms . . . We'll let you know in a week . . .

Undaunted, she went to the bank for more quarters, then sealed herself inside a booth. She tore through the Classified listings. The cheapest and the most outrageously priced. Eighteen of her twenty calls were answered by machines. The other two places were taken.

Shikata ga nai, Suki thought. Out of luck.

She shuffled off, her spirit crushed.

She shuffled right into a street pole and was sufficiently stunned that she bowed, beginning to apologize.

But then she saw the tattered flyer pasted to the pole:

APARTMENTS NOW—GUARANTEED!

TWENTY-ONE

The realtor wore a shiny suit. His shirt was stained and one button, popped, showed a soft belly with tufts of black hair. He wore a string tie with gold and pearl clasp. He'd worked hard to cover a bald spot, but too much hair had traveled south, now lushly sprouting from nostrils and ears.

His name was Jorge.

Whore-hey.

And Suki's *hara* told her that this was a man she might deal with.

He was pitching to the room, the desks around them likewise filled with hungry realtors, foreign-looking, all watched by a slick-looking white in the back with pounds of gold around his neck and a foul-smelling cigar.

Jorge flipped through a huge spiral binder. There were rooms for only five hundred a month—in *convenient, central* parts of town. There were studios, some with bay windows, in *quiet, historical* buildings, for only six hundred a month. Eight hundred to a thousand would rent a one-bedroom with *fireplace* and view of the *world-famous* Golden Gate Bridge.

Any one of these treasures, he promised, was hers—upon completion of the forms and payment of a viewing charge . . . first and last month in advance . . . plus a one-month finder's fee.

Suki followed her *hara* and pitched to the room, crying "Yes!" and "Lovely!" to each photograph he showed. All of them were lovely. All of them had their attractions. And he was such a good salesman she found it hard to choose. She set a hundred on the desk and implored him to pick a place for her.

Jorge gawked at the money. "Just twenty—"

But the white man roared, "So show her *now!*"

Jorge's car was parked a half block down. An '81 convertible, worn down in a dozen spots to large patches of dainty lace rust. The floor was littered with plastic foam cups and bags with golden arches.

On the dashboard was a glitzy plastic bust of Jesus. Jorge slapped the crown of thorns. A cigarette slid smoothly from the figure's painted lips.

He kicked back, smiling at her, not a body to pitch to in sight. "All right," he said. "Tell Jorge what it is you really want."

"I be a desperate woman," she said.

Jorge blew Jesus a kiss. "Thank you, Lord."

TWENTY-TWO

She didn't dare keep him waiting.

A minute late, and who could tell in what direction the spirit would lead him? Would he set off like a shark on the hunt the widow had programmed him for?

(He will not understand the why, but he will know the what . . . Oh, yes . . .)

Or would the spirit, overcome by a sudden rush of hate—

Suki waited by the bank, their luggage at her feet. No doubt, the Continental was still sighing with relief. She jingled the keys in the right pocket of her navy peacoat.

Front-door key.

Apartment key.

Jorge's humble abode. Theirs today, for one week, for just two thousand dollars . . . and a prepaid room for Jorge in the Hyatt, at ninety a night.

Saa . . . But it was perfect. As the spirit would see for himself if he came.

Three o'clock. Suki jingled the keys, already expecting the worst. Jorge would have a change of heart. Mr. Gold Chains would learn of their deal. Or—

Suki saw him coming now, just south of California. He was wearing a black leather jacket, the right side all vertical red and white stripes . . . the left, with USA over his heart—circled by glittering studs. His boots were red with steel toes brilliant in the midday sun. He'd found a white Stetson, which he wore cocked at a jaunty angle.

He also wore a wheel-sized spool around his right shoulder. He'd slung his arm through the hole, freeing his hand to lug six handled bags.

He came, crossing California, in a roller-hipped Marlboro walk, as if he were carrying nothing at all.

What he carried in his left hand, though, distressed her most of all. A thin, long box—about three feet. The size of a high-powered rifle.

He came, on time, and smiling.

He did not see, nor did she, the figure a half block behind him.

TWENTY-THREE

Kuni, unable to think through her pain, had set out for the one place she might find a few minutes peace.

Of course, the voices followed her—

I really loved you . . .

Jack . . .

Kiss!

—and people watched her as she passed.

But, as she recalled, or seemed to, the voices had been quieter at the Japan Center. Bonsai trees in windows lettered with familiar *kanji* . . . *Nihongo* sung sweetly to cooks at the grill . . . The leather-clad girl who had balanced a helmet and white-pink kimono . . .

What if she could find that girl and learn if *she'd* been born here—

Boots!

—or had devised some strategy she might be tempted to share?

Or if Kuni might watch the American boys once again with the Japanese girls . . .

Perhaps she might learn how they'd done it . . . or be assured that they *were* slaves and that Sister was right, she must

Kiss!

Post and Polk. The fever was beginning to burn through the Gulch. Two men-women in black wigs glared balefully at Kuni, hands on their red-leathered hips.

Kuni strolled past them in blue jeans. White Adidas on her feet. Haunted at the very end by the smallest things: sneakers . . . a sweatshirt . . . She might have relaxed . . .

The Japan Center was not far away. Perhaps she and the girl with the helmet might go for a—*spin*, that was it, on her bike. And the girl, a new friend, might say:

"Ah, nothing to it. You don't really have to be born here at all. There's no secret, you see, to American men. All you have to do is—"

KISS!

Couples parted, allowing her berth. And, truly, she was grateful. If she could get to the Center, and soon—

Kuni stopped. The voices stopped. The whole world had shrunk to one vision that could not have been, and yet was.

Swaggering up Polk Street, a tall man in a Stetson, a black leather jacket with red and white stripes, and red leather boots with twin glistening tips.

"No," she whispered. "Can't be!"

She hurried past Polk to a doorway to hide until the figure had passed her.

He waited for the light to change, swinging something the size of a rifle. He whistled "Dixie" cheerfully.

And Kuni, at once terrified and singularly hungry, followed him carefully, carefully.

KISS!

TWENTY-FOUR

Suki struggled to keep up with him.

There wasn't a chance of their catching a cab. Five had already refused them. One look at that box and off they'd run, slipping the locks on their doors.

But what did *he* care? He was fine, his energy abounding.

"Goddammit, I feel *good!*" he said.

He stepped up the pace, whistling "Dixie" again.

And Suki broke into a three-quarter trot, too proud to plead for a rest.

Mercifully, at Jackson, Polk sloped ahead in a gentle descent. Over the next rise, a half mile off, tall buildings half framed a blue slice of the bay.

He was forced to slow his pace, his lopsided cargo grown awkward. She kept up, two steps to his one, using the luggage for balance.

The Gulch was long behind them now. Here the street was densely packed with creamy bricks and rich pastels of Thai and Chinese restaurants, art galleries and hair salons, antique stores and packed cafes.

"I'm the *man.*"

"Yes, you are."

"Ain't no woman on earth ever met a man half the man I am."

"That right."

"I can chew glass and shit diamonds."

"*Hai.*"

"I can outdrink, outfight, outhunt, outfuck any man in this pussyboy town."

"You like god." Suki passed him, curling her lips in disgust.

Something hard and very sharp struck her brutally on the right buttock.

She nearly toppled, turning to see him retrieving one pointy-toed boot.

She dropped the luggage. Clenched her fists. The hell with the widow, the women in red. She wanted Hank back now. No more!

"You want play *now?*" She jerked her chin.

He looked enormously pleased with himself. "Now? Hell, a *real man* takes care of his business first."

Right on Broadway. There it was. The first, deceptive, gently rising portion of their climb. The main road veered right through a tunnel. They hung left and climbed for blocks past a nonstop succession of bay-windowed homes. Humming tracks for cable cars. And there, suddenly, sheerly, the *San Francisco* climb.

At the top even he was panting and wiping his brow.

Suki set the luggage down. She leaned against the breakwall that divided the road from the steep drop below, this one nearly vertical. Both sides were lined with angled cars a sneeze might neatly domino.

The city lay before them now in a chain of spectacular drops to the coast.

San Francisco. Even he whistled softly, admiring the view.

Or so she'd thought. Gradually, she realized that he was studying the windows of the crazy-angled homes while fondling the infernal box.

"Good . . . Good . . . Real good," he said. "All right, girl, which one is ours?"

Suki pointed to the left: a cedared hidey-hole with mostly boarded windows and a faded For Sale sign.

The house towered over its gingerbread neighbors like a swaggering, derelict uncle.

"Oh, yeah," he said. "This *is* the place."

Suki knew he'd just love the apartment.

TWENTY-FIVE

Kuni watched from between two parked cars until they had entered the building.

How could she ever have got it so wrong?

There was the problem—the Marlboro Man! Jack wasn't the bad kissing, *he* was. All muscle on the outside . . . pure baby fat underneath. Somehow he'd tricked her—and he was alive!

Kuni knew clearly what had to be done.

She would have to be more careful this time.

She would have to be stronger, much stronger.

Four o'clock now. She still had two hours to buy a red dress for the hunt.

Shocking, oh shocking, red leather.

And

BOOTS!

TWENTY-SIX

Downtown, Lacey's reflected the fever with an astonishing show.

In two windows Asian models prowled, in red leather dresses, like cats. To the Stones' "Satisfaction," they clawed the air with ruby nails and needily pawed at their loins. In each window were three mannequins, bulging beneath skimpy briefs. They had masks for their faces, of favorite male stars. Now and then the models used the mannequins as scratch posts. Or slipped their hands beneath the briefs. Tortured the torsos with fluttering kisses. And, finally, knelt for the deepest of all.

The crowd outside began to cheer as lights flooded the show windows crimson.

And Michiko looked proudly around her. Red leather dresses everywhere. And waist-length black waterfall wigs. She saw a few Caucasians whose eyes had been surgically slanted. A hundred more had Kabukied their eyes so artfully only a native could tell they were not Japanese.

The police couldn't possibly find her.

Not after she'd fixed her one problem: finding her dear Sister Kuni, who might somehow ruin everything.

TWENTY-SEVEN

Jorge's place. The digs of the divorced. Semifurnished with eyesores and orange crates. The rest of the building, deserted.

"Perfect," he growled. "This'll do me just fine."

The room measured twenty by twenty, its pine floor painted mocha. Jorge had made small, and poignant, attempts to ease the angst of bachelor nights by subdividing the room. Bricks and splintery planks formed a bookcase, marking off the living room. Inside this space were two pillows to sit on and a black rotary phone. A footlocker, covered with burlap and *Hustler* magazines, marked his sleeping quarters. A twin mattress was made up with gross floral sheets. By the door, a kitchenette with a small fridge and a hot plate.

The ceiling sloped up on two sides to a skylight. An odd touch of class in this desolate place. He truly admired the skylight. He yanked the footlocker out of the way. Pitched his gear atop the bed. And dragged the mattress seven feet, squaring it under the skylight, maybe fifteen feet above.

"Yeah," he muttered. "This'll do. Any luck and we'll get a full moon. Be real nice."

He drifted to the bay window. He stood without moving a very long time. Another man, another time, and she might have guessed he was stunned by the view. But the beauty below was beneath him, she knew. And she was not surprised at all when he raised his hands, positioning them as if he were holding a rifle.

"Bang," he said. "Bang, bang, dead, dead."

(Within limits, though, he can be managed . . .)

"Get to *work*," Suki said. "Work first, like real man."

He turned savagely toward her. "Well, clean this fuckin' place," he barked. "I ain't gonna live in no pig pen. And go on out and fetch me some beer!"

Then he stormed off to the floor just below.

Suki waited, listening. She heard him pounding on the doors. And then flattening one with the heel of a boot.

(He will know what to do, said the widow.)

Yes, but what in God's name was his plan?

TWENTY-EIGHT

Fifty feet of oily cable, wrapped about the wooden spool.

Bags full of pulleys, hooks, and parts she did not know the names of.

Nails, screws, nuts, bolts, hammers, wrenches, handsaws.

Four pairs of gleaming handcuffs.

Two knives: one short, with a finger-looped handle and a cruelly jagged edge . . . the other close to sword size.

Four boxes of shells for his toy in the box, each shell the size of her pinkie.

A black squarish *thing* with STUNNER lettered on the side.

She took a last look from the hall at his playthings, then shut the door behind her.

TWENTY-NINE

She'd been left nothing to clean with except a can of air freshener, sickly lemon-scented . . . two sponges blooming with fungus . . . and a mere sliver of hair soap.

And so she hiked downhill to Polk, her first moments of freedom since coming.

In a bar on the west side, well-heeled San Franciscans sipped at fruit-colored concoctions beneath a profusion of ferns.

Groceries lined both sides, with dewy displays of fresh produce.

She wondered: If she had been born here, a California girl . . .

She shook her head to clear it then of such futile thoughts.

She thought of Hank by the Sea of Japan, the finger he'd offered to papa.

Sannen kata ho.

Be strong.

Suki vowed, glancing fiercely at the lush pinkening sky: I will have him back again. There is nothing that I will not do!

She bowed then to his memory and marched briskly off to shop.

The way back up was easier. Yellow cabs weren't hard to catch when there wasn't a gun-toting psycho in sight.

After tipping the driver, she carried her bags and stood at the breakwall awhile. Again, the postcard-perfect vision fell in precipitous drops to the bay, now shimmering with hundreds of lights from the bridge.

Anything. She clenched her fists. *On my life, I'll have him back.*

From the house she heard the steady poundings of a hammer.

She thought Hank's name. No harm in that. Surely the thought of it was hers alone.

She bowed to the city.

Then, with all the strength in her, she willed herself to turn and bow to the thing that now worked in that house.

THIRTY

He met her on the landing, blocking her view of his workshop.

He held one hand behind his back. The angle squeezed the biceps, already well pumped by the hammering.

"Leave the beer," he growled.

She set the six-pack by his feet, where he'd jabbed at it with one finger. Colt 45. The man's man's beer, they'd told her at the deli. Cans. Real men liked to crush them.

"What's that stink?" he asked her. He poked his finger at the bag.

"Noodles," she said. "Chicken, rice—"

"Shee-it."

He grabbed her coat by one lapel, lifting her up onto tiptoes. His mouth was smiling, not his eyes, as he showed her the drill he'd been hiding. It was loaded with a half-inch bit. He touched her forehead with the tip, then withdrew a quarter inch as he squeezed the trigger.

The sound was terrifying. But if she resisted now . . .

This was Ted.

And he'd been called.

He was vile and hateful, but needed.

She hung there loosely, sipping air.

"I don't eat no Chink food, hear?"

"Yes, Master," she told him.

"Take it upstairs and get rid of the bullshit and bring me down the *meat.*"

"I will."

He set her down, stopping the drill as he did.

"And tomorrow mornin', crack o' dawn, I wanna smell *coffee* and *bacon*. I take my coffee plain and strong. I like my bacon crisp and *black*. Questions?"

"How like eggs?"

"Good question. I want the yolks as hard as rocks."

She was halfway up the stairs when he whistled at her.

"Girl!"

She turned slowly back to him, her molars rumbling as they ground.

"Yes, Master?" she said sweetly.

"Don't forget our little talk."

Suki bowed. "Happy time to play with you. After work like man."

He stormed back inside his room, sealing it off with the door he'd kicked in.

THIRTY-ONE

His energy amazed her. By midnight he'd been working, non-stop, for seven hours. Up and down the stairs he charged, to pace the room and measure things, then bang away some more.

Whatever he was building, snags in the construction taxed his patience to the full. He opened the closet and muttered, "Too small." He did the same with the bathroom. He measured off a corner section as if he were thinking of building a room. Then he spat in disgust. "No, they'll see it. They'll know."

Suki scrubbed and scoured and watched; listened to more of his labors below.

It had something to do with the bed, that was clear. But he scarcely looked at the bed when he came, or even his ferocious toys.

Angles and inches obsessed him. And the snags that still defeated him sparked the spirit's fury.

Through the night she'd heard explosive kicks of doors throughout the building as he rummaged for tools and solutions.

She heard the whine and woody buzz of an electric saw he'd found.

(He will know what to do . . .)

And it seemed that he did.
(The way will be the spirit's way . . .)
Not much chance of changing that.
(You must never oppose him . . .)
And yet—

The whine-buzz stopped abruptly. He sounded out a rebel cry and banged on the ceiling with something. Then she heard his footsteps taking the steps two or three at a time.

He charged in, jabbing at the bed.

"Gotcha," he said proudly. He knelt beside it and patted the floor.

And then he was off again, stopping at the doorway to draw one finger across the frame's top.

He looked at the dust on his finger and screamed:

"CLEAN THIS PLACE PROPER BY SUNUP!"

THIRTY-TWO

Three A.M. Exhausted, Suki stretched out on the pillows that Jorge had used as a couch.

The widow had been certain: The women would be drawn, as if by musk, in time. And the faster his spirit grew into itself, the more quickly the women would come. In which case, Suki feared—hearing him hammer and tinker below—they might arrive any minute.

Another fear, in its way worse: If their coming was delayed . . .

The women grew stronger with kissing, each stronger now by at least twice.

Had they found each other yet? If only she could know that much!

Suki's eyelids fluttered. She caught a final hazy glimpse of the long box on the bed.

Yes, the women could wait.

But could *he,* though?

Saa . . . She had about two hours left before the beast wanted its breakfast.

She allowed her eyes to close.

THIRTY-THREE

She awoke at the first pale suggestion of light.

Suki heard the absence first—of hammerings and sawings. Then she heard his breathing, low and steady, on the bed.

What she saw revolted her almost as much as it scared her: He was sleeping on his side, both arms around the rifle, with his right thumb in his mouth.

Without opening his eyes or removing his thumb, he snarled, "Make sure the bacon's *black*."

She slipped her shoes on, snatched her purse, and scurried from the room.

At the landing below, Suki stopped at the door he had managed to crudely rehinge. If she could steal a fleeting glimpse and learn what he was up to—

He bellowed like a raging bull from the bed above her:

"GIRL!"

She took the steps in record time.

THIRTY-FOUR

The headline read:

THREE BODIES CRUSHED!

The downhill path was perilous, but Suki speed-read on the stumble and ran.

Not two, or four, but *three* bodies . . . found in two different locations.

Sō . . . Michiko's and Kuni's paths hadn't yet crossed. And one of them was stronger now. Or, between them, they'd taken the two men . . . and there was a *third* woman in red. Either way—

Her attention was caught by a sidebar. A prominent San Franciscan had beaten a woman he'd met in a bar. The woman, a Caucasian who'd been wearing a red leather dress and black wig, had assured him she was Japanese. Later, though, in his apartment . . .

Suki trashed the paper.

She knew all she needed to know: Their time was shorter than she'd hoped.

THIRTY-FIVE

Not a cab to be found before sunup.

Suki trotted back up with his breakfast, lungs burning and legs aching.

She needed him well fed and *busy* today. The spirit was crazy, but it had a plan, and if *that* had a half ounce of cunning . . .

Halfway up, hope failed her. She dropped to one knee, wheezing. How many people must die here before the women came? And if they grew stronger and stronger . . . What could *she* do, though, to help him, in a city of eight hundred thousand? How could anyone find anyone who didn't want to be found? Michiko had probably been here for months. And—

"No apartment!" Suki gasped.

She took a long, slow drink of air, settling it down in her *hara*. She held it till she felt her pulse begin to slow a little. She let it out, slowly, ignoring the cries of her lungs for more air. Then, just as slowly, she took another sip.

Kuni had been here for one week at most. If she *wasn't* with Michiko . . . If she hadn't got lucky like Suki . . . Where would she stay?

A hotel!

Suki doubled her pace to the top of the hill.

THIRTY-SIX

He looked at her lazily from the corner of one eye. Yawned. And returned to the business at hand.

He'd moved the footlocker, topping it with Jorge's pillows for comfort.

He'd opened the window, but not for the air. He had his

elbows on the sill. He swung the rifle back and forth at prey
from the chart he had drawn on the wall.

NIGGERS
YUPPIES
CHINKS
GOOKS
JAPS
DAGOS
SPICS
BUMS
FAGS
DYKES
CABBIES
NUNS
SKINHEADS
PREGGERS

Beside each name were ten neat squares.
"Breakfast, Master," Suki said.
She turned away then, horrified.
"Set it down," he growled.
She did.
(Within limits, though, he can be managed . . .)
"Go," she said. "Play all day!"
"I'm on my fuckin' BREAK—y'all MIND?"
"Real man—"
He bolted to his feet, his neck a thick mass of cables.
She thought he was going to come.
Let him come.
But, instead, he tore the marker from his pocket.
He turned and scribbled Y'ALL on the wall, a single square
beside it.
Suki just managed the ghost of a smile.
"Need more big gun," she told him.
"No," he growled. "My bare hands."
He snatched up his breakfast, snarled something, and left.

THIRTY-SEVEN

There was no shortage of hotels in the Yellow Pages. One name was the same as another to her. The names of the streets meant as little. And she dared not risk second-guessing Kuni's choice of location or size.

Suki synchronized her calls with the building below of the devil's machine. When he stopped, he liked to hear her scurrying about the room.

She began with the A's.

"Hello, I looking for my friend. Please to see if Kuniko Kuroki . . . ?"

No.

No.

No.

No.

NoNoNoNoNoNoNo . . .

THIRTY-EIGHT

"Good morning. Hyatt Regency."

"Hello, I looking for my friend. Please to see if—"

"Just a minute, please."

Suki was connected with the Reservations Desk, where a high-pitched, lilting voice said, "Hello there. This is Peter. And how *may* I help you?"

Suki started over.

There was a second's silence while Peter checked the computer. Then he reported, "Sorry. Close but no cigar."

Cigar?

Suki said, "Sorry, but English . . ."

He laughed. "Close but no cigar means we have a name that's similar."

"*Aa.*"

"The last name is Kuroki, but the first name shown is *Connie*. Ha. Connie, Kuni. Sound alike."

"*Sō.* But no cigar."

THIRTY-NINE

Suki finished at ten. There were no more Kurokis, cigar-close or otherwise. She simmered with frustration, knowing Kuni just had to be in a hotel.

At the Continental, she herself had been asked for her passport. So how had Kuni managed . . .

(Ha. Connie, Kuni. Sound alike.)

What if Kuni, while offering her passport . . . Kuni, who'd hated Japan all her life . . .

She was starting to redial the Hyatt when he rapped on the ceiling and roared:

"I don't hear no workin' up there!"

FORTY

"Hello there. This is Peter. And how *may* I help you?"

"Hello, this be me again."

Suki asked if it was possible for a foreign tourist to use an American nickname. Could, say, a Kuniko Kuroki—

"Ah!" Peter saw her point. "Yes, sure, that could be done, at least on the short form I was checking. Naturally, on the *long* form . . . Let me check the other screen." Peter clattered a couple of keys. Paused. Then told her, "Bingo!"

"Cigar!" Suki cried, so excited she slammed down the receiver.

FORTY-ONE

They were taking a trip, he was certain of that.

And a long trip was just what he needed. A week, maybe two, off from dusting and scrubbing, cooking and following orders.

No, *orders* was too strong a word. And Cotter was sorry he'd thought it. Michiko's will *was* tempered steel and she *could* be —demanding. At least by lax American standards. But the thing about Michiko . . . Well, it was hard to say. When she moved her hand, he knew that he was born to please her. And, not so often now, but sometimes, when the moon was full, and he knew the meaning of witchcraft in bed . . .

Hard to get it up these days.

But that was fine. She'd move her hand . . .

Tired, more and more these days. And all his ribs were showing too. Bags under his eyes that could pack a box lunch. But when Michiko moved her hand . . . Surprising, how he could work on through the night. Like one of those battery ads on TV.

Sometimes she let him watch TV.

And all was well that ended—

Well, here they were taking a trip, fancy that!

He wondered where they were going.

He wondered why Michiko was carrying all of the bags . . . and all hers. Hers were, of course, superior. Made in Japan. Much stronger. Still . . . As long as she'd packed him some shorts for the beach!

He wondered, very vaguely, why Michiko was walking *behind* him. Almost as if to stay well out of view.

Whoops, there it was again. One of those Michiko hand waves. He felt his wonderings dissolve on the platform where they walked.

An announcement overhead. Their train would be here in two minutes.

He heard her whistling softly—Billy Joel's "Movin' Out"—farther and farther behind him.

Perhaps they'd ride in different cars. He wanted to ride in the back of the train. Stand at the windows and watch the tracks flutter out like two ribbons from under the wheels.

But first there was something he just had to do. He bypassed the last of the lines that had queued at the black strips on the platform.

On a devilish impulse, he trucked toward the end. His feet, for some odd reason, began to dog it a few yards away. But luckily, Michiko was there for him, as always. Again, he felt the surge of purpose that came when she moved her small hand. His feet got the message. They stepped up the pace.

Just in time!

Here it came through the tunnel, the smooth electric hum and whoosh.

The right way to start a real trip to remember was with a spot of good devilish fun!

"Hey!"

"Hey, mister!"

"Hey!"

Voices calling nervously. What did they think he was going to do—jump, when he'd just got to go on a trip?

Here it came now, whee, a train, with a wonderful rush of cool breeze on his face.

From the corner of his eye, he saw somebody charging—shot by a magical hand move into an ass-over-teakettle roll.

Thanks, hon, Cotter thought.

And then, with something like glee in his heart, he did what he'd just realized he'd always wanted to do.

He stuck his head around the wall at the instant the engine came barreling through.

This scared, as he'd been hoping, the conductor half to death.

But the "Boo!" was still frozen on Dave Cotter's lips as his head flew and bounced sixty feet.

FORTY-TWO

Michiko, for old times' sake, managed a scream—and a good one—at the sight of the head by her feet.

She continued to scream, on the heels of six women, all the way up the stairs from the platform.

Then, with a sigh, she turned left from the crowd and took the next steps up to Market. Where everywhere she looked she saw her hair, her eyes, red leather.

She whistled shrilly, caught a cab, and took off for her grand new apartment.

FORTY-THREE

On the way, Sister purred and continued to sort out vibrations.

One set was clearly Kuni's. Close.

And another, strong as musk. But not quite strong enough. Not yet.

FORTY-FOUR

The good news was that, since last night's kiss, the voices had grown softer. And there were interludes of something very close to silence. Kuni had slept for four hours last night. This morning she felt starved for *food*.

The bad news was there on the table beside her heaping bowl of soup.

THREE BODIES CRUSHED! the headline read.

Kuni folded the paper. Laid into her breakfast while drumming her nails on the page. Carefully, stealthily, she searched until she found a tiny corner of her *hara*, two inches under her navel. Here she might think safely, without awaking the voices. Thinking with each breath itself, thought distilled into airy sensation.

Breathing in: Three bodies crushed . . . Michi kissed twice . . . What's she up to . . .

Breathing out: Getting stronger each time . . . Already two ahead of me . . .

In: Say Sister lied and I wasn't called to join them . . .

Out: What if the plan all along was revenge . . .

In: If I kiss once this morning . . .

Out: And once this afternoon . . .

In: Then I'll be equal to Michi . . .

Out: And tonight I'll kiss *him* . . .

In: Yes, the Marlboro Man . . .

Out: And then—

In: I'll find—

Out: Mi—

In: chi—

Out: ko!

She felt the voices stirring then, quiet, dry rustles inside her, like leaves.

I loved you, Kuni!
Kiss!

Oh, Jack . . .

Kuni moaned, seeing now the Japanese girl with the helmet. Black leather jacket. New red leather pants. Her firm breasts rippling, as she moved, under a rock concert tee.

Kuni's throat began to throb. And then came the powerful churning below. Her own breasts heaved against the V of shocking, oh shocking, red leather. Her right hand drifted dreamily to the heated thigh at the cuff of one boot. She licked her lips and slashed the air with her left hand needily.

The girl came toward Kuni as if in a trance.

No! No girl! Bad kissing!

Kuni smiled and willed the girl to her.

FORTY-FIVE

He was on his *coffee break*—with his favorite toy, at the window —when Suki, risking everything, threw herself upon the bed, buried her face in the pillow, and bawled.

She kept wailing *"Haji!* Shame!" until he threw the rifle down and headed over in thunderous strides.

Well, now that she had his attention . . .

Suki sat up in one liquid move. Stopped the sobs cold with a sniffle. And folded her hands on her lap, head down.

"Sorry," she said. "Is okay."

"Oh, it is, is it? I work all day, I work all night, I try to relax for a minute—"

"Haji make me cry," she said. She sniffled, woefully shaking her head. The next part would be tricky, but she had to get him *moving* now. "My shame . . . to serve weak master."

"WEAK?"

She answered quickly. "Is okay. My shame balance with your shame."

He snatched her up in one fist with a yank. Her sweatshirt, drawn tight like a noose at her neck. Her face in his face. Her feet dangling.

Suki hung loosely and sipped at some air and told him again, "Is okay."

"SHAME?" he screamed. "My SHAME?"

"Red women . . . very dangerous . . . Is okay too scared to . . . hunt!"

"YOU'RE CALLIN' ME—"

"Even Colonel—"

"COWARD?"

He dropped her. She was glad of that. She'd expected him to throw her like a shot put through the wall. But the impact of the Colonel's name was beyond her reckoning. His eyes had a haunted and fugitive look. His grim mouth twitched and quivered. The use of his hands was a puzzle he could not seem to solve.

"I could whup his ass from the day I turned twelve. Don't talk to me of huntin'. Oh, the Colonel was fine with a grizzly. Look 'em right in the eye and then spit as he shot. But the ole woman turned him to jelly. Couldn't do nothin' but sit there and wait. So tell me who the hunter was when push come to shove. Who had the guts to stop talkin' and *do* it—sling a long rope 'round her neck and hoist her up in a jerky-foot dance?"

"You!" She did not say another word. She looked at him, horrified, and hating him with all her soul.

"Damn straight," he growled. "I was the man. Hank—"

Lightning streaked across his face. The left hand seized him by the throat, squeezing with steeled fury. He dropped to his knees, gasping:

"Oh, God—I knowed—y'all done it!"

"Grrr!" The right hand had him by the balls.

"TED! TED!" Suki screamed.

"What . . ."

"TED!"

"Who . . ."

"TED!"

"*Yeah.*"

Suki was behind him now, massaging his neck and his shoulders.

"You the man."

"Yes, I am."

"You like god."

"That's surely true."

"No one stronger!"

"That's a fact."

"You be world's best hunter!"

"Yep. And don't forget our little talk."

FORTY-SIX

His new shopping list ran a page and a half.

At two, when she came back, she found him just where she thought he would be: by the window, buffing the barrel of his gun.

But he hadn't been idle, as Suki could see. She dropped the bags at the doorway and gasped. The mattress had been mounted on a handmade wooden frame. Around the bed, a foot above, was a railing made of pipes. At the corners four lengths shot above it by about four feet.

Suki walked over and circled the bed.

He chuckled while she puzzled.

"Almost done," he told her.

It was like an abstract sculpture of the spirit that possessed him: crude, ugly, primitive. But what in the world was it *for?*

"Check it out." He joined her, proudly pointing out the features. He kicked the wood frame with the tip of one boot. "Rock solid," he said. She agreed. "Shake the rail." She tried, in vain. "Now take a look at this."

Suki knelt beside him. One side of the makeshift frame, she now saw, had been hinged. And his eyes were twinkling as he lifted the wood flap.

Suki cried *"Maa!"* leaning in for a look. The demon's real work had been hidden inside: a maze of cables, pulleys, and hooks rigged to what looked like a bicycle chain. A lone end of cable dropped through a hole he had drilled in the floor.

He slapped the flap down. Winked at Suki. Walked her 'round the other side. And positively beamed at a tattered and faded throw rug.

"Ain't it beautiful?" he asked her.

"But . . ."

He shifted the rug with his boot to reveal a flat handle of

some sort attached to more cable that led to the bed. He gave the handle a flick with his boot and Suki heard a brittle click.

"Hocus-pocus!" he growled. He kicked the wood frame. And, to her astonishment, the bed began to circle beneath the iron railing. "Get on the fuckin' mattress."

Suki said, politely, "Oh."

"Get on. Grab ahold of the railin'."

He was smiling as she did. Her small arms brought her hands just short of the full grip he'd desired. But his smile broadened as she looped her fingertips over and clenched. He tripped another hidden switch—and the iron railing, released from springs he'd compressed in the pipes, shot three feet up and then some before dropping and clicking in place. He laughed at her horrified look as she hung, gawking at the bed he'd set to spinning again with his boot.

"Spaghetti, huh? We'll just see about that."

Suki let go, dropping down to the bed, suddenly sick in her soul. She saw him, wrapped in steaming coils, turning the bed 'round and 'round like a fork beneath his screaming, outstretched prey.

"But, Master, how—"

He showed her. He'd built a wide but shallow drawer into the left side of the bed, near the rug.

"Cuffs'll be the tricky part." He slipped out one pair of four, dangling one ring from one finger. "But that's what I got this for." Out came the black thing lettered STUNNER. He hit the button, chuckling as blue lightning crackled from the head. He set it down. "And this," he said. Out came the knife with fingerholds and that cruelly jagged edge. And then the horrid swordlet.

Suki gulped. "But bed spin how?"

He shrugged, irritated. "Still workin' the bugs out of that one."

FORTY-SEVEN

Suki wanted to leave.

He would not.

Not just yet.

The phone in Kuni's room had rung and rung. He trusted his instincts: She'd be out awhile.

He had nothing but contempt for the details that still troubled Suki. How, for example, would they get in Kuni's room, unseen? And she'd be very dangerous. How were they going to—

Child's play. He refused to dignify the joke she called a *hunt* with a word of explanation.

Instead, he busied himself with his bed. Lovingly, he changed the sheets to the red satin ones she had brought him. He fiddled with the comforter, making sure it well covered both mattress and frame. He whittled the black candles' bases until they slipped, just so, into the ends of the vertical pipes. He checked and double-checked the other items with his list: Polaroid . . . lubricating oil . . . more hooks, nails, screws, pulleys . . .

He idled at the window, cradling the gun in his arms like a child.

Then, on a sudden impulse, he wanted to look nice. The hunt itself was trivial—but, still, the first show of his power.

He laid out a fresh change of clothes on the bed. He sniffed at the socks and the shorts. They were fine. He examined the blue jeans. He found a small spot that hadn't come out in the washing, and screamed.

She did what she could and then polished one boot while he brushed and rebanded his hair. She was just starting in on the second when he stuck his head out and bellowed:

"WELL, GET YOUR ASS IN HERE AND SHAVE ME!"

Ten minutes later, satisfied that he was dressed to kill, he charged down the stairs to his workroom.

His footsteps stormed across the floor.

Suki packed the Polaroid. Then, unable to trust him completely, she opened the drawer on the side of the bed and threw one of his toys in her purse.

He was waiting on the street, a metal toolbox in one hand.

He tapped the box.

He winked at her.

"Show time," he told Suki.

BOOK EIGHT
JULY, 1990
(Continued)
SAN FRANCISCO

ONE

Kuni shut the door behind her.

Safe.

She listened carefully, back to the door, before setting foot in the room.

They might be waiting anywhere, together or cunningly scattered: Jack's voice in the chandelier . . . Sister's in the minifridge . . . Hers—

But she heard nothing. And had heard nothing since that kiss: the Japanese girl underneath her . . . mouth to mouth . . . breast to breast . . . nipples stiffening in synch . . .

In all her life no kiss had been as sweet or half as hungry.

It broke Kuni's heart now all over again, the memory of that kiss's end. Blood and brains on the wall. And a sack of smashed bones.

Good kissing, though.

As sweet as wine.

And warm.

And like . . . a Sister's.

Mirrored arcs and supple curves . . . No rampant length of

meat below plunging, crudely, in and out, in a male sexual plunder . . . All silky-smooth and soft and moist . . .

Could it be, in the end, just as simple as that?

A natural end to the hunger?

Saa . . . At least an end to the voices, for now.

Kuni entered, glancing left and right. She could not remember having closed the bathroom door. But everything seemed
like a dream before—

Belly to belly . . . Silk to silk . . .

She sat on the edge of the bed. Floated back, her fingers
caressing her thighs at the boots.

A Sister's kisses were heaven and—

Aa!

Her fingers rose, slipping under the bands of her panties
and—

She heard a soft and furtive sound. Almost like the rustle of
leather.

Someone in the closet?

Jack!

> **Oh, Kuni, how I loved you . . .**
> **Of course, if I'd been born here . . .**

"Stop!"

She felt her throat begin to throb.

She was halfway to the closet when she heard the *meow* from
the bathroom.

"*Peaches!*" Kuni wailed.

She ran howling for the door, the gift already on the way.

She tore the door open and—

gasped, "No . . . Please . . ."

TWO

Suki and he had been waiting for over an hour when Kuni came
back.

Ample time, she had thought, to settle her thoughts in her
hara:

There really was no other way . . . The two women were
out of control, that was clear . . . And Kuni was no longer

Kuni, as such, but a walking instrument of evil Sakai Ito . . . Hank, dear Hank, her loving man, was in desperate need of her help . . .

By the minute she had grown still more resolute, immune to his growls from the closet. ("Where the hell is she? Goddamm it to hell!")

And when she heard Kuni's key in the door, she felt prepared for anything. She squared off in a flat-footed crouch, raising the toy she had brought.

She hadn't been prepared, though, for the anguished sounds she now heard from the bed: moans and weepy sighs . . . and then, shockingly, different voices:

"Oh, Kuni, how I loved you . . ."

"Of course, if I'd been born here . . ."

She felt her resolve start to crumble like sand, washed out in waves of sympathy.

What were they doing here? Kuni was sick. She was *uchi*, regardless of what she had done. She'd done terrible things, yes, but never as Kuni. The soft voices came from the woman she'd been, trapped somewhere inside her still.

Aa, though, he was waiting and he would not be denied.

She took a sip of air and did just what he'd ordered. She distracted Kuni with a soft kittenish mewling.

Then came the charge of footsteps and Sister's terrible, alien howl.

"*Gambatte*," Suki whispered, steeled again for anything.

Anything except the sight of Kuni's tormented expression.

"No . . . Please . . ." Kuni begged.

Please . . . Please . . . *Uchi* . . . Help . . .

The Stunner shook in Suki's hands. She blinked back the tears and cried, "Kuni!"

But, *aa*, she saw him coming then, over Kuni's shoulder. He had the drill raised. He was smiling.

Kuni whimpered, "Suki!" her eyes grown huge with confusion and pain.

But then they flashed with something else.

She'd seen him in the mirror!

Kuni sent her flying with a savage swat at the Stunner.

Suki caught a glimpse of the glistening coils as Kuni wheeled, shrieking "HANK!"

THREE

There he was, and look at him: a confused and cowering boy dressed up like a Marlboro Man.

Kuni slapped his Stetson off. Poked the USA patch on his jacket.

His eyes darted back and forth from the coils that lengthened and snaked in the air . . . to the drill at his side . . . to his hat . . .

"Where . . ." he blubbered. "What . . . Who . . ."

Oh yes, she was going to kiss him. But first there was something that Kuni had always wanted to do.

She hauled her fist over her shoulder to swing. She thought she'd knock him 'round the room, and start off by putting him through the back wall.

But something shocking happened first. Her fist was struck by lightning, which jolted up and everywhere, crackling through the coils' tips and her astonished eyes. Her body went into a mad spastic dance, her head snapping back to see crackling blue sparks.

Kuni dropped to her knees, dribbling puke, shit, and piss. The coils fell from her mouth to the floor, where the tips twitched, sizzling.

She heard Suki calling, "Ted!"

Looked up to see him rub his eyes.

"Ted!" Suki cried again.

"Who?" he answered, yawning.

"TED!"

"Oh, yeah," he said.

He held the drill up, smiling. He treated Kuni to a wink.

And—*Aa! Maa!*—here he came.

Helplessly, she whimpered:

"..........................

....

...........If............

....
..........................."

But then he grabbed her by the hair. Placed the bit between her eyes. And calmly squeezed the trigger.

She saw him smile in the spray of blood and brains and bone.

Finally, she saw a great flash of light as Suki snapped their picture.

FOUR

Michiko walked out of "The Washbag"—The Washington Square Bar and Grill—with a prize catch on either arm.

Total time for pickup: two minutes and thirty-two seconds.

And this in a roomful of red leather clones.

Michiko paused outside the bar. The men, in a daze, scarcely noticed they'd stopped. Their eyes dreamily fondled the mounds swelling over and out of the red leather V. Michiko savored the moment. Soon they would kiss and her power would grow. For now, the San Francisco air was very cool and very sweet. And tonight the air was sweeter still with the sure knowledge of *safety*. The streets, the bars, the small cafes, were packed with scores of look-alikes . . . while cops cruised by, in cars, on foot, with the most hopeless expressions. Across the street, a half block down, she heard a small crowd chanting: "No . . . more . . . Safe . . . Sex!"

Sister couldn't have been more delighted. But, having completed the pickup, she was off at work again—attempting to lock into Kuni's disturbing, but fading, vibrations.

Going . . .

Going . . .

Aa, maa!

Michiko shuddered violently and knew, in her *hara*, that Kuni was gone.

She brushed the men's arms off abruptly. She could not see through Sister's pain. Or through her own deep *haji*. Shame: to have forgotten that Kuni was a Sister. Shame: to have forgotten the noble dreams they'd shared. Shame: a Sister brutalized and wholly alone at the end.

The two men clutched at Michiko's hands, tugging her that way and this way. She sent them sprawling on their butts with a broad sweep of her arms. And, raising her hands to the heavens, she prayed:

"Help me! Tell me where he—"

Click.

Their vibrations locked at last.

Super-male.

Super-strong.

"Trouble . . ." Sister whispered.

"Oh, yes!" Michiko quite agreed.

She turned a stern eye to the crestfallen men.

"Tonight's your lucky night," she said.

And then she stormed off through the night in search of her own kind of trouble.

FIVE

"When's the Colonel comin'?"

"Soon."

"I ain't ready . . . Need more time . . ."

"Is okay."

"No! Cut her down!"

His fever was alarming—he'd been burning since the kill. The lights in the apartment had made him cry in anguish. And then the pressure of his clothes became unendurable. Now the moonlight on his naked skin brought coos and murmurs of relief. She risked lighting a couple of candles atop the bed's vertical pipes.

Something, somehow, had gone wrong. As if Kuni, in crying Hank's name at the end, had torched a keg of kerosene.

The magic word, the spirit's joy, now only fueled the fever. (Ted . . . *What* . . . Ted! . . . *What!*)

Hank . . . Ted . . . Who was he now, or was he both together? Divided once too often, a forced fusion of flawed halves?

He found some comfort at the window, where the gun he'd

polished shone. He cradled the rifle and rocked it while reciting the names on his list.

"Niggers . . . Yuppies . . . Chinks . . . Gooks . . ."

Halfway through the list, though, he set the rifle down. He shuddered uncontrollably. Wrapped his arms around himself. Then recoiled from his touch.

Finally, he saw the bed. And he approached it slowly, his eyes way out of focus. "She's comin' . . . Oh, she's strong now . . . Soon . . . But I'm the man . . . I *am* the man . . . I— How's this damn thing work? . . . Oh, yeah . . ."

He lifted one side of the mattress, withdrawing one strap of a seat belt.

"Don't forget to buckle up . . ."

He replaced the strap abstractedly. Then he sat on the mattress and yawned, leaning back.

"*When's* the Colonel comin'?"

"Soon," she told him. "How bed spin?"

"Later," he said. His eyes closed.

Forgetting his fever, she shook him.

He howled, "Oh, God Jesus, I'm on fire!"

"Please, Master, tell me! Tell Suki how bed spin!"

He smiled dreamily. "It'll be fun . . ."

Suki knelt beside the bed.

His skin was enflamed. Yet he shivered. She covered him carefully with a lone sheet. He turned his head from side to side and streams of sweat poured over pounding temples and down his scorched cheeks.

Suki whispered to him, with no real hope of his hearing a word.

"Listen me. Who you be now, I cannot know. But you the man. You the real man. *Sannen kata ho.* Be strong. You like warrior. You like god. This woman, she be nothing. Cannot hurt you. You the man."

His way or none, then.

Shikata ga nai.

Suki sprang to her feet. *Shikata ga nai?* No three words she had been taught seemed more hateful to her now. It can't be helped. It's *karma.* Fate. Accept, without emotion. Accept, without resistance. Accept, because you are a woman and men are the superior breed. Accept, because you are a *burakumin*. Accept with a shrug, say *Shikata ga nai.*

She clenched her fists, vowing *"No!"* in a voice she scarcely recognized.

I don't accept.

I won't accept.

This is California and how can life be hopeless here?

His way, yes. But it would work. Because she was going to finish the job.

Soon, he'd said. Michiko would come. And if she knew of Kuni's death . . .

Suki checked the front window. Across the road, in varied rooms, she saw men embracing their women in red. On the street, matching couples stumbled feverishly to their cars.

Sō . . .

She clicked the lock. Patrolled the room, securing every window.

Michiko would probably use the front door. And would pass by the workroom below on her way. The immediate threat was to Suki, not him. If she were surprised by Michiko . . .

How much time would she need?

Say an hour, with luck.

Surely the gods owed them that much.

Suki eyed the rifle longingly. If only she knew how to work it! Thank the gods she didn't, though.

His way or else, the old widow had warned.

She took a tiny sip of air. Settled it down in her *hara.* And moved, cat-footed, to the bed, where she eased the drawer open and replaced the Stunner.

On second thought—no disrespect intended to the widow—she helped herself to the demon's two knives.

Suki waited a couple of seconds till his breathing steadied. Then she raised the sheet as gently as if she were parting rose petals.

She set the handle of the short knife in his open palm. His fingers curled around it, the broken finger with a *crack.*

He had *something.*

Just in case . . .

Suki turned. Then wheeled around, hearing a soft silky rip.

She snatched the sheet over his knife's dreamy arc. He sighed and squared the handle between his legs, by his balls.

Gingerly, she draped the sheet over the tip of the blade. She smoothed the sheet around him, draping the flaps carefully over the wooden frame.

She could do no more for him.

She removed two of the candles, snatched the wicked swordlet, and locked the door behind her.

SIX

She'd lost count of the steps, and the incline was steep. But Michiko was climbing to heaven, for sure, and panting with excitement.

Musk.

The electric humming drew her up the hill.

And, for the first time ever, Sister was beside herself, unable to think through the hunger. In Michiko's *hara* Sister paced and pounded and cried:

KISS!

SEVEN

At the top of the hill, Sister suddenly stopped.

Michiko swooned, sighting his lair: the lawn, overgrown with weeds . . . cedar shingles, cracked and dangling . . . windows, boarded shabbily—except for the bay window there at the top, from which came a flickering candlelike glow.

Oh, he thought he was bad one, all right! How brazen and how obvious. Murdered Kuni, had he? Now sleeping in a haunted house.

She was going to enjoy this.

She started up the cracked steps to the door—when Sister stopped her, smiling, and led her around to the side.

There, she listened carefully. She glanced once at the drainpipe that rose to the roof.

She had no questions now.

Sister knew best.

She felt her throat begin to throb as joyously as her heart pounded.

The coils flew. They encircled the pipe, instantly starting to shimmy.

Hand and foot, Michiko followed Sister's delirious lead.

EIGHT

Aa, maa, what joke was this?

Suki studied his hellish contraption with a haunted and stricken expression.

Though the shades were drawn and the room was in back, she'd lit the room only by candles.

(If Michiko should see a light under the door . . .)

Now even the candlelight was more than she could bear. Each dim flicker shed more light on the impossibility of finishing what he'd begun.

Mounted from racks on the ceiling, directly under the bed, was the heavy wheel of cable. The wire ran up through a hole he had drilled, from which it would be threaded through the heart of the machine. Through a second hole the wire came back. It looped over one pulley and down through a second mounted in a makeshift frame he'd bolted to the floor. About seven feet from . . . the bike.

He was mad!

He'd found a ten-speed bicycle and stripped it of all but the pedals and frame.

He'd bolted this securely atop an angled stand, with butterfly supports to keep the thing from rocking.

And then—

he'd stopped . . . or been stopped. Unable to devise a way to rig the cable to the bike. Or at a loss, perhaps, for parts.

Suki pictured his smile as he labored away, his mind a circus of evil delights. Oh yes, he'd whistled while he worked, foreseeing the reddening carnage each time she pedaled the bike.

She fought a sudden rush of gorge.

But it was much faster than she was.

She retched until she thought she'd die, then wiped her mouth with the back of one sleeve.

Shikata ga nai?

There was work to be done.

His way or else?

Well, do it!

She wobbled back to the devil's machine, determined to figure a way.

NINE

Michiko knelt at the skylight, gazing down at the sleeping figure lit by moon and candle glow.

Murdered Kuni, had he?

What a sorry Sister *she'd* been, then!

He slept like a baby, with death just above him, in something that looked like—a cradle!

Naked as a newborn too. At least to the waist . . . where the sheet folded over what looked like one hell of a hard-on.

Well, look at all those muscles!

What a scary sight was he!

And look at the pride and the joy of his life—his stiffened Sister-crusher!

What better place on earth to be than here in San Francisco? The chilled air caressing her shoulders and hair. The full moon washing over all with its cool silvery light. And, below, hers at last: the Supreme Oppressor . . . revealed for what he was.

Flashes of Shinjuku nights flickered through her mind. Disco pounding. Lights pulsing. Faceless drunks between her thighs, shooting their loads with a few spastic moves before going home to their wives.

Michiko smiled grimly, shimmying out of her red leather dress. And then off came the lacy red panties. Naked except for the high leather boots that still drove her mad with their kisses.

Now!

Michiko's breasts ached fearfully, the nipples so stiff they might break with a touch.

She cupped the heavy, swelling mounds and, shivering, straddled the skylight.

She stepped back a couple of inches.

Reconsidered, moaning *"Aa!"*

Stepped forward one inch.

Back a half.

Finally, satisfied that her position was perfect, she took one last look at her target below. That arrogant, swaggering rise through the sheet. She felt the throbbing in her throat. And then the deep vaginal pulsing.

Kiss!

She touched herself. The touch too much, she sprang up with a scissoring move of her legs. And dropped fifteen feet in a shower of glass.

TEN

Suki was pacing frantically when she heard a brittle explosion above. And then a scream so shrill and piercing she pressed her hands to her ears.

The skylight—oh no, through the skylight!

She saw the swordlet by the door.

The hell with the widow! She started to charge—

But then he started screaming too, a spiraling scream with Michiko's.

And it wasn't his terror that stopped her.

Or even the heartbreaking sound of his pain.

What stopped her cold and turned her hard was what she heard him screaming.

ELEVEN

He awakened with a cry to hellish screams above him.

Oh, Lord Jesus, Mother Mary, Colonel, help me—

"COLLLLLONNNNNELLLLL!"

The woman shrieked like a stuck pig, hips locked to his in

agony, head back and spewing coils while one of her hands clasped his throat in a vise that closed and continued to close.

Windpipe going. Hernia. My fuckin' nuts is busted flat.

(Ted . . .)

He knew that voice. Whose was it, though?

(Ted, for God's sake—)

"HELLLLLPPPPP!"

(Get your arm out of there, fuck the knife, let it be, move your arm, oh, Ted—)

"I'm SCARED!"

The woman froze. The screaming stopped. She slumped, settling her weight on the knife . . . moaned and shuddered . . . and was still. She lowered her head. She was smiling through a mouthful of long, steaming coils. Suddenly, then, she sucked them in—and spat back the works in his face.

She gripped the side rails for support and started wrapping his skull in the slime, squeezing with each wrapping.

(Ted . . . Get with it, buckle up, Ted, get your fuckin' arm free—please!)

He worked his way to the straps of the seat belt he'd folded under the mattress.

(Come on, Teddy, you're the man!)

But the halves were a mystery he could not connect. Where was the courage to come from? It was hard enough to breathe, the coils now around his throat and spreading to his shoulders. And when she squeezed, oh, God—

"Daddy!"

The coils around his biceps now. And who could have guessed she'd come back, the ole bitch, with her smotherin' kisses, her hot rummy breath, hands touchin' me and clutchin' me while I'm lyin' in my bed, oh, mama, don't, I'm only *twelve* . . . Goddamn right I strung her up . . .

(Ted, please, you're the man . . .)

But the dim light began to fade and the small voice inside him grew faint as a ghost's.

He closed his eyes.

Hell, might as well . . . Go on, mama, do your stuff . . . Guess it all comes home just fine in the end . . . everythin' wrapped up real pretty . . . 'cept—

What the hell was the commotion coming up from the ceiling below? A god-awful banging, some bitch screaming—
What?
Can't be . . .
Must be . . .
Sounds like—

TWELVE

"HANK! HANK!" Suki screamed.

Long before the widow, the spirit had possessed him: *Ted* was invincible, *Ted* was the man. Yet which of them was screaming now? And which of them was stronger?

She crouched atop the wooden frame, ceiling plaster raining down from blows with the butt of the sword.

"HANK! BED! SPIN!" she screamed. "YOU THE MAN, HANK! YOU THE MAN!"

The wire that dropped from the hole in the ceiling waited like a jungle vine.

And Suki, still screaming and banging away, awaited his signal to jump.

THIRTEEN

       Hank!
What . . .
       Hank!
Who . . .
       Hank!
Me?
Yeah.
Click!
He fastened the seat belt over his sternum. Caught hold of the knife that impaled her and raised her a foot with a sharp, twisting stab.

"Kill *my* fuckin' cat?" he growled.

For one instant she lost it. The coils went slack. She grasped the railing, butt-upended, the blade cutting clear to her womb.

The instant was all that he needed. He freed his left arm, whipped the sheet from the drawer, and found what he was looking for.

FOURTEEN

Blue lightning crackled, closing in.

Sister screamed for Michiko to stop it—too late.

When the sparks connected, her body quite nearly jumped off the knife.

Regrettably, she sank again, and at a crueler angle. The lights went out completely.

(Michi!)

Silence.

(Michi!)

Zero.

Even the heartbeat, the pulse of *her* life, was slowing . . . slowly . . . much too faint.

Sister had no way of knowing what the beast below was up to. But, stripped of sight and hearing, she had the sensation of movement. Arm. Yes, Michi's left. Something happening to the arm. A dire sense of entrapment.

Now the right was being moved, but this with real effort as Michi came to.

"*Aa, maa,*" she whimpered. "Hurts . . ."

Her eyelids, leaden, fluttered once for a flash of the beast as he cuffed her right wrist.

Michiko tugged her hand. "Go 'way!" And then, to Sister's horror, she began to drift again, for keeps, on a lush, insensate wave.

(Michi! I command you!)

(Hmmmmm?)

(Michi! I implore you!)

(Bye . . .)

The same sense of entrapment clicked in on the right.

Through the numbed chambers of Michi's ears, Sister heard him chuckling.

(Listen, Michi, listen! Hear the laughter of men as they crush through all time. Hear them laugh as they crush from the cradle and on. Hear them laugh on the stage in Shinjuku, spilling their semen like piss in your womb. Go on, then, die, and let them laugh. Let them howl at the dreams of two Sisters!)

(No . . .)

The pulsebeat quickened. And through the body Sister felt a faint but vital surge.

(No . . . No . . .)

"No . . ." out loud.

The pulse grew stronger, steadier. Rhythmically, the surges swelled in power and duration.

"No!" Michiko cried.

Then, "NO!"

Her eyes shot open in a last electric jolt of rage.

The monster winked. Then pointed playfully over the side of the bed to the floor.

He jerked at something with his hand. The square railing she'd thought were sides of a cradle sprang upward two feet and then settled with solidly synchronized clicks.

Michiko tugged at the handcuffs and hung, arms outstretched as if on a cross. Her hips had been sharply reangled, the knife's tip inching out of her anus.

(Kiss! KISS!)

In agony, Michiko saw the monster wink again. Another movement of his hand. Another fateful-sounding click. And then he pounded on the floor.

(Hear them laugh as they crush . . . Hear them laugh on the stage . . . Go on, then, die and let them howl . . .)

Michiko took a slow deep breath—

(Twelve years on my back—for this!)

—and screamed *"Banzai!"* treating him to the full length and strength of Sister's rage. The coils shot and snaked and wrapped and squeezed from his skull to his waist, over and under the bed's useless belt.

To die was nothing next to this, the joy of slowly crushing—

But then she screamed, and screamed again, first in shock

and then in pain . . . as the bed beneath her jerked and swung in a slow savage arc.

FIFTEEN

Suki landed with a crash, howling in frustration. And cut to pieces by his screams and poundings on the floor.

The bed *could* be moved with the jungle-vine wire he'd failed to connect to the bike. Her weight, as she'd hoped, was sufficient, with the thrust of her jump from the frame. But the wire, greased, was too slippery to hold. She couldn't have moved the bed more than two feet before sliding in a streak and losing her grip altogether.

Shikata ga nai.

Oh, *shikata ga—*

Shit!

"HANK! HANK!" Suki screamed.

She saw him sitting on his rocker, back by the Sea of Japan. She saw him smile, grab his finger, singing, singing through his pain.

Oh, *sannen kata ho!* Be strong!

She wiped her palms on her blue jeans.

California! I can do!

Then she took a running jump, over the top of the frame, to the wire. Three fingers, trapped while wrapping it around one wrist for purchase, broke.

Then she let go, wrist snapping too. And she heard them both scream as she dropped.

The bed *swung!*

SIXTEEN

EEEEEKKK!

Seeing double this time, Suki picked the wrong wire to jump for. She landed hard, diver style, arms spread, on her belly.

Gasping for breath, Suki crawled to the wire.

Struggled, somehow, to her feet.

Encircled her unbroken wrist.
Jumped high and sank hard with a crippling snap.

SEVENTEEN

On and on his poundings went.
    But her hands were both ruined—there was no way to jump.
Shikata ga—
    No!
    She had more bones to give.

EIGHTEEN

Suki's perching was precarious. She stood on a couple of crates
barely balanced atop the wood frame. She wrapped the cable
she'd pulled over snugly from ankles to knees.
    Her hands screamed with each movement. She soothed them
with a song, his song. The words, for now, escaped her. But she
had heard the melody too often to forget. She wished she was in
Dixie, and she hummed it while she worked.
    And when she'd exhausted the last of the slack, she called his
name. Heard him call hers.
    With her heels she managed to kick the crates from under
her.
    Her legs shot out and up, then down. From her ankles to her
knees the bones went off like hand grenades.
    But she was sinking, sinking, *saa,* and though the way was
long and steep—and scarcely halfway there she heard a *crack*
that stopped his screaming—Michiko's scream went up and up.
    And so Suki sank and continued to sink until the ghastly *plop*
that stopped the screaming altogether.

NINETEEN

Red lights flashing through one window.
    Sirens whooping up the hill.

A pounding at the door—
"POLICE!"
—and an explosive kiss of solid oak and plaster.
Footsteps in the hall.
"POLICE!"
Be up here any second now. She wriggled over the top step, hauling her wrecked legs behind her. She inched across on her side to the door. She raised herself there on the butt of the sword, the need to know more powerful than her shattered skeleton's screaming. She inserted the key in the lock. Opened the door with a twist. Then, hitting the light, Suki crashed to the floor, blindsided by the horror.

Aa, maa, what had they done?

Footsteps coming up the stairs.
"POLICE! WHO'S THERE! POLICE!"
She pressed one palm to the sword's handle. She used her other hand to crack and curl the fingers around. It took both hands to raise the sword. But, done, she started snaking to him on her belly.

The bed had stopped at quarter spin. His head lolled over the side of the frame, one closed eye and half his mouth exposed through the slime-mummy wrap. The rest of him lay crazy-angled in a heap of bloody coils and Michiko's vital parts.

Michiko hung, lifeless, above him, head down. Suki saw, through a part in the black and crimsoned hair, the heart or a kidney slip out of her mouth and drop with a wet jelly-roll.

He couldn't have survived.

But if . . .

This much she owed him: If he was still It . . .

Pacings through the room below.
"What the hell . . ."
"Holy fuck!"
Now hammers clicking as the men climbed up the final flight.
"POLICE!"
He awakened suddenly, with a protracted moan. Gazed at Suki, upside down, with a glazed expression.

"Busted . . ." he said. "Back . . . broke . . ."

"Who?" she whispered. "Tell me!" She shimmied in, a half

foot more, rolling over on her side as she drew back the swordlet to swing.

"Just—me . . ."

"Where Ted!"

"Fuck—Ted . . ."

The lone eye winked.

She dropped the sword just as the cavalry came. Two men in
blue opened their mouths to scream "FRE—!" . . . and doubled over, retching. The others held guns that were blurs from
the shakes.

"Relax . . ." he whispered. "We get . . . one call . . .
Wanna meet . . . the Colonel?"

"*Hai.*"

"Good . . . Now get this damn slime . . . off my face."

The coils, unexpectedly, felt pleasantly warm and inviting.
She half wondered, for a second, what it might be like if
she . . .

"*Honey?*" he said.

Suki smiled.

"Behave self," she said sweetly.

ACKNOWLEDGMENTS

Special thanks to Paul Cotter of Crowley Webb and Associates, whose brilliant Obie-winning ad campaign inspired the one in this book.

Dōmo to Jeanne Cavelos . . . and Ron and Davi Dee . . . who were there every step of the way. We all have the phone bills to prove it.

And *maido dōmo* to Lori Perkins, my agent, for her unwavering belief and support.